DECORUM

DECORUM

KAAREN CHRISTOPHERSON

KENSINGTON BOOKS
www.kensingtonbooks.com

KENSINGTON BOOKS are published by

Kensington Publishing Corp.
119 West 40th Street
New York, NY 10018

All Kensington titles, imprints, and distributed lines are available at special quantity discounts for bulk purchases for sales promotion, premiums, fundraising, educational, or institutional use.

Special book excerpts or customized printings can also be created to fit specific needs. For details, write or phone the office of the Kensington Special Sales Manager: Kensington Publishing Corp., 119 West 40th Street, New York, NY 10018. Attn. Special Sales Department. Phone: 1-800-221-2647.

Kensington and the K logo Reg. U.S. Pat. & TM Off.

eISBN-13: 978-1-61773-522-6
eISBN-10: 1-61773-522-1
First Kensington Electronic Edition: April 2015

ISBN-13: 978-1-61773-521-9
ISBN-10: 1-61773-521-3
First Kensington Trade Paperback Printing: April 2015

10 9 8 7 6 5 4 3 2 1

Printed in the United States of America

To Betty J. Christopherson,
my mother and my biggest fan,
with love and gratitude

CHAPTER I

The Creaking Wheels of Life

❦

"Etiquette," says a modern English author, "may be defined as the minor morality of life." No observances, however minute, that tend to spare the feelings of others, can be classed under the head of trivialities; and politeness, which is but another name for general amiability, will oil the creaking wheels of life more effectually than any of those unguents supplied by mere wealth and station. . . . Be, therefore, modest and benevolent, and do not distress yourself on account of the mistakes of your inexperience; a little attention, and the advice of a friend, will soon correct these trifling errors.

—Decorum, A Practical Treatise on Etiquette
and Dress of the Best American Society,
Sold Only by Subscription, 1881, page 19

New York, New York, 1888

In the time it had taken Francesca to raise the field glasses to her eyes, the yacht was gone. In its place a spike of fire had shot skyward, followed by a blast of flaming debris and a spreading mantle of black smoke. An eternity had passed before an explosion tore the silence and the shock wave had jetted across the lake and left her flat upon the dock.

Francesca lay awake as she had done so many nights in the first year following the accident, when closed eyes could not blot out the images of wreckage and rent flesh that flickered across her mind. By day the assault of images was replaced by sensitivity to sound—the clatter in the street of two colliding carriages or the jagged household echo of an upended tea tray full of china—enough to send her fleeing to her chamber deep within the house. In the second year the explosions waned and images had begun to fade, but by then Francesca had accepted laudanum's blunting aid for sheer self-preservation and yielded all thinking and decision-making to the Jeromes.

Lately, though, Francesca had suspected an ogre lurking in laudanum's fog—a fear that staying longer at the Fifty-seventh Street mansion might mean an end to sanity altogether. At first the idea of leaving seemed laughable to someone who could barely rise from the divan to draw the curtain and see if the day were rainy or fine. Yet as the days wore on and the aspidistra on the corner stand grew limp with administration of the daily laudanum meant for her, she began to comprehend why Vinnie urged her interest in charity. As Francesca's unconscious wrestled nightly with leaving, the events of that deadly day threatened to rise again. Slowly, however, befriended by new resolve, rather than retreat from the memories, she welcomed them in silence.

Armed with a deck chair, a book, field glasses, and her father's old straw hat, she had determined to watch as the steam yacht bearing her parents and brother and their friends made its way from a neighbor's ten-room cottage and headed toward the house the Lunds had leased for the summer. Pleasantly weary from a morning of vigorous tennis with Oskar, she had declined the invitation to sail. The breeze from the lake had mitigated the late June heat and lulled her to sleep in the chair, the book fallen from her grasp. By the time she woke with a start, she couldn't tell how many times the whistle had signaled to her. The yacht had come within view, though still was many yards distant. She had risen, taking up the field glasses, and made for the dock.

The summer sun had dipped toward the western side of the lake, hot and yellow. Only the approaching noise of the engine had broken the stillness. She had stood upon the dock and pulled the hat brim low to check the glare. Even unaided she saw plainly the figures upon the yacht's deck, the ladies seated, the gentlemen walking or leaning on the railing. Odd to think of it now—her father's lean, linen-clad form, surmounted by flaxen hair, Oskar similarly built and similarly dressed, the ladies in shades of summer white and cream had comprised a vessel of tone-on-tone ghosts. When the whistle blew again, Francesca had taken off her hat and waved. Then she had raised the field glasses to her eyes.

Her scream might have come from someone else, tangled with the shouts of groundskeepers and house servants and the house's clanging alarm bell. Rushing, rushing, everyone flew past and she was swept up mechanically with the rescuers heading toward the lake until strong arms encircled her waist. Suddenly entrapped, she panicked.

"Let go! Let me go! Let me go! Papa!" She screamed and kicked. *"Papa! Oh, God! Oh, Jesus, help me!"* She reached toward the lake as if her extended arms could still save them. *"Mama! Oskar! Oskar! Let me go!"* She was hoisted toward the house, flopped over the gardener's arm as if she were a rag doll. Slowly, as each step drew her farther from the lake, her screams gave way to relentless sobs. *"Oh, God! Oh, Jesus! Mama! Mama!"*

How long the recovery had taken, Francesca could not remember. As word came that bodies were being brought ashore she broke free of the house and ran to the lakeside and, evading the rescuers, saw the body of her mother lying in the bottom of a rowboat—slits of gray-blue eyes fixed, lips parted, white-blond hair limp and matted, clothing disarranged. The lake-washed injuries might have been set in an alabaster statue. As shock overloaded Francesca's brain, she fainted.

She had awakened to the news that John had sent Harry to telegraph to the Jeromes. To summon the Jeromes seemed sensible to John, no doubt, though the choice would not have been hers. Childless, they had been attentive to her and her brother ever since the Lunds' arrival in New York when she and Oskar were children. Like many childless women, Maggie held firm opinions on child-rearing that had kept Sonia Lund's acquaintance distant but polite, and this only for the sake of Jurgen Lund's friendship with Jerry that emerged from their work together at the bank.

Their imminent arrival had galvanized Francesca. She remembered the sensation of standing outside herself, observing the world through senses newly sharpened. Throughout the night and into the morning, she moved, mechanical and steady, through the wretchedness and rituals of doctor, police, neighbors, servants, until all was as orderly as she could make it. The household was settling into a routine of working around grief—or perhaps working with it—as servants and staff and indeed the neighborhood began to take their cues from her. With a lifetime ahead of her in which to weep, she reckoned, she had answered all and turned no one away. By the time Maggie and Jerry alighted from the carriage from the station in Ithaca, Francesca had bathed and changed and met them at the door.

"I wired instructions to May and Evangeline to have your things ready before breakfast tomorrow," Maggie began when the perfunctory condolences had been exchanged. "John and Harry and Mrs. Howell will come with us, of course, to see to the house in the city. The rest of the servants will stay behind to close this house. We'll have to give the summer help their notice, of course."

"You'll do no such thing," said Francesca, offended but speaking with a quiet authority. "I've assured everyone that nothing will change for the foreseeable future. I won't see people turned out of their jobs and I won't allow you to undo everything I've done to make things as easy as possible for everyone."

"I don't expect you to know what to do at a time like this."

"This is hardly the time," said Jerry in a low voice directed at Maggie. "We have enough to get through with the immediate arrangements—"

"A young woman alone. That's ridiculous," Maggie cut in. "We'll handle it all."

"We wouldn't be having this conversation if my family hadn't been obliterated in the last twenty-four hours," said Francesca, her head beginning to throb, "or have you forgotten why we're gathered in the first place?"

"You see, Jerry," said Maggie. "This is just what we may expect. Fits of anger. Outbreaks of tears—"

"That's hardly fair under the circumstances," said Jerry.

"Certainly, John and Harry and Mrs. Howell must go," said Francesca, regaining something like composure. "They can leave as soon as may be and open up the house. We'll follow as soon as any business here is concluded. John will have everything ready—"

"You certainly aren't expecting to go back to Sixty-third Street on your own," said Maggie, looking at Francesca in some astonishment. "That would hardly be proper. We're taking you home with us to Fifty-seventh Street to look after you."

From that moment, no funeral wreath, no mourning brooch, no scripture verse, no yard of crepe, no obituary had escaped Maggie's interference. The well-meaning Jerry acquiesced to Maggie, failing to cushion the daily blows to Francesca's psyche as her life spiraled downward. Her only refuge was the church and her friendship with Vinnie and the Reverend Lawrence's family, associations Maggie dared not disapprove. Finally, in the busyness of the parish, Francesca began to realize that her only chance to save herself was to go.

At last the time had come. Francesca had excused herself from dinner, sensing the commencement of the evening's argument from the moment the footman appeared in the doorway with the dessert tray, and pleading a headache, had stolen to her bedchamber.

"I've put in all your last bits and bobs, miss—your underlinen and stockings and such, an extra pair of boots, a jacket..." the maid had whispered, the carpetbag full and the packing nearly finished.

"Thank you, May. My coat and hat?"

"Right here, miss, ready to go in the morning. Two mufflers and two pairs of gloves are in the bag. You'd best hurry now and get yourself to bed. Morning will come quickly."

The mansion was not large enough to swallow up the Jeromes' shouting. The hollow and lofty rooms only bottled up the friction until Maggie's words scraped across Jerry's frayed feelings like a match head across the bottom of his shoe. That Francesca could not distinguish the words from where she lay in bed mattered little. The recital was so frequent she knew it by heart.

"Can't you leave her alone?" Jerry had shouted, forgoing his usual conciliatory warm-up. "She's a grown woman—and a sensible woman, not to mention being sensible of her position."

"Yes, and it's thanks to you she's all too sensible of her position," Maggie spat back. "You've put it into her head that she can do things—manage things herself. She has no experience. She needs a guiding hand—"

"She's not a child, for God's sake," he retorted. "She's twenty-five goddamn years old. She would have had plenty of experience by now if you hadn't insisted that she come here so you could convince her that she's an invalid. You know as well as I do that she's going to have to manage her own life and that big house eventually. She can't hang on here forever, even to please you."

From the sanctuary of her bedchamber, Francesca could picture it all—Jerry pacing and standing over Maggie, glass of port in hand, addressing the top of her head or standing at the hearth or the sideboard and turning his back and yelling over his shoulder. Maggie would sit at her usual place, her face hard as granite, her eyes screwed into dark pinholes that shot darts of disapproval.

"Please me?" Maggie asked, in her familiar indignant tone. "You think it pleases me to see her frailty, her weakness day after day—"

"That's exactly what pleases you. You delight in finding a weakness and then driving a wedge into it. If you can't find a weakness you invent one. You want someone to manage and to disapprove of all at once. You can't face the truth."

"Which is?"

"That she doesn't need you—or me, come to that, or Edmund Tracey, or anybody else you think of so highly. She doesn't need your coddling. What she needs is to be left alone."

At five-thirty the next morning, Jerry's words reverberated through Francesca's brain as May helped her dress. They tucked folding money into the corset as May laced her up the back—six hundred dollars Francesca had scrounged from around the house. Francesca's worn nerves and wasted body had left plenty of room for the money around her frame.

"Remember," whispered Francesca as she pulled the skirt of dull burgundy plaid over her head and May secured it at the waist. "Mrs. Jerome may sound like she's giving you the sack, but I'm the only one who can sack you, and that's not likely." She held her arms out in front of her while May slipped the sleeves of the matching blouse over them. "She'll turn you out, though, after this. She'll call it insubordination—and something worse for me. But you know what to do."

"Yes, miss. John and Harry and Mrs. Howell are expecting me at the Sixty-third Street house."

"I'm sorry we couldn't send your box ahead." Francesca arranged the last coil of her thick white-blond hair at the nape of her neck and pinned it while May buttoned the back of her blouse.

"Never you mind, miss. It would've looked too suspicious. John will see to it that Harry fetches my box in short order."

"My old clothes have gone to Forsyth Street—you're sure?" Francesca rested her right foot on her dressing-table stool and laced the boot up to the ankle, then the left.

"Yes, miss," said May. "Mrs. Jerome thought it was a charity box for the settlement house. She even looked through it before Miss Lawrence came to fetch it. I was that nervous, miss, but Mrs. Jerome made no objection. I'm sure Miss Lawrence and Miss Reynolds will have taken it to the flat by now."

Francesca sat down on the stool, her elbow on the dressing table. She felt faint.

"I don't know whether I can do this," she said. "I seem to have lost my nerve. All I can think of is two perfectly good years wasted in this abominable place. I do so wish Aunt Esther could have . . ." She checked herself.

"There's no sense dwelling on that. Mrs. Gray could have done nothing in the midst of her own bereavement," said May. "You've done your best. You can't lose your nerve, now. You've got to look forward. Your mother and father would say so if they were here. Your brother, too, no doubt. Here, you must eat something."

May was right. Her family would have urged her to work out her own grief and move on. Yet the thought of leaving the only underpinning she had known for two years threatened to overwhelm her. This was all Vinnie's doing, she thought—all her doing, bless her. Her childhood friend had discovered the new settlement through the gossip of her father's New York parish and proposed a flat in Forsyth Street near the settlement house as Francesca's means of escape. In helping others, she would help herself, Vinnie had said. Now that the time had come, Francesca wasn't so sure.

"I'm not hungry."

"You're never hungry," said May, "and look at you. So thin and pale."

Francesca looked at the ghostly reflection in the mirror—the white skin with two ice-blue pools surrounded by dark circles.

"Them at the settlement'll think you're the one who needs the help, and not the one who'll be giving it," May said. "You won't last for the cab ride to Forsyth Street. I won't let you out of this house until you've eaten the rest of this bread and cheese, and finished the tea. But you must make haste. Miss Lawrence should have the cab drawing up at the corner at any moment."

Francesca stuffed the last of the bread and cheese into her mouth and washed it down with the tepid tea as May held up the woolen coat and slid it onto Francesca's shoulders. Francesca pinned the gray woolen hat, picked up the carpetbag and a small valise, extinguished the oil lamp, and followed May to the back stairs. They reached the basement kitchen only moments ahead of the footsteps that began the morning descent from the servants' rooms. Grabbing a shawl from a peg by the door, May stepped out into the cold gray morning and up the stone steps, opening the iron gate onto the street. She cautioned Francesca to stay as she ran to the corner to make sure Vinnie was waiting. At May's beckoning, Francesca quietly pulled the gate to, then ran on tiptoe the half block.

"You're here. Thank God," said Vinnie as Francesca settled next to her and May set the bags at her feet. Vinnie rapped on the cab's roof. "Forsyth Street, cabby."

"It's like a dream," said Francesca. "Shall I ever wake up?"

She turned and shouted as the cab pulled away from the curb.

"May, how can I ever thank you? I'll let you know how I get on. And I promise you, in a year we'll all be back at Sixty-third Street."

CHAPTER 2

The Accomplishment of Great Designs

❧

> To gain the good opinion of those who surround them, is
> the first interest and the second duty of men in every pro-
> fession of life. For power and for pleasure, this prelimi-
> nary is equally indispensable. Unless we are eminent
> and respectable before our fellow-beings, we cannot pos-
> sess that influence which is essential to the accomplish-
> ment of great designs.
>
> —Decorum, page 11

New York, New York, 1890

Tea. *Bloody hell*, thought Connor as he emerged from the hansom into the drizzly autumn afternoon. Couldn't this have been done at Jerry's club? Or at the fireside of a respectable little tavern? But no. Jerry Jerome had gone to a lot of trouble to persuade Mr. Worth to meet him at all, let alone cut him in on the deal. The deal, after all, was what brought him to New York. Since the deal was Worth's, Worth called the tune. A church vestryman and teetotaler, it was Worth who had suggested the Morocco Room.

The maître d' was expecting him. In an instant his hat, coat, gloves, and soggy umbrella were whisked away. Leaning for a moment on the walking stick, he surreptitiously flexed his right knee, which had been playing up—the damp weather, no doubt. Connor stepped away from the tearoom's entrance for a moment and moved a self-conscious hand over his dark wavy hair and adjusted the tie and the jasper stickpin. In doing so he trod on something soft and discovered a lady's kid glove underfoot. As he picked it up by its long and slender fingers, the faint scent of violets met his nostrils. He was recalled to himself when the maître d' cleared his throat, and Connor absently slipped the glove into his pocket.

The room before him glowed in red, gold, and black carpets, dark polished oak, and wallpaper strewn with russet poppies and gold acanthus leaves. With its potted palms and porcelain urns of hothouse flowers, Connor likened it to a high-class brothel.

He spied the table where Jerry and Mr. Worth were seated, by the ornately carved screen that separated the gentlemen's tearoom from the airier tearoom of the ladies with its alabaster fountain and cool white and coral marble. The men were in serious confabulation. A dispute, he wondered—about himself? If Worth was half the businessman his reputation foretold, it would take more than Jerry's word to give Connor entrée into the tight fellowship of dealmakers New York boasted. Could an immigrant upstart from the wilds of Colorado make New York sit up and take notice? It was full steam ahead between Worth and Jerome, with or without O'Casey. Better that it be *with* O'Casey. As he followed the maître d', he caught Jerry's eye and the latter rose, smiling.

"Connor, I see you've found us, and right on time," he said, extending his hand. "John, may I present Mr. Connor O'Casey, late of Denver, St. Louis, Chicago, and no doubt many points even I'm not aware of. Connor, this is Mr. John Ashton Worth."

The man whose hand met Connor's firm grip was impeccably barbered with a wreath of short white hair around a pink pate and a well-manicured set of white moustaches.

"Glad to meet you at last, Mr. O'Casey," Mr. Worth said genially. "Please, take a seat. Jerry tells me you're settling in at the Grand Central. I hope they're making you comfortable. Finding your way around all right?"

"Indeed, sir," replied Connor. "I'm finding New York much to my liking. I've been making a point of takin' in new streets almost every day—by carriage and on foot—until I can get the lay of the

land, so to speak. As far as the hotel"—he hesitated and smiled—
"the accommodation is only as good as might be expected. Where's
a respectable man of means supposed to lay his head when he was
in New York, in a stable? Horses were bedded down better than
most people I know—the Grand Central notwithstanding." *Pull
back, boy, pull back*, Connor thought. *Don't look too eager*.

"I couldn't have put it better myself," said Jerry.

Mr. Worth chuckled and pulled a cigar case from his breast
pocket, opened it, and offered it to Connor. A waiter costumed in a
caftan and fez arrived with tea. In the interval for serving refreshments, Connor's attention was drawn to the ladies' entrance to the
Fountain Terrace by a tall, slender young woman who appeared to
be joining a friend. He might not have noticed her, except for her
beautifully erect carriage. Her attire was somber black and dark
gray with a simple black hat covering most of her white-blond hair.
The fragments of her face he could see through the lacework of
the screen were enough to tell that she was delicately featured.
The friend whose table she joined was plainer, though not unat-
tractive, of smaller frame and darker hue and fussier clothes. The
Fair One—for so he thought of her—sat with her back to him.

"I can see Mr. O'Casey is already disposed to our way of thinking," said Mr. Worth, turning the offer of a cigar to Jerry. "Jerry
tells me you've been in timber and mining, Mr. O'Casey. Done
rather well for yourself, I gather." Had Jerry not told him, thought
Connor, the intervening months while the deal was brewing gave
ample time for investigation. Short of examining the books, Mr.
Worth was likely to know Connor's state of affairs nearly as well as
he himself. So much the better. The Midwestern timber, the killing he made in the Comstock Lode, his tight friendships with
Mackay and Daly, and part ownership of the lucrative Five Star
Mine would bear scrutiny. "Still active in those pursuits?"

"I keep myself apprised of what's happening in Denver and
Leadville," replied Connor, "but on the whole I would say I'm retired from any active involvement."

"A bit young to be retired," commented Mr. Worth. "You can't
be much past forty, if you'll forgive such a direct observation."

"Which is why I'm looking for a new project to occupy my

time," said Connor. "A man can't let his brain go to seed at any age now, can he?"

"So when I met Connor in Chicago last spring," interjected Jerry, "it seemed only natural to raise the subject of—"

"Of my little pet project?" asked Mr. Worth. Jerry made an affirmative gesture.

"Indeed, sir," said Connor, his attention straying momentarily to activity on the other side of the screen. The tall fair lady had risen and appeared to be searching for something. "A very interesting prospect, if I may say so," he continued, forcing his gaze back to Mr. Worth, "a luxury hotel in the heart of New York City." By now the lady had enlisted her companion in the search around their table and Connor's hand stole instinctively to his jacket pocket.

"People want to be pampered when they travel, don't you agree, Mr. O'Casey?" Mr. Worth asked rhetorically. "They are perfectly prepared to pay for it, but they want value for their money. Value in the service, certainly, but also in the quality of their surroundings."

"No doubt the Vanderbilts and the Astors would agree," Connor observed. A bit of a spoke in their wheel would do no harm—for the good of the finest luxury apartment hotel in New York. "What makes you think your 'pet project' will trump anything they might build?" Jerry and Worth exchanged looks.

"Well you might ask, Mr. O'Casey," said Worth. "I needn't bore you with a recitation of all the modern conveniences we intend to install in the way of electrical fittings, elevators, and private water closets. No doubt Jerry has catalogued these."

"He has, in detail," said Connor. "You can put modern conveniences in a barn and it's still a barn. What will make your establishment unique?"

"People want pleasant things, beautiful things to look at, just as they might collect for themselves in their own homes," said Worth, warming to his subject. "The Europeans understand this. Of course, they are in a better position to choose their ornaments and decorations, being surrounded by them."

Beautiful things to look at, Connor considered as the lady resumed her seat with a shrug of her shoulders, suggesting the futility of their search. "Wouldn't it, or couldn't it, be part of the attraction to have some rooms brought over wholesale and refitted and installed? A client might fancy boastin' to his neighbor that he stayed in the Louis XV Suite at the Excelsior."

"Excelsior?" Jerry laughed.

"It was the first thing that came into my head," said Connor. He could barely tamp down the thrill at the prospect of luxury on such a scale. It was not just the money that could be made. The chance to learn about fine things was being handed to him in a way he could never have imagined in the dark days of his childhood in Belfast, talking his way onto the first outbound ship that would have him, or the darker days in the lumber mills and the Montana mines as a young man.

"If this is to be as elegant as you suggest, the craftsmanship alone will be an enormous expense. Take these screens here," Connor said, toting up the figures in his head as he gestured toward the dark, carved wood that attracted his frequent gaze, "they must have cost a pretty penny, either to tear them out of some building in Marrakesh and import them, or to have them carved on the spot. What do you propose for your establishment?"

"You're quite right," said Mr. Worth. "I'm proposing that the laborers and craftsmen be hired either here or abroad and the work to be completed on the site—made to order, so to speak."

"I'm sure Mrs. Worth has catalogued many dealers in France or Prussia or Italy who could direct us to the makings of a Louis XV Suite, hasn't she, John?" asked Jerry. "Mrs. Worth has excellent taste, Connor—a great asset in this little enterprise."

"I believe she could be persuaded," said Mr. Worth, visibly pleased.

Could Blanche's knowledge and tastes keep up with those of the formidable Mrs. Worth? Connor wondered. If Worth's investigations had been as thorough as suspected, they would have uncovered his liaison with Blanche. Blanche may well speak of opera and art in three languages and impress Connor O'Casey, but when called upon to impress New York society, that might be another matter. Her manner may suit New Orleans or St. Louis, but would she invest herself in the social success of his business? Blanche could be dismissive and perverse when she chose. If she chose to be dismissive of a Mrs. Worth or a Mrs. Jerome? Well, then.

Mr. Worth summoned the waiter and ordered a particularly exclusive brand of Turkish coffee. As the waiter bowed and was about to melt away, Connor motioned him closer and said in a low voice, "I believe the lady yonder may have lost this." He retrieved the glove and handed it over.

"Thank you, sir. She said she'd lost it. I'll see that it is returned."

"I nearly didn't come," said Francesca, "but I didn't want to leave you wondering."

"You're only just coming from lunch?" asked Vinnie, pouring Francesca a cup of tea as the latter helped herself to cake. "I hope it wasn't as dreadful as the look on your face suggests. I wonder sometimes why you put yourself through this ordeal. You only have yourself to blame."

"I know," said Francesca with a sigh. "I thought with time things might improve between us."

Neither the substance nor character of Maggie Jerome's discourse had changed in four years. Francesca wished she had been stronger in those fatal hours following the worst calamity of her life. A year at the settlement had restored her to health and given her strength to return to her home. What remained was to see whether her relationship with Maggie Jerome could also be restored. Luncheons with Maggie had been a tenuous olive branch. Besides, scenes were more difficult in public.

"Maggie doesn't still blame you for leaving, does she?" Vinnie asked.

"It's more the fact that I deprived her of someone else to order around. She still harps about the flat—says it wasn't 'dignified' for a lady in my position to share a flat with two others in *that* part of town. And then, of course, there's Edmund."

Maggie quarreled with Francesca and Jerry by turns about Edmund Tracey. For Francesca herself, she gave Tracey credit for having withstood four years' interlude of illness and grief, and wanting her nonetheless. If Maggie would only let Nature take its course, however meandering and slow, all might be agreeably concluded. Still, by protesting so vehemently solely to stave off Maggie's meddling, Francesca worried that she jeopardized her chances of attracting a suitable man. At nearly twenty-eight, she feared that if something didn't happen soon, she indeed would be taking her comfort in old age in the work of the settlement house.

"Have the workmen gone?" said Vinnie, introducing a welcome change of subject.

"The last of them left this morning, thank goodness. I can't wait to arrive home this evening to fresh paper and paint and no scaffolding anywhere. I'm almost proudest of the kitchen, though Mrs. Howell was still fussing about the new stove when I left to meet Maggie."

"Has Maggie seen the changes?"

"No," said Francesca. "Nor will she anytime soon."

"You can't stop her from calling."

"Oh, can't I?" said Francesca with a sidelong look. "I've already planted that seed by saying that I'm attacking the other rooms myself. She wanted to help, of course, but I declined her offer with thanks. You and your parents must come for tea one day. But you come before then, certainly. I think you'll be pleased with the result."

The business of the hotel agreeably concluded, the men were chatting amiably when Connor perceived movement on the other side of the screen. The Fair One gathered up a small parcel wrapped in brown paper, a handbag, and an umbrella and turned to look around her, as if to check around her table one last time. Another waiter approached and proffered the glove, which drew an exclamation of pleasure and a nod from its owner. Connor tried to picture Blanche in the alabaster and wrought-iron sanctuary of the Fountain Terrace, gossiping with a society friend over tea, but couldn't feature it. The Terrace's elegant but restrained lines seemed contrary to Blanche's passionate nature. Hard to tell though, thought Connor, especially when "contrary" might be coined to describe Blanche's primary operating principle.

The companions walked and talked together, on terms of equality, yet how unequal. The Fair One seemed unaware of the attention she drew. She swayed as she walked and inclined her head toward her friend, listening, turning to look at her. He watched them move from the Fountain Terrace to the ladies' entrance and on out of the tearoom.

He continued to watch for a moment as if he half-expected to see them reappear, but the moment was gone. He began to wonder if he had really seen them at all.

How events do turn out, thought Jamie. He often dropped into a pensive frame of mind when he was performing mundane tasks such as this—brushing down his master's overcoat and topper, hanging the coat in the large mahogany wardrobe, and placing the topper in its leather hatbox—all giving the illusion of industry while the mind was busy elsewhere.

He had come a long way in two years, under the tutelage of a tough but not unbenevolent taskmaster. It never failed to amaze him that the whim of a moment that autumn of 1888 had made the difference between the likelihood of prison and the chance to make something of himself.

The man had appeared out of nowhere like an avenging angel of God, wearing a black top hat and a frock coat, and carrying a silver-handled walking stick. Jamie would never have guessed that a gentleman so finely turned out could run so fast and deliver such a blow. He thought he could outpace the man and escape with the purse. But the blow had knocked Jamie out cold. When he came to, he found himself covered with a blanket, lying on a hard settee in front of a roaring fire. A pair of dark brooding eyes loomed above him.

"What did you do a stupid thing like that for, boy?" said the man. "Not very good at sizin' up your mark, are you?" Jamie could not tell whether the man was more upset that he had been chosen as the mark, or that Jamie hadn't exercised better judgment by choosing someone else. "You've not been at this game long, have you, boy?"

"I'm not a boy." Jamie's head was splitting.

"If you've not been around long enough to be able to size up your mark properly or to know when and how to govern yourself, you're a boy—I don't care how old you are." He had poured a glass of water and extended it to the aching figure on the settee. "By the way, how old are you?"

"Seventeen," Jamie replied.

"Seventeen—sir."

"I don't call nobody 'sir,' least of all you."

"Considering I could've cracked your skull open for you or dragged you off to jail, I don't see's how you have much choice—do you?"

Jamie had sipped the water in silence. The man had turned away for a moment.

"Seventeen—sir," Jamie had said without looking up. The man faced him.

"Do you have a name you'd be willing to share?"

"James Lynch—sir."

"So, Mr. James Lynch, have you been in trouble before?"

"On and off, but not so's anyone could catch me."

"That's the trouble with that sort of game. Someone eventually does." The man stared at him, making Jamie uneasy.

"You're Irish." Jamie had nodded. "Where from?"

"Sligo," Jamie said, avoiding mention of his country-bred origin. Again silence.

"How long have you been here?"

"Not a year."

"Family?"

"None." The man raised his dark eyebrows. "None—sir."

The man went to the hearth and stirred the fire. With his back to Jamie, he said, "And what's your plan, Mr. Lynch?"

"Meanin' what, sir?"

The man turned and faced him. "Meaning now that I've spared your worthless hide, what do you plan to do?"

"I mean to go out West. Strike it rich."

"Doing what?"

"This and that." He sipped the water.

"Look at me, boy. 'This and that' don't count for much in this world without a plan. 'This and that will get you thrown in jail for sure. 'This and that' can get you killed."

"I can take care of meself well enough—sir."

"Like you've done so far, I suppose. Well, at least you've got yourself out of Ireland in one piece, I'll say that for you. When was the last time you ate?"

"I don't remember."

"You can't do a bit of 'this and that' on an empty stomach now, can you?"

The man had gone to the door and bellowed down the hallway for a servant, demanding a cold plate of food and a pint of beer. As Jamie ate, the pain in his head subsided and he realized the pain had been more from hunger than from the blow. He devoured the food like a feral cat. The man paced the room, observing him first from the mantel, then from the sideboard, where he poured himself a drink.

"Where are you from then?" Jamie had asked to fill the uneasy silence.

"Here and there," the man had said.

"No, really, sir."

"Really? Belfast."

"And how long've you been here then?" he said, omitting the "sir" without disrespect.

"I came when I wasn't much older than you."

"A long time then, sir."

"I'll overlook the remark upon me age. But, yes, a long time." He gave a long, deep sigh and crossed again to the mantel. "Are you interested in a job?"

"What kind of job?" Jamie had been surprised and skeptical.

"Valet," the man said, with a definite *T.*

"What?"

"Valet. Take care of me, my clothes, my belongings—understanding, of course, that what's mine is *not* yours—carry messages, hail cabs, do what needs doin', and be my general dogsbody."

"I don't go into service for no one," Jamie had said. "You can find yourself another dogsbody."

"So, the idea of regular food, decent clothes, a warm bed, and pocket money till you get on your feet doesn't appeal to you? I'll admit I'm no prize to work for. And the minute I catch you pilfering or otherwise causing disruption to hearth and home, I'll give you a hiding you'll never forget and throw you back out onto the streets where I found you. It does, however, seem preferable to a bit of 'this and that.' Think it over. You can sleep where you are tonight. Tomorrow morning I'll feed you. You can give me your answer then." The man disappeared into the bedroom, leaving Jamie to wonder at the proposition.

The cold, gray light of day and a bitter, blustery downpour had brought fresh perspective to the problem. Though the idea of being beholden to anyone was unpalatable, Jamie found himself inclined to prefer a life that, while not wholly independent, at least would afford him the basic necessities and a temporary relief from scrounging on the streets. A breakfast of steak and eggs and potatoes had been eaten in silence, with the man shoving extra portions across the table without ceremony or acknowledgment. When the dishes had been cleared and the last cups of coffee sat before them, the man spoke.

"Well?"

Jamie was about to ask for terms, but seeing the grave expression on the man's face, he admitted to himself that the man held all the cards.

"I'll stay."

"Well, then. You'll get half days on Wednesdays and Sundays— Sunday mornings so's you can recover from the night before and go to confession for the good of your immortal soul." Jamie couldn't tell if the man was serious. "You'll start at two dollars a week, plus you'll get your room and board. And I want no nonsense. I'll break your skull for you, boy, so I will, and no mistake. Now," he said, rising. "We'll see about cleaning you up."

"Yes, sir."

The man made for the door.

"Sir!"

"Yes," said the man, turning back.

"What's your name, sir?"

"My name, boy, is Connor O'Casey."

CHAPTER 3

The Subject of Confutation

Avoid opposition and argument in conversation. Rarely controvert opinions; never contradict sentiments. The expression of a feeling should be received as a fact which is not the subject of confutation. Those who wrangle in company render themselves odious by disturbing the equanimity of their companion, and compelling him to defend and give a reason for his opinion, when perhaps he is neither capable nor inclined to do it.

—*Decorum*, page 231

"What is it?" Tracey called in answer to the knock.

The knock came again. "What is it?" he called again, this time irritably.

The shutters flattened the room of plush and paisley into a pattern of gray stripes. A pile of clothes lay fermenting on a chaise of black horsehair that was draped with a fringed throw. A half-empty bottle of whiskey and a glass sat on the stand by the bed, a pool of drink in a sticky film on the green marble surface. A second glass had tipped over on the floor, the few remaining drops dried into amber spots on the thick rug. The stale memory of expensive perfume and cigarette smoke clung to every object in the room.

"Does Mrs. Ryder want her tea, sir?" The voice was timid. The social rituals had to be observed, even in an oven.

Edmund Tracey stirred and extracted himself from his companion's embrace, rose, and stumbled naked out of the alcove that held the ornate bed and into the adjoining sitting room. He fumbled through the rubble of clothing on the chaise to find something to cover himself. His long, collarless shirt would do. He ran his hand through his thick thatch of auburn hair as he made for the door and opened it without a word. The maid shrank back and looked confused, her arms loaded with the silver tray arrayed with afternoon tea.

"Does Mrs. Ryder want her tea, sir?" she repeated, then fixed her gaze upon the tray. The man eyed her for a moment, then turned his head toward the bed.

"Nell? Hey, Nell! Shall I have the tea brought in?" His tone was mocking. He made a graceful sweeping gesture with his arm.

The woman sat up. Her henna-red hair, disarrayed in the heat of lovemaking, sat in a ball on her shoulder and hung in clumps in front of her face like a ratty veil. Groggy, she drew up the sheet to cover her bare, sagging breasts and rubbed her pale face. As she came to, she took up the silk dressing gown from the end of the bed, pulled it on, and tied it tightly at the waist. The silk matted to her sweating form.

"Yes," Nell said, "have her bring it in." She rose and rearranged her gown, threw her head back, and squared her shoulders like an empress who had just donned her raiment. She moved to the bureau, picking pins from the knotted ball of hair on her shoulder.

Tracey stood aside and let the maid pass. She kept her eyes averted from the man and woman as she went to a round table and emptied the tray of its silver service, fine china, bread and butter, and jam. She turned, eyes cast down, to inquire whether anything else was wanted.

"That'll be all for now, thank you, Daisy," Nell said. The maid made a slight curtsey and escaped.

Tracey approached the bureau where Nell Ryder stood, put his hands on her waist, and nuzzled the hair she was trying to untangle. She smiled at his reflection in a curious, self-satisfied way.

"It's just as well. Anton will be home soon," she said.

"And how is dear Anton? As interestingly engaged this afternoon as I was?"

"Perhaps. I never ask."

"Not even ask him, in your good and wifely way, whether he has had a good day?"

"To that question I would no doubt receive a pleasant 'Yes.' And you have an engagement this evening, if I'm not mistaken."

He stood upright. She needn't have reminded him. To be caught thus between two undesirable circumstances, using one to seek relief from the other, was sapping his strength. He had come to rue the day she had fixed her roving eye on him. The timing could not have been more deadly. Tracey had been down to his last good suit and Nell had been down to her last gigolo.

"I'm glad Harold persuaded you to come out with us," remarked the female companion of a friend as Tracey joined them in a cab bound for a party at an unknown house. "Someone must take you in hand and cajole you out of this dreariness. You aren't in mourning, even if she may be. I'm sure you'll find amusement aplenty at Nell's. Everybody does—and I mean *everybody*."

The cut of the friend's evening suit pegged it as three years old—an offense Edmund Tracey would not excuse in himself. The girl was more fashionable, but her style was too emphatic for good taste. She was young, though Tracey deduced that her skill with unguents and corsetry had been acquired with much practice. Their confidence in a favorable reception at the Ryders' made it clear enough what sort of party this would be.

"Who is likely to be there?" Tracey had asked.

"Anyone," said the friend with a careless wave of his gloved hand. "Anarchists to antiquarians. Jurists to jugglers. Politicians to prizefighters. Thieves to thespians."

"Do they all dress?" asked Tracey, indicating their evening attire.

"Those who can, do," said the friend, "though I suppose it isn't strictly necessary. I'm sure our hosts will appreciate the effort."

"And our hosts?"

"He's an impresario," said the friend. "Always on the lookout for new talent or a promising production. His wife is equally on the lookout for new talent, which makes things interesting." The friend's words had been prophetic.

"Harold, that's terrible," the girl had said with pleasure. They all had laughed.

Tracey had liked the game at first. Nell Ryder had been beautiful in a vulgar sort of way. Such physical allure as she might continue to possess would be enhanced by more paint and rouge, which would sink into the smoky creases around her eyes and mouth. In the final analysis, nothing would give him greater satisfaction than to one day tell Nell Ryder and her whole posh, disreputable set to go to blazes.

He held her for a moment, motionless, eyes closed, with his face buried in the hennaed hair. How he could bear to continue, he could only wonder, but continue he must until his future was secure. He looked over Nell's head into the mirror and pressed his lips into her hair. Pulling her closer, he smiled and ran his hands under her breasts. She pushed his hands away and smiled again, then brushed her hair as he nuzzled her.

"I do indeed, my darling Nell," said Tracey, betraying a refined Southern drawl. He crossed to the nightstand and poured whiskey into the dirty glass and sat on the edge of the bed, sarcasm welling up and spreading unpleasantly across his face.

"How do you think you'll fare this time?" she asked.

"Oh, probably no better than at any other time."

"No? You certainly are a persistent gentleman."

"I am nothing if not persistent."

"My poor, poor pet," said Nell. She took the glass from his hand and drank from it, then poured him another and handed him the glass. He put his hand to her face and turned it to kiss her on the mouth. "I wish I could help you," she continued. "I wish I had some magic potion to make rich but recalcitrant ladies fall in love with you." She took the whiskey bottle and drank from it.

"I wish you had, too."

"The Magpie hasn't made any headway on your behalf?"

"No. They don't seem to be getting along again, which makes things very awkward. I keep being invited to attend every possible function, but nothing ever comes of it. The Magpie billows and coos but the Chickadee only gets annoyed. I'm afraid it is only a matter of time before the Magpie tires and gives me up to my luckless, penniless fate."

"So you haven't bedded her down to keep her interested in you?"

"You don't understand, my dear Nell. If I slept with the Magpie, she would consider it a betrayal of her Chickadee, not a token of my loyalty to herself."

"How awkward. She certainly doesn't allow you to play to your strengths, does she?"

"I think I frighten her."

"You haven't done anything stupid, have you?" Nell asked in a mocking tone.

"I think if I were to make serious advances she wouldn't know what to do. She would have neither the nerve to accept nor the courage to be indecorous enough to tell me to go to hell. Even thirty years of marriage to that bore Jerome hasn't driven her to seek more interesting company. She's a dried, shriveled-up shell with no seed and no imagination. I seem to fascinate her, which is enough to hold her and plenty for me to cope with."

"But would you bed her down if it were—necessary?"

"Since I do not think it will become necessary, my dear Nell, I would sooner refrain from speculating on any such action. Flattery and attention are crumbs enough to satisfy her meager appetite— thank the Lord." He poured another glass.

"My poor pet." Nell went to the table and drew two cigarettes out of a silver box, placed them both in her lips, lit them, and brought one to Tracey. "She still believes you're dripping with money?"

"To which 'she' do you refer? The Magpie or the Chickadee?" he asked, drawing on the cigarette and exhaling a plume of smoke. She liked to see him squirm and it took all his power to deprive her of the satisfaction. Their mental arm wrestling was a game for which he had little strength. He drew on the cigarette again. Nell's were expensive cigarettes. His one consolation was that she only paid for the best.

"Either, I suppose. I was referring to the Magpie." Nell considered him. "She does still think you are dripping with money, doesn't she?"

"Positively dripping." He couldn't look at her. He studied the bottom of the glass and then held it up and tapped the bottle she held with the glass's rim. She poured him another.

"Meaning that she'll be offering you none?"

"Positively none."

"Then I take it you need money."

"Don't I always need money?"

"Always, my poor, dear Edmund." Nell crossed back to the bureau and took a purse from the top drawer. He did not watch her as she pulled out the wallet and thumbed through its contents. She replaced the wallet in the purse and the purse in the drawer. He drew on the cigarette and kept his eyes fixed on nothing.

"Will a hundred do?"

"Two hundred would be better."

"I'm sure it would."

The oft-repeated scene was wearing him down. Though Edmund Tracey had long believed—indeed from childhood—that someone else should have the trouble of paying for his keep, to have to ask for money and have it meted out chafed at his image of himself as an independent man. He should not be kept, but be served.

"You know if I give you more you'll only spend more." She held out the money. He stirred and looked at her. She made no move toward him, but fixed him in her gaze. She expected him to come to her. The picture irritated him—the dyed hair, the traces of rouge and powder, the erect carriage draped in silk that clung to her still-shapely form, the knowing look, the money in her hand, the purse in the bureau that held more.

"Well, do you want it or not?" she said, smiling, shrugging her shoulders a little, still holding out the money.

"The question is, Do *you* want it or not?" he said.

"Want what?" she replied in mock innocence.

"To continue these lovely afternoons in each other's company."

"Let me put it this way: I've become as dependent on you as you have on me."

He lingered a moment, then rose grudgingly and went to her, taking the money from her hand. Before she could let her hand drop he caught it and pressed it to his lips.

"You are a picture, Mrs. Ryder."

"You are a bastard, Mr. Tracey."

CHAPTER 4

Awkwardness and Effrontery

The most appropriate and becoming dress is that which so harmonizes with the figure as to make the apparel unobserved. When any particular portion of it excites the attention, there is a defect, for details should not present themselves first but the result of perfect dressing should be an elegant woman. . . . A modest countenance and pleasing figure, habited in an inexpensive attire, would win more attention from men, than awkwardness and effrontery, clad in the richest satins and costliest gems.

—*Decorum*, page 264

Connor daubed his lips with the linen napkin as the waiter brought two brandies. The light from the globed chandeliers cast a warm glow over the fluted columns and ornate plasterwork of the Fifth Avenue Hotel's dining room. Chatter floated upward to the coved ceiling and merged into a general din before descending over several hundred patrons.

Blanche was in high spirits, and truth be told, his own spirits were no less high. Connor had just had the pleasure of sharing an excellent meal with a stylish woman in the dining room of her hotel and the night still held the promise of pleasures to come.

The day had been a good one. A small, private celebration was in order.

Connor raised his glass to his lips and fixed Blanche in his gaze—the plain black watered-silk dress, the whiteness of her shoulders and her slender arms, the bisque-white complexion framed by sleek black hair swept high at the back of her head.

"Are those pearls quite right for you, do you think?" he asked, regarding the necklace he had just presented to her. She fingered the three long strands and gave him a questioning look. "Maybe I should have chosen something brighter, something with more sparkle." He loved to taunt her, if just a little. Her happiness was evident in her eyes and this gave him pleasure. Though he knew his generosity would be rewarded, he was conscious of his own happiness in pleasing someone else. The anticipation had grown even as he stood in Tiffany's and peered into the glass case earlier that morning.

"Oh, no," Blanche exclaimed. "I love them. They're the finest pearls I've ever seen. To be understated is to be elegant, you know. Don't underestimate your taste, darling."

"All the same, maybe we can find some little sparkler to hang from them. Spruce 'em up a bit. What do you say?" She acquiesced with a gracious nod.

"Now, what's this all about?" she teased. "I've told you all about my little triumphs. You can't have been opening accounts with dressmakers and boot-makers and milliners as I have done today. I'm sure you haven't the least interest in my battle with Mrs. Van So-and-So over a dress-length of sapphire silk, or that I was two steps ahead of Mrs. Humbug in obtaining the last of the green shoe leather." Connor chuckled at this. "What have you been doing that you should look so satisfied with yourself?"

"Today, my dear Blanche, I have officially become a major investor in the forthcoming Hotel Excelsior, the finest apartment hotel in the City of New York." He leaned back in his chair and took a large swallow from the brandy glass.

"Oh, darling! How simply marvelous. We shouldn't be sitting here quietly talking about dressmakers. We should be out dancing somewhere."

"In due course, Blanche," he said in hushed tones. "It's a step in the right direction, wouldn't you say? We can't go larking about and spoiling the effect, now, can we? You're the one who's always telling me that triumph needn't be showy to be triumph, aren't you? You and your understated pearls?"

"You're right, of course, darling." She laughed. "Plenty of time to celebrate when they've seen what a superb partner you are. What is your first move?" She swirled the brandy in its glass and brought the rim to her lips.

"They—or we—are still looking for premises. I'm to scout about a bit, make some inquiries, look for a sizable plot of land at a good price—and the best location, naturally."

"Perhaps I can help," she said eagerly. "I might hear of something to your advantage. You never know whose wives I might run into in my travels about the city and to whom they might be connected."

"Yes," he said. He often wondered what sorts of "connections" Blanche might make in New York, if left to herself. He was glad that she was striking out on her own in a mild way. She was like an exotic flower, after all, and needed sun and air. When he had pressed her about her prior associations with New York—her family, her friends, her favorite haunts—she left him with the feeling she had not left the city the last time on favorable terms. Whether on account of her family or herself or her connections, he wasn't sure. Society's rites and rituals were circumscribed and unyielding. Her association with him was enough to put society on its guard and for this he blamed himself. Society as a whole could not welcome Blanche until she received calls from women who mattered, or who mattered by extension from their husbands. Even so, Connor was not yet familiar enough with society to know how far back its memory stretched and whether society had learned to forgive— or how much. They finished their brandies.

"Shall I order another bottle of champagne to be brought up?" he asked.

"I'm light-headed already," said Blanche, smiling, "though whether from the champagne or the pearls, I couldn't say. More champagne and I shall be good for nothing." Which, as Connor knew well, meant that she would be good for anything.

As they crossed the lobby to the elevator, Connor gave a nod to the concierge. A regular dollar or two had ensured that any inconveniences decorum might dictate as to how a man and woman spend their time alone would be avoided. The concierge telegraphed a look to the desk clerk, who looked the other way.

As Blanche preceded him into her suite, Connor handed the maid an envelope and whispered out of Blanche's hearing, "On the pillow."

The evening breeze billowed the window curtains and the room was fragrant with Blanche's scent. She began to hum a waltz and sway her body in time to her own music until she sang in full voice. Gathering up a handful of skirt, she made pirouettes around the sitting-room chairs. She floated up to him as he stood at the fireplace, his elbow resting on the mantelshelf as he pulled his cigar case from his breast pocket. In three-quarter time, she stepped before him and caressed his cheek, gave his ear a playful tug, and ran her fingers through his beard. Her hand slipped to his shoulder, then his arm, until her hand rested in his. Blanche's touch electrified his frame, her soaring spirits an irresistible force as she waltzed him to the bedchamber door.

She stopped short. On the bed, freshly turned down, an envelope lay on the snowy, lace-edged pillow. Blanche snatched up the envelope and tore it open. In it were two tickets for the Halloween Charity Masquerade Ball given by the Ladies' Auxiliary for the Benefit of the New St. John's Hospital, a much-talked-of affair among Connor's business associates. A public ball, with hundreds of guests, and masked to boot—the perfect venue for society's first glimpse of his hothouse flower and his first opportunity to see how Blanche might fare. No pressure of invitations or visits. A public ball was no less important to their future, he must remind her. They must show themselves as players in this game. Public is still public.

"So, you'll get your dancing after all, Blanche, won't you?"

"Oh, Connor, darling! A ball! How simply wonderful! I shall ado-o-ore it." Her being seemed to explode in joy. She sang herself around the room, folds of skirt in one hand, the tickets in the other hand like a flag. As she approached him, she untethered the watch chain from his waistcoat. He shed his jacket and Blanche sang and sang and pulled the knot of his tie free and pushed her body into his. Her singing was only arrested by his kiss. He grabbed her around the waist and lifted her—lighter than usual? he wondered—and swayed her toward the bed to the humming that buzzed in his ears. She laughed as he tasted the soft flesh of her neck. He was beyond thought, beyond care, beyond worry. At that moment, the only thing that mattered was Blanche.

Chapter 5

This Trial of a Woman's Patience

❦

A lady's choice is only negative—that is to say, she may love, but she cannot declare her love; she must wait. It is with her, when the time comes, to consent or to decline, but till the time comes she must be passive. And whatever may be said in jest or sarcasm about it, this trial of a woman's patience is often very hard to bear.

—*Decorum*, page 179

John tapped lightly at Francesca's dressing-room door.

"One moment," said the lady as May wrestled the last pin into the thick coil at the nape of Francesca's neck. May opened the door as John remained in the doorway.

"Mr. Tracey has arrived, miss," he said in his usual quiet tone.

"Now?" Francesca turned from her dressing table, where a small enameled clock displayed three-thirty. "I didn't expect him for at least half an hour. Show him into the drawing room, please, John. I'll be there in a moment."

"Yes, miss," said the manservant, and retreated.

"What on earth can he be thinking?" said Francesca half to herself and half to May, though the grip on the pit of her stomach told her that she knew the answer already. "Vinnie won't be here till four o'clock, and she'll probably be late, as usual."

The uncooperative autumn weather had required a change of plans. The rain had begun at two o'clock and the planned drive through Central Park with Vinnie attending as chaperone had been abandoned in favor of tea at Francesca's house at four. For once, she was annoyed with herself for being more than punctual. After five years of pursuit Edmund knew this habit well.

Why should she be so skittish about a few minutes alone with Edmund Tracey? It's not as if they had never been "alone" before, dining at a public restaurant or together at home with the door ajar within a long earshot of a friend. How many times had Francesca craved being truly alone with him? Too many to count. The moments in his embrace, to be overcome by his kisses, the play of his lips, the brush of his moustache around her ears and neck were all too few and left her unsatisfied. His smooth freckled hands with their long fingers, graceful and adept, had always fascinated her. His sunny freckled face and auburn hair belied the cool blue eyes, whose look seemed to expose her every feeling before she herself was even aware and sent her into a tailspin of confusion and delight.

When she was alone, her resolve was so strong to move steadily forward, to be healed and made whole and use the brains and heart God gave her for some good. There seemed to be no room for a decoration like Edmund Tracey and it suited her. His lukewarm enthusiasm for her interests in music and charity was exercised the way many men of her acquaintance exercised enthusiasm for women's interests, as an entertainment to keep them out of trouble. She would stand for none of that, Francesca would think to herself. Anyone whom she might marry would have to credit her and her interests with more import. She would dismiss Tracey from her presence and her life. Next time. Next time she saw him she would do it. Then he would come, sunny smile spread across his handsome face, with eyes and lips and hands full of implicit desire fulfilled, and she was undone.

It's only Edmund, she thought as she made her way down the hall to the landing at the top of the stairs. As she descended, she could see through the open door his shadow moving to and fro across the drawing-room floor as he paced. She halted on the third step, took a deep breath, and walked the final gauntlet to the drawing room.

"Hello, duchess."

There was that smile again, drat the man. Her body turned to water—water into which Edmund Tracey plunged an electric current.

"You're very naughty," said Francesca.

"Yes, most of the time." The smile grew wider.

He met her halfway across the room and circled her waist with his arm before she could protest and with his other hand guided her face toward his and kissed her warmly on the mouth. Whether he released her from the kiss or she him, she couldn't think. She laid her head on his shoulder and felt the smooth-shaven chin against her forehead as she drank in the masculine scent of shaving soap and pomatum. Reluctantly, she remembered herself and peered over his shoulder to the pianoforte, where her eyes rested on a sheaf of blood-red roses in a chrysalis of baby's breath and tissue, cinched with green ribbon.

"Oh, how beautiful," she said, breaking the embrace and gathering up the roses in her arms, drinking in their fragrance. She touched each silky rose, firm and tight on its stem. "Thank you, Edmund. They're perfect." Blood-red roses—no man with any sense of decorum would present a lady with such a blatant display of passionate love unless he meant to follow through. The qualm in Francesca's stomach was likely to prove right.

"I thought we should have a few minutes before Vinnie arrives," said Tracey. "I think it's high time we settled a few things."

"Oh?"

"Now, don't pretend not to know what I'm talking about, duchess." He drew up close to her. "This interview has been a long time in coming."

"Edmund—"

"Now, hear me out—and take those silly things out of your arms and look at me." He took the roses from her, replaced them on the piano, and took both her hands in his. A roar of thunder shook the house. Rain torrented against the windows. "How long have we known each other? Too long to pretend there's no attachment between us. There is a decided attachment, isn't that true?"

"You've been a good friend to me, Edmund—"

"Friend? I had thought—had hoped—that after all this time I would have become more to you than that. Besides, do you usually kiss your friends with such determination?"

"Oh, Edmund. You're teasing me."

"Of course, if it will help ease the situation."

She pulled her hands from his, strode to the fireplace, and turned and faced him.

"This is so difficult," she began.

"Why?"

"Now you hear *me* out, Edmund. Please." He gestured as if to give her the floor. "You have been a good friend to me, when a friend was what I needed most. You left me alone when I needed that, too. You didn't demand anything of me or ask me questions."

"I didn't know what else to do."

"I know. In fact, I marvel that you haven't given up on me after all this time. I've often asked myself why." He nearly interrupted her, but she held up a hand, begging him to keep still. "You were wise to stay away, when I was living with the Jeromes."

"I was afraid you thought I had abandoned you."

"No, not really. I wasn't fit to be seen. I never would be until I could go out on my own and get back on my feet. I know the settlement house wasn't exactly your cup of tea, but you didn't fight me over it."

"I admit that at first I thought you may have been foolish not to let Maggie and Jerry take care of you. I do know how protective they can be, though. It can't have been easy."

Protective? More like smothering, she thought. The rain continued its relentless patter against window and street.

"Eventually, I came to see it as a sign of strength," he said.

"Did you really?"

"I know it took a great deal of courage to walk away from them with no guarantee of success. I also understand the anxiety they must have felt when they realized you were gone. It's a natural reaction to want to protect someone you care for deeply."

Always protection. The protection of a man's name. The protection of a family and a home. Maybe even protection from herself, she thought. Where was this protection the day Mother and Father and Oskar went boating? No one protected them—or her from grief.

"And do you want to protect me?"

"I know better than to answer that. What I want is to somehow make up for a part of what you lost—and more, if I can," he said, as if he could read her thoughts. "More than a friend or a brother. I think you're ready for more and I believe you know it too. You're ready for what a married life can offer you, for what we could experience together as husband and wife. For a life that's no longer hedged about by chaperones and proprieties."

"Edmund . . ."

"Yes, duchess, for a full life together."

Francesca would have stopped her ears if she could. Edmund had hit upon two themes that cut her to her marrow—to live in the bosom of a family and the "full woman's life" to which Maggie always referred with a lowered voice. If he understood these, could he fail to understand her desire for a full life in other ways as well, to push the limits of her talents and her personality? If not Edmund, then who? Would more time and consideration make the least bit of difference? Was she being foolish, standing in her own way when she could have at least this part of what she wanted? Maybe engagement and marriage were the last, best answers.

"Duchess? Shall I kneel?"

"You're teasing me."

"No, not about this." He came forward and took her hands again. "Francesca, I offer you my heart and my hand, my soul and body. Will you marry me? Will you consent to be my wife?"

Could she leap over this last hurdle—and survive? If she faltered now, would there be anyone else six months from now, or next year, or the next? Would she come to her thirtieth year with no one? As Francesca looked into his earnest face, she heard the clatter of hooves. A cab had pulled up outside the house, followed by the snap of the cab door.

"That'll be Vinnie," said Edmund. "It's now or never, duchess. What'll it be?"

The bell rang and John's footsteps made their way down the hallway. The inner hallway door opened, then the front door, and Francesca heard Vinnie's greeting and complaint about the weather. "Miss Lund and Mr. Tracey are waiting in the drawing room, Miss Lawrence," she heard John say. Yes, it's now or never.

She threw her arms around his neck and held him to her, as if for dear life. He nuzzled her hair and then kissed her mouth.

At that moment, Vinnie burst into the room.

"Vinnie," Francesca said before her friend could utter a word. "You'll never guess what just happened."

$\mathscr{C}$HAPTER 6

The Inconveniences of Society

$\sim\!\!\gg\!\!\approx\!\!\sim$

There is the most delicate shade of difference between ci-
vility and intrusiveness, familiarity and common-place,
pleasantry and sharpness, the natural and the rude, gai-
ety and carelessness; hence the inconveniences of society,
and the errors of its members. To define well in conduct
these distinctions, is the great art of a man of the world.
It is easy to know what to do; the difficulty is to know
what to avoid.

—Decorum, page 26

A good deal of dickering took place before Connor and Blanche agreed upon the characters for their costumes for the charity ball. Connor nixed the Harlequins, Columbines, Brunhildes, Siegfrieds, Raleighs, and Elizabeths that were in vogue this year and Spanish gypsies were "not fine enough." Blanche settled on Marie Antoinette but failed to persuade him to sacrifice his buccaneer for Louis XVI. Blanche was to engage a costumer and settle on designs, fabrics, and fittings with minimal interruption to the Hotel Excelsior's progress. And if the expenses for visiting gowns and reception gowns were slipped in among the costumer's charges, no matter. Connor's bank account could stand the strain.

"Don't worry, darling," Blanche had assured him when he cross-questioned her about costumers. "I'll find the best places. By the time we're done, Blackbeard himself won't be able to tell you from a member of his crew."

The parts of New York that catered to those for whom costumes, characters, and impersonation were a way of life were not the finest in town, nor would their clientele necessarily be on Mrs. Vanderbilt's guest lists. Connor might not approve, but he could not disapprove of what he did not know. Blanche felt as if she'd been sprung from a trap.

Though her father's family had come from money, he himself had been a younger son, the renegade—a musician and composer whose work made him a frequenter of opera houses, theaters, music halls, and mansions. With an artist for a wife—and she reputed to have come from Spanish gypsy stock—the bohemian life of artists' studios, salons, and the adoption of personae as the situation dictated were as familiar to Blanche as if they had been inscribed on her personality from birth. The gifts of money her father's mother had intended for her and her sisters' education financed the family for two years in Europe, where indeed the young and striking trio of Blanche, Teresa, and Harriet received an education beyond anything their grandmother would have imagined—or approved. With the preoccupation of survival and the desire to rise in the world, Blanche had given not a moment's thought to the withdrawal her spirit had undergone when deprived of the color, noise, odor, and sensation of the life she had known. The chance to reacquaint herself with the theatrical costumers and the world with which she and her family had been so familiar was intoxicating.

Though the theaters that catered to the elite had begun their great migration uptown many years before, the Bowery still boasted good entertainment. Blanche picked her way through the dirty back streets and fetid, trash-strewn alleyways. She jostled with handcarts and horse-drawn vans and stopped at shop after shop, referred on to street after street until she found what she sought.

Down a blind alley, recessed into a windowless wall of dingy brick, was a door bright with red-, green-, and yellow-painted panels and a brass knob and knocker. Above the door, a black sign with bold red letters edged in gold proclaimed ATELIER MAXIMILLIAN. She gave the knocker a brisk rap. A peephole door snapped open and a spectacled eye appeared and raised a bushy eyebrow. The door was flung open by a portly man in plaid trousers, a brocade waistcoat, and a white collarless shirt, with a smattering of grizzled hair on top of his head and sticking out over his ears.

"My dear Mrs. Alvarado," the man exclaimed as he took her hand and kissed it. "How do you do, my dear lady?"

"Hello, Max, darling."

"You should have wired that you were in town. How long it has been since we've had the pleasure. Come in. Come in."

"I had a good job tracking you down," said Blanche, stepping over the threshold. "You seem to have moved shops several times since we last met."

"Yes, well, you know how it is," he said, still smiling. "The fortunes of war, one might say. The modern bill collector is such a relentless breed of bloodhound."

"The Oriental and the Neue Stadt still not paying up?" asked Blanche sympathetically.

"Oh, my dear, the list gets longer and longer. But let us not speak of unpleasantness. Come on back and let us become reacquainted."

He led her through a rabbit warren of rooms crowded with costumes hanging from every hook and pole, mounted a narrow staircase, and skirted the perimeter of a workroom flooded with light from three tall windows. Three women ran three sewing machines that kept up a steady rat-tat-tat as a man cut a pattern at a long table. Fabric was stacked to the ceiling, scraps of braid and lace were trodden underfoot, and trays of notions were set higgledy-piggledy on shelves. The proprietor admitted Blanche to a small glassed-in office and indicated a shabby wooden chair. She sat down and drew off her gloves.

"Now, my dear, may I offer you refreshment from my somewhat limited stores?" he said, opening a small cabinet containing a single bottle and two glasses. "Gin or gin?" This invitation she declined and Max, glass in hand, sat down with a creak at the well-worn desk.

"What brings you to New York and to my humble establishment, my dear?"

"I arrived here several weeks ago to join a gentleman who has just concluded a rather lucrative business deal. We are expecting to be caught up in a number of social engagements. One of them happens to be a masked ball."

"This wouldn't be in aid of the new hospital," ventured Max.

"The Ladies' Auxiliary Ball, yes. My friend and I want completely original designs, you see. Naturally I wouldn't rest until I had found you." Max beamed.

"You understand, my friend is a very busy man and couldn't possibly be bothered to come here, but mightn't you be able to send someone to his hotel for measurements and fittings and such like?"

"Say no more, dear lady. We shall send a man accoutered as the most respectable of costumers for the highest of high society. Simply tell me where and when."

"You are a darling, Max," she said as she took a folded piece of paper from her handbag. "Here is the gentleman's name and address and a list of the types of fabrics and accessories we shall require. You can arrange for wigs and shoes and such, as always?"

"Of course, my dear."

"Naturally you and I shall consult as to the finer points, though the lion's share, darling Max, will remain in your capable hands. Here's a little something on account," she added, pulling her wallet from her bag and handing him several bills.

"You're too generous."

"You don't possess a telephone?"

"Alas . . ."

"Then I'll wire you as to an appointment time for Mr. O'Casey and for a time when you and I might consult here again."

"Certainly."

Blanche rose and Max hoisted himself to his feet. They retraced their steps through the workroom, down the stairs, and squeezed among the costumes to the door.

"Until then," said Max. "Charmed to see you again."

"Likewise, darling," she said, giving him her hand. She turned to go, then stopped. "And Max," she said. "For heaven's sake, make sure you pay your workers."

It was one-thirty and Blanche was hungry. She turned down a side street where she used to know a smaller, quieter luncheon room, hospitable to ladies, that served excellent though simple fare. Until today she had resisted visiting her old haunts and renewing old acquaintances. At any moment she expected to be introduced to Connor's associates and thus be released into the boundless surge of the mainstream. Her search for Max brought the old longings back to her. Besides, she couldn't wait for Connor forever. Her step quickened. She saw the sign: THE BLUE IRIS TEAROOM.

The decor had changed little since she was last there, a lifetime ago it seemed. Chinaware in patterns of blue were still displayed on a shelf that ran around the entire room—vases, porcelain ladies in blue dresses, flow-blue cups, saucers, plates, and English china teapots of all descriptions. A hodgepodge of familiar historical prints still occupied the walls. A small china vase with a few cuttings of the season's last chrysanthemums sat on each linen-covered table. Mismatched chairs were brought into greater symmetry with identical deep russet and blue-violet upholstered seats.

Ladies were lunching alone at several tables. A neatly frocked waitress in a white apron and cap showed her to a table toward the back. Blanche deposited her jacket and handbag on an empty chair and sat, taking in the whole room. The moment she closed her menu the waitress was at her elbow, took her order, and departed. Blanche relaxed.

That evening Connor congratulated her on her luck with their costumes and said that he was glad she had found in the Blue Iris a small retreat. She took advantage of this approval and included a stop at the Iris whenever she ventured out.

One afternoon after an unusually good visit with Max, she decided to celebrate at the Blue Iris. Seated at what was becoming her usual table, she had ordered her tea and cakes and had pulled from her handbag the small notebook to review the day's progress when an arrival at the front of the room caught her attention.

A woman entered wrapped in a dark paisley shawl with a dark oversize soft velvet hat with a heavy broach at one side. So flamboyant a costume would have made most women look ridiculous, but something confident and familiar in the woman's posture carried off the ensemble. Blanche could see the profile of a white chin, smiling lips, and straight nose beneath the hat. Blanche sat arrested.

"Is everything all right, madam?" inquired her waitress.

"Yes, everything is fine, thank you," answered Blanche, caught a little off guard.

"Shall I bring you fresh hot water?"

"Yes, if you please," she said to send the girl away.

By then the woman stood by a table unwinding the shawl and laying it across the back of a chair and unbuttoning her coat. She sat in the frame of the tearoom's front window, the fading after-noon light casting her in silhouette. A waitress drew up to take her order. The order completed, the woman's glance followed the re-treating waitress and then took in the rest of the room, stopping one by one at each table. Blanche waited. Surely the flamboyant style was unmistakable. The gaze passed lightly over Blanche. *Probably a mistake*, she thought as she breathed again. Then in an almost imperceptible moment of recognition, the woman's look re-turned. She looked away and smiled from under the hat, then turned again toward Blanche. This time Blanche saw an amused smile spread across the woman's face. Relieved, Blanche smiled in return.

Neither acknowledging the other, the women took their tea and cakes in silence. Finally, the woman made a show of drawing out her purse to pay her bill. She handed the girl the money, rose, wrapped herself in the coat and shawl, and left without another look. As the waitress retreated to fetch a tray from the sideboard, she passed by Blanche's table.

"The lady asked me to give you this, madam," she said, proffer-ing a card.

The card read,

MRS. ANTON RYDER
20TH STREET, GRAMERCY PARK
NEW YORK, NEW YORK

CHAPTER 7

Imperfections

❧❦❧

Supposing the gentleman to be accepted by the lady of his heart, he is, of course, recognized henceforth as one of the family.

The family of the engaged lady should endeavor to make the suitor feel that he is at home, however protracted his visits may be. . . .

But protracted courtship, or engagements, are if possible, to be avoided; they are universally embarrassing. Lovers are so apt to find out imperfections in each other—to grow exacting, jealous, and morose.

—*Decorum*, pages 187 and 188

The drawing-room table was arrayed with gleaming pink luster china, silverware, sandwiches, and seedcake. Vinnie and her brother, Michael, her friend and Michael's fiancée, Anne, Maggie and Jerry Jerome, and Vinnie's parents, the Reverend and Mrs. Lawrence, had been invited to tea in anticipation of the engagement ring, the prelude to the official announcement and the party to follow.

Vinnie had not greeted the news with her usual gushing abandon. For ten years they had watched their friends marry and become occupied with families and children. Their spinster status seemed to cement their friendship and made spinsterhood not look so very dim. Vinnie could only picture a year of busyness ahead with little time for her. A veil of experience was about to come between them that she could not penetrate until her own marital fortunes changed. She would be the spinster friend, powerless, without status or vocation, and doomed to a life at home. When this melancholy overtook her, Vinnie wept for the loss of a friend—and her own foolishness. If twenty years' friendship had taught her anything about Francesca, Vinnie would be enfolded in the bosom of a new family.

"Edmund is late," said Maggie, peering between the lace curtains.

"No, he isn't, not yet anyway," said Francesca. "You're early, you know."

"We must all be early, then," said Jerry, looking at his watch. "What did his note say?"

"Just that he'd been detained," said Francesca. "He didn't give a reason."

"Business, no doubt," said Mrs. Lawrence kindly.

"Yes," said Maggie. "Gentlemen are always letting business detain them."

"I'm surprised he didn't use the new telephone," said Vinnie, then wished she could call back the remark. Edmund had made such a fuss about the telephone. A modern convenience, he had said, one that everyone would have sooner or later. Why have one now when there weren't that many people to talk to? "Maybe he couldn't find a telephone himself," she added, trying to make amends for her unkindness.

"Here he is at last," said Maggie as a hackney carriage drew up. "Dear Edmund."

John moved past the drawing room to answer the insistent sound of the knocker. Tracey showed himself into the drawing room, pushing both doors open and leaning into the room with a look of boyish mischief on his golden, freckled face.

"Ladies!" he said, his smile wide. "Good afternoon!" He straightened his tall frame and pulled the doors closed behind him. "Hello, my duchess." Francesca went to greet him and he put both hands on her waist. "You all won't think me too forward, will you, if I show a little more affection than usual to my fiancée, whom I haven't seen in four days?" Without waiting for an answer he drew her to him and kissed her full on the mouth. He embraced her in a bear hug and held her for a few moments, then kissed her mouth again before releasing her. Only then did he shake hands with each gentleman and lady.

"Edmund, dear, it's so nice to see you," said Maggie, extending her hand. Tracey took the offered hand ceremoniously and kissed it.

A bit overdone, thought Vinnie. Tracey's ardor seemed barometric rather than passionate. The pressure of his frequent presence was the indicator of attachment rather than passionate protestations of love. Still, he had pursued Francesca doggedly. He was handsome, charming, and well-mannered, which certainly added another mark on the credit side of the ledger. His infrequent references to money hinted at family resources from Louisiana gentry. Perhaps she was selling Edmund Tracey short.

"You're in good spirits," said Francesca.

"Why should I not be? To spend the afternoon in the company of my own duchess and her lovely court."

"Silly," said Francesca with a rueful smile. "You've been to your tailor, I see."

"Does it become me?" He held open the front of his warm brown jacket to show off it and the brown-on-brown striped waistcoat beneath it.

Francesca tugged on the bottom of the waistcoat as if to straighten it. "Very well indeed," she said, then suddenly encircled his waist in a quick, hard embrace.

"Well," said Tracey with a broad smile, "this is more like it." As he folded his jacket around her and held her, he pulled a small velvet-covered box from his pocket, took Francesca's hand, and placed the box snugly in her palm.

Overdone, Vinnie thought again. Francesca, though warm-hearted and generous, was rarely this demonstrative, her affection reserved for private moments. Was Vinnie unconsciously hoping this open affection masked some other feeling?

"Well, go on, duchess, open it," he said, smiling and nudging her gently. Before she could move, he took the box from her and said, "Allow me." He opened it and turned it to face her. The ring was indeed beautiful, two large, round, and lustrous opals side by side, a garnet filling the gap between them at the top and bottom, the whole setting surrounded by seed pearls and mounted in rose gold.

"Edmund," Francesca exclaimed, "it's exquisite." He took the ring and placed it on the middle finger of her left hand.

"An old custom," he said, "for an engaged lady. To follow decorum, you know."

"Such fine taste," said Maggie. "I would have expected no less, Edmund. It's *lovely*."

"And so unusual," said Francesca, gazing at her finger. Vinnie and Anne rose from the settee and joined Mrs. Lawrence and Maggie in exclaiming over the beautiful ring. Even Mr. Lawrence and Michael agreed and offered Tracey congratulatory handshakes. "Don't you think so, too, Jerry?" she asked, going to the chair where Jerry was sitting and extending her hand.

"Very nice," he said flatly.

"That, dear duchess, is why I have been absent for so long. I was determined that the next time I saw you it would be with ring in hand to seal our betrothal."

Betrothal possibly, thought Vinnie. *Proposal definitely*. Francesca had evaded Vinnie's queries up till now, which had given the latter small comfort that her friend had not yet made up her mind. The ring seemed to put the matter to rest.

"I was having the ring made up specially and it took a little longer than I anticipated. Am I forgiven?"

"There's nothing to forgive, dear," she said, admiring the ring. "I see you've observed more than one tradition."

"Indeed?" he asked.

"Yes. Opals are for hope, aren't they," Anne broke in, "and garnets for constancy? Very appropriate, Edmund. So much nicer to have a ring with meaning, don't you think?"

Anne *would* be happy for her, thought Vinnie. She doesn't know how to be any other way these days. Anne and Michael radiated joy. Never had two people been more suited to each other or more thrilled at the discovery of it. The wedding plans catapulted forward, with no problem insurmountable and difficulties addressed with humor. Yet those things that should be common to engaged men and women were not there for Francesca and Edmund. Their relationship lacked vitality. Francesca's quiet warmth flickered in Edmund's presence when incandescence should have filled the room.

Why did Francesca look a little sad as she showed the ring? Then the irony of Tracey's choice struck her. Francesca's mother had always been one for interpreting the language of flowers and portents of gemstones. Opals might represent hope, indeed, and garnets fidelity. But opals held a double meaning. Opals could mean misfortune and pearls, tears.

CHAPTER 8

Devotion of the Stronger Sex

Since women prefer, as a rule, to conceal their womanly weaknesses and disabilities as far as is practicable, it is impossible for individual men to judge of the strength or weakness of individual women. Thus, when a man rises from his seat to give it to a woman, he silently says, in the spirit of true and noble manliness, "I offer you this, madam, in memory of my mother, who suffered that I might live, and of my present or future wife, who is, or is to be, the mother of my children." Such devotion of the stronger sex to the weaker is beautiful and just. . . . It is the very poetry of life, and tends toward that further development of civilization when all traces of woman's original degradation shall be lost.

—Decorum, page 17

Francesca had nothing of the Miss Havisham about her, but, untouched and shrouded in dustsheets, the very personal chambers of her parents and brother threatened to upset the balance she had struggled so hard to achieve. The house's other sixteen rooms had given ample vent for her energies. Lighting had been modernized and the new telephone hung in the back hallway. The kitchen had been refurbished and bathrooms overhauled with porcelain fixtures and black-and-white tile. The servants' rooms, too, had been given fresh paper and paint, curtains and quilts. Eventually she could avoid them no longer. The time had come to go through the last of her family's belongings to make the house ready to receive her new husband.

John helped her. Jurgen Lund's manservant and head of the servants' hall, he had moved with the Lunds from Denver to New York when Francesca and Oskar were children. He had dispatched the rescuers to the lake and sent the footman Harry for the doctor and the police on that awful day and knew better than anyone the devastation that followed in the wake of the Lunds' deaths. He had kept the devastated household together, moving mechanically. Now, if she lost her nerve, John would keep her to her task.

Her parents' honey-and-primrose bedroom felt otherworldly— the carved oak bedstead, the tall oak bureaus, the shaving stand, all hovering specters beneath their dust sheets. The Labradors, Coal and Chalk, obediently followed from room to room, their nails tapping on the parquet between the carpets, their acute noses sniffing at the fading scents beneath the coverings. Determined to vanquish the ghosts, Francesca tore away the sheets and turned out closets, bureaus, and trunks, separating clothing for charity, for the servants, and the few things she would keep. John followed behind her, lifting, moving, cleaning.

"I'll keep these," Francesca said as she fingered the beads on her mother's bodices of black velvet encrusted with jet beads, plain blue-gray velvet, and blue moiré.

"I remember that blue one, miss, for the mayor's reception." Then, as if reading her mind, "Any of them would look well on you, if I may say so, miss."

Three of her father's flannel suits would become jackets for her, his neckties crazy-quilt pillows. Small personal items she chose for Maggie and Jerry, and for John and Harry and the cook, Mrs. Howell, and for her own maid, May. Her favorite items of her father's would go to Edmund—a stunning gold pocket watch on a stunning chain, and two heavy gold rings—a signet and a deeply carved crest her father had used as a seal.

"John, I don't believe I've ever told you how much I appreciate everything you've done for the family these last four years. These can't have been easy years for you. I'm very grateful."

"You've said it many times," he said with a slight smile.

"Have I? It seems to me I never say it enough."

"It may seem so, miss."

"It has been important to me that you've been here, to see to things. At nearly twenty-three—I was mature, yet immature in many ways. There are so many things I wish I could have done to shield you all, and make things eas . . ."

"You needn't say, miss. I understand."

Their progress was more rapid than she expected. Granted, a heap of questionables lay on the bed, but the worst was over. All had been excavated amid quiet reminiscences and even a little laughter.

In the week following, Francesca launched an assault on Oskar's room. Fastidious in neither furnishings nor clothes, it was her brother's exercise equipment that brought her low, so evident was vitality of a young life cut short. The rings and a punching bag still hung from the ceiling, the well-used tennis rackets displayed on the wall, the dumbbells, baseball bat, and golf clubs—somehow she would find a place for these. She felt where Oskar's long fingers had molded the fabric lining of the boxing gloves and batted at the air, then turned her fury on the punching bag. When she stopped, her face was glowing and her arms were sore. *I could have used that punching bag at the Jeromes'*, she thought. The decision now was whether to leave it in this room or have it removed to her own.

Her father's study was last. Might Edmund change this room with the cocoon-like oak paneling, its dark blue-papered ceiling strewn with gold-leaf stars and bordered with paper in patterns of gilt crenellation and Greek keys? So many men used their libraries as showplaces of masculine bravado for drinking, cigar smoking, card playing, and deal-making. Jurgen Lund's library had been for work and study—a private haven for a gentle and private man. Francesca and Oskar had regarded it a privilege to share it, to read aloud to him or to study with him as he worked, times of quiet companionship. The trio would leave Sonia reading or sewing in her little butter-colored sitting room until the family assembled there for evening devotions.

The desk and bookcases had remained locked except for one bank of open shelves that held the well-loved and well-worn books—Shakespeare and Dickens, the great poets, classical mythology, Tolstoy and Caesar's *Gallic Wars,* modern machinery, sports, religion, and science in English, Latin, German, French, and Norwegian. The massive desk had been specially designed so that Oskar and Francesca could study there, with specially made chairs and footstools. The desk and all the books would stay. She couldn't imagine any man objecting to a fine collection of books.

Jurgen's presence was everywhere as if he wanted to speak to her. She drew up her special chair and remembered how it was. Three gleaming white-blond heads bent over their work on a winter evening. Their father holding some small mechanical curiosity under the lamplight, explaining its intricacies and pointing to tiny parts with his pen, three pairs of gray-blue eyes straining to see. "Move, Oskar, I can't see; your head's in the way" and "Move yourself, silly, you're just a girl," she could hear them say and Jurgen's gentle rebuke, "Let Francesca see, too, Oskar. Girls can know things."

As Francesca unlocked drawer upon drawer she found to her amusement that this reserved, fastidious man was a pack rat. The drawers were crammed with small glass jars, old cigar boxes and pipe tobacco tins, tea tins, and matchboxes, all neatly labeled in Norwegian—broken jewelry pieces, lengths of watch chain, mismatched clasps, thousands of objects from a jeweler's lens to a glass jar filled with nails, screws, nuts, bolts, and washers.

In the back of the center drawer, she found several packets of well-thumbed letters in Norwegian tied with blue ribbons. Francesca pulled two or three from their envelopes to look at her mother's writing and the signatures, glimpsing phrases, spilling flower petals and carefully replacing them before tying the letters up again. She found another envelope in this drawer, and in it a folded paper containing two locks of baby-fine hair the color of tow, each tied with a white ribbon, and a longer, coarser, thicker white-blond curl. Across the paper in Jurgen's neat, precise hand was written, "Sonia, Oskar, and little Frankie."

The discovery took her breath away and tears, to which she had not yet given way in all this project, suddenly sprang into her eyes. She sat in her father's chair, holding the locks of hair—her mother's, her brother's, and her own—the last physical remnant. Grief exploded inside her in wave after painful wave, purging and cleansing her psyche, until her sides and shoulders ached.

Exhausted and hungry, she rang for tea. She needed sustenance to complete her task—the largest and deepest desk drawer. Francesca turned on the desk lamp in the fading afternoon light, and over tea and sandwiches pulled several folders from the drawer and stacked them at one side of the desk. Page by page, she quickly grasped each account and determined that most of the business contained there had already been dispatched. Notes on subjects of interest, jokes and funny stories, and articles on current affairs, literary criticism, and psychology she threw away without regret and set aside the business files for more careful scrutiny.

As she came to the end of the drawer, a folder bearing the uninformative label "T.—E. F." emerged. She laid it flat upon the desk and, the second half of her sandwich in hand, began to leaf through it as she had all the others. The first sheet was a page torn from a ledger, titled "J. K. Shillingford, Expenses" and whose first entry was listed as "$20—advance on expenses" and dated March 10, 1886. There followed several other entries, some for fees at a rate of eight dollars and fifty cents a day, others for reimbursements of direct expenses for transport and lodging and indicated a business journey to Baton Rouge and a place called the Felicianas in Louisiana.

Louisiana. A distant alarm bell began to ring in her mind at the mention of the destination of this Shillingford. Few Southerners were among their family acquaintances and none who had called Louisiana home. The engagement of Shillingford may, of course, have had something to do with business at the bank where Jurgen and Jerry were colleagues. Yet she had a sinking feeling. She dawdled over a dish of rice pudding, decided the tea in the pot had gone cold, and rang for more.

She was roused from her reverie by John's appearance with the tea. As he quietly withdrew, she moved the ledger sheet to the left-hand side of the file. Next were invoices and an envelope filled with receipts, mainly railway ticket stubs and inn receipts and handwritten chits for meals that documented the ledger entries. Buried among the receipts was a business card presenting "J. K. Shillingford, Detectives" and an address on Bleecker Street. Loath to go on, she put down the envelope and began to pace, stalling over paintings and books.

When she could avoid it no longer, she came back to the desk and looked again at the folder. Four items of correspondence followed, each in its envelope, as was her father's habit, to keep all pertinent dates together—the envelope's postmark, the date upon the letter itself, and the date received, which he noted on all business letters. These she passed by and took up a short but more formal-looking document, typewritten, headed by the same name and address as on the card, with the addition of the title, "Contract," and signed by her father and Shillingford. With increasing dread, she picked it up and read it.

Date: March 10, 1886

Client: Mr. J. Lund
       East Sixty-third Street
       New York, New York

Agreement: Mr. J. K. Shillingford, Detectives, to undertake investigation of Mr. E. F. Tracey at the rate of $8.50 per day, additional expenses to be reimbursed upon presentation of receipt. Client to be invoiced.

CHAPTER 9

The Real Thing

꿍

A perfect gentleman instinctively knows just what to do under all circumstances, and need be bound by no written code of manners. Yet there is an unwritten code which is as immutable as the laws of the Medes and Persians, and we who would acquire gentility must by some means make ourselves familiar with this.

The true gentleman is rare, but fortunately there is no crime in counterfeiting his excellences. The best of it is that the counterfeit may, in course of time, develop into the real thing.

—*Decorum*, page 15

Tracey couldn't wait to see the expression on Nell's face when he told her that Francesca had finally accepted him. He lulled himself to sleep the night before rehearsing what he would say, how he would look, even what he would wear to irritate her most. When he told her the next day, he thought Nell betrayed shock—that momentary widening of the eyes, the mouth about to form the words, "Oh, God," and stopping just short of the "Oh." She used the seconds it took to pour them tea to regain her composure. When she sank onto the chaise, her attitude unpleasant, he thought he had reckoned accurately.

Nell smirked and sucked playfully on a cigarette, and peered at Tracey through the haze of smoke with narrowed eyes. At ten-thirty in the morning she was unprepared for this visit. She was dressing and Anton had left for work only a half hour before. She lounged against several pillows, wrapped in her silk kimono with a throw over her feet. The hennaed hair piled on top of her head was neat enough, but her face was unpainted and sallow. In the glow of his triumph, she looked bloody awful to him.

"You certainly have a lot of gall, don't you, now that the dirty deed is done?" she said, drawing on the cigarette. "You must think rather highly of yourself."

It was true. He exulted in his achievement. He could scarcely believe it himself, his labors having been so long and fruitless. How much longer he could have acted the long-suffering lover he dared not speculate. The betrothal had given him renewed vigor with which he hoped to smooth out some of the more stubborn wrinkles in the complicated fabric of his existence. As much as he dreaded being married to Francesca Lund, the prospect of free-dom from his dependence on Nell Ryder made him almost giddy.

"I did tell you that persistence would pay off," she said.

"Are you trying to take credit for my good fortune?"

"You certainly couldn't have done it without me."

"And just how do you figure that?" he asked. He went over to the table where the breakfast tray had been laid out and helped himself to a piece of toast. He slowly, deliberately spread it with a gooey gob of marmalade and watched her out of the corner of his eye. She crushed out the cigarette in an art glass dish and took an-other from the silver box on the side table. She held it aloft before setting it in the perfect *O* that was her lips. He grinned and bit into the toast and crossed to Nell, put one knee on the chaise and bent across her to retrieve the silver lighter and lit her cigarette. She was watching his every move. He enjoyed these games with Nell—but only when he was winning.

"If I hadn't urged you on and kept you in finery all these months you would have had to sneak back to New Orleans with your tail between your legs."

"I do not sneak anywhere," he said with mock indignation.

"No. That's true. Sneaking doesn't become you," she said, drawing on the cigarette and tilting back her head as she exhaled. "You do like attention, don't you?"

"When it's the right kind." Tracey chuckled and slowly licked the marmalade from his fingers, brushing the crumbs from his hands and examining the well-manicured nails.

"I suppose congratulations are in order."

"You needn't trouble yourself."

"I might wonder where you got the money," she began.

"What money?"

"The money for the ring." She was allowing him no emotional latitude. "I suppose there is to be a ring, isn't there?"

"You needn't trouble yourself about that either, my dear Nell. As it happens, I was able to turn your small contribution around sufficient to acquit myself quite creditably."

"Oh? Your game must be improving," she said. He laughed at this. "Or you chose the right dog, or horse, or rooster, or *rat* for once." Nell drew on the cigarette, expelled the smoke, and then ground it out—quite viciously, Tracey thought. She was irritable, like someone rudely rousted from a much-needed nap. "You certainly are strutting around like a peacock. And what of the peahen, or should I say the Chickadee? Is she happy?"

"Most assuredly. She was overcome by my generosity and good taste. The Magpie was enraptured, too, which reinforced the rosy picture of our forthcoming wedded bliss."

"You may spare me the sentiment. I can picture it all quite nicely, thank you. What about money? I mean, how do you think you'll be fixed?"

Tracey knew what lay behind the question: any hint of money in quantities sufficient to shift the delicate balance of their relationship. Nell liked dependents in all sizes and proclivities. She didn't take kindly to any of them walking away under his own steam.

"I expect to do quite well. I'll admit there may be an obstacle or two. I dearly wish that Jerome would leave matters well enough alone." Tracey's tone became more serious. "The Magpie clings to the old-fashioned method of running a family's affairs and would like nothing better than for the Chickadee to leave all of those worries to me."

"Nothing would suit you better."

"Indeed, nothing would. Unfortunately, Jerome may be henpecked, but it doesn't prevent him from having opinions or acting on them. Through his offices my beloved is not so pliable as she once might have been. It would have been so much easier if I could have—"

"Exerted your charm forcefully enough to get her to marry you earlier? Yes, she certainly was smitten when you first appeared, wasn't she? However, there's no sense talking about what might have been. You should be looking at today and tomorrow, darling, not yesterday. You may have the Magpie to champion your cause, but I think you should prepare yourself for some unpleasantness. Jerome won't let go easily."

"Since you have already taken credit for my present good fortune, what do you suggest for my future financial happiness?"

"You should try to get control of all of it, of course, darling. You may succeed, but I doubt it. Next best thing would be to get a large portion."

"Your confidence in me leaves me speechless."

"I know how touchy you can be when you don't get your own way. You're like a little boy. Women only like little boys when they're adorable and need mothering, not when they're spoiled and temperamental. If you're not careful, you may find yourself sent to bed without any supper."

Tracey felt the balance shifting again, out of his favor. Nell's picture of reality did not conform to his ideal. Frustration began to rise inside him at the thought of the work involved in bringing Francesca to heel. Charm grew tiresome and Nell was right about his temper. *These women with their money,* he thought. Of all of them, Nell Ryder was the worst. Suddenly he felt as if he were no closer now to his goal of independence than he was before. *That's ridiculous,* he thought. Of course he was further ahead. He was just casting his mind back to the happy thought of life without Nell when she interrupted his musings.

"I assume you'll need money until the wedding. You certainly can't let yourself begin to look careworn. We must make the little Chickadee proud, mustn't we?"

His expression confessed as much. He would need Nell's money.

"I do wish you could manage to buy things for her without my money. Oh yes, the ring. You did manage that, didn't you? A hopeful sign."

"The most hopeful sign," said Tracey, "is that a year from now you won't have to worry about my buying anything that isn't purchased with my own money. Until then, my dear Nell, I expect we shall continue as we have always done."

"What do you mean, 'until then'? I expect to continue a good deal beyond that."

"Now, what did you really want to see me about?" Jerry said. If she looked as sheepish as she felt, Francesca thought, he had exposed her motive.

The waiter had cleared away the plates and scooped the crumbs from the linen cloth. They were waiting for coffee and dessert. Francesca had asked Jerry to take her to luncheon to discuss business. Jerry seemed a little impatient at having been corralled in the middle of a workday when all her innocuous questions could have been dispatched at another place and without appointment.

"Jerry," Francesca began, "do you remember when the Burnhams were married a couple of years ago? Freddy didn't really have any money of his own, did he?"

"No. The Burnhams did have money at one time, and some property here and there, but nothing much to speak of anymore. They were—they are—very respectable people, though, with a good reputation. Freddy held up his end of it and got a good job, did reasonably well and proved himself reliable. In the end that was good enough for the Tomlinsons—at least for Rachel. Why?"

"They seem to be very happy, don't they? They haven't had many obstacles to overcome, aside from Mr. Tomlinson's initial disapproval. I mean, the money part of it has worked out amicably, hasn't it?"

Jerry leaned back in his chair and crossed one leg over the other as if settling in.

"I believe Rachel and Freddy had a marriage contract worked out before they married, which probably left most of the control of the money in Rachel's hands. It's not uncommon, Francesca, and isn't something you should be afraid to ask about."

"I feel terrible even thinking about such a thing. You'd think I didn't trust Edmund."

"Do you trust him?"

"Of course I do." She knew the answer was too quick the moment the words left her lips. Doubt had taken on a persona that hounded her since the discovery of her father's file. It had always puzzled Francesca that she could have known Edmund Tracey for five years and yet he had betrayed to her so little about himself. He had given her no reason to doubt him in any aspect of their relationship; she had only concluded by process of elimination that the money must have been her father's chief concern. Jerry's scrutiny was at once unnerving and comforting.

"Then you have nothing to worry about." He watched her and waited. "And your interest in marriage contracts is purely academic."

"Yes," she said, then hesitated. "No. No, it isn't academic."

"You shouldn't feel bad about it, Francesca," he said again. "Many women with fewer means than yours have marriage contracts. It makes sense to have financial arrangements worked out well in advance. If it's any comfort, I think your father would have brought up the subject much earlier than this if he were here."

"Do you think so?" That Jerry's thoughts echoed hers brought small relief.

"I do. Marriage contracts come in all shapes and sizes, just as people do. There's no reason that one such agreement couldn't be worked out amicably between you and Edmund. You could choose to manage all your money and only give him money when he needed it."

"An allowance? That sounds so humiliating."

"I know it probably sounds like the harshest of your choices. If you have some measure of confidence in his ability to manage, but feel that his only problem is that he doesn't have much money of his own, you might consider settling a sum on him—either in one lump or an annuity paid out regularly. Let him manage it while you control the rest."

"That seems more fair."

"Fair?" Jerry straightened, put one hand upon the table, and met her eye. "Seems more generous than most men of limited means deserve. If a man hasn't discovered some way to earn a living, a sudden infusion of his wife's capital won't change him."

"Maggie would think this whole discussion is ridiculous and unnecessary."

"My dear, for everything that Maggie believes is ridiculous and unnecessary, I can produce at least three things she swears by that are equally ridiculous and unnecessary."

Such a family discussion played out fleetingly in Francesca's imagination. "No doubt, she thinks I should simply turn everything over to Edmund at marriage and let him have the entire management."

"That can be done, too," said Jerry, leaning back and folding his hands in his lap, "if you wish it."

She hesitated. "I don't think I do wish it. In fact I'm sure I don't."

The arrival of cake and coffee gave her time to gather her wits. She reproached herself for not having pressed Edmund about money and family, particularly early on when these subjects might have been less volatile. Having come this far in seeking Jerry's counsel, she could only continue.

"What's happened, Francesca?" Jerry asked sternly. "What prompted this?"

"I've been going through Father's study. I wasn't sure about the business papers he had locked in his desk. I almost threw them out wholesale, but then I decided to go through them all myself and consult you on anything I didn't understand."

"Sounds reasonable. What did you find?"

She didn't answer him immediately, but worked at the cake and took a sip of coffee as if to clear her head. Jerry stopped, fork poised in midair, and looked at her.

"Something serious?"

"Apparently Father was having Edmund investigated. Nearly five years ago now."

She could almost hear a hundred questions rattling through his brain as Jerry allowed an interval for cake and reflection.

"I'm not surprised," said Jerry, with forced nonchalance, she thought. "You were young when you first met, you know, and very passionate about young Edmund, if I remember rightly. He was certainly paying a lot of attention to you, even then. If there had ever been an understanding . . ."

"There wasn't. Not then."

"To the rest of us it looked very much like there might have been. Your father naturally would have been concerned. Quite frankly, he probably would have had any young man investigated if he wasn't from a family of your parents' own circle. To have a young man from halfway across a continent show interest in his daughter." He took a sip of coffee. "Well, put yourself in your father's shoes."

They finished their dessert and the waiter replenished the coffee. She knew not how to proceed. Fearing Jerry's wholesale disapproval, she felt obliged to guard Edmund's reputation now that she had agreed to spend her life with him. At the same time she sought relief in tumbling out the few new facts as she understood them to have Jerry dispel her fear. She waited for Jerry to probe as he saw fit.

"Did the papers show that the investigation had been completed?"

"No. The investigator—a Mr. J. Shillingford—had charge of the case. Case." She sighed and felt the long breath go out of her. "That sounds dreadful. His correspondence with Father up until Father died appeared to produce nothing conclusive. At least, nothing extraordinarily bad, if that's what Father was looking for. Not related to Edmund himself."

"That sounds like a lot of hedging, Francesca, what does it mean?"

She unfolded a tale that was not unfamiliar to a War veteran like

Jerry. The Traceys had owned a large plantation in the Felicianas in Louisiana before the War. Edmund's grandfather had swindled the original plantation owner out of the land. The original owner suffered straitened means and borrowed money from Edmund's grandfather at high interest. When the man couldn't pay, the Traceys foreclosed. The family grew to exercise unwelcome influence. Edmund's father went missing shortly after enlisting in the Confederate army. His mother sold everything except a small parcel with some outbuildings and put food on the table through black marketeering. She may have sold secrets to the Union.

"Certainly, Edmund would want that kept quiet," said Jerry. "Many families survived as best they could. As you say, there is nothing against him personally. Or is there?"

"He gambles," she said reluctantly.

"So do a lot of men. So do I, come to that. And we've been to the races with him."

"Apparently he has done so from an early age with mixed success."

Jerry had restrained himself admirably, Francesca thought, but now the cloud that passed over his countenance looked about to burst into a storm.

"No wonder he's so evasive about where he gets his money. And he must get it from somewhere. He's never asked you for money—or has he?"

"No, never."

"Is he still living at the Brevoort?" Francesca nodded. "Not an extravagant place, but respectable. It could be that he knows how to live within his means. That's something at least, though I confess I don't like a habitual gambler. You were right to consult me, and you may be right about settling something on him that he can manage himself and remove yourself from his dealings. That is, if you are still determined to have him." He waited, but she could give no answer and met his eye with a determined look. "If you're having doubts, better to act on them now than regret them later. Was that all?"

"Only one thing. In Shillingford's last letter to Father from New Orleans, he said that he had uncovered another line of inquiry that he wished to pursue. If what he surmised was indeed borne out, it would be not only of interest, but also of importance."

"Did he say anything about the nature of this line of inquiry?"

"No. He didn't wish to commit himself on paper until he had gathered all his evidence. If Father wished him to pursue it, he was to wire a further twenty dollars. There was no receipt for a wire transfer. The letter was dated in late June of 1886, shortly before the accident."

"So we can assume that Shillingford never finished the investigation and that your father never knew what he was after."

"It would seem so. I tell you, Jerry, I feel so despicable and disloyal. I never would have thought to do any of this if it hadn't been for the papers. I'm sure Father wouldn't have pursued such a line unless he thought it was in everyone's best interests."

"It's understandable that you should feel that way when it involves someone you love," he said, though his words conveyed no comfort.

"I thought you'd like to see the papers. I'll send them around to the bank in the morning. I'd sooner that you kept them anyway. I don't think Edmund has been in Father's study above twice, but eventually he'll have a right to be there and, I suppose, a right to know what's in the desk. I'd rather not have them in the house."

"Yes, I'll keep them for you." He finished his coffee. "And I think we should pursue the marriage contract as soon as possible. There should be nothing at all suspicious about doing so. If Edmund has half the knowledge of the world that I give him credit for, he won't be shocked and should have no objection. You haven't been engaged long, but I'll feel better if we can get the contract nailed down."

The waiter arrived with the check and Jerry pulled his pocket book from his breast pocket and leafed through its contents.

"I wonder if Shillingford is still operating in New York," he said.

"As a matter of fact, he is," said Francesca. "I checked."

CHAPTER 10

Formality

❧

A gentleman should not be presented to a lady without her permission being previously asked and granted. This formality is not necessary between men alone; but, still, you should not present any one, even at his own request, to another, unless you are quite well assured that the acquaintance will be agreeable to the latter. You may decline upon the ground of not being sufficiently intimate yourself. A man does himself no service with another when he obliges him to know people whom he would rather avoid.

—Decorum, page 36

The charity ball was in full swing when Blanche and Connor arrived at the Academy of Music at nine-thirty. A traffic jam of fine broughams and landaus mixed with a crush of hansom cabs outside the imposing edifice, just as a traffic jam of people crowded inside the imposing entrance. Connor was amused and heartened by the delight that overspread Blanche's face. Her dark eyes shone and her ivory complexion flushed as her look darted from one carriage window to the other. Connor gently tugged on her arm.

"No you don't," he said as she appeared ready to bound from their carriage. "You'll get your slippers all dirty. I'm sure they've not been able to clean up after the horses. Best to sit tight till we pull up to the curb and I can help you down properly."

"Don't worry," she said, smiling. "Here, let me look at you."

She played at tidying him up, tugging at the ruffled jabot, smoothing his moustache, securing the scarf around his head, pulling down the eye patch, and fluffing the plume on the tricorn. As she smoothed his beard, with her hand still upon his cheek, she kissed him.

Atelier Maximillian had certainly delivered, Connor had to admit, and with a minimum of fuss. Once or twice the tailor alluded to people or instances that seemed to Connor a bit "off." Blanche merely laughed, but Connor was uneasy with this familiarity and wondered what Blanche might be getting up to. Still, the man delivered the goods and Connor credited Atelier Maximillian with making him look far less ridiculous than he felt.

"No need to worry. It'll be wonderful. I'm certain of it." She kissed him again.

Connor descended the carriage steps and offered Blanche his hand as she bent her white-wigged head low, squeezed the skirt of her enormous blue satin French ball gown through the carriage door, and swept into the Academy's main lobby. Sumptuous costumes were everywhere. Hogarthian shepherds and shepherdesses, Chinese nobles and Persian harem girls, cavaliers and Puritans, medieval knights and Renaissance damsels, and the predicted Harlequins, Raleighs, and Brunhildes were displayed in stunning variety.

Blanche stood still as if soaking nourishment from the atmosphere—the scent of perfumed bodies, the sight of rich finery, the glitter of lamplight, and the strains of the music that emanated from within. Even as he watched, she seemed to become conscious of herself, and her black eyes took on a worldly, self-indulgent, and slightly mischievous look. A seductive smile emerged as her face disappeared behind the covering of blue satin, as if she knew it would only add to her allure. Connor's offer of his arm broke her reverie. They entered the ballroom.

The massive room glittered gold and white. The orchestra section had been floored over and made level with the stage, creating a mammoth dance floor. The stage had been converted into a miniature Venice of the Renaissance, with bridges, streets, and the Doge's Palace with its heraldic pennants and shields. The boxes were perfect Venetian balconies, with revelers hanging over the railings. In the tier above, the orchestra was striking up a waltz. People began to break off into pairs, gracefully stepping to the downbeat and ending each measure in synchronized pirouettes. Hundreds, perhaps thousands, of people crowded the dance floor, boxes, and tiers.

Suddenly, Blanche turned to him and squeezed his arm to her. Her eyes were expressive, even behind her mask. "Thank you for this," she said. "You have no idea what this means to me. It's absolutely splendid." She turned back to the scene before her and seemed to devour it.

John Ashton Worth and Jerry had said that their wives wished to be introduced. Neither they nor their wives, however, had mentioned introduction to a companion, nor had Connor hinted at such a companion—or that she would be glad of such an introduction. Blanche had remained undeterred.

"After you've paid your respects you might ask them to join us for a drink later on," she had said, somewhere between request and demand.

"Let me see how it goes first," he had told her, encircling her in his embrace. "You forget that I haven't met half these people myself yet. If they don't appear to be very favorable toward me, it won't help if there are two of us to contend with. We've got to build it step by step. We've got to be the bigger people and show them we know how it's done. If we go rushing in and make a mess of things, they'll take us for the hooligans they may think we are already." She nodded her resignation. Connor well understood her longing for acceptance. He hadn't reckoned on how much he himself longed for it and what he might sacrifice to get it.

A Sir Walter Raleigh and a Falstaff in the company of a Cleopatra and an Empress Theodora were the figures he was to look for and finally spied them on the other side of the horseshoe. They were laughing and nodding, the ladies fanning themselves, the gentlemen bringing them champagne punch. He wondered for a moment if he'd ever find a place among them, secure and accepted. He decided they should plunge in as best they could.

"Would you like to dance, Blanche?"

"I'd adore it."

As luck would have it, the waltz ceased, but without a word or a grimace he guided her to one of the many squares that was forming for a country dance. When a waltz was offered again, Connor put a commanding hand at her back above her waist as Blanche took several folds of her skirt in her left hand and he took her right. They stepped out and joined the dancers in a dizzying progress around the floor.

They had nearly reached the miniature Venice when Connor saw a tall, slim woman dressed in a gown of shimmering gauze, the deep décolleté adorned with rough-cut gems in gold necklaces, the bare arms cuffed by bracelets above the elbows. A large jewel was suspended from the center of a jewel-encrusted conical headdress and hung down on her forehead like someone out of the *Arabian Nights*. Instead of a mask, a filmy veil covered the lower half of her face. She danced with a seventeenth-century highwayman swathed in a large hat, a large mask, and a large cape. As the couple turned, Connor saw the white-blond hair in a knot at the nape of her neck and he realized where he had seen her before—the Fair One from the Morocco Room. In an instant she and her companion had turned and sailed across the dance floor.

"Do you see someone?" Blanche cried over the noise. "Do you see someone you know? Your business associates? Where?"

"There. Raleigh and Falstaff." He nodded in the general direction.

She strained to spot them. "With the Egyptian something-or-other?" Connor nodded. "They've seen us. Are you going to speak to them?"

"I'll have to pay my respects at some point, yes."

Only by his introduction to Mrs. Jerome and Mrs. Worth could he gauge the likelihood of a favorable turn in the path of Blanche's social destiny. The music ended and he led her back to the far side of the ballroom.

"Would you like some refreshment?" he asked. "I could do with something myself." He could see behind her mask that the light had gone out of her eyes. She looked away and took his arm. He wrested a vacant seat for her on the main floor, from which she might observe the room. He would wrestle with the Jeromes and the champagne punch alone.

The corridors were choked with people as Connor picked his way to the Worths' box. Ascending the stairs, he was met by two women who weren't looking where they were going. The smaller one was saying, "Your hair's coming down in back. Shall I help you?" to which the taller one said, "No, that's quite all right. I can do it. I won't be a moment." Her head bent slightly, one hand holding up the wayward tress, she nearly toppled into Connor. He looked up into the unveiled face of the Fair One, the Scheherazade of the dance floor.

"Oh, pardon me." The voice was darker and fuller than he expected. She moved.

"The fault's mine." Connor moved.

"Oh, I'm so sorry." She moved again.

"I beg your pardon." He moved again. Even with the patch over one eye he was well able to note the flawless complexion, the thick fair hair, the full bosom. He returned her look of cool irritation with a provocative smile, removed his hat, and with an exaggerated bow let her pass. She made her way down the hall, her elegant figure swaying ever so slightly as she gathered up the tress, the one flaw, the little vulnerability in this otherwise perfect picture and disappeared. He made his way to the Jeromes' box.

Mrs. Worth was cordial. Connor admired people like the Worths who were not easily ruffled by anyone. His self-effacing remarks upon his own dancing abilities made her laugh and her eyes twinkled in her soft pink face. Odd, Connor thought, that this woman, whom her husband credited with so much taste, should be swathed in a costume that could have been knocked off by a tentmaker for Sears, Roebuck, and Company. Still, he liked her.

Mrs. Jerome was cool and hardly moved when introduced, save fanning herself with a peacock-feather fan. Only when the other ladies removed their masks did she follow suit. She was handsome enough, but her smug self-importance did nothing to enhance her looks. Jerry was his affable self. At Mrs. Worth's offer of a seat, Connor accepted.

More than once he caught himself glancing toward Blanche, conscious of not wanting to appear to her to be having a rip-roaring good time. She watched the dancers, moving her feathered fan gracefully to and fro, looking now and then in his direction. He began to feel sorry for her seeming isolation, this blue satin hothouse flower in society's formal garden. He was about to excuse himself to Jerry when he noticed a woman had pushed through the crowd and appeared at Blanche's side. She was dressed as some garish circus character—perhaps a female lion-tamer, for she carried a whip. Her chat with Blanche was brief, but despite their formal attitude, it seemed the encounter was deliberate and not mere civil courtesy of two ladies abandoned by their escorts. Then, as quickly as she had come, the woman melted into the crowd. When he came to himself, he realized that Mrs. Worth and Mrs. Jerome had seen his distraction, and had turned to see where he had been looking.

"Have you made many acquaintances since arriving in New York?" Mrs. Jerome asked pointedly.

"A good many, thank you, ma'am, but only through the kind offices of your husband and Mr. Worth—in connection with the hotel, don't you know," replied Connor, a bit uneasy.

"New York offers such a variety of acquaintance," she continued. "One never knows what kind of person one might be meeting."

"In the most innocent of circumstances," added Mrs. Worth, with sincerity, Connor thought. "I declare, we can be such fusspots when it comes to judging our fellow man."

"Nonetheless," said Mrs. Jerome, "proper introductions can save a person a good deal of trouble, don't you agree, Mr. O'Casey?"

"I do indeed, ma'am," he said.

"In my limited experience of Mr. O'Casey," put in Jerry, "I find him to be a reliable judge of character, regardless of the circumstances. He's put us off a couple of shady characters already, isn't that so, John?"

"Yes. I thought I was a good judge of character myself," said Mr. Worth. "But when O'Casey said we should have these people investigated, we did, and he was right."

"That's all well and good in business," said Mrs. Jerome. "But one can't have everyone one meets investigated now, can one?"

"If that were the case," said Connor, beginning to feel a little testy, "half of New York would be spending its time investigating the other half and the city would grind to a standstill. Introduction is the best way, of course, but sometimes a man—or a woman—has to take a few things on trust." Connor acknowledged them all with a tip of his plumed tricorn. "John, Jerry, Mrs. Worth, Mrs. Jerome, gentlemen, ladies, I must be leaving. It was a pleasure meeting you. If you'll excuse me."

Relieved to be exiting the Golden Horseshoe, he felt strained by this short but important encounter and he still had Blanche's cross-questioning to face. For the moment he shook off speculation about what they might be saying and walked through the lobby and out into the street for a breath of air. He removed his hat and dug in his pocket for his handkerchief and was just blotting the perspiration from his brow when he saw the highwayman remove his cape and place it around the shoulders of the veiled Scheherazade. She looked defiantly at Connor, turned to her escort, and smiled. They walked to the corner and back past him to the far end of the Academy, then back again to the entrance. Connor somehow knew she was keenly aware of him. As they neared him, Connor allowed his attention to be diverted to the street. As they reentered the building, he turned to look at them. To his immense satisfaction, she looked back.

CHAPTER II

Rightly Appropriating the Money

❧

In all money matters, act openly and honorably. Keep your accounts with most scrupulous exactness, and let your husband see that you take an honest pride in rightly appropriating the money which he entrusts to you. "My husband works hard for every dollar that he earns," said a young married lady, the wife of a professional man, to a friend who found her busily employed in sewing buttons on her husband's coat, "and it seems to me worse than cruel to lay out a dime unnecessarily." Be very careful also, that you do not spend more than can be afforded in dress; and be satisfied with such carpets and curtains in your drawing room as befit a moderate fortune, or professional income.

—*Decorum*, page 202

Francesca decided to speak to Edmund Tracey about the marriage contract herself. She overruled Jerry's suggestion that he himself or her lawyer be present. The suggestion seemed heavy-handed. Besides, surely Edmund would be reasonable. Instead she hit upon the idea that the Reverend Lawrence, Vinnie's father, who would perform the ceremony, might come to luncheon to discuss the wedding. As long as they were talking "business" she might ask

Mr. Lawrence for a few moments alone with Edmund. Mr. Lawrence was happy to put himself at Francesca's disposal. Tracey, too, was eager to "get the ball rolling."

Mr. Lawrence, satisfied with Tracey's intentions, set appointments for Edmund's instruction in the Lutheran faith so that he might be a regular communicant well before the wedding the following Christmas, 1891. Mrs. Lawrence was volunteered to help with the church arrangements and Mr. Lawrence would guide them through the spiritual aspects of their nuptial. The initial business concluded, he excused himself to her father's library, leaving them in the drawing room, the door ajar. Edmund began.

"I thought that went rather well, didn't you?" he said.

"Yes. I'm so pleased."

She realized, now that the moment had come, that she felt a little uncomfortable.

"What was it you wanted to talk to me about, duchess?"

"Well," she began. "I must admit to feeling a bit awkward, but I thought we had better make a start. It's the subject of finance."

He gave her a quizzical look.

"Oh, not of the wedding. Heavens no, that's my bailiwick. No, I mean finance in general, yours and mine, after we're married."

He seemed nonplussed and didn't speak for several moments. Walking to the fireplace, he drew his cigarette case from his inside jacket pocket, opened it, seemed to think better of it, slapped the case shut, and replaced it in his pocket. Francesca chose not to fill the silence.

"Certainly," he said at length. "Frankly, I no doubt should have introduced the subject myself. It was remiss of me. Forgive me, duchess."

"That's quite all right," she said. "I thought we might begin to talk about how we're fixed and how we might manage it."

He drew a sharp breath. "Certainly," he said again, "how we might manage it. You must have given some thought to the matter or you wouldn't have raised it."

"Yes. Some."

"Well?" He stood with his back to the fireplace and his hands clasped behind him.

"Well, the house, for instance. It is the house where I grew up and I'm attached to it, of course, but it doesn't follow that we must live here. I don't mind the idea of moving to a different house. And the house is part of our collective wealth, so to speak, so that is one thing I thought we should at least begin to think about. You've never expressed a desire one way or another about where we might live."

"That is because I have no objection to living here and thought it was understood."

"Oh. Splendid," she said, forcing a smile. "If at some later date we want to move to a new home, we can talk about it then."

"Of course. I am glad to hear that you are so amenable." His expression did not exude gladness. He stood looking at her as if he hoped the subject was ended.

"Naturally, I assume that no matter where we live, you would want to add a servant for yourself," she continued.

"Yes, I will. Perhaps more than one, and of course I shall probably have certain opinions about any changes or additions to the household in future."

"Naturally, I would consult you. But for the most part I would expect that the majority of the household arrangements would be left to me."

"Of course. But I'm glad you would consult me. Is that all?" He said it as if he had one foot over the threshold and only a word of extreme import would arrest him.

"No." She felt awkward and feared she looked and sounded the way she felt. So again she confessed as much. "I'm so sorry, Edmund. This is so very awkward and tiresome—"

"Very tiresome," he broke in.

"—but necessary, if we—if I—am to understand our relative positions in money matters."

"May I venture a guess that we are discussing your money, rather than mine?" Light had gone out of him and good humor had followed.

"You've never talked much about your occupation, except vague references to business that has kept you occupied. I assumed you

were a man of independent means and that business was more of
an amusement. Of course I have no objection whatever to a man
having no profession, as long as he has the means to support such a
lack of profession. Clearly"—she gestured toward Tracey's elegant
new suit—"you're able to support yourself. So I'm sure I needn't
worry about how our money is managed."

"Of course, you needn't worry." He continued to face her. She
waited for him to say more, especially to divulge his occupation or
explain where he got his money. This time he took the cigarette
from its case and lit it. Neither she nor her mother—nor any
woman—would allow smoking in the drawing room, but she felt
helpless to voice her wishes, not wanting to use an awkward moment to begin to nag him. She did, however, take it as a small act
of rebellion.

"You seem to be implying that I might be a poor manager."

"No, not at all," she said with genuine feeling. "It's just that
since under normal circumstances my money would come under
your jurisdiction, I would like to know what plans you might have
and how I might be consulted."

"Normal circumstances? How I might consult you?" He shook
his head as if he were straining to understand her. "I believe it is
customary for the husband to take over management of the finances completely—to relieve the wife of the burden, of course. I
fail to see why any consultation would be necessary."

Francesca could hardly believe her ears. Though she far from
claimed to understand how the world worked, she couldn't help
but remember what Jerry had told her that awful day when he
brought home the first balance sheets for her to learn to read.

"Look at this," Jerry had said, putting before her a sheet of
paper with figures on it. He was sitting at his desk in his library.
She had just brought him a cup of coffee. "It's your bank statement. I want to give your whole portfolio a good going-over. I
could use some help. Why don't you pull up a chair?"

"Help? From me? Why?"

He stopped fussing with the papers on his desk and looked up
at her. "You're a woman of means, Francesca. You're young and

relatively unprotected. Even if you weren't attractive, your money will be." Jerry's blunt recital of her situation made her feel vulnerable, naked to everyone but herself.

"But I don't know anything about banking and figures and things. Besides, I've got you to look after everything for me."

"You of all people should know that I won't always be here to help you." Yes, she of all people knew how fleeting life could be. "Francesca, there are two things that make people crazy—having money and not having money. If they haven't any money of their own to control, they want to control somebody else's. When it comes to money, if someone says he has your best interest at heart, don't you believe him—not anyone. Even me. You don't have to be a banker to learn to read your own statements. If you don't understand something, question it. Keep questioning it until you're satisfied that you've gotten the right answer—not necessarily the answer you want, but the right one. Don't let anybody bully you. You're a bright woman. No one has the right to make you think otherwise. You have a right and an obligation to be a good steward of the means that have been left to you."

Now, facing the man she intended to marry, she said, "It is my money, after all. And we never have discussed what sort of settlement I might make on you at marriage."

"Settlement?" He seemed genuinely surprised. "What sort of settlement were you about to propose?"

"I hadn't thought of any particular percentage—"

"Percentage?" He stood at the fireplace with his foot on the fender and his elbow on the mantel. "Am I to believe that we've known each other for more than five years and yet the trust you bear me only extends to the management of a percentage of the whole?"

"But even a percentage would be a generous sum, considering the whole. I think it only wise that the majority be held against catastrophe."

"Held by you?" It was more statement than question. His displeasure was evident, though he governed himself impeccably.

"Presumably, yes," she said, adding hastily, "This is why I wanted to talk with you, Edmund, because I wanted to know your expectations and intentions, so that we might work out any differences and come to a workable agreement."

"My expectations, as you call them, were that we would be following the modern—and legal—custom of my taking over the management of our, how did you put it? Our collective wealth." His tone was condescending and sarcastic. It grated on her. "Of course, I have no objection to your keeping a portion for yourself, as I expect you will have your own expenses and, as you say, you will have a household to run."

"Do you expect me to have an allowance of my own money?" She stared at him in incredulity. A deep flush crept over her cheeks and her whole body suddenly felt over-warm. Defensiveness and indignation rose in her that took all her strength to suppress.

"I believe that it is the custom in many households." He drew heavily on the cigarette and expelled a plume of smoke into the air.

"Let me get this clear. Am I to understand that your expectation was that I turn all my money over to you and let you then parcel it out to me?" Her voice rose. She hated her own reaction, but she could hardly believe what she was hearing.

He tossed the cigarette end onto the hearth. "My dear duchess, there wouldn't be any 'letting' about it. I would have the management." He changed his tone. "Either you yourself or Mr. Jerome have had the management of your finances until now. As your husband, I see no reason not to take that burden from you. Not that you haven't managed nicely up until now, with Jerry's help, but I can hardly expect you to take an active interest once we're married."

"I'm afraid it's quite the contrary. I am very interested and expect to continue to be." She felt quite cross now and looked for a way to exert her control. "And since the sum in question is no inconsiderable one, I feel it may be necessary to draw up a marriage contract."

It was he who looked incredulous this time. "Marriage contract? So that I may not exercise my right as head of our household?" He was angry now. "So that I may come to my wife with my hand out?"

"Of course not, Edmund." She felt bludgeoned by guilt as well as anger. "I understand what a difficult position this is for a man. That is why I'm suggesting a generous settlement be made on you that you may control without asking me. For heaven's sake, I don't want you to have to come to me whenever you want something."

"Certainly not," he said. She thought he looked like a whipped puppy.

"But by the same token, I don't want to come to you to get permission to use my own money. That's absurd."

"Many a marriage is run on such absurdities."

"That's true. And some of them are amiable, and some of them are not."

"Your assumption is that ours would not be."

"I didn't say that."

"But you do think it. There must be some question in your mind. Well, I see where I stand."

"That's nonsense. I only want to be practical when so much money is involved." Francesca could feel all self-control slipping away. She feared that if they went on much longer she would commit to something she would later regret. His situation, it appeared, was not as easy as she had thought.

"We're both overwrought. I'm so sorry, Edmund. We have plenty of time to work out something that will be to our mutual advantage. And this whole discussion in no way diminishes my regard for you." As she said this, there was a momentary qualm in the pit of her stomach that belied her words. "I understand this is quite common, to talk about the money side early on. We're bound to have differing views. Please don't be angry." She came to him and put her arm through his. She could feel the tension in his frame. "I know you are, and I don't blame you. Please think about it, and let's talk again at another time. Perhaps Jerry or Mr. Grimly will have some ideas."

"Who's Grimly?"

"My family lawyer."

"That's just fine. Let's let the whole world in on our private concerns." He loosed himself from her grasp and made for the drawing-room door.

She ignored his remark. "We can talk about it again when you're—"

"When I'm more reasonable? Since I believe I am being as reasonable as any man can expect to be, I hardly think the passage of time will make a difference. But if you wish to take up the subject later, I shall try to be as reasonable as possible so that we may dispense with this disagreeable subject."

"I do agree," she said, "that the sooner we deal with this, the better." She followed him out to the entryway. "Will you say goodbye to Reverend Lawrence?"

"You make my excuses for me, duchess," he said, taking his hat. "You may as well become accustomed to it."

Francesca's account of her first interview with Tracey on the marriage contract disturbed Jerry, though it did not surprise him. Francesca's early exposure to the grimmer side of her fiancé's personality was not a bad thing. This information, together with the unanswered questions left by Jurgen Lund's papers, concerned Jerry enough, however, that he hunted down Mr. Joshua Shillingford, private detective, to see what he could learn.

Jerry mounted the steps to a second-floor office on Bleecker Street, situated above a tobacconist's shop. He expected a ramshackle establishment of peeling paint and draperied in dust. Instead the tidy reception room was bathed in whitewash and stocked with a plain, serviceable suite of oak furniture.

A bespectacled, no-nonsense young woman in a shirtwaist verified Jerry's appointment in her engagement diary, took his hat and coat, and begged him to have a seat. Mr. Shillingford was in conference with another client. Indeed, he could hear muffled conversation within over the staccato of the typewriter. Five minutes before his appointment time, all conversation ceased. At ten o'clock precisely the door was opened by a short, slight, middle-aged man with piercing blue eyes, wearing a slim-fitting dark gray suit, a very white, stiff collar, and a conservative dark-blue necktie.

As the receptionist rose and said, "This is Mr. Jerome, your ten o'clock appointment, Mr. Shillingford," the man stepped forward and with a crisp "How do you do," gave Jerry's hand a strong though not overbearing handshake. Shillingford ushered Jerry into a larger office bathed in light from two half-shuttered windows. Shillingford's previous client had disappeared, apparently through a discreet side door.

Shillingford looked more like an accountant than a detective, Jerry thought as he sat before a massive oak desk. The desk was nearly naked except for a small metal lamp, a blotting pad, one folder, writing implements, and a thin sheaf of writing paper. The two oak cabinets bore cryptic alphabetical markings on small white cards labeling each drawer. The man sat, took a sheet of paper, placed it on the blotter, and fixed Jerry in a steady gaze.

"Now, Mr. Jerome," said Shillingford in a somewhat reedy voice, "you said in your communication that you wished to inquire about an investigation I was undertaking several years ago for Mr. Jurgen Lund of this city. You mention briefly your relationship to Mr. Lund, sir. Would you please elaborate on your interest in that investigation?"

"Certainly. Mr. Lund and I were not only business associates, but our families were close friends, so close that when the Lunds died tragically nearly five years ago their daughter, Miss Francesca Lund, who was then twenty-three years of age, came under the care of my wife and me. She officially came into her money at twenty-five and has since moved back into the family home. In the course of going through her father's papers recently, she came across a file that he had apparently been collecting on Mr. Edmund Tracey, mainly as a result of an investigation. His papers indicate that you are the man he had engaged for the purpose." Jerry unbuckled the leather briefcase he had set on the floor, pulled the file from it, and laid the briefcase on his lap and the file on top of it.

"The nature of my clients' business is, you will understand, strictly confidential," began Mr. Shillingford. "However, since Mr. Lund is no longer with us and a considerable interval has passed, I feel I am at liberty to answer at least some questions."

"I understand and I'm grateful."

"Mr. Lund never told me the reason for his interest in Mr. Tracey's background. His instructions were merely to conduct as thorough an investigation as I could. He also asked that I conduct it personally, rather than assign it to one of my operatives. I knew of the deaths of Mr. Lund and his wife and son, of course, as it was reported widely in the newspapers. But when he died, and not knowing to whom I should apply for further instructions, there seemed no occasion to pursue it further, so I let the matter drop."

"As I would have done in your position, Mr. Shillingford. If Mr. Lund placed his confidence in you, I see no reason to gainsay his confidence." Jerry perceived a slight relaxation in the man's shoulders, though he continued his businesslike demeanor. "I have reason to believe that a resumption of the investigation is more necessary, I might even say, more urgent than it was five years ago." Shillingford nodded, took a pen from the stand in front of him, dipped it in the ink, and began taking notes. "At the time Mr. Tracey had begun to court Miss Lund, the Lunds were concerned that they could get little information regarding Mr. Tracey's background, his connections, or his finances. I believe Mr. Lund engaged you to fill the holes, so to speak, in the event that Mr. Tracey should ask to marry Miss Lund. Naturally, if your investigation unearthed unfavorable evidence, he would have refused his daughter's hand." Shillingford's pen scratched across the surface of the paper.

"To cut a long story short," Jerry continued, "after a period of absence from New York after the Lunds passed away, Mr. Tracey returned and renewed his attentions to Miss Lund and recently prevailed upon her to marry him. Now that she has claim to all her money, and now that she is in a relatively unprotected situation it is even more urgent that we find out whether Mr. Tracey is the fortune hunter Mr. Lund feared him to be. Mr. Tracey has been approached about a marriage contract, to which he reacted badly. Miss Lund brought her father's papers to me and would be much relieved to have her belief in her fiancé's character vindicated. For her peace of mind, I'm asking you to resume the investigation under the same terms as before, with an additional consideration for the time that has passed, of course.

"What concerns me most is your last letter to Mr. Lund, dated June of 1886, from New Orleans. In it you indicated that you had come upon a line of inquiry that you felt it essential to pursue and you asked Mr. Lund for further instructions. Mr. Lund was meticulous in his record-keeping and I see no copy of any letter from him to you, nor a copy of a wire or a receipt for one. Did you receive any communication from him on the subject of pursuing that line of inquiry?"

Shillingford laid his own file open and transferred a few papers from one side to the other until the essential elements in the case fell in line before him. "I have reviewed my notes and correspondence with Mr. Lund at the time and I see no record of correspondence from him, so as I have said, I considered any official business to have been concluded upon his death. I do, however, remember much of the case and am reminded of further details from my notes. I had not pursued a case in Louisiana before, and consequently took particular care, not being altogether sure how that part of the country manages its affairs, and with War sensitivities still running high, even after twenty years.

"I will not take up your time with the early part of the investigation, since you have Mr. Lund's papers, but I had reason to believe that Mr. Tracey had been married before."

Shillingford waited as Jerry sat in stunned silence for several moments. "Married?" he said finally. "Whatever happened to Mrs. Edmund Tracey?"

"That, Mr. Jerome, is what we shall endeavor to discover."

CHAPTER 12

An Inconvenient Hour

Should you call by chance at an inconvenient hour, when perhaps the lady is going out, or sitting down to luncheon, retire as soon as possible, even if politely asked to remain. You need not let it appear that you feel yourself an intruder; every well-bred or even good-tempered person knows what to say on such an occasion; but politely withdraw with a promise to call again, if the lady seems to be really disappointed.

—*Decorum*, page 72

"Don't pout. It doesn't suit you. If she's half as soppy as you say, she won't want her poor hubby to have to come to her every time he wants money. She'd probably settle a lump sum on you rather than give you an allowance." Nell's voice bit on the last word.

Tracey leaned on the drawing-room mantelshelf, flexing his hands on the edge as if to hurl it through the wall. His right hand was inches from a whiskey glass, his third that afternoon. He examined his visage in the mirror that hung above the fireplace. Did his face convey rage or could he satisfactorily conceal it? This was generally followed by grabbing the glass, downing the contents, and stumbling to the table to pour himself more.

Nell was stretched out on the divan, hugging her kimono

around her. She crushed out the stub of the cigarette in the ashtray, then casually lit another.

"This isn't getting you anywhere." She took a glass of whiskey from among the bric-a-brac on the side table and sipped it. "I don't see what you're complaining about. It still means you'll get money. Isn't that the point?"

Tracey straightened himself. He walked to the window, tugged sharply at the curtains, looked outside, then jerked them back into place, and walked back to the mantel.

"I don't know what you were expecting," Nell resumed. "A contract is quite typical. That doesn't mean all is lost. If the Chickadee will negotiate, you should get a tidy sum."

"That's not what I wanted. The soppy ones can keep a man on the shortest leash."

"True. But if she's madly in love with you, you still have a good chance of controlling a substantial percentage. So what are you worried about?" He made no reply, and without looking at her took the decanter from the table and poured himself another drink.

"Oh, so that's it. Don't tell me she's fallen out of love with you already." Tracey downed the whiskey. "Goodness me. You're losing your touch, Edmund dear. I hope you haven't gone and done anything foolish."

"If I were worried about doing anything foolish I wouldn't be here, would I?" he snapped.

"No, I suppose not," she admitted. "But when you get your back up, you can be quite nasty. You haven't frightened her or anything? No fits of anger?"

"I have behaved myself admirably." He had, he thought. He felt and behaved the way any self-respecting man should feel and behave. Why shouldn't he show his indignation when that indignation was just?

"So you say. Women tend to take a very different view of things. Does she know you are 'displeased'?"

"Yes," he said sheepishly.

"Was she displeased with you?"

"No. I don't think so. She was quite understanding of my situation."

"Without even knowing what your 'situation' is? My, my. She is generous. If she wasn't angry with you—or even if she was—you're probably all right. You have such a way with you." She was taunting him. He rolled his eyes and sighed again. "Still, it would be prudent to be as attentive as you can manage, especially through the negotiations."

"Then you think I should agree to this."

"I don't see how you can do otherwise. The more cooperative you can be, the better. If you're too obstinate, Jerome will step in and protect her, and then you will be on a short leash. And breach of promise is such a bore. It's too bad you don't have anything to bargain with—except your sweet self." She gave him a seductive smile.

"You really do go too far, Nell."

"Do I?" She changed her tone. "I'm sorry. It really must be dreadful for you." She rose from the divan and walked up behind him, set her cigarette on the mantel, the ash end hanging off the edge, and began to rub his shoulders and arms. "Think what it will mean," she said softly. "You could be set for life, especially if you learn a bit more self-restraint."

"Could I?" He took a drink. "And how shall I restrain myself when I'm used to spending money?"

"Other people's. Not your own," she said. He looked at her grimly over his shoulder. "I know, I know. Perhaps it's better this way," she said with a shrug. "At least the bulk of the money would be reserved for a 'rainy day.' That doesn't mean you could never get your hands on it. All sorts of things could happen, you know. Accidents. Incompetence." She took up her cigarette and drew on it. "Insanity. Lots of things."

He turned and faced her. "That's not so neatly done."

"Oh, it can be tiresome, I agree. Still, the main thing is get her to the altar as expediently as possible. And for God's sake, don't do anything to alarm the Magpie. She's your main ally. Just remember, we all have our little crosses to bear."

Shillingford had secured carte blanche to pursue the investigation in any way that would promise results. Knowing the hostilities toward Northerners that still persisted in the South, and that his own previous foray into Louisiana might be remembered, he recruited a fresh face and engaged another former Pinkerton colleague to assist him—a native Georgian named McNee. Shillingford would undertake the investigation in Baton Rouge and New Orleans and leave McNee to penetrate the outer parishes. Operatives in New York would keep tabs on Tracey there.

Shillingford assumed a persona of a clerk in the employ of an Atlanta law firm whose practice settled old estate claims. McNee was to be a civil engineer, for which he had trained before joining Pinkerton's, employed by the same firm to plat the land and investigate associated documentation. Their story for why the efficient little Yankee should be employed by an Atlanta firm was that to include a Northerner among its employees might squelch any questions if a claim had Northern connections. A good clerk was the next best thing to a lawyer, and Shillingford was to have been reputed to be the best.

Their mission was simple. Find out as much as possible about Tracey and his wife—whether she be fiction or fact, and if fact, alive or dead. Their separate tasks were straightforward. Shillingford would search for the records. McNee would search for the grave.

Connor had begun joining the gentlemen of his business circle on Thursdays for a long though not always leisurely business lunch at the Union League Club, to which he hoped to gain membership. Their lunches began at one o'clock and sometimes barely wound up in time to dress for dinner. At first Blanche had complained mildly, then she had thought better of it. After they were married, this might be a nice little homely pattern for him. In the meantime, she could certainly find ways to amuse herself. So one Thursday when she was sure that he would be well entrenched at the Club, she pulled the calling card from its hiding place among her lingerie and decided to visit Nell Ryder.

Connor had enough bloodhound in him to enable him to quickly sniff out the fact that the Ryders' marriage was founded on mutual appreciation, respect, and trust—they appreciated that they both were incapable of fidelity, respected each other's privacy, and trusted each other not to noise it about. Hardly the makings of an acceptable acquaintance. Outside the Fifth Avenue Hotel, she hailed a cab for Gramercy Park.

Blanche stood for a moment in front of the house as the cab clattered away behind her. It stood in a row of imposing stone edifices on a street that had been one of the city's finest, though it had begun to suffer erosion of moneyed families to newer and grander premises. At first glance the flat facade was nothing remarkable with its plain rectangular windows and long, well-scrubbed staircase. Then she noticed the unusual modern renditions of natural plant life that were carved in the stonework around the front door. A handsome carved stone planter sat just inside the gate. It almost didn't matter what kind of reception lay behind the polished oak door. To stand in that familiar front hallway, to take off one's coat and hat and sink onto a familiar chair was too good to pass up. She mounted the stairs and rang the bell.

The maid who answered was very young, small, and neat.

"Good afternoon. I'm here to see Mrs. Ryder," said Blanche, producing her visiting card and depositing it on the small silver salver the maid offered her.

"Won't you step in for a moment, madam, and I'll see if Mrs. Ryder is at home." The slight, straight figure mounted the stairs.

The handsome foyer had undergone a change. A new paper of warm browns and beiges in lilies and leaves accented by gilt and royal blue adorned the walls. A lush brown carpet ran from the edge of the black-and-white tiled floor of the entrance. On a low marble-topped cabinet stood a white-marble card receiver carved as a stylized calla lily. Blanche rifled through the ten or so cards and noted only one or two names that she could place.

The maid was gone an unusually long time. If the verdict had been dismissal, she would have been down forthwith. Blanche heard voices at the top of the stairs, but out of sight. The maid, unhurried, descended.

"You may come into the drawing room, madam. Mrs. Ryder will be with you in a moment."

The girl slid open the double doors and ushered Blanche into a rich and chilly room, dull in the fading light of an autumn afternoon. It smelled at once of patchouli and cigarette smoke. The maid quickly stirred a few dying embers to life in the grate and put on more coal. She then pulled the switch on an electric table lamp whose only value lay in its modern design, not in illumination. She left the room and pulled the doors to behind her.

The lamp cast a garish yellow light on a steely gray velvet divan that sat at an angle across the corner of the room near the front window. The brown and royal blue of the entrance bled into the drawing room, but in peacock blues and greens. A piano stood near the divan, the keys toward the window. Against the opposite wall was an enormous Rococo-style cabinet, ornate and gilded and very gaudy. On the other walls hung paintings of the modern type, with bold interpretations of ordinary life. In spite of the room's style it lacked warmth. The place reflected perfectly the colorful and dark personalities that inhabited it.

Blanche had known Nell Ryder from a lifetime ago. Among the more risqué element of artistic society that Blanche's mother entertained ran Nell's parents, who commissioned Roberto Wilson to compose the incidental music for many performances, which first brought the Wilson girls and Nell Montagne together. Not until the girls were grown did friendship with Nell become more central to Blanche's life. Such innocence as either girl possessed was lost among the properties and costumes. When Europe beckoned the Wilsons, Nell predicted Blanche would be painted in Paris. Confronted with the question on her return Blanche replied coolly that Nell had been mistaken—she had been painted in Florence. The girls laughed. Finally marriage sent them in opposite directions in geography and fortune—Blanche with Alvarado to South America and ruin, Nell with Anton Ryder to Europe and prosperity. In the separation of their destinies, correspondence faded. Since returning to New York, Blanche had heard a guarded remark that she "simply must meet Mrs. Anton Ryder. Her husband is an impresario, you know. Brilliant man. They're rich as Croesus, but do you think they are accepted? Hardly." Great was Blanche's surprise when it turned out to be her girlhood friend.

Presently Blanche heard the creak of stairs and she felt her pulse rise. Then came the footfall on the carpet, and then the tile, and then a hesitation outside the door. Blanche rose, and in that moment the door slid open.

Nell stood with her hand on the door handle, the other hand holding closed the neck of a loose-fitting dress, her russet hair carelessly pulled up and knotted on top of her head. In the harsh glow of the electric light her powdered face had a ghostly aspect seared through by sealing-wax red lips that curled into a knowing smile.

Her look lasted an eternity. Blanche was transfixed. When Nell spoke, anticipation was broken and speech took its place as if it were the most natural thing in the world.

"Darling," exclaimed Nell, pulling the door shut behind her back, "let me look at you." She stood for a moment more, surveying Blanche. "My God, you're a sight for sore eyes." She came forward and grasped Blanche's hand and greeted her with a kiss on each cheek. "You can't imagine my surprise when I saw you at the Iris."

"Yes, I can. I was just as surprised to see you."

Nell stepped back to look at Blanche again. "You look well. Very well indeed."

Blanche did look well and knew it. It pleased her that she had worn better than Nell. In the room's harsh light, Nell's hennaed hair only made her look sallow and the little creases that were beginning to show around her mouth and at the corners of her eyes were more pronounced.

"So do you," Blanche said politely.

"Nonsense. I look like hell."

Blanche ignored the remark.

"I may have caught you at an inconvenient time."

"No more than usual," she said with the same knowing smile. She crossed to an overstuffed chair and sat, drawing up her slippered feet beside her. She took a cigarette from a silver box and placed it in a holder and lit it. She held the open box by its lid and extended it toward Blanche, who declined.

"I can come back another time."

"Not at all." Nell relaxed a bit as she drew on the cigarette. "I'd rather have you here at an inconvenient time than not have you here at all. You haven't had any tea, I expect. Would you like some? Or would you prefer something stronger?" Without waiting for an answer, she rose and rang for the maid. As she returned to her chair, she said, "Good heavens, darling, do make yourself comfortable. You are welcome, you know. Truly."

"I wasn't sure. It's been so many years."

"I thought we parted on perfectly friendly terms." She took another drag on the cigarette, which made her face screw up into a curious grimace as she eyed Blanche.

"We did indeed," said Blanche as she drew off her gloves. "But you know how it is, the years pass, and I'm afraid I'm a horrible correspondent. I thought you might not want to see an old friend. I didn't even know you were still in town until I saw you at the Iris. I thought perhaps you and Anton had gone off to Paris or something."

"We had, shortly after you left. We were there a couple of years, as a matter of fact, dear Anton having quite a number of business dealings there. But one gets homesick, doesn't one? Yes, of course, you know what that's like, poor darling. Well, you certainly look like you've landed on your feet."

"Yes, fortune seems to have taken a turn in my favor at last." *Enough explanation for now*, she thought. Nell was never a good confidante—or rather, she only kept the confidences that suited her. The Ryders observed their own decorum. "How is dear Anton?"

Nell threw her head back and with her upturned face in full profile placed the cigarette to her lips and drew on it. "My dear Anton continues to be one of the kindest, most considerate, and understanding individuals on the face of the earth."

"I'm very happy to hear it." Blanche finally smiled. She was beginning to relax, but only beginning.

"Yes, he is a sweet man," Nell said more naturally. "Growing a bit of a paunch, though I must say, poor dear, and a little fleshy in the face. Other than that, you'd certainly know him."

"I'm sure I should. Out and about on business this afternoon, no doubt," Blanche chuckled. She waited to see if this familiarity would be well received. The years may only have made the Ryders more circumspect in discussing their marriage. Nell's reaction would signal that Blanche was either considered an intimate or an outsider.

"No doubt—somewhere." Nell smiled.

"And his business is just as varied and interesting as it always was?"

"Probably even more so than when we saw you last." Blanche was satisfied.

They were interrupted by the arrival of tea. Another diminutive young woman, who appeared to struggle to erase the look of intimidation on her face, arranged the silver tea service and china on a low table and left the room. Both women sat forward to pour.

"Allow me, darling, you relax," said Nell. "Milk and sugar, if I remember correctly." She prepared the cup as Blanche took a piece of cake. "You should have looked me up earlier. Anton had it from Max that you were back."

"It would have been impossible to look you up, even if I had thought you were in New York," Blanche said reluctantly. "I haven't been mistress of my own activity as much as I would like. You see, I'm not alone on this trip."

"So that was the man—at the Auxiliary Ball?" Nell laughed. "You could have brought him along, darling. It would have been perfectly all right with me."

"But it may not have been all right with him."

"Oh, I see. No wonder I haven't seen you." Nell drew again on the cigarette and squinted at Blanche through the smoke. "I hope I didn't make things awkward for you when I spoke to you at the ball."

"Not that I've noticed. You caught me at a good time. He was paying his respects to some business associates."

"Goodness, how dreary for you."

"Not really, Nell. He actually has some very promising prospects here in the city. My job is to help him smooth the way."

"You won't make me believe that I'm witnessing Blanche Reformed. Well, he's either terribly amusing or he has buckets of money." She crushed out her cigarette. "Knowing you, he has buckets of money."

"He certainly has the means to make himself a success. Only a few rough edges that need a bit of smoothing and polishing."

"Introductions?"

"None yet. He's only just made the acquaintance of the wives of his business associates, but we're hopeful that the calls will come in due course." Though Blanche refrained from disclosing much about his business or social ambitions, Nell's curiosity clearly was roused.

"In the meantime, you should bring him along. Anton knows absolutely oodles of people it might be useful for you to know. I leave it open to you, darling, to come to any of our little soirees that might suit you both."

"We're usually much engaged in the evening," said Blanche.

"The invitation stands nonetheless."

CHAPTER 13

To See Rather Than Talk

❧

In visiting picture-galleries one should always maintain the deportment of a gentleman or lady. Make no loud comments, and do not seek to show superior knowledge in art matters by gratuitous criticism. Ten to one, if you have not an art education you will only be giving publicity to your own ignorance.

Do not stand in conversation before a picture, and thus obstruct the view of others who wish to see rather than talk. If you wish to converse with any one on general subjects, draw to one side out of the way of those who wish to look at the pictures.

—*Decorum,* page 150

Plans for the Excelsior were moving apace. Commitments for financial backing were settled, garnering for Connor an eighteen percent share. With Jerry and Mr. Worth in for equal sums, they made a triumvirate with fifty-four percent. Inclusion among this elite and tight-knit crew was an enormous and well-earned coup. Documents of incorporation were drawn up. The triumvirate and three more major investors—with a carefully selected tie-breaker yet to come—would make up the board of directors. When stock was finally issued, the triumvirate would be the principal shareholders.

Connor reveled in his newfound success. He vented his excitement to Blanche in endless recitals of the intricate workings of big business. A small notebook he carried in his breast pocket was filling rapidly with jottings of his ideas and particulars of the Grand Central and Fifth Avenue hotels that he liked and disliked. Suitable premises had, as yet, eluded them, with a plot on Madison Avenue near Central Park a tantalizing possibility. Where he felt out of his element was in the intricate world of artists, craftsmen, and decorators, but was nevertheless determined to take part in these deliberations too. Announcing to Blanche his desire to learn more about what constituted fine art, he allowed her to steer him toward an old and reputable establishment known simply as Venables'.

Venables' establishment consisted of a reception room connected to a set of three spacious and high-ceilinged showrooms on the ground floor. A grand staircase at one side of the second of these rooms wound up to an open gallery. A doorway hung with a gold portiere next to the staircase led to the office, which adjoined a large room for receiving, crating, and wrapping. Paintings in heavy gold frames, double- and triple-hung or more, spread over walls, archways, and doorways, with smaller paintings cheek-by-jowl going up the stairs.

The frontmost room, which could be seen from the street window, was devoted to popular genre paintings. The second room was awash with landscapes, seascapes, and cityscapes. The third room held still lifes. Upstairs were the figure paintings and portraits. A statue or bust rose majestically upon its pedestal. Here and there an upholstered ottoman invited the viewer to sit and contemplate. The gallery was bustling with activity.

"Good morning, sir. Good morning, madam," said the eager young man who accosted them the moment they entered.

Connor dearly wished to bolt ahead and explain that he was Connor O'Casey, *the* Connor O'Casey who was acquiring land on Madison Avenue to build the finest hotel New York had ever seen—but he restrained himself.

"I'd be obliged if I might have the privilege of speakin' to Mr. Venables himself."

"He's with another client at the moment, sir. Have you an appointment?"

"Mr. O'Casey has only recently settled in New York and is desirous of becoming acquainted with the city's finest art dealers," said Blanche. "Naturally, Venables' Gallery is at the top of the list. I myself am acquainted with Venables' reputation from my previous residence in New York. I am happy to see that the intervening years have been kind."

"Indeed, thank you, madam."

"I realize we have no appointment," she continued, "but perhaps if Mr. Venables might grace us with a few moments for introduction, we would be most grateful." Connor produced his visiting card on cue.

"You've rather caught us at sixes and sevens today, I'm afraid, madam. Mr. Venables's engagement diary is full and we've just received a new shipment from Europe a day early, which Mr. Venables is endeavoring to oversee himself. Perhaps I may be of assistance." A new shipment. What unbelievable luck. It was like going on a hunt and being in at the kill.

"We certainly don't wish to be any trouble. May we know what has just arrived?" Blanche said smoothly as Connor felt an almost imperceptible squeeze against his arm.

"Some paintings acquired by our agents in France for clients here, and a healthy selection of Académie paintings and some very new works, madam."

"Oh, how splendid," said Blanche. "We won't detain you. In the meantime, we should be delighted to take in your collection, if you will permit us."

"Certainly, madam," said the assistant, examining the card; handing them each a catalogue, he departed.

As assistants came and went, Connor noticed that certain of Venables' clients gained admittance behind the portiere to the workroom. He caught glimpses of elegantly attired patrons covered in bits of straw and dust, magnifiers in hand, bent over paintings for minute examination.

"They might be at sixes and sevens," Connor whispered, "but seems to me we've come on the right day. How do we get a look in?"

"We should look around. You did want to look at art, you know. The more you learn, the better you'll be able to converse with the owner when the opportunity presents itself. If the opportunity comes, a well-placed word in reference to the hotel and its future decoration may go a long way toward gaining us admittance. It wouldn't do to be too pushy. Come along. Let's see what we have here."

O'Casey attacked the catalogue as if it were the racing form. With only a question or two he quickly picked up the formula of artist, medium, school, and provenance. The genre paintings came first, the easiest to explain and understand, unencumbered by the allegory, mythology, and history. He remarked enthusiastically to Blanche upon their light and color and composition, an enthusiasm that she shared as she amplified his observations. Connor was captivated by the boldness of these paintings that transformed an ordinary field or figure or vase of flowers from the mundane into something more vibrant than the original.

A racecourse and a painting of the St. Lazare train station in Paris so captivated Connor that he asked to have the latter taken from its upper berth for a better look. Connor stepped forward to examine it minutely, then stepped backward to take in the entire view, the assistant hovering at Connor's elbow and extolling Degas and Monet. He fixated on the contrast—the smooth flesh of the horses and silks of the jockeys on a shimmering field of golden light, and the steely blue-gray of the smoke-filled station with the black iron behemoths and delicate buildings materializing through the mist. Blanche asked if they might see more work by these artists. The assistant answered in the affirmative and conducted them upstairs.

"These are some of our finest works by these artists, sir," said the assistant as Connor prepared to pounce on more paintings. The young man drew Connor's attention to two pastels of ballet dancers and an oil of a nude. Blanche smiled and stifled a snicker. The assistant left them to browse.

"Where are you going?" she asked as Connor headed for the stairs.

"To look at my paintin's again. Well, they're as good as mine. I don't want anyone else to buy them."

"I doubt very much that Venables' will suddenly be invaded by droves of connoisseurs itching to buy pictures of train stations."

Connor wasn't sure he agreed with her, but acquiesced.

Finally, they were joined by Mr. Venables himself, a robust little man with frazzled hair, a raspy voice, and a quick manner. "My dear Mr. O'Casey, I believe," he began as he peered at Connor above his spectacles, seeming to forget whether to look through or over the spectacles to read Connor's card. He extended his hand. "I do apologize. We're in something of a muddle today. So sorry. I hope you haven't been inconvenienced."

"Your assistant has been most attentive," Connor answered. He exerted himself with businesslike charm and after a few polite questions steered the conversation back to the two paintings that by now were becoming obsessions. The proprietor was on the point of conducting Connor and Blanche down to the beloved paintings, when the assistant met him halfway up the stairs.

"Your noon appointment is here, Mr. Venables—about the Redon and the Ravier. We'd be grateful for your attention."

"I'm so sorry, sir, madam," Mr. Venables said, turning to each. "Duty calls, I'm afraid. Pray continue your perusal and tell my assistant to call me if there is anything else in particular you would like to see."

As they descended the stairs a young woman came into the second gallery and met Mr. Venables at the bottom step. She was tall and fair—the Scheherazade whom Connor had seen at the ball, but no highwayman accompanied her. Instead, the smaller, darker young woman of the afternoon tea was again her companion along with a third young woman who was plainer still. Before he could make further assessment, Mr. Venables whisked the ladies into the workroom.

A rose among the cabbages, thought Connor. *Three times now she's been where I've been*. He began a mental list of what he knew about her—the dancing, the art. He speculated upon the circles in which she might travel. Did she know people he knew? Had they missed each other in other places? Had she been at dinner anywhere he dined with Blanche? Had he passed her in the park on their afternoon drive?

Denied the pleasure of further appraising this woman, Connor was about to protest that he had had enough cultural stimulation for one day. He wanted to pack up his paintings and go home, when the assistant met them and announced that a crate containing another work by one of his favorites had just been unpacked. Would the gentleman and the lady care to step into the workroom for an advance look before it went on display? Connor's eyes sharpened and his chest expanded; he squared his shoulders and followed Blanche as the assistant held back the portiere and guided them in.

Venables' workroom was a hodge-podge of elegance and industry, nearly two full stories high with large windows on the two outer walls and a loft with bookcases and cabinets and stairs and catwalks that marked the circumference. Near the double doors that opened out onto the alley were workbenches equipped with vises and clamps, with pulleys, chains, and hauling tackle overhead. Well-worn cabinets held tools. The smell of straw and solvents for repairing and cleaning fine art hung in the air. Wooden barrels held scraps of frame molding while fresh supplies in every style and thickness stood against the wall.

A section was screened off where an enormous oriental rug covered the rough wooden floor and easels were arrayed like soldiers waiting for duty. A Franklin stove stood in the corner, in front of which stood two chairs and a low table crowned with a costly set of Wedgwood that held the remnants of tea. Nearby stood a well-stocked liquor cabinet and a hutch that protected fine crystal. Wealthy clients wore bits of straw like badges of honor, part of the select set who were privy to the inner workings of the gallery. Several parties were examining paintings, but their placement was so skillful and the service so individual that an air of exclusivity and discretion belied the high degree of activity.

Two easels were prepared for Francesca against a backdrop of dark velvet. A small, brilliant still life of a vase of flowers and a landscape of a sunlit classical arch hemmed in by trees and shaded hedges were secured by the assistant's gloved hands. The strong primary hues of the still life with its golden ground and jewel-like flowers beckoned her from across the room. Immediately she knew this would hang where she could see it the moment she entered the drawing room. The landscape—cool and sunny, solitary and refreshing, with its fresh hedges and pebbled path—would go in the study. To mentally transport these works and see clearly where they should live was a sure sign that they were meant to be hers.

A striking couple entered the workroom, she handsome, he not handsome but arresting in appearance. As the newcomers entered, all the parties quickly turned to look and just as quickly returned to their own activities. Mr. Venables detached himself from the ladies with a bow and directed the couple to another easel beyond. The woman was pale with jet-black hair and black eyes and a look of unabashed self-satisfaction, elegant in deep blue and with a large fur muff. He was equally dark—dark of feature and of mood.

The lady passed first and Francesca dropped her gaze. Just as the man came upon her, just before she turned back to her paintings, Francesca caught him out of the corner of her eye. He looked at her directly and touched the brim of his topper. She quickly faced the paintings, face flushed. Anne uttered, "Of all the abominable cheek." Vinnie repressed a smile. Francesca instantly recognized his impertinence, if not his face. She had seen him at the charity ball.

A packing crate had been pried open and a large canvas taken from its linen shroud and placed upon the easel. The woman's exclamation of pleasure drew all eyes toward them. The painting was indeed exquisite, a small cottage on a brilliant and thickly vegetated cliff overlooking a misty azure and aqua sea. Francesca, too, looked at the painting with its brilliant yellow light and then back at her own beloved Ravier. It seemed puny for a moment until it drew her into its cool pathway. She looked at the Monet again and cocked her head.

"He's looking at you," Vinnie said at Francesca's shoulder. "He is." Anne pressed Vinnie's arm as Francesca turned to the Ravier, but Vinnie would have none. "She's quite something," she persisted, "she sparkles like jet. You should look."

"I saw her quite adequately, Vinnie, thank you," said Francesca. "You shouldn't whisper about people so."

"I'd stop whispering if you'd start looking." Anne pressed Vinnie's arm again as the jet woman glanced over her shoulder and the dark man looked openly at Francesca, who was trying to maintain her dignity—and Vinnie's—in spite of the flush she could feel rising in her cheeks.

"Are you here to look at paintings or people?" she said.

"Oh, bother the paintings," said Vinnie. "The people are much more interesting. Mr. Venables seems very interested in them."

"Of course he does," Anne said. "They are customers, after all. Professional interest is not the same as being nosy." Francesca supported Anne's sentiment with a stern look at Vinnie, who rolled her eyes and continued unabated.

"I think the man has more than a 'professional interest' in Francesca."

"Mr. Venables?" said Francesca, just to irritate her.

"Oh, he's back looking at that painting again," said Vinnie, ignoring Francesca.

"As he should," said Anne.

"He looks very interesting."

"Everyone and everything is interesting to you, Vinnie," said Anne, lowering her voice with each syllable. The assistant rejoined the ladies.

"Who is that over there?" Vinnie inquired of the assistant, while Francesca and Anne looked on, horrified. "I mean, what artist are they looking at?"

"That's a Monet, miss."

"Oh, a *Monet*," she said with emphasis. At that, Francesca expressed herself satisfied with the Redon and the Ravier. The assistant motioned to Mr. Venables, whose back was turned to them. It was the gentleman who caught the assistant's eye and drew Mr. Venables's attention to them. The latter excused himself with a bow and invited the ladies to follow him. Before disappearing into the office, Vinnie turned to look over her shoulder.

"He's looking at you again."

"Stop it, Vinnie."

CHAPTER 14

A Good Stock of Information

❦

*Still it is a sober truth, of which everyone should feel the
force, that, with the single exception of a good conscience,
no possession can be so valuable as a good stock of information.*

*Some portion of it is always coming into use; and
there is hardly any kind of information which may not
become useful in an active life.*

*When we speak of information, we do not mean that
merely which has direct reference to one's trade, profession, or business.*

—Decorum, page 48

Jerry stood in front of the tall windows of his office at the Merchants and Mechanics Bank and peered between the slats of the
dark oak shutters and looked down onto the street, Shillingford's
letter in his hand. He had steeled himself for a result like this,
much as one steels oneself for the death of a loved one after a prolonged illness. But as with death, however long anticipated, the
announcement came as a shock just the same.

Registered letter to Mr. W. T. Jerome, New York,
New York, from Mr. J. K. Shillingford, New

Orleans, Louisiana, November 20, 1890, In re:
Investigation of E.F.T:

> *Dear Sir:*
> *We are pleased to report progress at this early date.*
> *Specifically, we have confirmed that the subject in ques-*
> *tion wed Henriette Genevieve Agnes Letourneau at the*
> *Church of the Sacred Heart of Jesus in Ascension*
> *Parish, Louisiana, on 4th February 1884. This cere-*
> *mony followed an earlier civil ceremony performed by a*
> *justice of the peace on 15th January in New Orleans.*
>   *Other discoveries are noteworthy: a death certificate*
> *for the father, Charles Montague Letourneau, dated 3rd*
> *June 1884, at Maywood Plantation, the family prop-*
> *erty in Ascension Parish. In addition, a death certifi-*
> *cate for Henriette Letourneau Tracey and a stillborn*
> *child, a boy unnamed, is dated 9th June 1884. All the*
> *deaths were certified by a Dr. Andrew Warren, whom*
> *we are now seeking for information concerning the cir-*
> *cumstances. We intend to pursue inquiries into who*
> *might gain by these deaths and how. Should you wish us*
> *to cease these lines of inquiry based upon our current*
> *report, please wire instructions to this effect.*
>   *I am continuing the investigation in New Orleans.*
> *Operatives are assisting here and in New York to bring*
> *this case to a thorough, rapid, and, we hope, satisfac-*
> *tory conclusion. I will wire you of an address where I*
> *may be reached. I am,*
>   *Your servant,*
>   *J. K. Shillingford*

Jerry dearly wished he could have confided in Maggie. He
wished she could be more circumspect and more considerate of
another person's situation and feelings. But such had not been the
case in nearly thirty years. When she did find out about Shillingford
and Tracey, they would row. The thought of it made him weary.
   The real question, of course, the preservation of Jerry's home

life notwithstanding, was whether to tell Francesca this crumb of information or to wait for more evidence. What he really wanted was for Tracey to be discredited. He was not good enough for Francesca, but in the absence of evidence to the contrary, there was no good reason to prohibit her marriage. Having been married and widowed was no crime, though hiding the fact may be suspect. Jerry dearly hoped for sufficient evidence to the contrary.

What a mess a life could be—a once-proud family broken by war, divided loyalties, betrayal, deprivation, desperation, and defeat, all the makings of bitter resentment and bolstered by an attitude of wanting the world handed over on a silver salver. Jerry's sympathy was fleeting, however. Having given her pledge, Francesca would be loath to break it. Though she had come to him about Tracey, Jerry did not want to push her into defending her fiancé against unsubstantiated accusations.

He had no choice. Until Shillingford could produce evidence to vindicate Tracey, Jerry must keep the matter to himself. He could only reply to Shillingford to conclude his investigation with all due speed.

Blanche had nagged Connor, in a mild way, into setting a regular luncheon date with her on Fridays. A mild nagging did Connor good, now that their life was becoming more settled. Most men expected it, didn't they? Besides, a too-contented Blanche, she reasoned, would make him suspicious, as if she didn't need him. And Friday luncheon with Connor helped to stanch any questions he might have about how she spent the rest of her week, especially her regular Wednesday visits to Nell.

One Friday, Connor couldn't make it. A crisis in the land deal for the hotel had arisen and the investors needed him for the negotiations. Blanche knew it couldn't be helped, but it peeved her nonetheless. The tiny seed of rebellion, already planted in the fertile ground of her isolation, flowered in the shape of an unexpected visit to Nell.

The maid took Blanche's card and went to inquire as to whether Mrs. Ryder was receiving visitors. That Blanche had caught Nell at an unguarded moment was evident. As she waited in the entry hall, she could hear voices in the drawing room—Nell's, the maid's, and a man's. Silence, then Blanche heard, "Yes." Blanche made her entrance, hand extended toward Nell, who was sitting in the overstuffed chair, feet drawn up in her characteristic pose.

"Nell, dear, forgive me for intruding. . . ."

A gentleman rose. He was tall, well built, with thick, short auburn hair and a thick moustache. He was thoroughly composed, his posture careless. He faced her, absently slipping his fingers into the watch pocket of his waistcoat. He betrayed no emotion, but in the brief moment of surprise and recognition, Blanche thought she detected an expression of pleasure in the deep blue eyes and the sunny-freckled face. Then, as quickly as it had come, the pleasure disappeared into a reserved and disinterested countenance.

"Hello, Blanche."

The sultry drawl took her breath away. She felt a gripping pleasure and thought her knees might buckle under her. For a moment she thought how awkward she must look, but it didn't matter. She withdrew the hand still extended toward Nell and offered it to the man.

"Why, Edmund," she said, letting her confusion flood the room. She looked at Nell. "Nell, dear, I had no idea . . ." her voice trailed off.

"Nor did I," said Nell. "Mr. Tracey's little surprises never fail to entertain."

Tracey's look apologized to Blanche for Nell's remark. He took her hand, kissed it, and returned it to her side before he let it go.

"You're looking very well, Blanche. Are you well?"

"Yes. Very well indeed. Thank you, Edmund. You look well, too." Blanche's feelings overwhelmed her, her mind crammed with questions. Where had he been? Where did he come from? Did she still move him as deeply as he did her? Surely Nell would assume that Tracey's prior acquaintance with Blanche was intimate, as Blanche assumed his current acquaintance with Nell was no less so. What must Edmund Tracey be thinking of them both? The overriding question was how the three of them came to occupy the same room.

"Do sit down, dear, and you can tell me how on earth you know dear Edmund. Edmund, be so good as to ring the bell. We may as well have some tea. Unless you prefer a different sort of libation. You both look as if you could use a drink."

As Tracey crossed the room Blanche thought how well acquainted she once had been with the strong back and broad shoulders. She was sensible of the freckled hands as he pulled the bell, and remembered how those hands had caressed her. He was the only one who ever loved her without judgment, and whom she felt justified her love. When they parted, she knew she would never feel that way with anyone else.

Blanche had seen Connor O'Casey as a man with ambitions and appetites, not unfeeling or unkind yet rough and worldly. He was good to her, as any man with means can be good to a woman. Perhaps she had expected too much of him and thus of her own powers to mold him into an image she could adore. Edmund roused her as if from a long slumber. Here was an idol ready-made, who could draw from her adoration. She wondered why she ever thought she could marry this man with whom she had spent this last, arduous year. Oh yes, she remembered. The money.

Tracey went to the liquor cabinet and poured a large bourbon and extended it and said, "Blanche?" She declined and he offered it to Nell.

"Well, if you don't need it, dear," said Nell, "I certainly do." There was an awkward silence until Nell changed the subject.

"What brings you here on a Friday, Blanche darling? You're always welcome, of course, but this is a bit unusual for you. O'Casey occupied?" said Nell. Then, turning to Tracey she said, "Mr. Connor O'Casey is Blanche's gentleman friend, Edmund," giving a barely perceptible emphasis to "friend."

"O'Casey," he said, pondering the name, "O'Casey. Oh, yes. I believe I have heard that name. Does he not have business dealings with a Mr. William Thomas Jerome?"

"William?" asked Blanche as she made herself more comfortable.

"Known as 'Jerry' to his friends and associates," continued Tracey.

"Oh, really? Yes. Why? Do you know Mr. Jerome?"

"He knows the Jeromes intimately, don't you, darling?" offered Nell, smiling. "Though among their friends there are others whom he is about to know better." She chuckled. He consumed his drink, but Blanche recognized the little habits of manner that signaled his displeasure and concluded that his relationship with Nell was one of dependence. Money. Always money. She pitied him for that, even as she tried never to pity herself.

"Oh, let's not make this any more difficult than it needs to be," Nell cooed with an edge of sarcasm. "Do tell Mother how you two met."

"It's quite simple." Blanche surprised herself by stepping into the breach to save Tracey the necessity of a polite reply. "You remember, Nell, how I spent so much time in the South after Alvarado died? Well, Mr. Tracey being Southern, it can hardly surprise you that he and I might cross paths."

"But the South is such a big place, is it not, Edmund?"

"Indeed it is," Blanche continued. "But we were both in New Orleans for a time. Besides, circles of like-minded people are generally smaller than one thinks, no matter where they are. It's not unusual for such people to find each other."

"True," said Nell. "And I'm sure you two were very 'like-minded.'"

"New Orleans is as cosmopolitan a place as you'll find anywhere and a natural draw," Blanche continued, deflecting Nell's last statement. "The port is always bustling and the French influence is so cultivated. It's really quite an interesting place. Mr. Tracey used to come to the salon to play cards, didn't you, Edmund?" she said. "You brought a letter of introduction with you, didn't you? I can't remember now from whom."

"Another like-minded person, no doubt," said Nell.

Blanche would get nowhere by defending him, even mildly. Despite the thousand questions that invaded her thoughts, to linger was to no purpose and she might make matters worse. The sooner Tracey faced it and told whatever story he chose about his previous life with herself the better. She consumed her tea and cake. Tracey spoke little, ate nothing, and drank bourbon. She felt homesick for his embrace and the shelter of his body. Nell, curled up in the chair like a contented cat, held her plate of cake in one paw under her chin and ate it with the air of having been caught doing something naughty. As soon as she could do so politely, Blanche left.

CHAPTER 15

A Complete Stranger

In good society, a visitor, unless he is a complete stranger, does not wait to be invited to sit down, but takes a seat at once easily. A gentleman should never take the principal place in the room, nor, on the other hand, sit at an inconvenient distance from the lady of the house. He must hold his hat gracefully, not put it on a chair or table, or if he wants to use both hands, must place it on the floor close to his chair.

—*Decorum,* page 79

To lubricate the priest's memory and powers of speech, Shillingford arrived at the rectory with a gift of two bottles of very fine sherry and a bottle of very old bourbon. Father Marcel had come to the Church of the Sacred Heart of Jesus as a young cleric and had spent all his career there, so he knew well the tumultuous history of la Famille Letourneau.

A darkness came into Father Marcel's expression at the mention of the Maywood Plantation. He had had no meaningful contact with the Letourneaus since the death of Henriette. Hospitable though he was, he stated firmly that he still was bound to the confidentiality to which his profession held him, even after all this time. Shillingford chose a roundabout probe, avoiding reference to the fact that a young woman's reputation might be ruined by Henriette's husband. The priest replaced the glass stopper in the sherry decanter and, his own glass in hand, took his seat opposite Shillingford in front of the fire.

The priest embarked on an interminable family history—the arrival of the patriarch, Georges Letourneau, and his French bride, Elodie DuLac, in Ascension Parish and the establishment of the Maywood sugar plantation. The son, Charles Montague, and his regrettable marriage to Celestine, who nearly bankrupted the family in luxurious living. Charles's debauchery with a slave woman, and his cowardly escape to France during the War. The account was peppered with comments on Georges and Elodie's generosity to the Church and the marked contrast in the behavior of their children.

"The first fruits of Georges' and Elodie's labor came here, as it should. They gave sacrificially to the Church," he said, and sipped the fine sherry. "What remained of their wealth they put back into Maywood and the sugar business, so despite the fact that they had very few debts and came to have enormous property and slaves, there was very little actual capital, you see." He sipped the sherry again. "The younger generation don't know what sacrifice means. They spend it all on pleasure and forget God." Shillingford noted the fine carved paneling, the comfortable furnishings, and the thick rug in the priest's study. He noted equally the priest's fine linen, meticulously kept, but a little threadbare at the neck and cuffs. At one time, at least, Father Marcel had indeed benefited from their patronage.

"Slowly Maywood came back, but it would never achieve the greatness it had known in the old days, especially since the slaves had been freed."

"And what of the sons? I assume they were raised to take over the business."

"Hmph, business." The priest dropped into musing again. "Henri Gerard and Philippe should have made it their business. They should have made eternity their business. There was much they could have repaired besides Maywood." The priest appeared to want to say more, but held his tongue. "Their relationship with

Charles Montague was less than a father might hope for. Their relationship with Celestine was somewhat better. They exhibited the same social tendencies as she, which she simply put down to her sons' high spirits.

"Etienne was a different breed. He tried to keep up with his older brothers in mischief, but one sensed that his heart was not in it. I believe he felt some burden for his brothers' behavior and the family's reputation. He even asked me once about the Church, and I believe with a little encouragement he might have made the Church his career. Worse villains than he have become some of our most revered saints, you know. But Etienne Letourneau died prematurely. He was out hunting with his brothers. A gun discharged accidentally. He was killed." The priest sighed, looked into the fire.

"I see." *A hunting accident*, thought Shillingford. This chilling bit of news shed new light on the Letourneaus. "You mention only the three boys. What of the daughter?"

"Ah, yes. We come to Henriette. Henriette was born after Charles Montague returned from France. A sad business. Celestine died in childbirth. Montague was prostrate with grief. He gave generously to the Church to have her remembered there and doted upon the little girl as the last remnant of her mother. Henriette was a petite thing, doll-like, with dark hair and black eyes, and tiny feet, I remember. She used to flit about everywhere. *Le papillon*, the butterfly, they used to call her. Her father put her in the Ursuline Convent School in New Orleans. When she finished her schooling at thirteen she went back to Maywood.

"She was the little princess. Their father treated the boys more like vassals than princes, so there was bad blood from the beginning. Except for Etienne. He and Henriette were closer in age. When he was killed, she was overcome with grief.

"Then a young man from an Anglo family appeared and set the Letourneaus on what I believe was their final path to destruction," said the priest.

"Edmund Tracey," said Shillingford.

"Yes, Edmund Tracey. He had been an acquaintance of Henri Gerard, the eldest. Charles Montague disapproved. He felt Tracey

was a bad influence on his sons. I believe it was the meeting between Tracey and Henriette and her infatuation with him that
sealed their fates. Henri Gerard brought the Anglo to Henriette's
coming-out ball. She was barely fifteen."

"You were present at the ball?"

"Naturally. I was always invited to all the important family cele-
brations. The Anglo made himself agreeable to her, an impression-
able young girl. He had no right, of course, and should have been
thrown out then and there. But Henriette was always determined
to have anything she wanted and she wanted Tracey. Eventually
they married." *A skillful omission of detail*, thought Shillingford, *and
a baby is no small detail*. The path from coming-out ball to matrimony appeared to be a short one for Henriette and Edmund
Tracey. "I blessed the union on condition that any children would
be raised in the Church in spite of his Anglo heritage. The entire
episode was dreadfully hard on Charles Montague. It broke him.
He died only a few months after they married."

"And they lived at Maywood—Tracey and Henriette?"

"Yes." The priest's face grew hard and drawn.

"And Henriette herself died shortly thereafter?" asked Shillingford.

"Yes." Father Marcel rose and went to the hearth and made
rather a business of stirring the fire and laying on more wood. He
decanted more sherry for each of them and resumed his seat, staring for a moment into the crackling flames. When he finally spoke
he did so haltingly, without looking at Shillingford.

"It was so queer," he said. "All of it, so very queer. I had been
there for her father, of course, only a few days before. Everything
had been done decently, properly for him. I was called to administer the last rites. He was *in extremis*, but he managed to kiss the
Cross. Yet for Henriette, I was not called." He stared into his glass.
"She lingered for a day or two, yet I was not called. There would
have been plenty of time for her—to ensure her everlasting peace.
After she died, there was no wake, no vigil, no rosary, no leave-taking
of any kind. I fully expected the burial to be in one of the family
tombs, with Charles Montague and Celestine. But Henri Gerard

said no. A year and a day had not passed since Charles Montague's death. That was his defense for his reprehensible actions.

"Maywood has a little city of tombs in the countryside where Georges and Elodie had constructed monuments for the family, to keep them dry throughout eternity." The priest made a feeble smile, then continued, "Henri Gerard insisted that she be placed there as quickly as possible. She would not have received Christian burial at all, had I not intervened when I heard of her death and had proven equally stubborn in insisting that the dead must at the very least be entombed with the proper words.

"When I arrived, the coffin lid was bolted down. I was not permitted to see let alone anoint the body. I was shown the death certificate signed by the doctor—Dr. Warren—which Henri Gerard declared to be enough. He and Tracey and I transported the coffin on a wagon to the graveyard. The ground in the little grove of trees was overgrown and thorny, like some forgotten place. My whole being revolted at the thought of laying Henriette to rest there. But Henri Gerard threatened to turn me out altogether, so I helped them pull the wagon up next to an old box tomb. Do you know what that is?"

"I believe I've seen them."

"They're horrible things. They look like they should be a box on top of the ground, but they have no bottom and are dug deep. It took the three of us to budge the stone slab. The moment we opened it the air came up cold and damp and stale. Henri Gerard and Tracey dug it even deeper until all they hit was mud. We lowered her coffin in that awful muddy hole and I gave her Christian burial. Then I was sent on my way."

"Philippe was not there?"

"He had left for France."

"And since then?"

"Nothing. That was the last contact I had with the Letourneau family and Edmund Tracey."

CHAPTER 16

The Most Unreserved Friendships

❧

If you call to see a friend who is staying at lodgings, however intimate you may be with him, wait below until a servant has carried up your name and returned to tell you whether you can be admitted. . . . These decent formalities are necessary even in the most unreserved friendships; they preserve the "familiar" from degenerating into the "vulgar." Disgust will very speedily arise between persons who bolt into one another's chambers, throw open the windows and seat themselves without being desired to do so. Such intimacies are like the junction of two electrical balls—only the prelude of a violent separation.

—Decorum, page 72

"How are you observing Thanksgiving, gentlemen?" inquired Mr. Worth. The investors were concluding a business meeting in rooms newly leased for the purpose. Their three partners had left. Only the triumvirate of Jerry, Connor, and Mr. Worth remained.

"Nothing special," said Connor, sensing an invitation. "I shall probably have dinner at the hotel."

"You'll do nothing of the sort. Mrs. Worth and I are gathering the holiday waifs for a celebration at our house. We'd be pleased if you would join us. We conduct a rather homey affair for Thanksgiving—lots of family and lots of food. A glorified Sunday dinner plus games for any grandchildren who wander through." Connor had heard about dinner with the Worths. Unlike most of their peers who hid the children away whenever they entertained adult guests, the Worths prided themselves on including children at dinner.

"That's very kind of you, sir. In fact, I may be engaged—"

"And you, Jerry?" interrupted Mr. Worth. "You're not exactly a waif, but we'd be pleased to have you and Maggie and Miss Lund."

"Thank you, John. I'll have to consult with the Jerome Entertainment and Mission Committee."

"Oh?" said Mr. Worth, with an amused grin.

"Maggie and Francesca will spend Thanksgiving morning slaving away at some mission," Jerry said, "cooking meals and feeding the poor. By the time they get home they won't be able to stand the sight of turkey. I may have to eat the whole unfortunate bird myself."

"Then perhaps you'd better come, Jerry. It sounds like you're a waif after all. I leave the invitation open, though Isabel will see to the formalities, I'm sure. We dine at four o'clock, but people begin arriving around noon, so you're all welcome anytime."

"Thank you. I'll consult with the Committee and let you know."

"What about Mr. Tracey?" asked Mr. Worth. "It appears I must become accustomed to including him, too." His tone had an edge.

"Yes," said Jerry, attempting a show of enthusiasm. "Miss Lund has recently become engaged to a Mr. Edmund Tracey, Connor. None of us are quite used to the fact."

"Isabel would be happy to see Miss Lund again," said Mr. Worth, passing over Edmund Tracey. "You should have seen Mrs. Worth and Miss Lund the last time we came together, O'Casey. Thick as thieves they were, talking art, music, religion, and books. Isabel nearly forgot that she had other guests."

"Talking about some obscure musical notation or literary quotation or some desert hermit or mountaintop mystic, no doubt," chuckled Jerry.

"No doubt," chuckled Mr. Worth. "Though I must say, Isabel is like a new person after one of her 'Lund episodes.' Can't stop her talking about Miss Lund's accomplishments and interests."

Connor looked dubious. *Jesus,* he thought. *Probably a member of the Women's Christian Temperance Union and a suffragette to boot. Thank God she's engaged.* At this moment he felt his bachelorhood keenly.

"Don't worry, O'Casey. The Worth billiard room is the male bastion—unless of course it's taken over by a gaggle of children. In which case we retreat to the library."

"Children I can take," said Connor. "Mountaintop mystics, I'm not so sure of."

"I don't blame you, sir," said Mr. Worth, laughing again. "Any children of your own—in your own family, I should say?"

Was this a slip, or was it meant to be funny? thought Connor. This was not the first sidelong reference to his personal life that he had endured from his colleagues. Had he been married, of course, the question would have been an innocent one. But for a man who was well known to be not only single but eligible, the question held more than innuendo. Connor had successfully dodged all mention of a family. Yet his increasing intimacy with his colleagues had already made him privy to the everyday doings of wives and children and grandchildren. He had not reciprocated with a recital of his own commonplace, and certainly not about Blanche.

Jerry and Worth knew about Blanche, of course, and had construed correctly what his arrangement with her might be. They freely dropped names of suitable women whom their wives and society had thoroughly vetted and offered, in so many words, to effect introductions. They had hinted that Blanche had also been vetted and found wanting. If Connor wanted to keep a bit of something on the side that was his lookout, but if he aspired to the circles in which their wives and daughters traveled, then an acceptable wife was the only alternative. Connor had never contemplated a divided life and the thought of it now displeased him. One woman, acceptable only to him, was all he ever cared about. But now, even elevating Blanche to the rank of wife might not be enough to excuse their prior conduct or to remove the stain with which they had so clearly marked her character.

Connor chose to take Mr. Worth's question at face value. "No, sir. I don't have much experience of children, but am, in general, favorably disposed."

"Splendid. Then you'll fit right in."

"Thank you, sir, I look forward to it." Connor felt he could not say otherwise.

"You know, John, your talk of Isabel and Francesca makes me think I should push the Mission Committee a bit this year," said Jerry. "It would do Francesca good. She needs more people who share her enthusiasms. She still stays so bottled up." *So long as she keeps it bottled up around me*, thought Connor. "I'm afraid Maggie and I are no match for her artistic passions. If she didn't have the piano and the opera—"

"She's playing the piano again? Splendid. Can we persuade her to play, do you think? Isabel would love it."

"She's taking piano and singing lessons again, yes," answered Jerry.

"Marvelous. Then we shall persuade her," said Mr. Worth.

"Yes," said Jerry. "She tends to take refuge in things rather than people—books, music, God, though I suppose God is a person after all and not a thing. She does take great satisfaction in helping people who can't help themselves. She's developed a passion for this new settlement movement and has thrown a good deal of her time and financial support behind it. I was a little dubious at first, but I honestly think that it's had a wonderful effect on her. But she prefers to remain in the background, and not in the limelight. Maggie's always trying to get her to take center stage."

"Well, we must work on that then," said Mr. Worth. "She has much to give and much to teach. Isabel would be delighted to help, I'm sure."

"Sounds as if Maggie and Isabel would make ideal conspirators."

Blanche was testy. She was standing in Connor's hotel suite at the Grand Central, in her hat and coat, watching him as the young valet Jamie helped him prepare to go out. "So, why can't I go?" Connor had hoped to avoid confrontation. Now that she was here, he was determined not to work himself into a lather. He would have the final word.

"You know very well why you can't go. You weren't invited." He was unruffled as he preened before the mirror. Jamie buttoned the collar onto Connor's shirt and buttoned the shirt at the neck as Connor inserted the jasper cufflinks.

"And why wasn't I invited?" asked Blanche, more as a statement than a question. "Because they don't know I exist, that's why I wasn't invited. And why don't they know I exist?" She raised her muffed hand and let it fall. "Because you didn't tell them."

Connor turned to her. "They know you exist all right. They saw you at the charity ball, didn't they? Can I help it if none of the ladies have come to call? You can hardly expect me to simply pop up and say, 'Can I bring a friend?' now, can you?"

He turned back to the mirror. Jamie handed him his necktie.

"No, but you could have been more chivalrous about it and said, 'I'm sorry, Mr. Worth, but I have a previous engagement. Mrs. Alvarado and I will be eating our *lonely* Thanksgiving dinner at the hotel'"—here she gestured melodramatically—"'while others more fortunate gather with family and friends.' Perhaps you could have troubled yourself to tug harder at the old man's heartstrings and managed two invitations instead of one."

"That wouldn't be proper, Blanche, and you know it. Besides, you wouldn't like it. It's their children and grandchildren. It wouldn't be right, havin' you come."

"What's that supposed to mean?"

"Meaning that I know how you feel about children. You couldn't stand being there more than five minutes before they'd drive you stark-starin' mad." As long as he had known Blanche, she had avoided the subject of children, whether from a barefaced dislike, a fear of encumbrance, or the failure to produce her share, he couldn't tell.

"And you like them, I suppose?"

"As a matter of fact, I don't mind the little beggars." He pinned his tie with a jasper stickpin. "At least I have more patience round 'em than you do. And I'll not have you go insulting the children and grandchildren of an important business partner and blowing this carefully cultivated relationship to smithereens." Jamie held the waistcoat as Connor slipped it on and buttoned it. Jamie strung the watch chain through the buttonhole and attached the jasper fob as Connor flipped open the watch and checked the time against the clock on the wall. He snapped it shut and put the watch in his pocket.

"Do you mean to say that you think I don't know how to behave?"

"Oh, you can behave, Blanche. It's just that you've no power to dissemble. Your displeasure winds up written all over your face, no matter what sugary sweetness comes out of your mouth." Jamie helped him on with his coat. "Nope. This time it's on me own. If all goes well, your chance'll come soon enough."

"And what am I supposed to do while you're cultivating your relationship?"

"You'll think of something, I'm sure."

Blanche was furious and deeply hurt. Connor's refusal had been so cavalier. He left her at home as one might leave a pet dog. He never would have come this far if it hadn't been for her. She had subordinated her own desires for Connor's sake. Ungrateful wretch. Now that he was on the point of making his first real entrance into society he didn't want her there. Selfish bastard. She couldn't get out of Connor's hotel room fast enough.

Outside the Grand Central Hotel she hesitated. She dreaded going back to her room, the reminder of her predicament—the clothes Connor bought her, the jewelry, the paintings and bric-a-brac and the interminable isolation. Her usual refuge at the Iris was distasteful now, a shabby substitute for the society she longed for. Nell had cooled since discovering Blanche's former association with Tracey. In any case, she had assured Nell that she would be well occupied for the day, hinting that this might be her groundbreaking occasion. She couldn't go to Nell now and admit defeat.

She walked on past the hotel, determined to work herself out of her present misery. A reckless and ridiculous thought surfaced on the murky waters of self-pity—all the more appealing for its reck-lessness. She remembered an idle comment someone had made at Nell's one afternoon—about a small and somewhat less-than-smart hotel. A careworn place that once pretended to be chic, but had long since given up pretending.

"How humiliating it must be, poor darling. I wouldn't wish such a place on my worst enemy," an all-knowing someone had said that gloomy afternoon.

"Yes," answered a sardonic someone else, "to be in such re-duced circumstances. And such a charming gentleman. It's too cruel."

Men are bastards, thought Blanche. Her fury rose at her predica-ment with the immovable Connor O'Casey. To Blanche, her situa-tion defied logic and deserved sympathy.

"Such a shabby little place it is." The voice crept up through Blanche's consciousness. "Hardly the sort of place in which to 'en-tertain,' shall we say?"

She stopped to collect herself in front of a door, to the right of which was a brass plate. She looked at it blankly. Jeffers. Jameson. Brier. Stanley. Names that meant nothing to her. She conjured up the party at the Worths' with Connor standing in their midst, the solitary recognizable figure. Fresh pain shot through her anger. She put a gloved hand to her mouth and extended the other to steady herself against the wall.

"Are you all right, madam?" Blanche felt a firm and gentle hand tug on her arm. "Can I help you in some way?"

She pulled her arm free, not unkindly, and turned without look-ing at the woman who addressed her and threw back a "No, I'm quite all right, thank you" as she continued down the street. She stumbled on, pushing past numberless others hurrying some-where.

"And where is this wretched hotel?" swam the voice of the sym-pathetic soul.

"Somewhere in SoHo, I think," echoed the all-knowing.

"Do you recall the name of the place?" asked the voice.

Do you recall the name of the place? insisted Blanche's own thoughts.

The pace of her recollection picked up with each determined footfall.

She hailed a cab and made for the street in SoHo, confident that once there she would know the name of the hotel when she saw it. The cab clattered its way along the busy avenue, fashion yielding block by block to a more careworn gentility. As the cab picked its way through a jumble of horse-drawn conveyances, Blanche strained to give attention to both sides of the street. "There!" she called out, and knocked on the roof. The cab drew up.

As she entered, she felt larger than her surroundings, as if she might bump her head on the door frame. Her confidence expanded into the dingy lobby, where the lethargic clerk unfolded himself and addressed her with something like respect. Her query was answered shortly. She mounted the long staircase, breathless with anticipation. She stopped in front of Number Ten and, without hesitating, knocked. A stir indicated life within. A few steps ended in an abrupt turn of the doorknob and the opening of the door an eye's breadth before it opened fully.

"I hoped it wouldn't be long before you found me," said Tracey.

CHAPTER 17

Many Foibles of Manner

A young man or woman upon first entering into society should select those persons who are most celebrated for the propriety and elegance of their manners. They should frequent their company, and imitate their conduct. There is a disposition inherent in all, which has been noticed by Horace and by Dr. Johnson, to imitate faults, because they are more readily observed and more easily followed. There are, also, many foibles of manner and many refinements of affectation, which sit agreeably upon one man, which if adopted by another would become unpleasant. There are even some excellences of deportment which would not suit another whose character is different.

—*Decorum*, page 26

As the cab sped toward the Worths', Blanche receded further and further from Connor's consciousness. The wide boulevards, green parks, and fashionable squares whetted his appetite for more than a festive dinner. Thanksgiving would be an auspicious occasion, he was sure—a baptism, a confirmation. Yes, he would mark November twenty-seventh as his birthday. Though the real date of his birth eluded him, the year, 1847, was burned into history—the year that pushed Ireland over the precipice. Today would be a day of renewal, a day of great things. Connor even dared to picture himself dandling Worth grandchildren on his knee, children who might one day look favorably upon their old Uncle Connor. The cab pulled up in front of an imposing stone structure with turrets and balconies and leaded glass and wide steps that swept up from the street to massive double doors of dark-stained oak. Old gas lamps on the front of the castle-like mansion were the only hints of warmth. A moat and a drawbridge would not have surprised him.

He rang the bell. A footman answered the door and with a cordial but businesslike manner ushered Connor in and took his hat, coat, and stick. Humble the gathering may be, he thought, but not the surroundings. Everywhere were the fruits of wide-ranging interests—magnificent ornaments gathered from their travels with none of the vulgar curiosities of distant cultures so often displayed on a pianoforte under a bell jar. The royal blue carpet contrasted with the warm yellow of the carved oak paneling. Chinese porcelains of all sizes with nature scenes and stylized flowers adorned the mantelpiece above a crackling fire. A magnificent sideboard of intricately carved tiger oak offered a host of nooks and crannies for displaying more chinoiserie. The graceful staircase swept up to the top of the landing, where an exquisite Tiffany window depicted Oriental flowers, birds, and insects.

The house was not in the state of chaos Connor had expected, as several of the littlest Worths had just gone down for their afternoon naps. Mrs. Worth greeted him. She was stylishly dressed, if a bit overdone, he thought, but was an attractive woman, round, soft, and white-haired with piercing dark eyes.

"I'm so glad you could join us, Mr. O'Casey. I hope our humble family gathering won't tax you too much, being a bachelor."

"May I compliment you on your wonderful home, ma'am." Connor was shown upstairs to the drawing room. The kind of home he could see himself in, he thought, presided over by a woman of taste and accomplishment. And where does one find a Mrs. Worth—or more to the point, a Mrs. O'Casey—to find the right bits and bobs to adorn a man's life and home and do him proud? "I understood from Mr. Worth that you're an exceptional collector. It's clear to me now that he was being modest on your behalf. If time permits, I'd be pleased to have a tour."

"The pleasure would be mine, Mr. O'Casey, I'm sure," she said, much gratified. "And if the day gets away from us today, perhaps I may have the pleasure on another occasion." Another occasion? A good sign, thought Connor.

He followed her to a sprawling room of dark, fumed oak where the light of two large fireplaces danced merrily against the high polish. Her heels clicked on the parquetry between the thick Persian rugs. East had moved West, with dark medieval European pieces mixed with the contemporary.

The older Worth grandchildren were strewn across the floor, absorbed in puzzles, maps, building bricks, and games, except for one little girl of six, clearly bored, half-reclining in an overstuffed chair and absently stroking a cat. The men lounged in comfortable chairs, chatting or reading the newspaper. The eldest daughter and granddaughter were the only adult females in attendance. The gentlemen rose as Mrs. Worth introduced the ladies, two sons, and two sons-in-law, who in turn introduced the scatterlings, who sprang to their feet and came forward to shake Connor's hand.

One of the younger ones was a freckle-faced boy of eight with strawberry blond hair, wearing a paper sailor's hat and sporting a homemade sword. "You look like a pirate," he said to Connor.

"Jeremiah!" said Mrs. Worth as the rest of the children giggled and adults suppressed smiles—except for Jeremiah's mother, Mrs. Edith Blackhurst, who shot Jeremiah a look of reprimand.

"And so I am, Master Jeremiah," said Connor, amused, but glaring at him soberly with his dark, disturbing eyes. This bit of frankness gave Connor courage. "I've sailed the Seven Seas and plundered and pillaged, too."

Jeremiah turned to his siblings and cousins. "See, I told you," he whispered.

"We Worths teach our young ones to size people up from an early age, Mr. O'Casey," said the eldest son.

"Heavens, Frederick," said his sister, Mrs. Blackhurst. "What will Mr. O'Casey think?"

"It's amazing how accurate they can be when they're not burdened by adult biases and misconceptions," said Connor. "They've got only their gut instincts to go on, beg pardon, ladies, so off they go." Frederick laughed at the remark.

"Then perhaps we should take their accounts more seriously," said the senior Mr. Worth, smiling as he strode across the room, followed by the remaining Worth women.

"We should at that, Father," said Frederick.

"Don't encourage him, Mr. O'Casey," said his wife as she came up and stood beside her husband. "He's bad enough on his own. I'm Mildred Worth, Frederick's wife." Mr. Worth senior completed the introductions, presenting Linton Blackhurst, Edith's husband, and the Worths' younger daughter, Margaret, married to Samuel Curry. First impressions all round seemed favorable. Connor couldn't know that only hours before, the elder Mr. Worth had given the family its marching orders.

"Of course I know his reputation," Mr. Worth had said. "And yes, I know about this woman of his. She was not invited and, God willing, he'll have the good sense not to bring her along. If he does, we'll know what we're dealing with."

"But Father," protested Margaret. "How are we to explain such a person to the children?"

"There's nothing to explain, my dear. No one need know anything about him other than that he is a business associate of mine. He's a big fish, and likely to become an even bigger fish."

"Or simply more fishy," chimed in Frederick.

"And," said Mr. Worth, paying no heed, "I'd rather he swim in this pond than jump the dam and wind up in someone else's pond."

"Father, for heaven's sake."

"Edith, he's done absolutely nothing to offend thus far. He has bent over backward to accommodate me at every turn. He's got a very good head on his shoulders and has wisely pointed out particulars where we might have put a foot wrong. He's no fool, even if he is a bit lax in the morals department. And he's a friend of Jerry Jerome's, whose friendship I'd like to keep. Besides, there have been many sound men of business—and politics, and the law, and any other profession you can name—who have had the misfortune to suffer from their own little personal weaknesses of one kind or other."

"*Little?*" Margaret exclaimed.

"Personally, I think he's a lost soul in some ways," said Mr. Worth.

"Oh, Father, you're worse than Mother," said Edith.

"Thank you, my dear."

"But Father, do you have to drag him into our drawing room?"

"Yes, my dear Edith, I do."

"Well, I, for one, am willing to give him a chance," said Frederick. "He might prove quite amusing."

"However much I appreciate your support, Fred—and I do—I still expect you to be polite to Mr. O'Casey," said Mr. Worth.

"I wouldn't dream of being otherwise, Father," Frederick said, more seriously. "I'm curious about Mr. O'Casey, to see whether he's the devil incarnate that Edith thinks he is."

"If this is important to you, Father," said Linton Blackhurst, who had been listening in silence to the family harangue, "then I'm with Fred. If he makes a gaffe he hurts no one but himself. If he comes off well, so much the better for all of us."

"Thank you, Lin. My point exactly," said Mr. Worth. "Innocent until proven guilty."

So, unbeknownst to Connor, he had leapt over the first hurdle—leaving Blanche to sulk at the hotel, much to the collective relief of the Worth women—and spent the afternoon charming the family.

Thank God for the children, Connor thought: amiable buffers to awkwardness and an endless topic of conversation. Whenever possible, he queried the children directly regarding their ages and interests, their schooling and subjects. In turn, they plied him with questions about sailing, which eventually led to other kinds of travel, then to questions about distant shores. It ended with Connor sitting in a club chair with an atlas open on a large ottoman and the children gathered around, pointing to places on a large map. To most of their questions Connor could formulate a reasonably accurate answer and for those that he could speak to from experience he had a ready fable fit to entertain. He feared he might have overstepped the bounds of decorum, but the children's pleasure, Connor's willingness to answer anything they asked, and the tranquility of the warm fire made wholesale disapproval nearly impossible.

"Have you ever seen John L. Sullivan fight?" asked Jeremiah's elder brother, Vaughan, as more of a challenge than a question.

"I have, sir. And shook his hand, too." Connor allowed both his Irish pride and his accent to swell as he lapsed into soliloquy. "I saw him fight his famous bout with Jake Kilrain. Blistering heat we had that day. It was so hot the willow trees themselves were perspiring (I beg your pardon, ladies). Paint was fair peeling off the sides of buildings. The birds in their nests were fanning themselves against the heat. Yet for all that, three thousand strong we were, standing and shouting and nearly passing out from the heat ourselves. And it was in this heat that the great Sullivan laid blow upon blow with his bare knuckles, jabbing and thrusting until the life was nearly battered out of poor Jake Kilrain. Seventy-five rounds they went—more than two hours, until Kilrain could stand no more. Afterward, I pushed my way to the front of the crowd and clasped the bruised and bleeding hand of the great man himself in my own two hands and blessed him for a fine fight. He looked me in the eye and said in a hoarse voice, 'God bless you, sir.'" The children were spellbound. The women sat in rapt attention. Connor was pleased with the effect. Even the men could not help but admit to a slightly elevated respect for the man whose hand shook the hand of John L. Sullivan.

Edith was reserved, though not uncivil, throughout the afternoon and seemed to laugh in spite of herself. Now she looked at him and Connor caught her.

"Sizin' me up, Mrs. Blackhurst?" said Connor.

"Yes, Mr. O'Casey," said Edith. "It's the way of the Worths." The adults laughed.

Connor made no bones about his own lack of education or his great pleasure to be making up for it now. What he wanted was some guidance, a hint directed at Mrs. Worth senior for the promised tour of her collection of art and antiquities. He asked intelligent questions and plainly accepted her kind correction and filed the facts away.

He felt as if he were living a portion of childhood he had missed, plying Mrs. Worth with questions in an unabashed, unyielding, but good-natured manner. Curiosity had been his faithful companion since he scrounged for pennies at the Belfast shipyards, watching, asking, practicing, using everything his brain could absorb. When a merchantman took on this clever lad of twelve, he felt as if he had graduated from a rough schooling on the docks to a floating apprenticeship in the ways of the world. Every port and people, custom and marketplace, landmark and back alley, vice and virtue fired his imagination and sharpened his judgment. His break came at twenty, when opportunity converged with his preparation and his ship docked in San Francisco and his own golden gateway to a new life. Until now, he regarded his education as only useful to himself or to those in whom he had an interest, and a business interest at that, certainly not a family of children.

In its way, this confrontation with the Worths' grandchildren was a greater test than passing muster with their children. Though whether his own children might one day be ashamed of their papa had never worried him before, he was relieved to think there were things in the recesses of his past that could be of interest and use beyond simply earning a living. If curiosity and a love of learning were his few noble legacies, they would be enough.

Faint, irregular wails from the nursery foretold the arrival of the three remaining Worths, rousted for a wash-and-brush-up. *It's a pleasant sound,* thought Connor, lusty and full of life, a sound full of promise. He wondered if he would be any good at holding small children. Surely a man can get the knack. He amazed himself for wondering such things.

As the dinner hour approached, the wails grew closer. Connor and Mrs. Worth met a servant in the hallway, about to announce dinner. She made the announcement herself and paired the women with escorts, handing Connor to Edith and Mildred to Mr. Worth, and choosing her bachelor son, Clayton, for herself.

Minty-green watered silk lined the dining-room walls and hung in graceful folds at the tall leaded glass windows and gave a sense of breathing space for the long table set with twenty-two places. Light from the alabaster fireplace danced off the two cut glass chandeliers and flickered off the etched crystal goblets and glasses. Sequestered on more formal occasions, today the children scurried around the table, looking for their places, spotting their special dishes or cups or silverware.

Before the party could be seated, the bell rang. As the table filled up, Connor noticed the four empty places and reminded himself of the Jeromes and Miss Lund and her fiancé, whom he had forgotten in all the commotion. Mr. and Mrs. Worth excused themselves briefly to greet their new guests. Connor took his place. A small skirmish broke out next to him, where Jeremiah was determined to displace an older sibling.

"Let Jemima sit next to Mr. O'Casey, Jeremiah, and you come down here so I can help you cut your food," said Mildred.

"But I want to sit here," said Jeremiah, cross and gripping the chair.

"Jeremiah," said Edith, "don't speak to your aunt that way, young man."

"He's fine here, ma'am. I'm happy to help him with his cutting," said Connor.

"See, I told you."

"Jeremiah, that's enough," said Edith. "You'll be eating dinner by yourself if you're not careful, young man."

"Then come down here, Jemima," said Mildred. Jemima acquiesced politely.

Connor bent down and whispered, "Apologize to your mother and your aunt. That'd please 'em." He gave Jeremiah a quick wink.

"I'm sorry, Mother, Aunt Mildred," he said, still vexed.

"Good boy," whispered Connor. Jeremiah looked up at Connor. The boy seemed more anxious to win the pirate's approval than that of mere female relatives.

Suddenly, a little group appeared at the dining-room door.

"The prodigals have arrived and await the fatted calf, or should I say, the fatted turkey," announced Mr. Worth as they entered— Maggie Jerome and Mr. Worth, then Jerry, Mrs. Worth, and Francesca bringing up the rear. The gentlemen, ladies, and children alike surged forward from the table to greet them.

Connor's eyes ran over the party. Naw, it couldn't be. Or could it? It's impossible. Francesca? Grievin' recluse? Bookish piano player? Francesca? Settlement worker? Bleedin' mountaintop hermit? Damn that Jerome. Connor hung back a bit to give himself time to observe, having had the advantage of Francesca by a few seconds, long enough to drink her in. Her hair looked like the foam on a good head of beer, he thought. He stirred himself in time to shake Jerry's hand.

"Connor, good to see you. You remember Maggie," said Jerry.

"Of course, Mrs. Jerome." He bowed slightly.

"Miss Francesca Lund, this is Mr. Connor O'Casey."

Francesca looked at him, her surprise evident.

"Yes, we've met. Miss Lund." He bowed. The alarm on Maggie's face pleased him.

"Mr. O'Connor. How very"—Francesca hesitated—"lovely to meet you formally, and how very unexpected."

"O'Casey, ma'am."

"I beg your pardon?"

"The name—O'Casey."

"You've met, dearie. Well, I declare," Maggie said.

"Briefly," Francesca said quickly, looking him in the eye. He met her gaze until she blushed. "Mr. O'Casey was good enough to help me with my hair." She smiled a smile of satisfaction.

"Helped you with your hair? Why, Francesca, whatever do you mean?" Maggie glanced at the others, as if trying to gauge whether they were as shocked as she.

"I very clumsily bumped into Mr. O'Casey at the charity ball and in doing so lost a hairpin. He retrieved it for me."

"Oh, so that's what you mean." Maggie laughed unconvincingly. "You must watch yourself, dearie, or you'll give these dear people the wrong impression."

"Francesca, you come and take this chair next to me," said Mrs. Worth.

"Oh, no, you don't," said Mr. Worth. "If we put you two together you'll keep her all to yourself and none of the rest of us will get a decent conversation with her. Maggie, you go down by Isabel. Francesca, you may take this place." He escorted her to a chair on the opposite side of the table from Connor.

Connor examined her, taking in every detail of her coarse, frothy hair, stubbornly held in place with pins that were even now hanging perilously. Her lips were full and pale, only a shade darker than her skin, a creamy pink-and-white, and her eyes a cool gray-blue. *She's a beauty,* he thought. *Gray watered silk may be fine for some, but she should be covered with diamonds and pearls. How could such a rose have blossomed among the cabbages of the settlement? Can such a one prefer their company to this? Huh, this rabble. Might she learn to prefer my company? Might she make my bed smell like roses and populate my life with little rosebuds?* Connor recollected himself. Francesca was chatting away to Samuel under Connor's gaze, something about the mission.

"How many hungry folks did you feed today, Miss Lund?" Connor broke in, his head cocked, demanding her attention, but refraining from adding sarcasm to his tone.

She turned to him reluctantly. "Nearly two hundred, Mr. O'Casey."

"Two hundred souls seekin' succor. A worthy cause. How many of you ladies were helping out with the cooking?"

"There were six of us."

"Do you enjoy that sort of thing, Miss Lund?"

"Very much, Mr. O'Casey. Have you ever been to any of the charitable establishments in New York?"

"I can't say that I have, ma'am. But I've seen poor unfortunates the world over. On the whole I find it rather depressing."

"Not nearly as depressing as for those who have to live it day to day."

"Granted, ma'am. But I've done my best not to have to live it day to day."

Before Francesca could reply, Mr. Worth gave the command to bow their heads in prayer. Connor would have ignored this command in favor of enjoying the view across the table, had it not been for the nudge from Jeremiah. With the "Amen" pronounced, the servants appeared carrying steaming bowls and platters of food. A large protuberance of harvest-time foliage from the centerpiece obstructed his view of Francesca except for her eyes. She merely smiled and turned her attention to the offered food and drink.

"Do you engage in any charitable work, Mrs. Blackhurst?" said Connor, trying to keep the thread of the conversation pulled taut. Edith's answer was carried away in a clatter of cutlery and china.

Blanche lay on her side, one arm outstretched, her hand hanging over the side of the bed. Tracey lay close up against her back, his arm around her, his face buried in her thick black hair. With her other hand, she cupped the hand that gently cupped her breast. They were awake, quiet, their breathing synchronous. It had been the kind of afternoon she had thought of often since finding Edmund Tracey again—the satisfaction, the exquisite release, the calm in its wake. Such had been many afternoons and evenings in those heated, desperate days when she had finally reached New Orleans from South America. Her reunion with Edmund Tracey in New York unlocked a door to her deepest self, a door that had remained bolted to all others.

Blanche seemed fated to be drawn to men who speculated. She had loved Alvarado passionately, and followed him to Argentina believing his story of a ranch and riches. Enchanted by the estancia, with its sprawling house, its cattle, and its gauchos, and captivated by her charismatic husband, she had been blind to his mounting debt. Seeing no way to escape utter ruin and disgrace, Alvarado had gone to the stables one night and had blown his brains out. Before the creditors could smell the blood, Blanche had fled.

For months she made her way across South America and the American South and landed in New Orleans. Humiliation kept her from seeking help from what remained of her family, promising herself that when she faced them again, whether in Milan or Paris or Newport, it would be with a husband and her fortunes restored. She had tried to survive in genteel poverty, hoping to trade on her knowledge of art and culture in a salon established with a friend. When Edmund Tracey walked in one day, hope rose. His breeding, his manners, his love of beauty, the ardor that boiled beneath a cool exterior drew her like no other man before or since. The heat of their liaison was so intense, it was as if a lifetime had been compressed into a few short months. Before long, however, they understood that although they complemented each other's strengths, they also magnified each other's shortcomings. They parted by mutual agreement, neither of them wishing to sully their relationship with constant disputes over money, and took their separate chances elsewhere.

Blanche kept her past as the merest sketch to Connor O'Casey and he never pressed her for more. He had swept her up with his winnings after an all-night poker game in Natchez, where he cleaned out the gambler who was her current lover. O'Casey had come south in that summer of 1889 to watch the pugilist John L. Sullivan fight Jake Kilrain. Blanche had fetched the men drinks, leaving the delicate scent of perfume in her wake, and with lowered eyes had sat silently in the background and watched the game over her lover's shoulder. Only once or twice had her eyes met Connor's across the table, as Blanche sat in the shadows, but her message had been clear. In the end the question resolved itself— the lure of O'Casey's means was sufficient to dislodge Blanche from her prior interest and transfer her loyalties to himself.

The clock in a distant hallway struck four. She could feel Tracey's mind and body stir.

"When does she expect you?" Blanche asked. She would not have minded lingering. After all, she had nowhere else to go.

"They're dining by now, I expect," he replied.

"Now? Shouldn't you be there?"

"We needn't worry. The invitation was open." He kissed her on the ear. "I can come at any time. As long as I appear before the party breaks up all will be well."

"How can you say that?" asked Blanche. "The Worths may be informal, but if I were engaged to you, my dearest, I should want you at my side the whole time. Women set great store by such things, you know."

"Do they? It would be different if you were the one waiting for me." He nibbled at her earlobe and breathed his hot breath into her hair as he drew her closer to him. Then, as if an unpleasant thought interrupted him, he threw himself on his back next to her. "I can't bear to be in their presence," he said. "Boring, tight-fisted, peevish pack of snobs."

"I know you hate it, darling, but you must make an effort." She sat up and drew the blankets around her. "Think how much better off you'll be." His situation pained her, not only because his engagement put him out of reach, but because it also reminded her of her dependence on O'Casey. "I hope you don't make a habit of this, darling—being late, I mean. How can she be convinced of your complete devotion if you're never there? Has she never questioned you about where you go or with whom you spend time?"

"Oh, yes, though she tries not to go on about it." He sat up and ran his hands through his auburn thatch. Grabbing his underclothes from the foot of the bed, he began to dress. He rose and retrieved his trousers from over the back of a chair. Blanche crawled across the bed and draped his cold shirt around her shivering shoulders and embraced him around the waist. Her move arrested him. She felt the tautness in his frame, the rigid muscles in his back.

"Is everything all right between you and your fiancée?"

"I almost wish she'd throw me over."

She squeezed him for a moment and then released him and relinquished the shirt as she pulled the blankets around her. He reached for her hand, held it and kissed it, then, sighing, continued to dress.

"What's wrong?" she asked.

His back was to her as he spoke. "Things are not turning out as I had hoped. It appears that I shall not be coming into the fortune I had expected. I am to make do with an annuity for my lifetime. She retains the principal." They were silent.

Blanche hated life when it was reduced to dollars and cents. It was always the same for people like them, like Tracey, like her. Tracey tucked his shirt into his trousers and put on his waistcoat, then sat on an ottoman to put on his stockings and lace up his boots. "Don't you see? I shall never be able to take any initiative on my own without going to her for the money first. If I were to find a . . . a business venture, or an investment of some sort, my paltry allowance would never cover it. I would never be truly free. What I expect from her can hardly make for the kind of freedom I'm looking for."

He looked worried now. *No, not worried*, thought Blanche, *but angry and on edge*. All this talk of business and investment. It had been the same as long as she had known him—a fantasy of a future when everything would be amply provided.

The clock chimed the half hour. Blanche began to be alarmed at Tracey's tardiness. She pulled her wits together and in the firelight began to dress. Tracey helped her to cage her slim figure in the corset. With each lacing, he jerked her body into alignment and pulled the stays tight with a snap. For a moment, she thought of a dog with a rat by the neck. It made her gasp. She shivered.

"You're cold." He made a move toward the fire to throw on more coal.

"Don't bother," she said. "We won't be here much longer." He threw the coal on anyway and pulled a chair closer. He stared into the fire as she finished knotting her hair.

"What would you do with the money if you had it?" she asked.

"The first thing I'd do is leave this miserable town. I have always hated it here. Stupid, filthy Yankee town with its barbarians and sham refinements. I knew I would hate it from the moment I set foot on Manhattan Island."

"Why did you come if you knew you'd hate it?"

"Because, my darling Blanche, this is where the money is. I had dearly hoped that I could make my fortune here, one way or other. I thought Maggie Jerome had more influence than proved to be the case. I thought she could introduce me to opportunity. Instead, she introduced me to my beloved." He nearly choked on the word.

Blanche had never heard his words so filled with spite. He hardly seemed to notice her, almost as if hatred were a lover with whom he was completely preoccupied. His loathing frightened her. She hardly knew Edmund Tracey anymore. She was afraid for him, afraid that he was so overtaken with his own pain that he would fail to understand the fine line he trod. In truth Francesca Lund had little to do with it. It was Edmund Tracey who would either make him or break him.

"You must hurry, darling," she said, as much for her sake as for his, to leave the gloomy room and its gloomier occupant. "You must cultivate these people. They may be able to help you, but you must at least make yourself agreeable to them." She tugged his coat on him like dressing a child and handed him his hat and gloves as she hurriedly buttoned her coat and pinned her hat.

At the door he stopped her and held her and kissed her deeply. How dearly she wanted to stay with him. How dearly she wanted to escape with him. But it was impossible. With effort she pushed him away.

"We mustn't linger," she said. "You must go."

The centerpiece was removed from the table only to be replaced by a huge epergne of candied fruit, cakes, and other sweets. The children had acquitted themselves well in the matter of vegetables, turkey, and gravy; they raided these delicacies and spied out their favorites, which the servants reached for them from the epergne's upper tiers. Exquisite squares of cake with colored icing, rich chocolates, sugary meringues, and meaty, nutty tarts were as much a delight to the eye as they were to the palate.

Everyone was talkative and genial. *Nary a stick-in-the-mud among 'em,* thought Connor as he surveyed the table. The look on his face must have been one of enjoyment for he caught Mrs. Blackhurst looking at him with amusement on her face.

"You like children, don't you, Mr. O'Casey?"

"I confess I do, ma'am," he said, turning his gaze back to the children. "You're lucky, if I may be so bold, ma'am. You and Mr. Blackhurst have done well. They're nice children, yours, and the others. Neither spoilt nor smarmy like some. Very nice children indeed."

"You're very kind," she said with a sincerity that surprised him.

"Not at all. It's the truth," he said.

"They're a bit forward sometimes."

"They're spirited and curious, not impolite, or at least I don't believe they mean to be. There's nothing wrong with confidence and curiosity. I'm sure they're a great joy." He was almost musing. When he surveyed the table again, he saw Francesca through the spidery, sweet-laden arms of the epergne, staring at him. He was so caught off guard that he hardly noticed when a servant came up to Mrs. Worth and whispered a word to her.

"Goodness," she said to catch everyone's attention. She hesitated, then rose and sent the servant away. Connor wondered for a moment what could have caught so self-possessed a woman off balance. She fumbled with the long strands of beads that hung to her waist and stole a brief glance at the time. As if by reflex, Connor consulted his own watch. Nearly four hours since he had arrived. An instant later, the servant ushered in a tall fair man with auburn hair who wore a sheepish look of apology as easily as he wore his finely tailored suit of brown wool. At the other end of the table, Mr. Worth rose. Connor looked across the table at Francesca, who sat upright in her chair and looked toward the door. Color crept into her cheeks as she looked away and fixed her eyes on the table in front of her. Then, as if to dismiss an unpleasant thought, she took a deep breath and cleared her countenance and rose. Her usual grace restored, Mrs. Worth took the man by the hand and drew him forward.

"Everyone," said she. "Edmund has just arrived."

$\mathscr{C}$HAPTER 18

To Attract the Attention of Others

❧

During the performance complete quiet should be pre-
served, that the audience may not be prevented seeing or
hearing. Between the acts it is perfectly proper to con-
verse, but it should be in a low tone, so as not to attract
attention. Neither should one whisper. There should be
no loud talking, boisterous laughter, violent gestures,
lover-like demonstrations, or anything in manners or
speech to attract the attention of others.

The gentleman should see that the lady is provided
with programme, and with libretto also if they are at-
tending opera.

—Decorum, page 152

It was one of those afternoons in late autumn when the sun is so
bright and the bursts of wind so sharp they give an edge of clarity
to everything they touch, as if the whole world were startled to attention. Francesca loved this weather. The air that filled the lungs
seemed purer, like water purified by a headlong journey over
rocks. It was the perfect day for a walk in the park. Instead, she was
going to the opera. Vinnie, Michael, and Anne were her guests.
Their objective: an afternoon performance of *Asrael,* the opera that
marked the beginning of the Metropolitan Opera's most peculiar

season to date. They chatted animatedly, recapitulating the newspaper accounts and hazarding whether *Asrael* could really be as bad as all that. Better to waste an afternoon in pleasant company than to go to the trouble of evening dress for nothing.

With much shedding of outerwear and smoothing of hair, they walked through the main vestibule and ascended the grand stairs to Francesca's private box. The brisk, bright day dissolved to dim memory as they were engulfed in the splendor of the Met, with its plush red upholstery and glistening crystal.

Francesca stood arranging the folds of her dress behind her, giving her plenty of time to let her glance encompass the hall before she sank onto her seat. The three ladies sat at the front of the box, Francesca to the right. Michael sat behind them, between Vinnie and Anne. Then commenced a show of consulting and commenting upon the program.

Opera glasses popped up like mushrooms. Francesca preferred first to take in the entire scene unaided and study the ripples of humanity nodding and chatting, waving to friends, and reading librettos. The box was nestled in the curve of the horseshoe-shaped tier, the orchestra whorling out beneath it. It afforded the ability to see a three-quarter back view of people. How amazing that the smallest bit of facial anatomy can betray so much emotion. A clenched jaw. A raised brow. A shy smile. The shimmering warmth and the buzzing conversation enveloped her. Francesca was serene and content.

"Francesca, look. That man," said Vinnie, seated on Francesca's left and trying discreetly to indicate a direction.

"What man?" Francesca stirred herself from her preoccupation.

"That interesting-looking man who tipped his hat to you at the gallery."

"Oh, that one," Francesca said. Bother the man. She was determined to pay Connor no mind, just as she was determined not to tell Vinnie that she had discovered who he was, which would only result in an endless barrage of questions. "Where is he?" she asked as she continued to survey the crowd, her opera glasses before her eyes.

"He's over there, about four boxes to our right. He's been staring at you for the last ten minutes. He'll look at you through the glasses, then take them down, then put them back up again. I know it's you he's looking at."

"That's ridiculous."

"How impertinent," Vinnie said, with obvious relish, bringing the glasses to her eyes. "It's almost as if he's trying to catch your eye."

"It certainly would be impertinent."

"He's with a lady."

"Oh?" She wouldn't admit curiosity. Being in the company of ladies and one gentleman who was not hers made her feel exposed. Edmund's absence annoyed her. Business, he had said. And here was that infernal O'Casey in company with a woman to whom she had not been introduced—nor would be, with any luck.

"Why on earth would he be observing me if he's with a lady?"

"Well, she's gone out," said Vinnie. "He's been taking the opportunity to observe you while she's gone—and with the glasses."

"Vinnie, for heaven's sake."

"Oh, dear. She's back now. He can't look at you anymore. He's paying attention to her." Vinnie put her glasses down.

"I should hope so." To try to catch her attention while in the company of another woman? No matter what the other woman might be, his conduct was inexcusable.

"She's quite something. The woman who accompanied him at Venables'."

"Oh, really?" Oh, bother. What should she care who this dreadful man might take to the opera? It was none of her business—and none of Vinnie's.

"Foreign looking. Very dark. He's really not so much to look at, though." Vinnie put the glasses up to her eyes. "Maybe he's not so bad—more interesting than handsome."

"Vinnie, put the glasses down."

"Well, he's talking to her. He's not paying any attention to us. Oh, wait. He's looking this way." She put the glasses down and fiddled with her program. "He's looking at you, I tell you. He's sitting to her right, so he can look past her and observe you."

"Vinnie, stop it."

The lights dimmed. The concertmaster rose and called for the tuning pitch. A cacophony of sound rose from the pit and fell again. The conductor entered, accompanied by applause. Gradually, the sound died away and the overture began.

Francesca let herself be carried away. Music was half-opiate, half-incense to her, especially music like this. She could empty her mind and shut out everything.

"Francesca. Francesca. He's looking at you again."

"Hush, Vinnie, please. I want to listen." Her annoyance at Edmund Tracey resurfaced. His presence could have scotched this dreadful man's impropriety.

"But he is—and she doesn't like it."

"Who?" Francesca said dreamily, like someone trying to go back to sleep.

"The dark woman. The Jet Woman."

"Jet what?"

"She sparkles like she's wearing jet."

"Tell me later, Vinnie, I want to listen." The lights were making their final descent, but it was no good. Curiosity got the better of the cool and detached Francesca. As the curtain opened and all attention was drawn to the stage, she turned toward the infernal box to the right, only to be met by an impertinent smile that was becoming all too familiar.

Caught, she quickly turned her attention back to the stage. Oh, bother. *If I were given to profanity,* thought Francesca, *this would be the perfect time.*

The Letourneaus' lawyer had met his match. The more tight-lipped and insulting he proved to be, the more Shillingford calmly pummeled him with questions.

"I appreciate your position . . ." said Shillingford, ramrod straight on the hard leather chair that stood before the lawyer's desk, and looking like he was dug in for the long haul.

"I fail to see how the disposition of the will of Charles Montague Letourneau can make any difference in your investigation," said LeGros in a heavy French accent. "You have seen a copy of the deed, have you not?"

"I have. The deed was changed in 1884 to reflect the name of the current occupant of Maywood—Henri Gerard Letourneau. It was previously held by his father, Charles Montague Letourneau, who, I am given to understand, died in 1884. The will may have every bearing on the circumstances surrounding the transfer of the property and whether there were impediments."

"Has someone made a claim to the property?" asked LeGros.

"I take by your swift deduction that there was indeed an impediment."

"I am sure your investigations to this point have dispelled a good deal of the ignorance you profess. I see no reason to answer the inadequacies. The legal aberrations of the Letourneau family, then and now, are their business, monsieur, and neither yours nor mine. Has Edmund Tracey made a claim?"

"I make no claim to familiarity with the legal customs of this region, which I am attempting, through this interview, to ascertain. It would seem to me that the sooner you provide me with the information I seek the sooner the matter may be drawn to a close."

"That hardly seems likely, monsieur," said the lawyer. "It may be only the beginning."

"Would you prefer that I lay out before a clerk the matter of a dispute regarding Maywood Plantation? Or would you rather that I come directly to you, so that the discretion you are so keen to observe might be preserved?" Shillingford thought he detected a barely perceptible shifting in the chair of the gentleman before him. "It is Charles Montague's will that interests me and his original intent for the disposition of his property. To what lengths would you prefer that I resort?"

LeGros considered, then said, "I can give you its main provisions, after which you will leave this office and not return." Shillingford gave no answer. LeGros made no move, but retrieved the document's provisions from his memory.

"Charles Montague Letourneau left the bulk of his estate, including Maywood Plantation, to his daughter, Henriette Genevieve Agnes Letourneau, who, at the time of Charles Montague's death, was married to Edmund Francis Tracey. The sons, Henri Gerard and Philippe, each received considerably less in terms of fortune, consisting mainly of properties in New Orleans, but certainly each had enough to keep a prudent man comfortable for the rest of his life."

"What of the daughter's husband?" continued Shillingford. "Would he not have some legal claim to the property if it were last in his wife's name? I should imagine that in the case of property a husband holds rights over his wife, unless the wife holds the property in her own right, in which case he may likely inherit upon her death?"

"Likely, yes."

"I assume that in the event of the daughter's death, if her marriage produced no issue, and the husband forfeited any claim, the property would pass to the eldest of her brothers."

"Obviously your researches have failed to uncover the fact that there was a child."

Shillingford had not failed, of course. Despite the suggestion that he was anything less than thorough—against which his professional being revolted—he asked, "A child?"

"Hardly a fact to be spoken of in polite society, but yes, there was a child."

"And the child is now living?"

"The child was born dead, monsieur, and the mother died too."

"A husband, a child. Indeed these are impediments."

"I said, monsieur, the mother and child are dead. Regardless of the chain of events in the end, Charles Montague was cognizant of the"—he searched for a word—"*suitability* of either of his sons to manage the estate. He was also a pragmatist. His will was written before Tracey appeared and provided that if Henriette met with an untimely death by natural causes, the property would be divided between his surviving children, Henriette's brothers Henri Gerard and Philippe. But if her death could in any way be attributed to foul play, all rights would be forfeit, and Maywood would be given, with all moveable property, to the Church. Tracey seems only to have been a minor inconvenience."

"Then the husband made no claim?"

"Maywood came to him briefly upon the death of Henriette, but within days of her burial, he determined to quit the place and signed the property over to Henri Gerard."

"Signed over? A sum of money must have changed hands. Presumably Maywood, however reduced in circumstances, would have been worth a great deal."

"Presumably."

"You don't know?"

"I was not consulted, monsieur."

"Oh?" said Shillingford. "Henriette died as a result of childbirth, and the child died, too, so there was no living issue and no foul play?"

"That is correct, monsieur."

"Then where is Philippe Letourneau and why has he not laid claim to his half of the property?"

"As I said, monsieur, Charles Montague had reservations regarding his sons' fitness to oversee the property. It appears that his concerns were not unfounded. Philippe Letourneau left the country for France shortly after Henriette's death and has not been heard from since. Henri Gerard took over the property, as I have stated. I can make no further answer, monsieur. Charles Montague provided for each of his children according to the measure of his affection and his assessment of his—or her—abilities. What has happened to each subsequently and how he or she has disposed of what was bequeathed, I am no longer in a position to speculate or pass judgment upon."

"Oh?"

"Shortly following the reading of the will, I was informed by Henri Gerard that my services would no longer be required. Thus a relationship of many years was brought to an abrupt, and I need not say acrimonious, end." LeGros rose. "If I have given you the information you require, monsieur, I will presume this interview is at an end."

CHAPTER 19

The External Appearance

❧❀❧

"Taste," says a celebrated divine, "requires a congruity between the internal character and the external appearance; the imagination will involuntarily form to itself an idea of such a correspondence. First ideas are, in general, of considerable consequence. I should therefore think it wise in the female world to take care that their appearance should not convey a forbidding idea to the most superficial observer."

—*Decorum*, page 267

Blanche looked through the voile curtains and out into the street. She avoided the gilt mirror that stood on a tiny round table in Madame Pommier's millinery salon. At one time, she had been proud of her dark, exotic features, her thick, straight black hair, and the thick black brows that framed her large jet-black eyes. Now she was all too aware that the dark brows appeared more like wedges cut into her face, and that tiny lines were beginning to appear around her eyes and mouth. Her gaze swung back to the mirror. She sat absorbed, looking at the hair over her temples, and wondered if Connor could tell that art rather than nature had staved off the encroachment of a few silver threads. She examined her hands and twisted the large rings upon them. The hands, at least, were smooth and unmarred.

Giselle had gone to fetch another model for her to try. Mimi was engaged with another client at another tiny table. Madame was concluding a purchase. A fire crackled in the hearth. The women's dresses rustled softly as they brushed past each other, moving to and fro between salon and workroom. The lacy ruffle of French accents was interrupted by the hard, flat calico of American speech.

So absorbed was Blanche in her minute examination that she was startled by Giselle's return. *"Madame voudras bien essayer ceci?"* was uttered not quite as a question, not quite a statement, the hat presented and turning to and fro on the tips of her fingers. Blanche felt as if she were facing a doctor who was prescribing a new patent medicine. She gave the girl a sulky nod. Giselle stepped behind her and placed the hat snugly on Blanche's head.

Giselle's butterfly-like hands caught the crepe ribbon from the back of the hat. The ribbon *zzzipped* as she made the first tie under Blanche's chin and *zzzipped* again as she made the bow. She whisked up the hand mirror from the little table and stood behind, holding the mirror. Not so long ago a black hat resting atop the black hair with a black ribbon framing an exotic face with black eyes was very becoming. The crisp black bow under the chin emphasized the natural blush of her lips and stark contrast of the smooth skin. Blanche looked in the mirror, then turned her head from side to side to view the back.

"Un peu plus bas, je vous prie, Giselle."

The girl moved the mirror lower and tilted it upward. Perhaps it was the gray winter afternoon light coming in the window, or the somber green moiré silk oppressing the little room that caused her to appear ashen and tired.

She sighed. "I don't think so, Giselle, do you?"

"No, madame," said the girl.

"Is there nothing else to try? Something perhaps with a bit more color?"

"I will see if there is something with color, or perhaps some fur, that is still dignified for madame."

Dignified. The word struck like a coffin nail. *So that's what I've come to,* thought Blanche mockingly, *dignified.* She took up swatches of color from the table and held them one by one under her chin. The wine color looked well, she thought. Yes, like garnets that old women wear to bring brilliance to fading skin. The electric blue was not bad, though she could no longer carry off so strong a color with such a hard edge the way she once had done. Mutton dressed as lamb, Connor would say.

A slight commotion stirred at one table of the small salon as one of Madame Pommier's patrons prepared to leave.

"Oh, Madame, you are too, too unkind," cried a silver-haired woman of very upright carriage. "How can you say that this color no longer suits me? Why, half my clothes are in this green. I shall have to rout my entire closet and begin again. How am I to bear it? And how am I to afford it? Thank Heaven, Osgood is dead. The prospect of a whole new wardrobe would certainly kill him."

"Ah, but," said Madame, cooing and cajoling as she took the woman's arm and conducted her toward the door, "you certainly would not want others to associate Madame's taste in color with a time now many years past, would you?" The woman gave sullen assent. "Madame has made a bold break and has ordered a stunning new design in the latest shade. Madame will look fresh and new."

Mutton dressed as lamb, thought Blanche.

"But my green, Madame," whined the woman.

"Perhaps a splash of your green could be used as accent, but only accent. If one is to break with the past, then one must break indeed."

Blanche looked in the mirror. *Indeed, one must break with the past,* she thought.

She returned her gaze to the window. The squeak of the carriage springs, the thwack of the doors on the hansom cabs, and the sharp clatter of horses' hooves drowned out the foot traffic on the near side of the street. The clack, clack, clack was mesmerizing. The black masses of animal and conveyance swam before her in the gray light. She barely noticed when a cab pulled up in front of the salon and two figures emerged—a small young woman with chestnut hair, followed by a tall, fair woman with hair the color of flax.

Blanche stirred herself and parted the voile curtain for a better look. By the time she had collected her thoughts, they had entered the salon and were being greeted in the entry by Madame Pommier. She knew instantly to whom the velvety mezzo voice belonged.

"*Bonjour, Madame. Vous vous portez bien. Vous vous souvenez de mon amie, Mademoiselle Lawrence.*"

"*Mademoiselle Lund, quel plaisir de vous revoir.* And of course, Mademoiselle Lawrence. A pleasure. *Mimi, prends les manteaux de ces dames et apporte une autre chaise pour Mademoiselle Lawrence. Et sonne Marie pour lui demander de préparer le thé.*"

"*Oui*, Madame."

Blanche hadn't quite caught the mezzo's name. In the meantime, Giselle had appeared and drew Blanche's attention from the new arrivals. "Come and sit by the fire a moment while Mimi clears the table." Madame Pommier escorted them to a green-velvet settee. Mimi arrived with the extra chair and began clearing the small table of ribbons, fur, feathers, and other accoutrements of the millinery.

As the fair mezzo sat, her eye fell upon Blanche. For a split second she hesitated. Knowing she had recognized her, Blanche pretended not to notice, but surveyed the hat and motioned to the girl to help her try it on. Out of the corner of her eye she watched the mezzo sink onto the settee, her companion chattering quietly behind her. Then the companion, too, stopped and brought a gloved hand to her lips before lowering her eyes and sitting next to her friend. Their backs were to Blanche and she shifted her gaze. The maid's arrival with the tea tray would occupy the two women on the settee for a bit longer.

Blanche soon became engrossed in their interaction with Madame, hoping to catch the names and learn who this beauty might be who had so decidedly caught Connor's eye. She remembered herself and Giselle, who stood behind her with the mirror. For an instant, Giselle's reflection betrayed how accurately she read

Blanche's thoughts. An instant later, Giselle had resumed her expressionless demeanor. Having been thus caught with her thoughts exposed, Blanche regained her composure and threw Giselle a defiant look.

Before many minutes passed, the women rose and moved to the little table on the opposite side of the room. "Now, Mademoiselle Lund," began Madame as Mimi came forward with the hat, "let us see how it looks." The hat was made of black velvet and nestled easily on the crown of the young woman's head. Mimi secured it with a pin and attached a quantity of simple black netting edged in black lace to the front of the hat and let down a portion of this over the woman's face. She gathered up the ends and secured them to the back of the hat with another pin.

"Oh, Francesca, you look stunning," exclaimed the smaller young woman.

Francesca Lund. So that was the name of this beauty whom Connor admired—as yet from afar. Reluctantly, Blanche agreed. One wouldn't have guessed that such a fair woman could carry off black so well. The woman sat in profile, facing the mirror in front of her, turning and tilting her head to see the hat from all angles, Mimi holding the mirror behind her. She turned her head toward Blanche and looked at herself in the mirror out of the corner of her eye, then looked purposefully at Blanche. Their eyes met for a second before she turned to face the mirror once again. Blanche caught her own sour expression and an ever-so-slight smile from Giselle that again vanished. The women conversed with Madame and Mimi.

"Maggie will think it's ever so fine, Francesca. You look ever so smart and elegant." The chestnut-haired woman raised her voice slightly on the two adjectives. She stole a glance at Blanche, then resumed, "You've made a wonderful purchase." Madame Pommier gave a slight bow.

"You must remember me to Mrs. Jerome. It has been several months since she has graced my establishment. She has not found herself another milliner, I hope," said Madame, wagging a finger in mock reproof.

"You have nothing to fear from that, Madame. No, Mrs. Jerome was only saying the other day that she must consult with you."

Jerome. Maggie Jerome. It couldn't be, thought Blanche. Surely it couldn't be the Jerome that Connor goes on about day and night, the Jerome with whom he's making deals.

Suddenly Blanche felt sick and panicky. If indeed this woman traveled in the same circles as the Jeromes, it would only be a matter of time before she and Connor would meet. Blanche picked up one color swatch, then another, then handled the lace and ribbon. She spoke abruptly to Giselle and demanded a different hat, anything to get rid of the girl so she could collect herself. Her thoughts made a terrible racket as she tried to listen, to learn anything more. A flood of unpleasant scenarios between Connor and this woman played out across her mind. A snatch of conversation brought her back to herself.

". . . and we've received ever so many donations for the church . . . Mrs. Jerome was saying to the reverend only the other day . . . took all morning to make visits to the tenements . . . and teaching them their alphabet in English . . . there are some very talented seamstresses among the new arrivals, if Madame would consider . . . yes, of course, send them along and tell them to bring samples . . ."

Blanche breathed easier. Yes, yes. This was the one who would be Edmund's in due course. Church and settlement house would be his problem, poor darling. Such a woman could never occupy—let alone hold—Connor O'Casey. The image of this gravelly Irishman teaching a bunch of grubby little foreign children to speak English made her forget herself. She pictured him on a leash, kneeling in church at the fair woman's feet. A little bubble of laughter escaped her. The women at the other table stopped short and stared at her. She tried to stem her mirth, gave them an engaging smile and bit her lip, but to no avail. She pictured him sitting unhappily in a roomful of cradles, each containing a screaming infant, rocking a cradle with each hand and each foot, just out of reach of a bottle of whiskey sitting on a miniature altar. A peal of laughter shot forth. Never. Never in a million years would Connor O'Casey be satisfied with an innocent Sunday-school teacher.

"*Est-ce que vous vous sentez mal, Madame Alvarado?*" Madame Pommier had drawn up close to Blanche, her head cocked in a nononsense manner. "Is there nothing I can get for you?"

"*Si, Madame. Je crois que je vais commander un chapeau bordeaux.* Do you not think wine color becomes me well? I'm thinking of having a new frock designed in wine color and I shall need a smart hat to go with it."

"Of course, madame. Let me conclude with these ladies and I shall be happy to oblige you." Madame Pommier turned back to the other table. "Is there anything else I can do for you ladies?"

"No, nothing more for today, Madame," said the fair mezzo, relinquishing the hat to Mimi to be boxed and wrapped. As she rose, she faced Blanche and surveyed her up and down, not with the look of disdain that Blanche would have expected, but with cool curiosity. Blanche returned the look, but hers was half defiant, half mocking, and deliberately annoying.

The business was concluded in the privacy of Madame's tiny office. The coats and the hatbox were brought to the hallway. As Madame Pommier saw the ladies to the door to bid them farewell, she called over her shoulder,

"*Marie, hèle un fiacre pour ces dames. Ensuite, tu pourras débarrasser les tasses et refaire du thé pour Madame Alvarado. Au revoir, très chères. Ce fut un plaisir de vous voir, comme toujours. Ne nous privez pas de votre visite aussi longtemps la prochaine fois.*"

When Madame Pommier returned to the salon, Blanche was watching through the voile curtains as the women climbed into the cab. She smiled to herself.

"Now, Madame Alvarado. Have you made up your mind about what you might like?"

"I believe so, Madame. Can you dye a veil in this color?" she asked, holding up the wine-colored swatch. "I'm feeling a little frivolous."

CHAPTER 20

Marked Attentions

❧

A young lady [should not] allow marked attentions from any one to whom she is not especially attracted, for several reasons: one, that she may not do an injury to the gentleman in seeming to give his suit encouragement, another, that she may not harm herself in keeping aloof from her those whom she might like better, but who will not approach her under the mistaken idea that her feelings are already interested. A young lady will on no account encourage the address of one whom she perceives to be seriously interested in her unless she feels it possible that in time she may be able to return his affections.

—*Decorum*, page 180

"You sound as if you've got no faith in me, Jerome," said Connor, taking a cigar from the walnut humidor proffered by the hovering servant. The cut glass decanter of port followed. Connor declined it. "You've set me a pretty problem, looking for a venue for the Excelsior."

"You gentlemen wouldn't know of a good parcel of land that's going cheap?" Jerry asked with a chuckle. "Something stronger?" he asked, addressing Connor. "Don't be shy. The port is just a concession to Maggie, who would even proscribe our masculine post-dinner rituals with the 'done thing' and apparently the thing that's done is port."

The dining room began to cloud over as cigar after cigar was lit and the pungent plumes of exhalation hung in the air. The Jeromes' dinner party of old friends had been an amiable social stepping-stone. Mr. and Mrs. Cameron and a Mr. Blair and his sister, who had known the Jeromes for years, gave the gathering variety. The Reverend Lawrence and his wife and their daughter might quash some of Connor's more colorful storytelling, but no matter. Miss Lawrence was Miss Lund's bosom friend. The latter had come on the arm of Edmund Tracey. The Gages and the Monroes, whom he knew from the hotel business, rounded out the party. He suspected Miss Blair had been prompted to keep him occupied, she being a spinster and near his age. She was sensible and intelligent and tolerant of his plain ways and she and her brother were genuinely kind.

At Thanksgiving Connor had sized up Tracey as full of himself and patronizing. Truth be told, if Connor were engaged to a woman like Francesca Lund, he'd no doubt be puffed up as well. What man wouldn't be? Still, Tracey was condescending where Miss Lund was gracious. Connor had squashed bugs with better manners than Tracey's.

"There's plenty of land at the northern end of Manhattan," said Mr. Cameron from across the table, "if you can persuade some farmer to sell."

"It's not as easy as buying up some vacant field. I wish it were," said Connor, clipping the end of his cigar and accepting the match lighter from Charlie Gage, and passing humidor and lighter together to Reverend Lawrence, who passed them on to Mr. Blair. "The problem with lower Manhattan, of course, is that most of the choice land is taken, unless we try to buy out someone—or several someones—and pull everything down and start from scratch. We'd pay a premium, of course—top dollar for the land and again for demolition."

"Which is certainly being done," put in the reverend, helping himself to a thimbleful of port. "It's happening all over town. Progress, people call it, but I don't know." Several gentlemen nodded in agreement.

"At the other end of the scale, so to speak, is what you suggest, Mr. Cameron," continued Connor, "purchasing farmland cheap with nothing to demolish. No doubt eventually the whole of Manhattan will be covered with people living cheek by jowl."

"I can't feature that," said Mr. Blair with a chuckle. "The upper end of Manhattan will be farmland till doomsday."

"Then doomsday's coming," said Connor. "Mark my words. The trouble with being the first is simply that—being first. You've got water and sewerage and bringing up electricity and there're muddy roads to contend with to get patrons there, let alone the workmen and their gear to build the place. But more than that, there are no amenities that would entice a person to seek a good hotel in that district. That's the one advantage of pullin' down old and puttin' up new—the right location should have restaurants and shops and entertainment ready-made."

"O'Casey's right," put in Charlie Gage. "Our hotel restaurant has to be first class, certainly, and we can offer a few exclusive shops on the premises, but we can't do everything. A lot may be said for farm-fresh milk and eggs for breakfast, but when people are spending the kind of money we'll be asking, they'll want more entertainment in the evening than watching the cows graze."

"That leaves you somewhere in the middle," said Edmund Tracey, lighting his cigar and taking a whiskey glass from the proffered tray. "It seems to me that any venue that fronts Central Park would be an advantage, especially with a good restaurant in the hotel."

"Come again?" asked Jerry.

"Yes," said Reverend Lawrence. "I know what you're driving at. Many people like a nice stroll before breakfast or a drive through the park after dinner if the weather is fine. The absence of any entertainment in the immediate vicinity might be made up for if the hotel were on Central Park."

"Precisely," said Tracey. "If there are good stables nearby that can offer riding . . ."

"And good livery in general and cabs," said Mr. Monroe. "People have to be able to get around easily and stable their own conveyances. . . ."

Ladies' laughter came from the drawing room. Connor, who usually relished this masculine ritual following a meal, found it difficult to keep his mind on the debate. His attention swung like a compass needle toward Edmund Tracey. *What in God's name does a woman like her see in a man like him? He wouldn't spark her interest in other quarters. Perhaps that's it—a man can be all beauty and no brains just as much as a woman. The man's a bounder, and no mistake.* Interrupting these reflections Jerry rose and released the gentlemen to the drawing room where Maggie was supervising the arrival of the coffee.

Across the room the piano was unoccupied, an opportunity not to be missed. At least music, in whatever form, might be a pleasure he and Miss Lund could share. His repertoire was limited, having been schooled at the Academy of Taverns in Western Mining Towns. So far, however, he had been able to turn his limitations into opportunities to be schooled by the more refined. Scanning the room to make sure that none of the ladies appeared to be moving toward the piano, he slid onto the bench and began to look through the music piled to the side of the rack.

"Do you play, Mr. O'Casey?" called Miss Blair from across the room. The ladies' collective gaze turned toward him. It was the opening he needed.

"Yes, ma'am, though I'm afraid you'll find my schoolin' in music somewhat lackin'."

"Nonsense. Won't you favor us?" she said kindly. "You certainly don't mind, do you, Maggie? Pray, continue, Mr. O'Casey."

Connor had noticed in the pile of music a sheet of "Love's Old Sweet Song" and began to play it, though from memory. He refrained from singing, which might detract from any favorable impression his playing might create. By the time he reached the refrain he was so engrossed in the song that he was a little startled to hear Francesca's mezzo voice and looked up to see her standing by the piano. She sang the second verse, seemingly more for her own pleasure than for the benefit of the company. The party half-whispered, half-listened. Tracey stood near the back, his face red with displeasure. When she finished, Tracey moved to fetch coffee for himself.

"I didn't have you pegged as quite such a sentimentalist," said Francesca.

"What did you peg me as? Someone with a hide tough enough that nothing could penetrate?"

Francesca unabashedly looked him over as he sat there looking back at her. "No," she said after a moment, "no." She looked him in the eye. "I think you're all bluff."

In that fraction of a moment, a tiny, barely perceptible look passed between them—a depth of understanding that Connor would never have owned. *Bluff.* The word itself didn't matter. He had been called worse—much worse, and to his face. She seemed not to judge him at all, but the sincerity in the way she said it and the way she looked, not at him but into him, made him feel exposed—as if he were sitting at the piano stark naked. He felt unsettled and aroused by something unexpected in her. If she could unbalance him like that in such a simple yet penetrating way, what else might she be able to do to him? Was he mistaken, or was there not a tiny speck, an atom of attraction in her eyes as they rested on him? It happened so fast. In an instant the look was gone, leaving him to wonder if it had ever really happened, and at once to wish and to dread that it might happen again.

He maintained his demeanor with effort and tried to smirk. "Is that so?" was all he could manage, leaving the tenor of the next remark to her so that he might breathe.

"Yes. I believe that's so." He couldn't mistake the flush on her cheeks, though her eye was steady.

"And are you all bluff, Miss Lund?"

She considered again. "Rarely, sir. I am not sure I would know how to bluff."

"I expect not."

"I do think I have ample ability to call the bluff of others," she said quickly.

"That's a conceited reply, with all due respect, ma'am."

She laughed. "Yes, very conceited." Her laugh was mellow and pleasing.

"Do you do so successfully—call the bluff of others, I mean?"

"You, no doubt, would call it a mixed success. But I generally find my ability adequate for my purposes."

"Your purposes? Ah, yes. Most of your sex have 'purposes.' What might yours be?"

"I would not claim to be representative of my sex, Mr. O'Casey."

"You're being evasive."

"Am I?" she asked. "Oh, I suppose my purpose is merely to understand a person's character—the inner man, so to speak—rather than simply rely upon what comes out of his mouth. There's nothing devious in that, is there?"

"No," said Connor. "It's quite admirable. A lot of people wouldn't bother."

"You mean, a lot of women wouldn't bother."

"If you like."

"You don't think much of women, do you, Mr. O'Casey?"

"On the contrary, Miss Lund, I think of certain women often." *Especially at this moment,* he thought.

"I hardly think that 'much' and 'often' refer to the same thing in this instance," she said with perfect steadiness.

"Perhaps you're right, Miss Lund."

"And am I right about your being all bluff, Mr. O'Casey?" His fingers began to run over the keys in a series of chords and arpeggios, playing nothing in particular.

"Perhaps your assessment bears further investigation," he said. He thought she colored again, though her eyes remained fixed on him.

"Now you're being evasive."

"No, I'm not," he said. "Just allowing you the privilege of an unbiased assessment."

"So you would put the burden of assessing your character upon me? Do you never examine your character yourself?"

"Never. Why should I where there're plenty who'd do it for me?" She laughed at this.

"Then I shall be sure to lend my voice to the chorus when I have more information to go upon."

"Fair enough."

At the sound of her laughter, Tracey strode up and joined them at the piano. Neither his expression nor his tone was friendly.

"Perhaps you should lend your voice to the rest of us, duchess," he said, leaning past her on the piano so that he brushed her back and his face came up by her right cheek. "Mr. O'Casey would surely relinquish his seat to you for our entertainment."

"Indeed, I should have before now. Forgive me, Miss Lund." Connor rose and gestured toward the bench.

"Not at all," said Francesca. "Mr. O'Casey is more than capable of entertaining this crowd." She laughed again. There was kindness in her laugh.

"I'd be happy to accompany you, Miss Lund, if there's a bit of music we both know," Connor said, rifling through the sheet music again.

"I'm sure Miss Lund could manage "Dem Golden Slippers" or "The Man on the Flying Trapeze." Tracey was a troublesome bee buzzing around a rose, thought Connor. It was all he could do to keep his seat and direct his attention to Francesca.

"I'm sure your comment isn't meant to reflect upon Miss Lund's talents," said Connor. "I've heard enough of them to assume she's capable of a good deal better."

"I meant no slight on my fiancée's abilities, sir," Tracey drawled. "I merely meant that perhaps your repertoire was not as extensive as hers." Though Tracey's posture was easy, his eyes conveyed a warning.

"Edmund. That's not necessary," she said in quiet reproof.

"I'm sure it isn't," said Connor, referring to the comment on his repertoire. "I've had the pleasure of hearing Miss Lund sing at Thanksgiving, you know. She certainly deserves a more worthy accompanist than I. I'd be happy to give the piano over to you, Mr. Tracey, if you would prefer to accompany Miss Lund yourself. Perhaps your repertoire matches hers more favorably," he said, reckoning that Tracey might not play at all.

"I would sooner decline in favor of Miss Lund playing, in which she's equally accomplished," retorted Tracey.

Francesca blushed. "Stop, please. Let Maggie decide what type of entertainment she'd like to hear," she said, throwing the last comment over her shoulder toward the ladies sitting on the settee in rapt attention toward the scene being played out at the piano.

"If Miss Lund would favor me," said Connor more loudly, "I'd be happy to accompany her on the song I was just playin'."

"Do go right ahead, Mr. O'Casey," said Maggie, whose face betrayed a decided lack of enthusiasm.

"Then I'd be delighted," Francesca said, turning to face her audience, who by now were assembled in low chairs scattered around the drawing room. Tracey retreated.

"Edmund, do come and sit next to me," said Maggie. Sent to the corner where he should be. Tracey took Francesca's hand and kissed it before crossing the room.

Connor waited for a signal from Francesca to start. She nodded to him and he broke into the flourish of an improvised introduction. She took up the verse on cue.

Once in the dear, dead days beyond recall,
When on the world the mists began to fall, . . .

Connor glanced up and saw Tracey, looking as if a black rain cloud were hovering over him. *A minor obstacle,* thought Connor. The question was how to detach Francesca from this bounder without losing her good will. For the moment, Connor could only hope that Tracey would make himself objectionable and that she would see through the blighter and release him. Though Connor never gave Divine Providence a thought, he was struck by the feeling that he was now at this moment where he was meant to be, doing what he was meant to do. There was a fundamental rightness to the idea of spending the rest of his life with Francesca Lund. An enormous wave of comfort and desire overcame him. He could picture the two of them playing and singing in the evening in their own home, with their children tucked up in bed.

Just a song at twilight, when the lights are low,
And the flick'ring shadows softly come and go,
Tho' the heart be weary, sad the day and long,
Still to us at twilight comes Love's old song,
Comes Love's old sweet song.

Everyone had gone. Tracey was waiting to escort Francesca home. He sat cross-legged in a deep leather chair, alone in Jerry's library, staring out into space. One hand held a glass of bourbon. He drew on the cigarette he held in the other. The dinner had put him out of spirits.

He loathed Connor O'Casey. He had constructed a mental picture of a man not unlike the newspaper caricatures of the immigrant Irish—dark, unkempt, dull-witted, shiftless, loud, and inebriated, possessing neither heart nor brain. Indeed, Connor was dark of feature and dark of humor and put himself too much forward. If O'Casey were going to commit a social gaffe he was determined to do it deliberately and loudly. But Connor was not a bumpkin. Tracey was surprised at the man's erudition in matters of travel, business, and current events. This degree of polish he credited to Blanche at first, but as the evening wore on Tracey perceived that Connor's understanding went deeper than could be ascribed to Blanche. She may have given him outward polish, but his knowledge and opinions clearly were informed by experience gained in the School of Hard Knocks.

Connor's respectable impression on the rest of the party unnerved and irritated him. The Irishman's speech was very plain and sometimes pushed the limits of propriety, but there was no snickering behind the hands at his tales. Connor's reception merely confirmed Tracey's opinion that the rest of the party lacked judgment and taste, save Maggie Jerome, who possessed the redeeming virtue of being on Tracey's side.

Jerry Jerome had swept Connor into the tight fellowship of fortunes made, leaving Tracey to dangle stupidly on the fringes. Tracey never liked Jerome, but he could not escape the strategic position he held in relation to Francesca. Tracey might have been amused at his current predicament had it not caused him so much mortification. For to make himself agreeable to Jerry, who held sway over Francesca, Tracey was forced to make himself agreeable to Connor, who slept with Blanche. The mortification was multiplied by Francesca's apparent fascination with the man. Though he had no reason to doubt her loyalty, his self-regard would not let him leave well enough alone.

"So here you are," said Francesca. She stood in the doorway, smiling, adjusting a pin in her hair. She yawned and held her hand out as she approached him. Tracey didn't stir himself except to put the cigarette in his mouth and hold out his hand to her. She sat on the arm of the chair and leaned across him, removed the cigarette from his lips, and kissed him. She held the cigarette away from him, out of reach, and kissed him again more deeply.

"You're not going to give that back?" he asked with a rueful expression.

"No. That cigarette tastes appalling." She crushed it out in the ashtray of a nearby smoking stand and kissed him again as he put his hand on her waist and felt the crust of beads and pearls that adorned the bodice of her gown—the crust, the outer shell he seemed not to be able to penetrate of late. She looked into his face intently and smoothed his hair and ran the back of her fingers under his chin and along his cheeks. He questioned for a moment how he could ever have been worried about the evening's events, about the dreadful Irishman or Francesca's loyalty. For a moment, Tracey thought there was nothing to forgive or apologize for and considered letting the matter drop—but he couldn't.

Attempting self-deprecation he said, "I fear I've disappointed you."

She looked genuinely puzzled. "Whatever do you mean?"

"That whole business at the piano."

"With Mr. O'Casey?" She shook her head. "I don't think anybody was really paying attention. They were getting coffee." He searched her face for any sign of insincerity. "Besides, he was the one who provoked the situation." He knew she was being generous.

"I need not have responded as I did."

"Well, I suppose I need not have responded as I did either."

"No, you needn't have." A slight start in her eyes hinted that he should check the reproof in his own voice.

"I'm sorry, dear. I was just trying to be polite." She sighed. "The poor man was simply trying to get on. He doesn't possess the same charms that you do, you know." He was unsatisfied with this remark.

"Dear, is something the matter?" she continued. Tracey rose and went to the low bookcase where the tray of glass decanters stood and poured himself another bourbon.

"Edmund? Did I say something?"

Tracey could feel the ire swelling in his chest. He could only picture her ease with the man, her manner, her laugh, her attention to O'Casey and her reprimand of himself. If he turned and looked into the face that he knew was overspread with incredulity he would explode. He threw his words at her.

"What should it matter to you whether he gets on or not?"

"Well, it doesn't really. I was only trying to be polite."

"Do you find him charming?"

"I find him an oddity, if you want to know the truth." Her voice had an ever-so-slight ring of defensiveness.

"I do want to know the truth," he said, turning toward her.

"What do you mean? I thought he was funny to listen to. He did have some amusing things to say."

"And I had nothing amusing to say?"

"You were a little quiet, but you often are in a large party. I know that. So am I, usually. Neither of us has the talent for conversing easily with everyone. I understand that and there's no harm in it."

"But it does tend to make one appear dull," he said.

"Nothing of the sort, unless one makes a big flap about it."

"You certainly weren't your quiet, restrained self."

"I don't understand."

"You found his talents attractive."

"Mr. O'Casey simply hit upon something I enjoy, something I feel at ease about. Had he not sat down at the piano, you probably would never have heard a peep out of me the whole evening."

"But you were attracted to him."

"I was attracted to the music."

"The music wasn't your usual style."

"Does it have to be? I enjoy sentimental songs just as much as the next person."

"I wasn't referring to the music."

"Then I don't know what you're referring to."

"To your making yourself agreeable to that man. It's not your usual style to go exposing yourself to other men."

"Exposing myself? What on earth . . . ?" She stood. "I was singing and making conversation. How was that to be construed as exposing myself?"

"Did you not see how everyone watched you? How you drew everyone's attention and left me to stand by and watch the two of you? My fiancée?"

"You sound as if I were conspiring with him against you." Her voice rose. "Good heavens, you can't suppose I have an ounce of interest in that man."

"You made me look like a fool."

"You didn't look a fool. Your only foolish behavior is occurring now, as we speak. You're making an absolute mountain out of a molehill."

"So now my judgment is in question."

"Oh, for heaven's sake," she said.

"You weren't the one who sat back with the others and had to listen to their remarks."

"What remarks?"

Tracey really could not think of any to cause her contrition and bring her to heel. In truth, nothing untoward was said, only compliments. But the focus on Francesca and Connor O'Casey together was more than he could bear and he meant to make her feel the weight of his displeasure. He chose not to answer her directly.

"I wish in the future you would not draw so much attention to yourself."

"You usually complain that I don't put myself forward enough. You always want me to sing."

"But I don't choose to have you make a spectacle of yourself."

"A spectacle?" she cried. "What on earth did they say?"

"It is of no importance. If you are ready, I'll see you home."

"Have you seen this Dr. Andrew Warren?" McNee asked, handing back the copies of the death certificates to Shillingford. They were seated in a private room above their rendezvous at Mills's country tavern, their evening meal and an oil lamp in front of them.

"No. But I must see him. He seems to be the only one left who can tell us what actually happened in June of 1884—save Tracey and the brother, of course."

"Yes. I inquired of Mills about the brother, Henri Gerard. An unsavory character by all accounts. A regular tear-'em-up at one time. Now pretty much keeps to himself."

"Got religion, did he?" asked Shillingford.

"Either religion or the fear of God. Speaking of religion, Mills says the priest has something against the family. Apparently there was enough of a regular flow of money from the Letourneaus to the Church that the bishop considered recommending Father Marcel's elevation to monsignor. When the current generation failed to live up to the parents' standards, the priest's chances were greatly reduced."

"No wonder I had a difficult time with him—protecting the names of the father and grandfather, at the same time despising Henri Gerard and Philippe. He conveniently omitted the business about the child. Perhaps he considered Henriette to be the last hope of the family redeeming itself with the Church—and his prospects."

"Not unlikely," agreed McNee.

"Clearly even Father Marcel regarded the circumstances surrounding her death to be suspect. To the best of his knowledge no one except the brothers and Tracey—and Dr. Warren, of course—witnessed the deaths of Henriette and the child. There was no wake or vigil, no administration of last rites, no normal activity surrounding the death of a Catholic. Why the haste?"

"There is the custom of letting the remains rest in the crypt for a year and a day before room is made for another body," said

McNee, "but this is a family burial ground with many tombs scattered about, not a single crypt or oven vaults aboveground. Plenty of room for everyone. Maybe they were afraid another interment so soon after Charles Montague Letourneau's death would draw undue attention to the matter." McNee considered. "But would it? Wouldn't it be more noticeable not to follow the normal rites of the Church and not to inter the bodies in the normal way? The Church would be up in arms. Now, there's a row for you right there."

"From what I understand," said Shillingford, "with the Church on the side of the family there wouldn't have been much the law could do to intervene. I can't imagine that the journey to the Letourneau cemetery twice in the space of a week would have made any difference to three able-bodied men. I assume three—Henri Gerard, Philippe, and Tracey."

"You mean four, don't you—with the priest?" asked McNee.

"No," said Shillingford after a moment's thought, "the priest said three—himself, Henri Gerard, and Tracey. Philippe had left Maywood for France."

"The lawyer could shed no further light upon the situation?"

"None. He was discharged as soon as he read the will, a will that left everything to Henriette."

"Henriette?" asked McNee, surprised. "A bit unusual. And she was alive then—when the will was read, I mean?"

"Yes."

"So, we must indeed try to find the doctor," said McNee. "I'll see if our host has anything to say about him." McNee produced a rude map. "Perhaps it's time I paid a visit to Maywood Plantation. Maybe Mills knows the quickest way to the graveyard."

CHAPTER 21

The Obligation of Silence

⟨❦⟩

*There are few points in which men are more frequently
deceived than in the estimate which they form of the confidence and secrecy of those to whom they make communications. People constantly make statements of delicacy
and importance which they expect will go no farther and
will never be repeated; but the number of those who regard the obligation of silence even as to the most particular affairs, is extremely small.*

—Decorum, page 227

McKetterick's hosted a special brand of secular Christmas musical
extravaganza, sparing no expense in costumes and scenery and live
animals. Indeed, the theater made most of its money during the
Christmas season, which carried it through the year's more medi-
ocre offerings. The theater itself was at the bottom of the list of respectable entertainment, a stifling hellhole and firetrap, with cramped
seating and decrepit balconies and an alley full of bleating livestock—
which only added to its charm.

Vinnie Lawrence, who enjoyed a good laugh, had persuaded
Michael to take Anne and herself and their more incorrigible
friends to McKetterick's, followed by the splurge of a late supper
at Louis Sherry's. Vinnie didn't care that many in the parish would

criticize this raucous entertainment for a parson's daughter. She had so little opportunity to be the object of delicious gossip that McKetterick's suited the purpose perfectly. Michael Lawrence nearly sacrificed a limb to give Vinnie her wish and emerged victorious. The evening promised to stoke the fires of gossip well into the New Year.

The street was sporting a lively traffic jam of hansoms, private carriages, and foot traffic when the Lawrence party's carriages pulled up. The narrow sidewalk was a mass of undulating humanity. They had missed the initial melee; one of the theater's front doors was already hanging by a single hinge and another looked like a fist had gone through. Extra house staff were hired for the occasion, their muscular bodies straining at McKetterick's livery—gatekeepers through which the seething and excited throng passed. Their attempts to weed out the troublemakers only created bottlenecks clogged with merry patrons. Scalpers did a brisk business. So did pickpockets.

The Lawrence party flung itself into the fray, forming a human chain with the gentlemen leading "like parting the Red Sea," shouted Michael—a pathway closing up tight behind them as soon as they were through it. With so much jostling around them, no one took any notice of the ladies unbuttoning their coats and thrusting hands down their bodices to retrieve the tickets. The party was carried through the cramped lobby, swept up the shabby stairs, and deposited in the front two boxes almost before any of them could draw breath. Flushed and excited, the young people settled above the mayhem that was the orchestra. Above them in the balconies, two tiers of overheated spectators waved, shouted, and fanned themselves with stage bills.

"Say, Lawrence!" shouted one of the friends who peered around the wall that divided the two boxes, cupping his hand next to his mouth to make himself heard. "What's the chance of escaping at intermission for a quick smoke?"

"Nil," Michael shouted back, "There's nothing quick in this place."

"Except a cutpurse," said a companion in their own box, who had just noticed her bag was missing.

The buxom girl laughed. "Someone took the bait. You were right about keeping nothing of value in a purse. I stuffed it with torn newspaper." The girl put both her hands on the top of her bodice as if adjusting it. "Let them try to get my purse." Everyone laughed.

No need to be demure in this place. Vinnie extracted her opera glasses from their little bag and surveyed the crowd. She began at the top and slowly made her way around the tier, laughing at the antics of the occupants, and disappointed that she could see properly only the people nearest the railing. The second tier, the story was the same.

As she began to peruse the back of the orchestra, her eye caught a set of dark and striking features atop a tall figure making her way down the near aisle. Each man she squeezed past looked her up and down. Unruffled by this attention, she kept her progress as if she were out for a Sunday stroll. Her hair was black and exquisitely knotted at the back, a large Spanish comb rising from the knot. She wore a slim black dress, a brightly colored shawl thrown carelessly over her shoulder.

It's that Jet Woman, Vinnie decided, *Mr. O'Casey's paramour.* She couldn't wait to tell Francesca. She watched the woman pick her way down the aisle to a row near the front of the house. Vinnie looked for the empty seat and expected to find O'Casey next to it. Instead, she saw the head and shoulders of a man in evening clothes who looked oddly familiar. The Jet Woman stood at the end of the row and shouted to her companion. The man turned his head at the sound.

"It couldn't be," Vinnie whispered, dropping her opera glasses in her lap. "It just couldn't be." She put the glasses up to her eyes again. One by one men rose and women pulled their skirts closer to let the woman pass. The companion rose, turning toward her— and consequently toward Vinnie. As the woman brushed past him to take the seat on his other side, the man pulled her toward him and kissed her low on the jaw under her ear. She smiled as she took her seat. The man sat down, showing by his posture that he was devoting to her his full attention.

Vinnie suddenly felt sick. She wanted to cry. She wanted to run.

She wanted to tell someone, everyone. Yet she could tell no one that the man she saw was Edmund Tracey.

The theater became unbearably hot. She felt drenched inside her dress and suffocation leapt across her chest and up through her neck and face. Cold perspiration sprang onto her forehead as pain grabbed at her eyes from behind. She dropped the glasses and pressed her gloved hands to her temples. The noise in the hall merged into an incomprehensible mass. The lights and people began to spin. Michael's voice saying, "Vin, are you all right?" was the last thing she heard.

When Vinnie woke, she was at home in her own bed. Her mind and body were in such misery that she couldn't trouble to remember how she got there. Anne was sitting at the foot of the bed. Michael stood by the door, ghostlike in the dim gaslight. Her father stood behind her mother, who continued to soak a cloth in cool water, wring it out, and apply it to Vinnie's spinning head. The doctor had been sent for. Vinnie couldn't think. She couldn't speak. She was seized by a violent crying fit that so hurled her stomach that she vomited into a bedside basin. Exhausted, she fell back onto the bed.

Michael's disembodied voice said, "She seemed just fine when we arrived."

"It was terribly hot in the hall," Anne's voice said. "There was a lot of noise and people moving about everywhere."

Her mother's voice swam to the surface. "I knew I had misgivings about this for some reason. All you young people gallivanting off to that dreadful place. Then to become overheated and be dragged out into the cold air. What on earth were you thinking, Michael?"

"We couldn't very well leave her there."

"Now, Mother," said her father, patting her mother's shoulder. "I'm sure Michael and Anne did their best."

When at last the doctor examined Vinnie, he concluded that she had caught a chill. Her overheated state had made her vulnerable to illness. The Lawrences must keep her warm, lest her chill turn to pneumonia. Vinnie's confinement was like being in prison. She was permitted no visitors, which would only incite restlessness and rebellion. Only Francesca's plea to join her and Anne in hosting a celebration New Year's Day kept her in minimal check. When the first cough made its debut from deep in Vinnie's chest and threatened this enterprise, she determined to wait it out and put up with the hot eiderdown, mustard plaster, bland porridge, dry toast, weak tea, and a room that smelled of camphor.

The tumult in Vinnie's mind and her enforced silence found vent in imagination and tears. As much as she wanted to unburden herself, for once she dared not give voice to her fears. She turned the scene at McKetterick's over and over again in her mind. There was no mistaking the easy stance and the charming smile. It was Edmund all right—and the exotic-looking Jet Woman. The memory of the look they shared, the kiss, the movement of their bodies as he pulled her closer embarrassed Vinnie, even as she lay there in the safety of her bed. She wished that even a fraction of the passion Edmund showed toward that woman could be genuinely bestowed upon her friend. Vinnie was ashamed of him. She hated to admit it, but on the surface at least, Mr. Connor O'Casey stacked up much better than her friend's fiancé.

McNee stood in the shade of a tree at the edge of a clearing and took a canteen from his light pack, swished a gulp of water around in his mouth, spat, then took two good swallows before replacing it. He knelt and extracted a map and laid it out on the grass, taking off his hat and wiping his forehead with his sleeve as he prepared to refresh his memory on this parcel of Maywood Plantation.

The sun was at midday's height. He lifted to his eyes the binoculars that hung around his neck and surveyed this part of Ascension Parish as far as their sight would take him. The Letourneau family graveyard lay in his direct line of sight. The little city of the dead, peopled by stone angels and saints, rose in the shelter of a modest stand of live oak trees, engulfed in tall grass and vines. An oversized gray temple tomb with its Corinthian columns commanded the center and dwarfed even the pediment tombs and barrel vaults with their crosses and obelisks, each of which diminished in size until the graves in the outer edges were reduced to a few plain box tombs and overgrown coping graves.

He made for a pile of decaying logs in the shelter of a small stand of trees. He would eat his midday meal hunkered down among the logs for protection and ponder the problem of the lock. He pulled his grub from the pack and drew a slim flask from his pocket. A box tomb, the priest had said. Only two or three of these were visible above the encroaching grasses. Might one of them contain a clue that would lay to rest any question of Edmund Tracey's motives and veracity?

He would sit back for just a minute more, he thought, and then get up. As he leaned back, his head bobbed a time or two and he forced his eyes open for a second and squinted at the dappled sunlight through the leaves, only to let his head fall forward on his chest. In a moment, he was fast asleep.

One of the first things a detective learns is, Never fall asleep on the job. This principle floated up from the recesses of slumber when McNee heard the unmistakable cock of a shotgun and felt both barrels nudge him against the back of his drooping neck.

"On your feet—real slow-like," said the deep, drawling baritone over McNee's left shoulder. McNee chided himself for being caught so completely off guard, but let it pass in favor of riveting his full attention on the situation at hand. As he stood, his canteen tumbled to the ground and he half-bent down to retrieve it.

"Leave it. Put your hands in the air." Again, McNee complied. "Now move off about five paces." McNee did so. "That's far enough." The man's speech was careless, but McNee detected a hint of refinement, as if the man were capable of proper speech when he cared to exhibit it.

"All right. See that patch of dirt?" McNee could just see out of the corner of his eye the double barrel of the shotgun indicating a bare patch of earth in the grass to his left. "Now you're goin' to take that gun out of your belt with two fingers of your left hand and you're goin' to toss it over there, gentle-like. Two fingers, mind, or I'll blow your head off."

CHAPTER 22

Impatience and Heedlessness

❦

The desire of pleasing is, of course, the basis of social connection. Persons who enter society with the intention of producing an effect, and of being distinguished, however clever they may be, are never agreeable. They are always tiresome, and often ridiculous. . . . They thrust themselves into all conversations, indulge in continual anecdotes, which are varied only by dull disquisitions, listen to others with impatience and heedlessness, and are angry that they seem to be attending to themselves. Such persons go through scenes of pleasure, enjoying nothing. They are equally disagreeable to themselves and others.

—*Decorum*, pages 22 and 23

Blanche had wheedled out of Connor that the Worths' invitation to Christmas dinner had arrived. She had also wheedled out of him that the woman she saw at Madame Pommier's millinery was the same Miss Lund who attended the same Jeromes who were guests at Thanksgiving, the same Miss Lund who was engaged to Edmund Tracey.

A change had come upon Connor, though he tried to conceal it—the introspection, the distraction, the obvious effort to show

enthusiasm for anything that interested Blanche. She had attributed it to the press of business and the hotel, but she soon realized
it was something else. He seemed a little lost, absorbed in reverie
from which she found it hard to rouse him. Even in the midst of
their lovemaking he was absent from her.

With this new invitation, she was determined to stand her ground.
She had a right to complain, didn't she? She had given up Thanksgiving, hadn't she? She was a respectable widow. If she didn't stand
up for herself, Connor would certainly never respect her.

"Oh, no you don't, not this time," Blanche fumed, "I will not be
left behind again."

"It's not my party, Blanche. I didn't make the choices. You'd
hate it anyway. The place'll be crawling with kids, just like it was
at Thanksgiving."

"That's not the point. You promised me that once you broke in
with these people you'd see to it that I would be introduced. I
won't let you shove me in a cupboard as if I don't exist. You've had
your chance—two in fact. What am I supposed to do by myself
while you're eating your Christmas pudding?" Her face was hard
and her words were sharp.

"I'm sorry, Blanche. Truly. The Worths asked me again for
Christmas dinner—and did not include any guest of mine in the invitation. It'll be just like it was, only worse. Kids'll be crawling all
over and shouting and showin' off all their presents. You'll go mad."

"If you can stand it, so can I."

"You wouldn't last an hour."

"Well, the whole party can't be made up of children. Who else
will be there?" Blanche tried to make the question seem natural.

"Whadaya mean?"

"It's a straightforward question. Who else was invited?"

"Just a few friends of the Worths."

"Who are they?"

"Some people you wouldn't know." The comment stung.

"*Who?*"

"What are you on at me about?" he snapped. "Probably the
Jeromes and maybe a few other people, that's all. How should I
know?"

Question, evasion, question, evasion. It was infuriating.

"I want to go."

"It's a bit late for that." His irritation showed more and more. She didn't care.

"Then decline. Say you can't go. Say you're sick. Say anything." She choked back her last words and turned away.

"I can't do that," O'Casey said.

"Why not?"

"It'd insult them."

"Decline!" Blanche lost her composure. "Decline and tell them you're spending your Christmas with me!"

"I can't do—"

"So help me, O'Casey, if you don't either decline or get me invited, I'll find out where they live and I'll come and make a spectacle of myself."

"You'll do no such thing," said Connor. He grunted as he rose from the divan in her sitting room. "You'll ruin everything."

"If you don't take me I swear to God that when I'm through, they'll be glad to see the back of you."

"Don't go threatenin' me, Blanche." His voice had dropped to the low growl she knew well—the tone he took on just before the real shouting began. He took one step toward her and pointed at her. "Don't you dare try it with me."

She picked up a china figurine and hurled it with all her might at Connor, who ducked just before it went crashing into the mirror above the mantel. Two more ornaments were sacrificed before he could grasp her around the arms. Desperation welled up in her chest as she flailed about. She could hardly breathe. Anger choked her.

"I won't be treated like this! I won't! I won't!" she shrieked.

"Stop it, Blanche!"

She kicked him.

"Damn you!" He threw her against the settee. She could see on his face the pain his maneuver cost him. She sprang to her feet and rushed toward him. He grabbed her wrists before her hands could reach his face. He backed her toward the settee and tripped her up to let her fall back upon it.

As he let her go, she grabbed the front of his waistcoat and pulled him on top of her. Using the only weapon she had, she planted her mouth across his mouth and entwined her leg around his. The friction of her leg inched up her skirt as she held him in a firm grasp that she knew he would have no inclination to break. He tried to pull away, but the attempt was half-hearted. Anger and frustration seared through her.

"Take me," she said as she grasped at his mouth with hers. She grabbed the waist of his trousers and continued to pull at him so that he gave in and fell heavily upon her. "Take me with you."

"I can't."

"You can," she said, every movement of her body enticing him onward. "You can, and you will."

Shillingford sat on the edge of the bed in his modest hotel room and by the light of a small oil lamp deciphered the scrawl that was as lanky and tousled as the Georgian himself. The thought of McNee's body in some remote hollow, the fear of discovery, of careful planning gone awry shot anxiety and weariness through the detective's frame—but McNee was alive. That was something at least. He fingered the thick letter in his hand. How could anybody—even McNee—wax philosophical for four pages on the subject of defeat? He lay back on the bed and prepared to be astonished.

> . . . My first assumption was that my discoverer was none other than Mr. Henri Gerard Letourneau himself. You will recall Mills's description of the man—a nocturnal animal who sleeps like a cat and prowls like one, too. Then I thought perhaps it was someone who had stewardship of the property, someone in Henri Gerard's employ. Again I surmised that had this been the case Letourneau would have employed a man with no more scruples than himself to patrol Maywood—a wild dog to complement the prowling cat. If he were, he would have had no scruple in dropping me where I

stood. Only with great difficulty did I collect myself and begin to divide my wits between self-preservation and pursuit of our investigation.

Get on with it, thought Shillingford.

Now he questioned me in earnest about my business at Maywood. I found the man's attitude peculiar—he showed curiosity aplenty, but no contempt, as might be expected of one who defended the place.

He pummeled me with questions about you, as one who already knows the answers. He knew of your interviews with the priest and LeGros. When I bristled and asked him the reason for his interest in our business, he produced proof of his being the law hereabouts. A few days after you and I entered this jurisdiction, Dr. Andrew Warren had gone missing. His purpose was to find out whether I was there in search of the doctor to question him or to dispose of him myself.

At this point I discovered what had so interested my captor in my pack. The map I had drawn from Mills's information clearly indicated the old Letourneau cemetery on the Maywood property. This, coupled with the doctor's disappearance, redoubled my captor's suspicions about our business. It appears the doctor was wary of our presence in the neighborhood. Friend Mills had tipped off Warren and soon thereafter the good doctor had been seen leaving the livery stable that keeps his horse, where he had saddled up and was last seen heading toward the Maywood road in a pouring rain.

The lawman wished to know whether his investigation and ours might in some way be connected. Guessing the answer before I asked the question, I inquired if he had learned anything from Henri Gerard. My captor had been unsuccessful in that quarter and was searching the premises to satisfy himself.

Under the watchful eyes of the double barrel, I pro-
duced my card. After a short verbal parry during which
he failed to extract from me the exact nature of our in-
vestigation, he asked if we suspected foul play in con-
nection with the Letourneaus. Though he maintained his
professional demeanor, I suspected that he, like many
we had questioned, would like nothing better than to
have something to pin on Henri Gerard Letourneau.
Before he released me, he warned that while he would
not stand in our way, he refuses all aid. The only time
he will acknowledge us is if we come up with hard evi-
dence.

I will attend on you shortly, so that we may confer.
Yours sincerely,
M. McNee

CHAPTER 23

A Wiser Opinion of Men

In mixed company, among acquaintance and strangers, endeavor to learn something from all.

Be swift to hear, but be cautious of your tongue, lest you betray your ignorance, and perhaps offend some of those who are present too.

Acquaint yourself therefore sometimes with persons and parties which are far distant from your common life and customs. This is the way whereby you may form a wiser opinion of men and things.

Be not frightened or provoked at opinions differing from your own.

—Decorum, page 52

"So, you got your wish, then." Connor dropped the letter on the table in front of Blanche. "Happy now?"

She swept it up triumphantly. "Of course. I knew they couldn't resist another poor homeless waif on Christmas."

Though she reveled in her triumph over Connor, the invitation had cost Blanche dearly. She asked no questions as to how he had engineered it, but, forewarned to expect a call, she received Mrs. Worth and her daughter Edith at teatime one afternoon. Connor's stress upon the importance of this meeting and the consequences of any misstep had unnerved her. The ladies were cordial and impeccably correct, but Blanche felt their scrutiny keenly. She could practically hear the gears turning in their minds, noting every aspect of her dress and toilette, her deportment and manners, her expressions, her taste, searching for any objection that might justify excluding her. With great effort Blanche overcame her natural acerbity and desire to display her wit and made do with elegance and etiquette. They stayed half an hour.

"Just remember who she is, and where you are, and who you're talking to while we're there," Connor warned.

"You never cease to amaze me, the way you think I don't know how to behave."

"Yeah, well, just remember that you know how to behave when the children start screaming and carrying on."

"You underestimate me. I may surprise you."

"I think not," said Connor.

On Christmas Day, Blanche was in hell. She contained her displeasure at being introduced to the Jeromes and gave Mrs. Jerome a fishy handshake. The noise of children was deafening and the disapproval of the adults palpable. Nothing, however, could compare to her displeasure at meeting Miss Lund. Still, she was determined not to give Connor the satisfaction of seeing her misery. Mr. and Mrs. Worth had received her with cool cordiality. Edith Blackhurst's disdain, Frederick Worth's amusement, and Margaret Curry's and Mildred Worth's curiosity could hardly escape her as she traversed the gauntlet of Worth guests.

Francesca acknowledged that they had seen one another before and were now fortunate to finally meet. Was there a sudden exuberance in Connor's address upon meeting Francesca? Was he going out of his way to establish familiarity by his unoriginal bromide, "So, we meet again . . ." that trailed off into reminiscences? Blanche forced herself from looking at Connor as he looked at Francesca, but she knew how his eyes could feel, as if his eyes were hands. The amusement in Francesca's eyes annoyed her. Did Miss Lund find Connor amusing on his own merit or in the idea of his attachment to herself?

To make matters worse, Blanche had not anticipated the surge of emotion Edmund Tracey's presence produced in her. He showed indifference at the charade of their introduction, equaled only by his indifference toward Francesca. Blanche was embarrassed for Edmund's discomfort just as she was embarrassed at having to be seen with Connor in Edmund's presence. He stepped forward and briefly took her hand, then retreated. She checked herself as her eyes followed him, almost of their own accord. An involuntary flush suffused her face. The room was very warm.

Blanche observed Francesca's attire minutely—nothing out of the ordinary, though it suited the woman perfectly. Francesca's complexion radiated warmth, heightened by the Russian green frock and the jet that twinkled around her neck and ears. Or was it Connor's attentions that gave her cheeks rosiness—or the crush of these abominable children?

Blanche had been saving the new wine-colored dress and hat for an occasion when this stylish apparel could be put to good use. Connor thought the velvet unlikely to withstand the rough and tumble of a Worth family dinner. She shrugged off his comment, saying that it was simply a muted tone of a Christmas red and that velvet would serve for anything. Within an hour of their arrival, the dress had been threatened by the grubby little hands and crumb-encrusted little faces longing to press themselves into its soft folds.

Blanche sought refuge in the company of the ladies near the fire and soon discovered that she was joining a conversation on Sunday sermons. No subject could have been more ill-suited to her knowledge or experience. She dearly wished she could have hidden long enough to take a deep swallow of gin from the thin silver flask hidden beneath her skirt. Mrs. Jerome was speaking.

"I said to the reverend, I said, 'Reverend, it is all well and good to preach about how to resolve the moral dilemmas in our day-to-day lives, but it is the Bible that must be preached. People just don't know the Bible anymore. If people knew the Bible they could figure out the moral dilemmas for themselves.' Then he said to me, 'Mrs. Jerome,' he said, 'if all I did was preach from the Scriptures like a Bible study, the Moral Dilemma Faction would be up in arms, saying that I care nothing for the moral and ethical problems they face every day.' So we are quite divided on the subject."

"I certainly agree with you, Maggie, that people don't know the Scriptures anymore the way they should, especially these young people," said the elder Mrs. Worth. "So caught up with their telephones and fast trains and scientific expeditions. It's no wonder they favor the moral dilemma over plain preaching, poor souls."

"One has to move with the times, Mother," said Mildred. "One can't stand still, even for moral dilemmas."

"I know, dear, but it does seem we're moving away from the fundamental things of life with such rapidity these days," Mrs. Worth replied. "There are so many more distractions than there ever were. It seems that every invention meant to make for convenience and to give us more leisure only gives us more time to get into trouble, and we seem to be able to do so with increasing ingenuity."

"Hence the moral dilemma, Mother," put in Mrs. Blackhurst. "I couldn't have stated the problem more cogently myself." The younger women smiled and nodded their support.

"But what about real progress in the sciences," offered Margaret Curry, "medical advances and such? Surely you can't think that discoveries—what about this germ theory, for instance?—that they can create a crisis of conscience."

"I think I was a much happier person when I didn't know about germs," said Mrs. Worth, to the general amusement and dismay of the younger women.

"I do agree with you though, Isabel," pursued Mrs. Jerome. "People do seem to be able to get themselves into trouble in the most ingenious ways. I blame education for a good portion of it. I believe there are some things that mankind simply wasn't meant to know. God set the world in motion and mankind shouldn't go tinkering with it."

"I suppose you would extend that to the education of women, Maggie," said Miss Lund.

"Now, let's not begin that sore subject, dearie," Mrs. Jerome retorted, looking a bit embarrassed.

"You yourself have done quite well, Francesca," Mrs. Worth cut in, "balancing the spiritual and the temporal. You always seem so at peace with yourself."

"Oh, Francesca never has to grapple with that sort of thing, any moral dilemmas I mean, do you, dearie?" The Jerome woman seemed to comment for Blanche's benefit.

"You make me sound like an empty-headed fool, Maggie. Of course I face them. All the time. One cannot count oneself as human without having faced some sort of dilemma of action or conscience, wouldn't you agree, Mrs. Alvarado?" Blanche was at once grateful and resentful of a civil question being asked from that quarter.

"Yes, I would."

"And wouldn't you agree," continued Francesca, turning toward Blanche, "that simply being a woman requires that one be even more vigilant with regard to these dilemmas? For men are always getting away with things that women could never do in a million years." Blanche might have taken this remark as a decided breach of decorum, had it not been delivered with such innocence and sincerity.

Jerry Jerome, who overheard the last remark, broke in before Blanche could answer. "And what on earth does a man do that you would ever want to do?"

"Work. Vote. Go out late at night alone. Escape to one's club. Escape halfway around the world—"

"Dearie, really," broke in Maggie with a nervous laugh.

"And not be dependent," said Francesca.

"You could hardly call yourself that, dearie." Maggie shifted in her chair and fumbled with the long chain of little ornaments that fell from around her neck.

"When I marry I might be." Blanche's ears attuned themselves to this remark. "Certainly for most women it's true. Everything she has might be her husband's. Now there is a moral dilemma for you. If she remains single and financially independent, she's subject to the censure of society for being unmarried. If she marries, she gains the approval of society but loses her independence. Is that not a dilemma, Mrs. Alvarado?"

"Most definitely, Miss Lund." A thinly veiled comment about

Miss Lund's engagement to Edmund, or a deliberate insult directed at her? How odd to have such a dilemma in common when this protected beauty had not the least idea what dependence really meant. How odd and how ironic, thought Blanche, to have chased across half the world in pursuit of a man to whom to shackle oneself in marriage in hopes of being forever free of being dependent. Now here she was in the presence of a young woman at risk of losing her independence by virtue of the very same shackles. Blanche had expected to have to brazen out the evening somehow, but she hadn't expected the conversation to strike so deeply at the heart. She was miserable.

Blanche caught Connor's eye as he and Jeremiah pored over a new picture book on the Orient and shot him a look of distress.

"Jeremiah," he said. "I'm sure Mrs. Alvarado would enjoy looking at this new book you have here." Hardly the rescue Blanche had envisioned. The suggestion was clearly unpalatable to Jeremiah, who threw Connor a look of one who had just been ordered into the presence of the wicked witch.

"But we haven't finished looking at it," the boy protested. "We missed a part at the beginning, and we have a whole bunch more pages to go."

"We can pick it up again after you've showed it to Mrs. Alvarado," Connor assured him. Jeremiah clapped the book shut on his lap.

"Jeremiah, show the book to Mrs. Alvarado," Mrs. Blackhurst insisted. Jeremiah proffered the book and pushed the ottoman beside her chair and sat upon it.

"Have you ever been to the Orient, ma'am?" asked Jeremiah politely.

"No," said Blanche with an edge of sarcasm, "have you?"

"No, ma'am," he said seriously.

"Lots of young people travel the world, you know," said Blanche, recovering her civility.

"Yes, ma'am." Jeremiah brightened. "Mr. O'Casey's been to the Orient, and he wasn't much older than me."

"Than I," corrected Blanche.

"No, ma'am."

"Yes, Mr. O'Casey has been absolutely everywhere," she said, throwing Connor a look of disdain before returning to the book.

"Mrs. Alvarado is herself well traveled, I believe," chimed in Frederick Worth. The entire room looked at him and froze. Mrs. Blackhurst shut her eyes. Samuel Curry coughed. The elder Mr. Worth, who was pouring a glass of punch, stood upright. Mildred Worth nearly choked. Blanche looked at Connor to supply a graceful way out.

"Mrs. Alvarado knows Europe like the back of her hand," said Connor. "She has a sister who lives in Italy with her husband and family."

"I understand you lived in South America for a time, Mrs. Alvarado," said Linton Blackhurst, betraying knowledge that he should not have had.

"Yes, my late husband was from Argentina and we lived there for some years." The room breathed again.

"It is reputed to be a very beautiful part of the world, is it not?" he continued.

"Much of it is."

"And very hot?" asked Frederick Worth.

"Only if one is unable to adapt to it, Mr. Worth," Blanche said. "One does find relief in the mountains when the atmosphere becomes overheated."

"Yes, adaptability is certainly a virtue," the younger Mr. Worth replied, "especially when traveling where one is unaccustomed."

"The highlands are coffee country, I believe, Mrs. Alvarado," offered Francesca.

"Not so much in Argentina, though other parts of South America produce many excellent varieties. Many people prefer South American coffee to the Turkish or other Far Eastern varieties. We were ranchers." Again Blanche was obliged to think well of the woman for her civility.

"What did you raise?" asked Francesca.

"Cattle and horses."

"Mr. Worth is a devoted connoisseur of Turkish coffee, are you not, John?" asked Jerry.

"Let's just say a 'devotee,' Jerry," replied Mr. Worth. It was he who provided Blanche with a graceful exit. "Mrs. Worth has just acquired some very interesting artifacts from South America. Pre-Columbian, I believe, aren't they, my dear? Perhaps Mrs. Alvarado would be interested in seeing them."

"I'm hardly an authority, but I should certainly be happy to see any of Mrs. Worth's collection, if she would be kind enough to oblige me," said Blanche with more grace than she felt. She was glad of the escape. With Connor left behind conversation about her would be stanched.

"I'd be delighted," said Mrs. Worth as she rose. "If anyone would like to join us for a brief tour, you would be most welcome."

Blanche remembered the child who was supposed to be entertaining her. He had sat mute and wide-eyed. "Thank you for sharing your book with me," she said as she nearly slapped his hand shut in the picture book. Jeremiah retreated to the safety of Mr. O'Casey.

Edmund, who had been watching Blanche from the other side of the room, reached Mrs. Worth just as Francesca rose from her chair.

"I don't believe I've seen these particular objects, have I?" asked Francesca. She smiled at Blanche, as if she were sensible of Blanche's precarious position and meant to exert herself in being friendly. It was insufferable.

"No, dear. I don't think you usually go in for this type of art, but you may find it of interest, so do come along." Blanche and Edmund looked at each other in veiled horror. To be "chaperoned" by Mrs. Worth was one thing. To be accompanied by the fiancée was quite another.

For the first time, Blanche wondered if the strain and mortification it cost her to gain acceptance were worth it. As she mounted the stairs beside the society matron whose acquaintance she had sought for so long, she felt even more cut off, as if it were the family who had been rescued and not she. Even Connor appeared to be relieved as Blanche cast him an unpleasant backward glance. Now with Edmund and the Lund woman following behind her, she felt trapped in an untenable situation of her own making. Behind her lay her old life with Edmund, who was about to shackle himself to this woman who had no business marrying him. In front of her lay a massive void she could not negotiate without O'Casey— O'Casey's name, O'Casey's money, O'Casey's growing respectability.

Blanche endured Mrs. Worth's pre-Columbian acquisitions in this new field of artistic exploration. To Blanche, they were no more than primitive and vulgar curiosities, with their broad and smooth-featured faces and their intricate and abstract decoration. The Lund woman compared their intricate designs to the jewelry her mother brought from Scandinavia and exclaimed over the work-manship. Such enthusiasm made Blanche sick. For a moment she sought refuge in Edmund's eyes. She could see he was as bored as she and the look between them confirmed the disdain each felt for these people.

The look he returned penetrated her being and made her every fiber and sinew aware of him. It seemed ages before she came to herself, so completely did she drink in his eyes and lips so that nothing else existed. The silence of their preoccupation made Francesca and Mrs. Worth look up from the collection. Blanche hoped she had recovered herself quickly enough to quell suspicion. But as Francesca looked from her to Tracey, Blanche knew it was too late.

CHAPTER 24

The Same Exalted Sentiments

It is an express and admirable distinction of a gentleman, that, in the ordinary affairs of life, he is extremely slow to take offense. He scorns to attribute ungentle motive, and dismisses the provocation without dignifying it by consideration. For instance, if he should see trifling persons laughing in another part of the room . . . he will presume that they are swayed by the same exalted sentiments as those which dwell within his own bosom, and he will not for a moment suffer his serenity to be sullied by suspicion. If, in fact, the others have been not altogether unwilling to wound, his elevated bearing will shame them into propriety.

—Decorum, page 12

Connor stared into space, a whiskey glass in his hand, a chaser of buttermilk on the bar. The tavern was a careworn Irish establishment he had found early in his solitary wanderings around New York. The heavy acrid smell of cheap tobacco hung everywhere. Smoke hung in ashen whorls that smothered the low light of the gas lamps. Chew collected in a brown, syrupy mash at the bottom of the tin pails or pooled in slimy puddles on the floor. The barroom was a dark shade of a forgotten color. The chatter was merry or contentious, the accent lilting or hard-edged, depending on its owner's origin. A small riot of children could be heard at the back door, waiting for their families' supper beer. Connor wandered there when he needed to think, away from any judgment but his own, with no demands and nothing to prove, where no one knew him or would think to look for him.

Until Thanksgiving, Miss Francesca Lund had been an abstraction, an anonymous beauty, no more than a mental dalliance and a chance encounter. He raised the glass to his lips and fixed his gaze on the large painting of an odalisque that hung over the bar. The woman in the painting returned his look, her fingers twisted in the fair hair that tumbled down in heaps of curls across her shoulders and between her ample breasts. The mental leap to the frothy-haired Miss Lund was not a long one.

Time was when such a picture conjured up an image of Blanche. More than an image—a touch, a scent, a rush, a release. But what did it amount to in the main? A few dresses, a few baubles, changing tweeds for evening dress, a room for a suite, a tavern for a restaurant, and a music hall for the opera, better and finer over more than a year, but there it stopped. The same old patterns simply became clothed in finer trappings. He had not realized this before.

He downed the shot and flexed his hand around the small heavy glass, kneading at it as if it were a lump of clay, working it until the glass was hot in his palm. Then he smote the bar with the glass and said, "Another. Leave the bottle. A round for the house while you're about it—and more buttermilk." The barkeep said nothing, but touched two fingers to his forehead in a semi-salute, receiving a jangle of coins tossed onto the bar in return.

Make no mistake—he liked Blanche. She'd been loyal and put up with his shortcomings and had done whatever he had asked. Despite her outward refinement, she found amusement in the seamy and questionable, in innuendo that made even he himself uneasy. She threw herself into each day as if tomorrow might not come. This passionate recklessness was part of her attraction, this ability to say to hell with it all and follow the day's good idea until she got bored with it. Then dawn would break and it would begin all over again. It could be exciting for a time, until one had to deal with the wreckage in her wake. Blanche needed managing by a firm hand, and yet, somehow she had managed him into keeping his eyes fixed on the details in front of him, not the future.

Consequently, he had not connected the future with her. Not really. In spite of her encouragement, her fitting him for better things, he had not stopped to consider whether her style was his style or her ambitions his. He had kept things simple and kept things moving and had ignored anything that looked like longing that might gnaw at his own soul.

The Deal had been the goal before, the brass ring. If he could only get there—get *there*—then he would prove to himself and the world that Connor O'Casey was equal to anyone. Here he was, soaring above his detractors, boldly facing out the possibility of failure. He *was there,* and now that he was, did he dare think what he was thinking? A different kind of belonging had entered the picture—a clannishness that hovered over every gathering like a great bulk and formed an invisible glue that cemented one to the tribe. Now there were children and grandchildren—the Worths', of course, not his. Now there were friends gathered around a table for a meal and an evening's entertainment—the Jeromes', of course, not his. He could build the finest mansion in New York if he wanted to, but what good was a cavernous mansion if it did not echo the laughter and tears of a family? Was there any point at all when a man had been content to live alone in a few small rooms? He was not content to die alone in a few small rooms, that was the point.

If ever there appeared to be a woman who looked to the future, who might be eager to form the next clan cemented to the larger tribe, it was Francesca Lund. Was liking Blanche—was gratitude—enough to glue the two of them to the tribe? Again, he raised his glass to the fair-haired odalisque, threw the shot down his gullet, and chased it with the buttermilk.

Then, there was all the church business. Connor was hardly looking to be reformed, but his instinct told him it drove deeper than that. The little twinges of discomfort Francesca stirred in him might be the disquietude of a soul long fallen into disuse, a moth-eaten part of him that needed tending. That he had probed his inner self enough to work that out made him uneasy, too, but he could picture no other woman to whom he could dare admit that he possessed so frail an object. No one ever said that possession of a soul would stand in the way of enjoying with her the awakening of those physical instincts that marriage would sanction. Quite the contrary.

But could he pull off such a coup? There must have been fifteen years between them and there were plenty of men nearer her age who could cut a fine figure. What of it? If she could shoulder all this, then she was the kind of woman with whom he could see himself growing old, in a mansion full of offspring, with a business to leave them, and a good name and a future. That was the brass ring—no, not brass, but gold.

He had been so deep in the problem of Miss Francesca Lund that he almost started when he discovered a laborer at his shoulder. This wouldn't do. This woman was making him soft in the head. The man put his hand on Connor's shoulder.

"We're much obliged to you for the drink," he said, looking Connor up and down, his comment bordering ever so slightly on a sneer.

"'Tis no trouble," said Connor, turning only his head to get a good look at the man and laying on his accent a tad thick. He poured himself another and raised it to his lips, returning his gaze to the row of bottles behind the bar and the long mirror behind them, above which the odalisque gazed at him.

"Won't you join us then?" said the man. It was a statement rather than a question.

"I'm obliged to you, but no. Thank you kindly."

"Might we at least know to whom we're to give our thanks?" The man stood with his hands on his hips.

"Give your thanks to God, then, if you must thank somebody. I need no thanks."

"Are you mocking us, sir?"

"I mean no disrespect. Another glass," said Connor. The barkeep plunked the glass down and moved on. Connor poured a

whiskey and shoved it toward the man, then poured one for himself and said, *"Sláinte."*

Before Connor could pick up the chaser, the man grabbed
his arm.

Connor looked at him full in the face. "I'd be obliged if you'd
unhand me."

"Would you, now? The gentleman would like me to 'unhand
him,' boys," said the man to his mates at the end of the bar.
"Afraid he'll get a crease in him and give over smellin' like toilette
water. Then his lady-friends won't find him quite so appealing."

His mates guffawed and whistled as the man stiffened his grip.
Connor made one last now-or-never attempt to retrieve his arm.
He pulled it out of the man's grip and poured himself another
drink. The man's expression instantly changed from mockery to a
squinty-eyed disgust.

"We don't take kindly to them as can't be social," he said, pushing Connor back by the shoulder with a jerk. Connor turned and
faced the man. They stood nearly eye to eye. "Them as can't be
social we generally try to make unwelcome."

"I don't take kindly to being manhandled by a stinking,
slovenly bastard like you," said Connor calmly. He drew up his
walking stick as he spoke and tucked the knob-handle under the
end of the kerchief that was around the man's neck and gave it a
playful flip, then tapped him once on the chest for emphasis.

"Dirty son of a *bitch*," the man began as he wheeled and threw
his arm back, winding up for a punch. Before he could deliver the
blow, Connor lifted his fist, which still engulfed the small, hard
whiskey glass, and threw a punch to the man's upper lip. The
room gasped as the man reeled backward. He made straight for
Connor's gut, only to receive an upper cut to the face with the
walking stick. Connor beaned him for good measure.

The man's mates rushed Connor. Each grabbed an arm. With
his face bloodied and his head spinning, the opponent was not so
light on his feet. He lurched toward Connor like a bear on hind
legs and lunged for his throat. Connor, who had not wasted his energy with struggling, poured all his power into the upward thrust

into the man's groin. Red pain and anger suffused the man's face as he fell to his knees, his hands clasped between his legs. Connor finished him off with a kick to the head.

The room rioted. Old wounds that had taken years of patient healing were wrenched apart as Connor was set upon by man after man. As the blows fell, the room spun into the likeness of the office of the Five Star Mine.

"They've waited to be paid for months," shouted Connor's friend and partner Walter West.

"This mine can't be profitable—" Prescott retorted.

"I don't want to hear about your damn profits," shouted Connor. "You're suckin' the lifeblood out of these men—"

"While you're up in your fine houses with your cut glass chamber pots we're down here—every damned day," shouted Walter. "We see these men when they come out of that hole. Like ghosts, most of 'em. Soon they won't be good to anyone—"

"The rest of us investors want to see the ledgers—"

"*Then see 'em!*" Connor threw ledger after ledger of the Five Star Mine onto the desk. "*Look at 'em!* What are you doin'? Holdin' their pay hostage until you're satisfied? Get your ass down here and manage it yourself if you're so damned concerned about profits." Connor lowered his voice. "There're union men sniffin' around here—"

"Then run 'em off."

"*You* run 'em off," shouted Connor, thrusting a forefinger in the man's face. "*You* explain to the men how they'd be better off without organization. I've worked in those mines and so's Walt. We swore that when we had the power to make things different for these poor sods, we'd do something—"

"You won't do it off the backs of the investors, I tell you. And we won't hear about you paying the men out of your own pockets this time. You're undermining our authority. It's about time you—"

A panicked foreman burst through the door. "They know Prescott's here with his men. They're comin' for him."

"They won't get past my men," he said arrogantly. "Get 'em back to work—*now!*"

"*You* get 'em back to work," shouted Walter. "*You* face 'em. *You* tell 'em."

A great rock sailed through the window. All three bowed away from the shower of broken glass. In a moment, Walter was on the floor, a head wound gushing blood.

"Walter!" Connor dropped to his groaning friend.

Prescott stepped to the broken pane, drew his revolver, and took aim.

"*You won't!*" screamed Connor.

He hurled himself at Prescott, knocking him off his feet. As he landed on the floor, a shot from Prescott's gun exploded into the air. Like a signal, the shot discharged a volley of bullets from the men outside to the accompaniment of cries from the angry miners. Connor struggled with Prescott as windows shattered in a hail of rocks and gunfire, and the sound of blunt force against flesh raged just beyond the office door.

Connor wrenched the revolver from Prescott's grasp and cuffed him across the head with the butt end until the man lay motionless. He crawled to Walter, took a handkerchief from his pocket, and tried to stanch the flow of blood.

"Walter. I'm here," Connor shouted above the din. "Stay with me, boy."

"Get out. Get outta the Five Star," said Walter, his eyes filled with anguish. "You're too good for Leadville." Walter raised his hand as if to dismiss Connor's aid. "Get out. Tell Ida . . ."

The miners burst in and hauled the unconscious Prescott outside and set upon him with rocks and hammers and finished him off. Connor threw himself over Walter.

"*Wait! Wait!*" he shouted. They seized Connor and pulled him off as a miner straddled the wounded man's chest and raised an iron rod. Amid Connor's cries begging them to stop, he could hear the dull, merciless bludgeoning. Thrown against the jagged ground, Connor suffered blow after blow, unable to fend them off with words and unwilling to raise a hand against them.

Now, in the din and mayhem of the tavern, the stick was ripped from Connor's hand and used against him, stomach, ribs, and head, but he had no chance to fall. Whipped into a frenzy, the tavern's patrons pressed against him, lifting him off his feet as they made their way to the door. With one great heave he sailed out into the street. Walter's words echoed through his brain. *Get outta the Five Star. You're too good for Leadville. Tell Ida.* The last blows left Connor O'Casey a bruised, bleeding, and unconscious heap.

"Jesus, sir." Jamie's tone was hushed. He was alarmed but relieved to find Connor lying on a cot, locked up at the Bummer's Hall. "What the hell do you think you're doin' picking a fight . . ." He was going to add, "at your age," but thought better of it. Jamie steadied the big man, trying to cushion Connor from further abuse, keeping one move ahead of the policeman who pulled Connor up smartly by the collar.

"Shut up, boy, and get me out of here," was all the reply his master could manage.

Connor's head and lip were cut and bloody and one eye was swollen nearly shut. Grime was ground into his coat and the sleeves were tearing from their seams. Jamie could only imagine how the shoulders had been wrenched in their sockets.

"All right," the officer had growled, "he's free to go. Get him out of here, lad. If I sees this ugly bastard again, ain't no amount of money'll get him out. Got that clear?"

"Yes, sir." Jamie had grasped Connor bodily, letting Connor drape himself over Jamie's slight but strong frame. The two men pawed their way past the tramps, drunks, prostitutes, and vagrants who shared the Tomb's large holding cell and walked quickly out the Franklin Street entrance and piled into a waiting cab—all before the morning's Police Court docket was complete.

Jamie had felt the bubbling undercurrent. Connor had been underfoot all day, not venturing out of the Grand Central Hotel. He had paced the sitting room or stared at nothing out of the window, a large cigar hanging between his fingers and thumb, its ash falling onto the sill. Jamie had gone about his business, doing and redoing the work of the wardrobe. He polished boots that already shined, brushed suits, and checked for the missing buttons he had sewed on but yesterday, all so that he would be within easy call. Surmising that his master might require a good drinking base, he ordered a simple evening meal of bread and cheese. At length, having eaten, Connor prepared to go out—not in his usual meticulous apparel, but old clothes that he kept retrieving from the odd lots that Jamie kept setting aside to be thrown away.

"Shall I get you a cab, sir?"

"No, not tonight. I'll see to it meself. You needn't wait up."

It was well past midnight when Jamie finally went to look for him. Despite being used to Connor's late hours, this night he sensed that something was wrong. He weighed the consequences of being absent when his master arrived against the prospect of his master being found dead in some alleyway. He found the burly cabby who was used to Connor's nocturnal rovings, and tucked a small derringer into his pocket, just in case.

The late hour prompted Jamie to skip the usual haunts and make straight for the Tombs, where disorderlies would be kept until their hearing the next day or until someone came to fetch them. Hospitals would be next, and then, if worse came to worst, the morgue. His foresight had been rewarded. He had located Connor at the Bummer's Hall within an hour of the latter's being picked up. The big man was doubled up on a stinking mattress on a rickety metal cot, a pool of vomit drying on the floor next to it. The crowded place smelled like urine and booze and unwashed flesh. Dirt and blood were ground into Connor's heavy coat. The cap and stick and cash had gone by the boards.

"Can't you keep out of trouble?" said Jamie, once they had made it to the cab.

"I didn't go lookin' for it," said Connor with effort.

"No, but it managed to find you right enough," said Jamie, matching Connor brogue for brogue.

"I don't need your lip now, do I, boy?"

"Well, you need lip from somebody, sir, begging your pardon. What am I supposed to do, may I ask, if you go getting yourself killed?"

"Just shut up and get me home."

CHAPTER 25

Our Gloomy Moods

❧

We should subdue our gloomy moods before we enter society. To look pleasantly and to speak kindly is a duty we owe to others. Neither should we afflict them with any dismal account of our health, state of mind or outward circumstances. It is presumed that each one has trouble enough of his own to bear without being burdened with the sorrows of others.

—*Decorum*, page 221

Francesca Lund let it be known that on New Year's Day, 1891, she would observe the old tradition of opening her home to receive guests. The Lund family home would again be a center of conviviality. No harkening back to her mother's days as hostess. This New Year's Day would be hers.

"Edmund will be here all afternoon to help and can protect me from any unwanted attention," Francesca replied with a wink at Jerry over the Jeromes' early New Year's Eve dinner, "and Michael and Anne will be here the whole time. It will be quite like two engaged couples sharing the duties as host. Vinnie and Anne and I will be trading places at the piano all afternoon and I've engaged the cellist whom you liked so much. Reverend Lawrence, Anne's father, various Messrs. Worth, and Jerry will call by"—at which

Jerry nodded his assent—"and Dr. Barton promised to come early and bring his mother to sit by the fire and drink tea. So you see, we shall all be quite proper." Maggie's objections were silenced.

The house was fragrant with good cooking and fresh greenery. Mrs. Howell had outdone herself in the kitchen. A festive display of pine and holly mixed with blood-red hothouse roses and carnations graced the entrance, drawing room, dining room, and banister.

The hostesses made a splendid trio: the diminutive, chestnut-haired Vinnie in creamy, chocolate-brown taffeta and velvet; the plainer but pleasant-looking Anne, whose deep green bengaline silk lit up her complexion; and the fair and stately Francesca in purple brocade with a collar that stood up at the back of the neck and plunged to a deep and narrow *V* at the bosom. Ear bobs and necklaces of cameo, pearl, or silver adorned each lady, and their lace fans matched their gowns. The patter of their soft kid shoes was masked by the elegant and provocative rustle of petticoats and the swish of heavy skirts.

At one-thirty the cellist, a Señor Grimaldi, arrived with his brother, a violinist, to take up their stations by the piano and began tuning up. Michael Lawrence arrived to take up his post with the ladies. John, all spit and polish in his crisp black suit and white shirt and white gloves, stood at the dining-room table, which had been extended to its full twenty-four-seat length, concocting punch in the gleaming silver punchbowl that sat surrounded by silver cups like a luxury steamer surrounded by a fleet of tugboats on a white linen sea. Gold-rimmed china plates and silverware sat at the opposite end of the table. The table was being decked with cold ham, roast beef, and fowl, condiments, breads, and salads. Cakes, chocolate éclairs, sweetmeats, and tea were to be served from the massive buffet. Bottles of champagne stood ready in ice buckets on the server with the rest in copper washtubs of ice and snow on the back porch.

An invisible policeman might have been directing traffic, so smoothly did the servants move from serving tray to dumbwaiter or staircase, Mrs. Howell and the scullery maid restocking refreshments on the trays as fast as the trays could be emptied. The pastry chef had arrived and was putting the final touches of decoration on the large cake. Two hired men replenished drinks. May stood by with the sewing basket should disaster strike.

Edmund Tracey had not come yet. Francesca thought she had made herself clear on this point. She so wanted them to be seen in society together, especially in the company of Michael and Anne, who looked so comfortable together they might have been married for years. *Edmund is always late,* she told herself. *There's nothing in it. He'll be here on time.*

True to his word, Dr. Barton arrived at two o'clock with Mrs. Barton, an elderly lady in stiff black bombazine whose wrinkled face beamed from beneath a lace cap that peeked out from beneath her black bonnet. Linton Blackhurst arrived. Two old business acquaintances of Jurgen Lund's who had known Francesca since she was a child paid their respects, downed large quantities of reception fare, and moved on. Waiters offered champagne. The Grimaldi brothers struck up a pleasant air. Anne and Vinnie greeted guests and inquired politely after wives, sisters, and daughters and ushered the gentlemen toward the dining room. Francesca renewed old acquaintances and effected introductions.

Many of Francesca's family friends wished to make Edmund Tracey's acquaintance. Francesca grew more and more embarrassed as she recited in turn a set of patent excuses.

"Why, I should have thought he could have used that new-fangled telephone contraption to ring you," one elderly family friend replied bluntly. "You mean you've not heard from him at all? He could have sent a message around at the very least." Each caller echoed every indignation Francesca felt, yet she felt forced to defend her fiancé.

By the end of the second hour, Francesca had ceased to blush at the mention of Edmund's name. The flush that bathed her face was a glow of mounting anger. She gladly took her turn at the piano and let Beethoven and Chopin drown the remarks while relinquishing the burden of courtesy to Vinnie, Michael, and Anne, but she couldn't hide from Vinnie and Anne the strain under which she labored.

"I'm sure he's only been detained," said Anne, putting on a brave face. "He'll be here soon." Michael Lawrence was indignant and made his views known to his sister and his fiancée, which Francesca could not help but overhear.

At last Jerry Jerome arrived, to Francesca's great relief. She would have drawn him aside had not Connor O'Casey followed on Jerry's heels. He looked under the weather, with a bruised forehead into the bargain, and leaned more heavily on his walking stick than usual. The small betraying cut at the corner of his mouth had not hampered his speech. The nerve of the man, to turn up in that state.

"Oh, so you've turned up," she said to Connor in a tone that made Jerry start.

"We caught up with each other—when was it, Jerome? Three? Four houses ago? Can't seem to shake loose of each other. Always easier to share a cab, as long as we're goin' in the same direction, don't you know." Francesca was ashamed at her own lack of grace. Yet she could not have handpicked anyone whom she was more loath to have intimate knowledge of her personal affairs. His look seemed to penetrate her embarrassment for Edmund. She grew redder still.

Jerry asked the dreaded question before she could prevent him. "Where's Edmund?" he said, as he and Connor scanned the room, expecting him to materialize.

"He's not here. He's been detained," she said as she met Jerry's eye.

"Detained?" said Jerry, pulling the watch from his waistcoat pocket. His anger was clear. Then, remembering himself, he said, "It's nearly four. I hope nothing's happened. Did he say when you might expect him?"

"No. No, he didn't."

"You have heard from him?" Jerry's question was almost a demand, not of Francesca, but of Tracey.

"No." Francesca took Jerry's arm and steered him toward the drawing room. "Jerry, you probably know everyone here," she said. "Would you do the honors and introduce Mr. O'Casey to anyone he may not know? Then you gentlemen must help yourselves to refreshment." Jerry did as he was bidden, but soon was cornered by Michael Lawrence.

Connor detached himself from this private conversation and made his way among the callers, greeting acquaintances and seeking new introductions. All the while, Francesca could feel his eyes follow her, with each offer of champagne, each introduction, each salute of recognition. His eyes followed her as she made for the dining room and spoke to John. As she turned, she was startled to find Connor beside her.

"I'm sorry about your fiancé," he began. She nodded without looking at him and fussed with the table. At the end of the room he intercepted her. He stood so close that she could have brushed her cheek against his shoulder. His baritone voice whirred in her ear—like the mesmerizing voice of the devil himself.

"I know it's none of my business—" he began.

"No, it's none of your concern—"

"You needn't put up with it—any of it."

"I don't know what you mean."

"You know perfectly well what I mean," he said in a low voice. "It'll only get worse, you know. Minor impoliteness. Indifference to your opinions. Opposition to your wishes. Now this. It wouldn't surprise me if you're on that path already."

"If you'll excuse me, I'm busy. I have guests to attend to."

The room was oppressive and hot. She turned away, eager to escape, but Connor blocked her path. The infernal man would not let up.

"Look at the men in this room," he said. "Any one of them would be better for you than he is. Any one of them would be kinder, prouder of you, happier to be with you, or at the very least would know where his duty lay."

"The duty, as you call it, for these gentlemen lies elsewhere, since the men in this room are married or soon will be."

"Not all," he said, his face close to hers. The two words smote her disbelieving ears.

"You can't be serious." The thought had never occurred to her that this man could have any possible interest in her. "Of all the barefaced impertinence. How dare you. How dare you," was all she could think to say. What unspeakable gall. She faced him, but before she could give voice to her anger he spoke.

"The man's a blackguard. You could do better."

"You are speaking of my fiancé, sir. Someone for whom I care a great deal."

"Do you?" He drained the champagne glass. "He's certainly displayed his regard for you this day, in spite of any finer feelings you may have for him. To be honest, I fail to see which is worse— his behavior or your judgment."

"How dare you," she gasped. "Get out of my house before I throw you out myself."

Connor set his glass on a tray and bowed. "Please make my excuses to Mr. Jerome and to your lovely hostesses," he said, and then more loudly as he kissed her hand, "It's been a great pleasure, ma'am. My warmest wishes for a very good New Year." He departed.

Never had Francesca felt so foolish, as if she had been the butt of some horrible joke while everyone around her laughed. To make matters worse, the dreadful Irishman, who at once fascinated and angered her, had spoken plainly what others only hinted. It couldn't be true. All Edmund's early protestations of love couldn't have been for nothing. Yet a man is defined by his actions. This afternoon Edmund's action had been reprehensible. For the sake of decorum and her reputation, Francesca hoped that in the later recitation of their New Year's calls, no one would be able to deduce that Edmund Tracey never came at all.

CHAPTER 26

A Slave of Women

❧

The whims and caprices of women in society should of course be tolerated by men, who themselves require toleration for greater inconveniences. But this must not be carried too far. There are certain limits to empire which, if they themselves forget, should be pointed out to them with delicacy and politeness. You should be a slave of women, but not of all their fancies.

—*Decorum*, page 24

"Where were you yesterday afternoon?"

Nell's confrontational tone took Tracey by surprise. She was pacing the peacock-blue, beige, and gilt drawing room in Gramercy Park.

"I had another engagement," he said.

"With whom?"

"I don't believe that's any of your business."

"Yesterday afternoon was our regular time together."

"I know. I apologize. I had planned to come, but something came up unexpectedly." Blanche's appearance in New York had indeed been unexpected; in some respects he and Blanche had picked up where they left off so long ago, though the complications of the intervening years made true resumption nearly impossible.

"Huh," she said with a toss of the head. "That's evasion if I ever heard it."

"Nothing like," he said. "I had some other things I had to do, that's all."

"You saw the Chickadee then?"

"I have seen her, naturally." His tone was unconvincing, even to himself.

"What *things* did you have to do?"

"Nell, I have apologized for not coming yesterday. I was engaged in business that could not be delayed. I don't believe I owe you further explanation. I do have a life apart from you, you know."

"What things?"

Tracey had only seen Nell genuinely angry once or twice, and not at him. Lucky, too, because her tongue could lacerate like nothing he had ever heard before. Hearing her unleash it on someone else made the comparatively mild sarcasm she used with him enough to make him squirm. This was different. There was a hardness that spoke of more than anger. Defensiveness would avail him nothing. He fell back on masculine incredulity.

"Nell," he said, approaching her, his hands spread in a gesture of supplication, "what's wrong?" He tried to put his arms around her, but she pushed him away. "I'm sorry that I wasn't able to let you know beforehand. It isn't as if neither of us has missed our engagement before—you as well as I."

"Where were you?" She wasn't budging. She stood with her arms folded, her pile of hennaed hair reflected in the gilt mirror. He turned away from her and ran his fingers through his thick hair. The opulent room with its gilt and art glass became gaudy and oppressive. How he could have stood this mausoleum for so long, he couldn't think.

"I was visiting friends. It was the only time that would suit."

"What friends?" Nell was annoyingly astute when it came to the question of "friends." Tracey tried to hide his discomfort.

"Do you happen to know everyone I know? Do you keep a list of my approved acquaintances?"

"Stop avoiding the subject. If you weren't with me—and you certainly weren't—whom were you with?"

He put his arms around her again and spoke more softly. "I thought we had settled that problem long ago when I became engaged. You know full well that nothing stands in the way of our arrangement, not even the Chickadee. Furthering my future prospects doesn't mean restricting myself to spending time with her, does it? God forbid that it should."

Nell broke from his embrace and marched to the other side of the room, arms still folded.

"You can't have it both ways, Nell," he said, trying to speak with authority. "I can't be here amusing you and be cultivating any other acquaintance or prospects elsewhere at the same time, can I? Do I have to account for the time when I am away from you?"

"When it's time normally reserved for me—time I've amply compensated you for."

He would happily have throttled her for that. She had never flung it in his face.

"What the hell does that mean?" He felt his body begin to tighten with anger, as if preparing to withstand a blow.

"You know perfectly well what it means." She eyed him viciously and retreated farther and paced back and forth in short steps like a panther. "You don't think I shell out that money for you to be entertaining your, your *friends*."

"What are you talking about?" he asked, maintaining his icy control.

"Don't try that with me. What kind of a fool do you take me for?"

"I never thought you were any kind of fool, until now." A thought struck him, far-fetched as it seemed to him. "Surely you can't be jealous of Francesca? I am engaged to her, you know, a situation encouraged by you, if you recall. That does put some demands on my time."

"Don't be ridiculous. I don't give a damn about that and neither do you. Marry her. Let her support you. I don't give a damn about your time, as long as it isn't time that belongs to me."

"I can't believe I'm hearing this. I've never seen you behave this way."

"You've never betrayed me before."

"Betrayed? Are you accusing me of disloyalty?" He had never been strictly faithful to Nell and was equally sure that she had seen other men besides him. She even seemed to take pleasure in watching other women be smitten by his good looks and Southern charm.

"What would you call it?"

"I don't know what I'd call it because I don't know what you're talking about."

"What a barefaced liar you are."

"All right, then, how have I been disloyal to you?"

She stopped her pacing. "Blanche."

Tracey tried to conceal his amazement. Was she just fishing?

"You can't be serious."

"Why don't you just admit it? You and Blanche are old friends, aren't you?"

"Yes. I told you that."

"Dear old friends. Intimate friends, wouldn't you say?"

"We did have feelings for each other once. But that was a long time ago. You seem to forget that her loyalty is elsewhere too."

"Loyalty. A blind man could see that you two still harbor feelings for each other. You've started seeing her, haven't you? I know you have."

"You know nothing of the kind."

"Then *where were you? Whom were you with?*"

"I'm telling you it's none of your damn business. You don't own me, Nell. I don't care what you think about our arrangement. I don't care about your timetables and your afternoon amusements. You don't own me. You never have."

"Oh, you're wrong, sonny. You're dead wrong. I own you from your felt hat down to the soles of your boots. And I can fix it so your loyalty to me will be guaranteed."

"Don't threaten me, Nell. It's a waste of time."

"Is it?" She leaned one hand against the back of the divan and placed the other hand on her hip. "Think again."

"If you think it's only the money, I'm perfectly capable—"

"Of finding someone else to support you? Yes, I'm sure you are, but you won't dare. You'll dance to my tune and like it. Or would you rather that your dear little Chickadee, your goose with the golden egg, learn a thing or two about her intended?"

"You mean about you? She'd never believe it. I'd only have to deny it."

"Would you? Then maybe I can offer her a more potent bit of scandal. How do you think your Chickadee would receive news about Henriette?"

Tracey stood transfixed. Never in a million years would he have reckoned on such a threat from Nell.

"I'm sure you thought that little secret was safe. Oh, yes. That's right. That little problem was disposed of long ago." Slowly, Nell's anger metamorphosed into a superiority that nearly crackled. She became more self-assured, the posture he hated most. She tossed her head back and stood with her weight on one foot. "You didn't think I knew you were married, did you? Does Blanche know, by the way?" She waited.

He would admit or deny nothing. He wanted to stop his ears— or her mouth—yet he was dying to hear how she had dredged up that long-buried bit of his life.

"Who said I was?" His voice was steady.

Her words were blade thin. "Let's not be coy." She crossed the drawing room to the table next to the overstuffed chair, drew a cigarette from the silver box, and lit it so quickly it seemed to have been accomplished in a single motion. "You don't cover your tracks as well as you think."

"Why should I be covering my tracks about anything?"

"You can be tedious, Edmund."

"I'm sure I don't know what you mean."

"Stop it," she said as she drew on the cigarette. She walked back to the fireplace and made as if to flick the ash into the hearth, but it fell onto the rug. She tossed her head back again. "You could at least do yourself the dignity of admitting it gracefully."

"I admit nothing," he said. A smirk curled itself in the corner of his lip as he considered the absurdity of his situation. He suddenly felt amazingly relaxed, like one who has just witnessed a fire destroy all he owns and feels a giddy release of an enormous burden before the shock sets in.

"I'm sure." Nell guffawed. "I don't know why I should expect any different tactic from you than the one you've employed for the last—how long have we been together now—four years? Five? You certainly haven't done too badly in that time. Had yourself a comfortable affair—more than one, I daresay. Hooked yourself a rich woman. You've evaded the law quite prettily."

"And why should I want to do that?" He felt silly and schoolboyish, but it didn't seem to matter.

"Oh, come, come, Edmund. You may as well admit it or we'll be here all day." She crossed to the sideboard and lifted a glass decanter. "Drink? You may as well be comfortable." She poured drinks for them both. As she handed it to him she said, "Now, let's try it again. Surely you wouldn't want me to go spreading ugly stories that aren't true." She crossed to her favorite chair. "I'd much rather spread ugly stories that are true."

"To be married isn't such an ugly story."

"Indeed not. Marriage is such a fine, upstanding institution, don't you think? At least I've always found it to be so." She took another drag upon the cigarette and crushed it out. "Love, honor, and obey, you know."

By a circuitous route that avoided Maywood's plantation house and the crumbling village of the sugar refinery and the slave quarters, McNee and Shillingford picked up the road. In the years since Henriette's death, it had become a disused and overgrown track that wound through wild stands of trees and long-untended fields, giving way to patches of open country, then closing again where Nature had reclaimed her territory. The dark sky threatened rain and the black-on-black clouds surged overhead. The air was thick and close in spite of gusts that freshened it. Finally they came to the tethering place of live oak trees whose twisted trunks rose like writhing spirits and spread their supplicating branches heavenward. The men slipped from their saddles and secured the horses, grabbing their rifles, lanterns, and bags of tools. They made for the edge of Maywood's little city of the dead where the low box tombs were closest to the road. Stone slabs lay in weathered shards. Two headstones were barely distinguishable above the weeds.

They cleared away debris from one box tomb with a scrolled tablet at its head and raised the lantern's cover long enough to read the inscription. A name, though worn and dirty, was clearly inscribed and did not belong to Henriette.

"I hope to God this isn't it," whispered McNee as they regarded a second with an obelisk atop it. "I wouldn't put it past Henri Gerard to make entry nigh impossible." But hasty examination of the obelisk's inscription laid that cruel joke to rest.

"Your logic seems to have failed you," taunted Shillingford after two more box tombs yielded no result.

"I thought they would have taken the first tomb nearest the road," whispered McNee. "The priest didn't say where, did he?"

"Not that I recall."

Then McNee gestured toward the statue of an angel whose outstretched arms might have protected a grass-enshrouded box tomb, had the angel not been moved aside, as if rejecting whatever lay beneath the stone slab. The men applied their lantern's light to the slab. No name appeared upon it. They jimmied it loose with pickax and crowbar and put their backs into moving the slab.

Shillingford's spade hit something that was neither earth nor stone, that resisted but with extra force might yield. "Here," he said, and McNee drew closer to concentrate their efforts. They felt their spades scrape this surface and Shillingford pulled up the cover of the lantern again to give McNee light while he continued to dig.

They both stopped to look. McNee dug away with his hands and exposed a much-deteriorated length of wooden plank. He stepped back along the muddy trench that they had made and took up the spade again to resume digging. The coffin lid, which had been made of two heavy planks joined in the center, had collapsed. One side of the coffin had come free and was filled with dirt and mud. McNee yanked at the lid. Six years' burial was sufficient to ensure that whatever was buried in the coffin was well past putrefaction. Death is death nonetheless, and McNee was prepared to recoil at the sight and the dank smell. McNee pitched the planking out of the hole and Shillingford lowered the lantern. Both men bent to look.

At the side of the coffin that had caved in, up at the head, a tiny skull was just visible through the dirt, snuggled almost, at the shoulder of its companion in death. The larger skull leaned in toward the tiny head. Shillingford moved the lantern along the entire coffin's length. Though Mother Nature had done her best to return the bodies to dust, it was clear that the figure was not the diminutive *papillon*. The large figure had worn a waistcoat with silver buttons and a man's belt with a heavy silver buckle bearing the initials PRL.

"Jesus H. Christ," muttered McNee.

"Indeed," said Shillingford. "I think we have just found Philippe Letourneau."

CHAPTER 27

The Plainest and Simplest Words

*A man of good sense will always make a point of using
the plainest and simplest words that convey his meaning;
and will bear in mind that his principal or only business
is to lodge his idea in the mind of his hearer. The same remark applies to the distinctness of articulation; and
Hannah More has justly observed that to speak so that
people can hear you is one of the minor virtues.*

—*Decorum*, page 66

Epiphany Sunday came and went before Francesca Lund admitted into her presence the repentant Edmund Tracey. He was
quick enough to call following New Year's Day and brought flowers as a sign of contrition, but was greeted with the news that Miss
Lund had taken ill and was receiving no one. Francesca retreated
to her bedroom and lay upon the chaise, her brain playing again
and again the dreadful event and each disapproving look. Amid
prayers for guidance she cried herself to numbness. That she didn't
feel her usual eagerness to forgive bothered her almost as much as
Edmund's flagrant disregard. Ten days passed before she could
bring herself to send word that she would receive him.

She had been cool and dispassionate as she stood in the drawing
room. Edmund kept his remarks upon his behavior brief, applied

the requisite apology—omitting a promise to do better—received her forgiveness, and departed, all in the space of fifteen minutes. The episode fazed her so little that she wondered whether she should have offered him tea.

She took the dogs and went out. It was a pale, gray mid-afternoon. Snow had begun to fall in fat, quiet flakes. She made her way up Sixty-third Street and stopped when she came to Fifth Avenue. As Chalk and Coal investigated the shrubbery, she stood stupidly at the corner and looked up and down, deciding where best to enter Central Park. Her habit was to enter at the south and walk the park from end to end, but life had proved so contrary that she crossed the street and walked up Fifth Avenue and turned in at the Zoo.

The drab trees arched overhead, welcoming her into a peaceful, gray cathedral, whose lacy spray of branches vaulted skyward to hold up the light granite-gray ceiling. Beneath the colorless sky and the silent shower of white Francesca felt anonymous, invisible. As she glided along the path, she watched the world from a safe inner vantage point. The dogs' hindquarters swayed, tails erect, noses dissecting the air. Figures moved in the gray light as if in a dream. The world was muffled but for the crunch of her boots and the patter of paws on the packed snow, but troubled thoughts cut through unbidden.

When she reached the Bridle Path, she decided to make the Lake her destination to watch the skaters. A weekday when children were in school and men were at work would likely bring only a few ladies. She might skate herself if she was so moved. She hugged the fur muff to her and quickened her pace. The snow fell heavier and began to accumulate on the shoulders of her black woolen coat and hat. At the Lake, the skaters were indeed few and mostly ladies, with two gentlemen hustling to sweep the surface clear. She found a satisfactory vantage point and unsnapped the leashes and let the dogs run.

A heavy heart fired warmth into her extremities. She recounted to herself how much she had relinquished in the past few days. She had nearly relinquished the idea of marriage when Edmund proposed. Her acceptance, she thought, was a sign of her recovery, a desire to get on with the business of life. Perhaps in theory this was true, but her choice seemed to force her to relinquish other notions she held dear, especially marrying for love.

She pondered, for the hundredth time, what she might relinquish in becoming Edmund's wife. It wasn't so much the quarrel over money or his behavior, but how marriage to Edmund would change her. She was beginning to like herself less because she was less like herself around Edmund. Curbing her actions and words to keep him in an agreeable mood was taking its toll. She was anxious before each meeting and relieved when he was gone. Her endless mental recitation of their disagreements and the minutiae of his behavior left her sleepless and weary.

As Francesca watched the skaters, out of the corner of her eye, she detected the approach of a man, heralded by the odor of cigar smoke. She turned to see a dark mass of overcoat and top hat walking toward her. The infernal O'Casey approached warily (*as well he should*, she thought) and stood beside her. The only saving grace was that with him she needn't pretend. She felt herself flush nonetheless.

"Alone at last," he began, and was stopped by the unpleasant look she gave him. "No," he said, "that was in poor taste. I apologize." She said nothing. "I heard you were ill. I'm sorry. I take this as a sign you're feeling better."

"Yes, thank you." They watched together in silence.

"I'm sorry about New Year's Day. I had no right to speak to you the way I did."

"No, you had no right." She whistled to the dogs to bring them back within the tether of her call. "But your apology is accepted." She searched for something light to say. "I'm surprised to see you out for exercise. You must be feeling better yourself. You looked slightly worse for wear when I saw you last."

"I am, thank you. As to the exercise, I'm an avid walker. Keeps the limbs and joints limber. Stimulates the brain, too, don't you think?"

"Yes, for better or for worse." Francesca's thoughts strayed for a moment as she looked out over the scene before her. "Do you really enjoy a cigar? Wretched things. I don't like the taste myself," she said, not thinking.

"So you smoke cigars on the quiet?" he ventured cautiously.

She smiled in spite of herself. "No, I meant on a man's lips."

"I didn't think you'd tasted enough lips to know," retorted Connor easily, with a slight tone of mockery. She flushed and darted him a narrow look.

"Pipes are a much pleasanter form of tobacco smoking."

"For kissing?" Worse and worse.

"Yes, for kissing," she said, regaining her composure by degrees.

"I'll have to take up a pipe."

"It doesn't suit your—personality."

"Just what do you think would suit my 'personality'?"

"I'm afraid I'm at a loss to say, since I've not had the privilege of encountering anyone quite like you before."

"A deficit I shall endeavor to remedy."

"Don't trouble yourself."

"'Tis no trouble," he said, pausing until she looked at him. In spite of her calm exterior, her pulse rose and the winter atmosphere prickled at the rising warmth in her cheeks. She stood transfixed by his gaze, then came to herself as the mockery returned to his visage and he blatantly looked her up and down. "No trouble at all."

"And is this how you endeavor to make yourself agreeable to ladies?"

"I don't know any ladies—"

"I'm not surprised—"

"So it really doesn't signify, now, does it? You see, I don't believe in ladies, not really."

"What do you mean, you 'don't believe in ladies'?"

"Exactly what I said. I don't believe they exist. They think they do. They make men and even other women—especially other women—think they do. It's always been my belief that the idea of 'ladies' only exists to sell fashions and jewelry and all other manner of bric-a-brac to clutter up a man's life and keep him from smokin' his favorite cigar."

"So, you have no use for ladies."

"Oh, I didn't say I didn't have a use for 'em." He took a long draw on the cigar and exhaled in her direction.

She looked him in the face and then, with difficulty, looked him up and down. "And what might that be, Mr. O'Connor?"

"O'Casey, ma'am." He smiled.

"Yes."

"I thought you were a lady."

"I thought you didn't believe in them."

"No, ma'am. I'm the great emancipator. In my eyes, all women are equal. A woman is neither high, nor low. She's just a woman."

"And not the equal of men?"

"None that I've encountered."

"No woman that you've encountered or no man that you've encountered?"

"To clarify, no woman I've ever encountered has been the equal of any man that I've ever encountered."

"Not equal, but better perhaps?" asked Francesca.

He paused and rested the hand that held the cigar on top of the hand that rested on the handle of the walking stick. "Perhaps."

"Then she might be considered a lady?"

"No, never a lady, especially if she's better than a man."

"That makes no sense."

"Of course it does." He looked at her more squarely now, less mockery in his eye and in his tone. "How many women that you see in that blessed settlement of yours, scraping to hold a family together and put food in the mouths of their children, would you say were better than the men they cling to?"

"Most of them."

"How many of them would society dub a 'lady' for her pains? And how many women at your society tea parties couldn't begin to cope if the bottom dropped out of their lives and they were suddenly left to shift for themselves? How long do you think they'd last as 'ladies'? How many of your society ladies would sooner forget where they came from—from their lowly forebears? How many would rather die than have to go back to earning an honest living? Can you see Maggie Jerome behind a plow? I think not. Give me a woman rather than a lady any day. Women can hold their own where ladies cannot—or dare not."

"So you prefer a workhorse to a lady."

"What I prefer is a woman. A woman who isn't all lace and perfume and the latest gossip."

"The latest gossip I can understand, but I thought most men preferred the lace and the perfume."

"So they do. So do I, I confess. But most 'ladies' could no more survive in this world than the man in the moon."

"You greatly underestimate these ladies," said Francesca, her ire rising. "How many of them do you think are happily married, eh? How many? Is it not survival that makes them cling to loveless marriages? Is it not facing the world as it is? Is that so different from the world your so-called 'women' face? Is it not these ladies' own talents and abilities that keep their households afloat when the folly of their men brings the family to the brink of ruin? Do you think that half the women who sell themselves into that sort of slavery for the sake of survival do so willingly and willingly throw themselves into the 'protection' of the lowest form of man?"

"Men are fools and blackguards, I'll grant you that."

"What makes you think I couldn't take care of myself?"

"I think you could, as a matter of fact. I don't think you'd be afraid of it. I think you'd work it out somehow—and manage to keep your self-respect. You're not proud like the others. You're stubborn as a mule and got your head in the clouds most of the time, but not proud. But you also forget that you have resources other than money that most women don't have—not even your society women. You have an education—"

"So do other ladies."

"You're better informed than most. You've a certain practical knowledge of the way the world works, even from that blessed settlement, though you may lack certain experience. You know what work is and what it will yield and what that yield will pay for."

"So do other ladies, and many have wider 'experience,' as you call it, than I do."

"And what does your society call them behind their backs?"

"You're a filthy hypocrite. You'd compromise the first society lady that would give you a second look."

"I have done," he said dryly.

She looked at him in disgust and was silent.

"What do they say about you, while we're about it?" he asked.

This abrupt turn startled her and made her wary. "What do you mean?"

"What are they whispering behind their hands about 'Poor Miss Lund'? So lovely. So sweet. So accomplished. They can't understand why she hasn't hooked herself a more worthy husband. Ah yes, acute melancholia. Isn't that what the doctors said? Four perfectly good years lost, poor thing. If she only wouldn't show her brains so much. All those books. She'll frighten away all the good prospects. A man likes to know he's smarter than his wife, now, doesn't he? And Jesus, if she wouldn't be always talking about God, for Christ's sake. If she'd just give up the damn settlement and look more domestic-like. If she'd only just—conform."

Francesca felt like smoldering fury. She looked him in the eye, barely containing herself. He looked so smug and self-satisfied. She could think of plenty of names to call him, but name-calling was not only childish, it would have no effect. Effect. Of course, effect. Her mind stepped back and watched herself and him. The memory of him sitting at the piano, fidgeting with the music, flashed into her mind. He *was* all bluff, she thought. He wanted to see how far he could push before he got a rise out of her. How stupid of her not to realize before. Another memory followed—the memory of Edmund's jealousy that accused her of interest in Connor, an accusation she had dismissed for its absurdity, and yet . . . ? She relaxed as she had relaxed that night.

"Do you always swear and try your best to offend people?"

"Always."

"No wonder you're not married," she said.

He chuckled at this and drew on the cigar and blew out the smoke.

"I suppose so," he said. "You're not a reformer, by any chance, are you, Miss Lund?"

She laughed. "So that's what you're afraid of? A vigorous over-haul for the good of your soul?"

"Let's just say I'm not reform-minded."

She laughed again. "I venture to suggest that you'd be hard pressed to find a woman who wouldn't want to reform you, even if she vows to take you as you are."

"Oh, I'm always eager to improve myself, but it doesn't neces-sarily follow that improvement means reform."

"How so?"

"One can improve in education, in prospects, in station in life without changing the essential person," he said.

He had hit the mark truer than he knew. She thought of Edmund Tracey and his pervasive sullenness, his reserve, and his inattention to her. Edmund would never change. "I suppose that's true," was all she could say.

"Do I offend you?" he asked.

"Yes. Sometimes."

"How?"

"Your observations about my life and my associations, for one thing," she said evenly. "To be honest, I don't particularly care what you think of me, or what anyone else thinks for that matter. I don't care what you think about my life or my brains or my friends or what I can do or what I can't."

"Are you always this honest?"

She laughed. "I try to be."

"With yourself?"

She sighed and thought again of Edmund. "That's the hardest thing, isn't it? To be honest with oneself, to know what's right and to be brave enough to follow that path." She mused for a moment, watching the skaters. She looked at him and found him musing, too, as he dropped the cigar butt and watched it smolder and flicked snow on it with the toe of his boot. He took up the thread of conversation.

"So you don't like my swearing?"

"Not particularly, though I suppose it isn't the swearing so much as your choice of words."

"Come again?"

"When you take the Lord's name in vain."

"Oh. A sore spot then? I'm sorry."

"You see," said Francesca, not quite knowing how to give voice to a subject so private to her and wondering whether it was worth the effort with Connor, "my faith has always been important to me, ever since I was a small child. Not just religion, not just going to church. It's something much deeper than that. It's so much a part of my being I can't imagine life without God. In those awful years after I lost Father and Mother and Oskar, I don't think I would have had the strength to go on if I hadn't had the confidence that a wisdom greater than my own was at work. It frightens me to think that I might not even be here but for that. So you see, I will never excuse your making use of God, even thoughtlessly or in jest. You insult Him, and you insult the only member of my family I've got left." She roused herself and whistled to the dogs, who came at a dead run.

"And you can't afford to insult Him, Mr. O'Casey, because He represents the one thing you do believe in." She bent and snapped on the leashes.

"What might that be?"

She paused a moment and then said, "Redemption."

He stood silent.

"Or don't you believe in redemption?"

"Do you believe in it?"

"Are you afraid to answer?"

"Are you?"

"Never," said Francesca with a broad smile, her spirit soaring. "I believe in it with my whole heart and soul. Now if you'll excuse me, I'll leave you to contemplate whether you believe in it yourself. Good day to you." She turned and left him.

"I not only believe in it," he called after her, "I'm countin' on it."

CHAPTER 28

Intending to Be Absent

❧

When you are going abroad, intending to be absent for some time, you enclose your card in an envelope, having, first, written p.p.c. *upon it;—they are the initials of the French phrase, "pour prendre conge"—to take leave, and may with equal propriety stand for* presents parting compliments.

—*Decorum*, page 74

Mrs. Lawrence was plumping the cushions on the black horsehair settee when the sound of a cab pulling up outside arrested her attention and drew her to the window.

"Who is it, Mama?" Vinnie asked.

"Francesca, dear."

A moment later, Vinnie, Anne, and Mrs. Lawrence were greeting her.

"What a relief to see you up and about, dear," said Mrs. Lawrence. "A little pale perhaps," she said, holding Francesca's chin and examining her face, "but it looks like you're on the mend. Brava. I've been telling the girls we don't see as much of you as we'd like. Do come and warm yourself. Such a bitter day. You must be frozen through. Violet, bring some tea, would you please?"

"Don't trouble, Mrs. Lawrence." The maid took away Francesca's coat and muff.

"Nonsense, dear, it's no trouble. It'll give you something warm to put your hands around." The ladies sat and Mrs. Lawrence recounted the callers for the day. Vinnie hinted at gorier details before reproof in her mother's eyes checked her. After a short interval Mrs. Lawrence excused herself to see to the family's dinner. "You will stay, dear, won't you?" she asked as she paused in the doorway. "We'd so love to have you." She departed.

Vinnie might have had an electric current running through her, so alive was she to every word Francesca uttered, to every look and gesture. Francesca politely redirected Anne's artless questions about the wedding back to Anne herself, who chattered with enthusiasm. Minutes ticked away until Michael breezed through the front door, home from work, and Anne led him by the arm in search of Mrs. Lawrence.

"I wanted to talk to you," Francesca said when the parlor doors were closed.

"I thought maybe you did. Is everything all right? You do look so pale."

"I've been thinking a great deal over the last few days," she began. "I must get away for a while, and I hoped you would consider joining me."

Vinnie was not shocked by this proposal. She half-expected it. Perhaps some fresh intelligence had come to Francesca, that she knew about Edmund and the Jet Woman after all. If Francesca knew, however, this sudden desire to leave New York betrayed nothing. Vinnie probed gingerly.

"Get away. What do you mean? Like when Agnes went away for her rest cure?"

"Not exactly. I just can't seem to think about anything clearly anymore. Not here. Not now. Everywhere I turn I encounter someone or something that causes me to doubt myself, my actions, my reasons for my actions."

"Have you spoken to anyone else about this?"

"No."

"Not even to Edmund?" Vinnie held her breath and waited.

"Especially not to Edmund. In fact, Edmund is one of the reasons I must get away."

Vinnie could have burst for joy, but bridled her tongue with heroic self-control. "It was about New Year's Day?" was all she said.

"New Year's Day, Christmas Day, Thanksgiving Day, every day in one way or other. It isn't simply the resentment and embarrassment. I find I like him less and less. I do care for him, but in a more detached way, as one might feel toward a friend, not a fiancé. What's more, I feel myself changing in the most distressing ways. I must get away to see if this really is the person I'm becoming—whether I'm the cause of our difficulties, or if the person I'm becoming is caused by the difficulties—because of Edmund."

"You seem to me as you always were—just a little sad, perhaps, but that's perfectly reasonable given everything . . ."

"Given everything I've been through? Yes, I suppose it is reasonable, but that's years ago now, Vinnie. It retreats further and further into the past every day. Not in some maudlin way, but more peaceful, more accepting. I miss them all now as much as I ever did, but it's funny how I'm able to draw strength rather than grief from the memories. I was so proud to be back in the house, so sure of my ability to make a life for myself, to decide for myself. So I decided to marry Edmund. But having come so far, shouldn't I be happy? Shouldn't I like myself more? Shouldn't Edmund and I be happier because of each other?"

"Yes, you should be very happy," said Vinnie. "It grieves me to see that you're not."

"Then why am I not? Why all this doubt and turmoil? I can't seem to fix on a reason except to blame myself. What should I have done? What should I have been? I turn it over and over in my head: What could have changed him so?"

"I don't believe it's you, Francesca. I really don't," said Vinnie in earnest, wanting to spill out everything she knew, but she dared not. Francesca must arrive at the conclusion by herself—with any luck—to end her engagement to Edmund. Yes, it was best for her to get away, and if Vinnie needed to push her along, she would do it. "I think you're very wise. I'm sure things will become clearer if you put some distance between you and New York. And Edmund."

"And that dreadful Irishman."

"Mr. O'Casey? Has he been imposing himself on you?" This was an interesting prospect.

"Not exactly. But he does seem to emerge at the most inconvenient times. Every time I walk away from a conversation with him I'm more confused than I was before."

"You don't mean that you're interested in him?"

"*Interested?* Good heavens, Vinnie, how can you suggest such a thing? I'm an engaged woman." *Too quick an answer,* thought Vinnie, *and much too pat.*

"That doesn't mean you've had your eyes and ears cut out," said Vinnie. "I think he's nice, and he's very funny. I like being around him. I always get the feeling I should be scared to death of him, but I'm not. Not at all."

"Don't tell me *you're* interested in him."

"Good gracious, Francesca, don't be silly. Could you see *me* as Mrs. O'Casey? A scalawag and a parson's daughter? Wouldn't *that* be a scandal?" She paused and thought. "It's funny, though. I can see him with you."

"*Me?* Don't be ridiculous. Besides, you see what havoc he causes."

"*I* like him. Don't you?"

"I don't dislike him. But you see what happens—the moment he's even introduced into the conversation he creates absolute bedlam. I must go, Vinnie. Don't you see?"

"Yes, I do see."

"You don't think I'm simply running away from a problem?"

"I don't think you're running from a problem as much as looking for a solution. I think you're giving yourself a chance to consider your decision before . . ." Francesca looked up and searched Vinnie's face. "Before it's too late."

"It's not cowardly?"

"No. I think it's wise."

"Will you come with me?"

"Where?" Vinnie asked, trying not to grimace until she heard the answer. "I mean, of course you know I will. But where will we go?"

"I saw this advertisement in the newspaper some time ago when I was thinking about honeymoon venues," said Francesca, pulling a leaflet and a dog-eared newspaper cutting from her pocket. "I've been carrying it around forever. It looks so interesting."

"What? Baniff? Barnff? I don't know how to pronounce it, let alone know where it is."

"Banff, Vinnie. Read on."

"The wilderness? Do we have to leave civilization altogether to be able to think?" Vinnie began to wonder what she had agreed to.

"No, look, Vinnie," said Francesca as she shoved the leaflet into Vinnie's hand. "I went to the booking agent's just before I came here and inquired and they gave me this. It's quite exclusive. The accommodation is first class—a new hotel. The Canadian Rockies are supposed to be breathtaking. I think it's just the atmosphere I need—clear air and vigorous exercise. Spring must be beautiful there."

"But it's so far."

"It's no farther than Paris or Rome or Vienna. And it will be a whole different set of people, Vinnie, people with different tastes and interests and ideas." There was relief in Francesca's voice.

"I don't doubt that." Vinnie was dubious as she looked over the description of snow-capped mountains. "Just we two, alone?"

"I've thought about that. Do you remember my aunt Esther, Mother's friend in Boston? I might persuade her to join us. May would come and tend to us and Aunt Esther would bring Rosemary. I'm sure Mr. Worth could help me hire a private car."

Vinnie's heart sank at the thought of the expense. Her family could by no means bear this expense, but Vinnie pressed on.

"When would we go?"

"Perhaps May. I haven't really thought that far ahead."

"How long would we be gone?"

"Six weeks, eight, ten, I don't know. I'd love to get a good taste of summer."

"I don't know what Mama and Papa will say," Vinnie said honestly.

"Well, one thing you can tell them for certain," Francesca said, no doubt reading her friend's thoughts. "You would be my guest. You can tell your parents I insist upon treating you. Are you game?"

"Oh, Francesca, I couldn't. . . ." Vinnie could and would.

"You don't sound so certain."

"Oh, no, no. I'm just so surprised. I'm certain you've made the right choice. As for Banff," she said, looking at the advertisement and dreading the prospect of a prolonged winter and a cold spring, "I hope you're just as certain when you see all that snow."

Francesca left before dinner. They agreed that Vinnie would not mention the plan to her parents until Francesca had secured Aunt Esther. Vinnie was not easy with this promise, however, especially with the silent burden of Edmund's infidelity she would carry all the way to Banff. She decided to tell her parents, hoping that if they knew, Vinnie would gain her their support and encouragement.

Mr. Lawrence was home by now and in his study. Detaching her mother from the dinner preparations she went to the study and rapped lightly upon the door. Once inside, Vinnie tumbled everything out—the journey to Banff, Edmund's behavior, Francesca's self-doubt, Aunt Esther, Mr. O'Casey, and the terrible charge of Edmund's affair with Mrs. Alvarado. It took much questioning before the facts lay in comprehensible order.

"This is a very serious charge you are leveling against Mr. Tracey, Lavinia," her father said, "one for which there is no proof other than your observation. We have no way to permit Mr. Tracey to answer the charge without making him look as if he's a condemned man already."

"I know, Papa," said Vinnie, who by now was in tears. "You have no idea how this weight has been pressing upon me. I've tried so hard not to say anything or cause Francesca any more distress. I haven't said a word to a soul. I'm so glad you know."

Mr. Lawrence rose from the desk and held his daughter, who fell sobbing on his shoulder.

"You've been a good friend, dear," Mrs. Lawrence said, as she smoothed Vinnie's hair and rubbed her back. "No one could ask for better. I must say, I'm proud of your forbearance, especially that you've been able to keep it from Anne and Michael."

"Yes, I agree," said her father. "You judged rightly to let Francesca draw any conclusion to break her engagement, not merely on a single piece of evidence that might be explained a hundred ways. Your mother and I will keep our eyes and ears open. If anything further comes to our attention, we will consult with Mr. Jerome, who is the one person who can be trusted to have Francesca's very best interests at heart."

"I thought about going to him. . . ."

"I'm glad you didn't. You must focus your attention on your friend. You let us worry about Mr. Jerome. And if Francesca is able to convince Mrs. Gray to accompany you on this journey, then of course you must go."

Registered letter to Mr. J. K. Shillingford, New Orleans, Louisiana, from Miss E. Neumann, Shillingford Detectives, Bleecker Street, New York, New York.

Dear Sir:

In re: Surveillance of E. F. T.

Per your instructions, we report that the subject has removed from the Brevoort Hotel and is now resident at a lodging house in SoHo. Further inquiry revealed that the subject is paying privately to continue to have mail and messages received at the Brevoort, where the subject calls regularly to collect them.

The subject is in regular company of a married woman of this city at her own home, and most recently another woman who visits the subject's lodgings.

Finally, the subject is seen to regularly visit a telegraph office near subject's lodgings. We can personally attest to the subject wiring money to St. Louis to yet another woman, whom we found to be a Mrs. Helene

Terrey. No address has yet been ascertained. We suggest
the dispatch of an operative to St. Louis immediately.
   We believe the subject's suspicion has not hitherto
been aroused. We suggest that surveillance be continued.
   I am,
   Yours faithfully,
   E. Neumann (Miss)

"Indeed," said McNee, reading over Shillingford's shoulder, then taking the letter from his hand. "Looks like I must purchase a ticket to St. Louis."

"Yes, with all due speed," said Shillingford. "I'll take care of things here. I quite agree with Miss Neumann that we dare not lose Tracey now. I'll wire her to confirm keeping someone on his tail—and I'll wire our progress to Mr. Jerome."

CHAPTER 29

The Proprieties

❧

The proprieties in deportment, which concerts require, are little different from those which are recognized in every other assembly, or in public exhibitions, for concerts partake of the one and the other, according as they are public or private. In private concerts, the ladies occupy the front seats, and the gentlemen are generally in groups behind, or at the side of them. We should observe the most profound silence, and refrain from beating time, humming the airs, applauding, or making ridiculous gestures of admiration. It often happens that a dancing soiree succeeds a concert, and billets of invitation, distributed two or three days before hand should give notice of it to the persons invited.

—Decorum, page 113

The way Miss Blanche had talked, thought Jamie, she might be running the show, telling Mr. O'Casey what to do and how to arrange everything to best advantage. For whatever Jamie might think of Miss Blanche personally—and it wasn't his business to be thinking things—he had to admire her knowledge of manners and dress and what was proper, when propriety was called for.

An opera party followed by a late supper at Louis Sherry's—

Delmonico's new venue being not yet opened—was on the docket for the evening, Connor playing host to his ever-widening circle of friends. The Worths, the Jeromes, the Gages, the Calloways, and assorted others would be there.

Connor and Blanche had had words. Clearly, Connor had his fill of Miss Blanche for the present. He snapped his impatience as she barged into the bedroom and headed for the wardrobe, ready to rout all of Jamie's thoughtful work. It was two o'clock in the afternoon, for God's sake, didn't she have preparations of her own, Connor barked, she ought to get a move on. He had been dressing himself for more than forty years, he barked again. He and Jamie would do just as well by themselves. Blanche was dismissed. He would call for her later. Holy Mother of God.

Connor usually enjoyed the rituals of dressing and was particular about clothes and the impression they would create. Tonight, however, presented a new predicament. Having divested himself of Blanche's help, Connor was between a sartorial rock and hard place. To play host—not only to his most important business associates, but also their wives—transformed an otherwise enjoyable preparation into an exercise of sweat and tears. The Met would take care of the entertainment. Sherry's would take care of the food and drink. If they could only dress Connor O'Casey. Having arrayed himself to the best of his ability, Connor turned from the mirror and faced Jamie.

"You're not goin' like that, are you?"

"What do you mean by that?" Connor snapped.

"You look like you just stepped out of a brothel—sir."

"And who the hell asked you?" he said. "So, what's wrong?"

"It's that waistcoat, sir. It's too shiny, sir, and too, well, loud."

"And what do you mean by 'loud'?"

"You look like a bloody pimp, sir."

"Jesus! Since when are you an authority on formal attire for formal occasions?"

"Since I been watching other people, like you told me. Makes me as much an authority as you—sir. Gentlemen always wears black or white—mostly white," said Jamie, unbuttoning and removing the offensive waistcoat and holding out the white silk brocade.

"You're working yourself into a lather over nothin', Mr. O'Casey, sir. If you don't ease up a bit, I'll have to take you apart and put you back together again proper. And no amount of diamond studs'll make up for you smellin' like a pig. A fine impression you'd make then." Jamie cooed and clucked like a mother hen and tried to smooth the ruffled feathers of Connor O'Casey. "So why don't you let Miss Blanche help you like she always does? She can see you're put together right."

"Miss Blanche isn't here. I don't need Miss Blanche to help me. I can do it myself. Can you get this damn tie to work?"

"Will you just put your hands down and let me take care of the tie?" Jamie turned Connor around to face the mirror and pulled up a stool to stand on behind him while he tied the tie, made all the more difficult by Connor's fidgeting hands over collar and shirt studs. Jamie stopped and stared over Connor's shoulder into the glass. Connor caught Jamie's look and, with a frown, relented.

"There, sir," said Jamie, hopping down and smoothing out Connor's shirtfront and buttoning the waistcoat again. "You look a right picture."

"Don't be daft, boy."

Why get so het up over a simple formal costume of black and white? In no other attire did Mr. O'Casey create such a strong impression. Why muck about with perfection? What could possibly be so important about a dinner party with business associates that Connor O'Casey should work himself into such a twist?

A brilliant thought struck Jamie. "Why not wear that diamond ring you bought yourself? The one from Tiffany's. It's enough to create an impression, but not gaudy-like."

Connor considered. "Fetch it then," he said.

"What about that fob with the little diamond in the end of it?"

"Fetch it." Jamie rummaged through Connor's jewelry box and found the fob and attached it to his watch chain. "Pleased with yourself then, Mr. Lynch?" asked Connor, surveying himself in the mirror.

"More pleased with you, sir. Just enough glitter, but not too much. Miss Blanche would approve." Jamie winced. It slipped out before he could call it back.

"I don't want to hear another word about Miss Blanche," said Connor, smoothing the shirtfront under the waistcoat. "We've done all right on our own."

We? thought Jamie.

"You think I'll keep for another six hours?"

"Yes, sir."

"Right, then. Get me hat and coat and get me a cab."

Jamie helped him on with his scarf and coat and handed him his topper, gloves, and stick.

"Now off with you." Connor took one last look in the mirror, adjusted his hat, tugged at the ends of his sleeves, and squared his shoulders. Jamie ducked out and dashed down the hall and was just at the head of the stairs when he heard Connor pull the door to. He knew exactly how long it would take him to reach the hotel's front door and tell the doorman, "A cab for Mr. O'Casey," and have the cabby pulling up at the very moment that Connor emerged from the hotel with just enough time to tip the doorman as he breezed past. Jamie heaved a deep sigh and watched as the cab trotted away into the dark night.

All this fuss and bother. He'd never been so bad as he was tonight. His nerves were all shot to smithereens. And no Miss Blanche to look after him. If ever there was a man who needed taking care of in an everyday way, it was Mr. O'Casey. A valet couldn't do it all, even a good one. What he needed was a woman's touch to see him right.

As Jamie trudged up the stairs, his weary brain began to tick over with an entirely new thought. *No Miss Blanche, eh? No Miss Blanche. Holy Mother of God, let's hope the next one's as good as the last one.*

So at home at the opera was Blanche Wilson de Alvarado that it might have been her own drawing room. She had hired a man to wait upon them and gave him orders from behind the half-opened fan of expensive black lace. Her insistence upon command may have robbed Connor of some of the pleasure of playing host, but Blanche needed to score an unequivocal social victory among his peers if she was to remain in his good graces.

Blanche's ease with the Gages and the Calloways turned to recalcitrance with the Jeromes. Though she well understood how important Jerry Jerome had been to Connor's ascent, she disliked the Jeromes and repaid Jerry's affability with restraint and gave no attention to Maggie at all. She bent her efforts toward repairing her relationship with the Worths and courting the Gages and the Calloways, on whom she had yet to make an impression. Connor had offered himself up as a sacrifice to mollify Maggie, who seemed to soften toward him, albeit slightly.

Francesca Lund and Tracey, being lesser lights in this social constellation, occupied the party's outer orbit. Blanche was glad that the woman who had shown her such courtesy at Christmas seemed content to remain in the background. Still, Blanche was uneasy with Francesca there. Connor's eyes often strayed to that outer orbit and rested upon the translucent neck and shoulders and the soft well between the breasts. The white-blond beauty in icy blue-gray and her engagement ring as her only adornment contrasted sharply with her own shining black hair and attire of blue-black and sparkling jet. But this was Blanche's night to shine, she reminded herself, and with the Gages, the Calloways, the Worths, and the Jeromes within her sphere, she was determined to burn brightly.

With difficulty she kept her eyes on Jerry's face or watched the stage as he spoke, for it was too easy for her own gaze to wander and light upon Edmund Tracey. Tracey sat at Francesca's shoulder, legs crossed, a hand in his trouser pocket, an arm resting on the back of Francesca's chair. Occasionally he ran his fingers along the nape of her white neck. *A gesture of possession rather than affection*, thought Blanche.

The four hours between Blanche's departure from her hotel with Connor and the last curtain call passed uneventfully. When Sherry himself stepped forward to greet Connor as the party was ushered into the elegant private room with its silver fixtures, she ceded control, as any wife would.

As soon as waiters arrived with their gleaming trays of champagne flutes, Connor began to make his way around the room. He greeted each lady with some question or snippet of information that reflected her particular interest—a garden club event, an announcement of a lecture, or a new exhibit at the Metropolitan Museum. Blanche coveted Connor's ease among his company. She did not mind, she told herself. The evening afforded her the opportunity to query the guests themselves. She was skilled at conversation, and the opera, the dinner, and the hotel business provided ample subjects.

Francesca and Tracey had been collared by Mrs. Worth to become better acquainted with Mrs. Calloway. Connor drew up between this lady and Francesca, and made a genial offer of more champagne. Blanche, who was speaking with Mr. Gage and Mr. Worth, could only catch a phrase or two—superb soprano . . . Academy of Music . . . next season . . . no piano in the room. Out of the corner of her eye, she caught Tracey. He was such a poor dissembler, poor lamb. She wished she could give him a hint that he was doing himself no good by sulking. Blanche was comforted to think that she might be the only creature in the room who could claim his affection and wished the thought of it were enough. It was Francesca's reaction to Connor that caused Blanche the greatest consternation. Did Francesca study his face more intently than was proper for an engaged woman? Perhaps it was her imagination.

At the announcement of the first course Blanche seized the opportunity to preside. She had fought with Connor days before about where she would sit. A commanding place at the foot of the table, where she would entertain Mr. Worth and Mr. Jerome, would have signaled a higher position in Connor's life. Connor, however, was determined that this honor would belong to Mrs. Jerome to ensure she had little cause to complain. Blanche's only consolation in sharing the head of the table with Connor was that seeing them together might solidify them in the minds of guests as a pair. Mrs. Worth sat at Connor's left.

"I hear from my husband you've purchased a new painting, Mr. O'Casey," Mrs. Worth said when the hubbub had died down and the waiters were serving the soup.

"Indeed, I have. Mrs. Alvarado and I were at Venables' recently and I acquired a handsome painting of a racecourse."

"A Degas," put in Blanche, seizing upon the remark. "I keep telling him he should acquire other more recent works by the same artist if his style suits, but Mr. O'Casey seems obsessed with that particular subject."

"Well, you can't blame a man for wanting his collections to reflect his interests," said Mr. Gage cheerfully.

"Thank you, Charlie," said Connor, raising his glass.

"I simply don't want him to find himself in an artistic rut," said Blanche. "We did consider a landscape, which he quite liked, but in the end he would have nothing but horses."

"I quite agree with you, Mrs. Alvarado, it is so easy to become fixated on one subject. But if one must have horses, are they well portrayed, that's the question," teased Mrs. Calloway, "not dissected into these dreadful dots and blotches?"

"I've seen the painting," said Jerry, "and I can vouch for it—an excellent likeness of horses."

"Jerry's an excellent judge of horseflesh, however portrayed," said Maggie, "as is Edmund, aren't you, dear?"

"I have some capacity in that arena, yes."

"Mr. Tracey is too modest," said Jerry. "He has been known to pick a winner for me on more than one occasion."

"I believe I know where Jerry gets his knowledge of horses," said Mr. Calloway. "Your people raised them, did they not, Jerry?"

"That's right. We had a large farm in Ohio, near the Kentucky border. Still do, or rather my sister and brothers are still there and run the business," said Jerry.

"How does Mr. Tracey come by his knowledge?" asked Mr. Calloway, directing his question to the gentleman.

"How shall I put it?" said Tracey in mock consideration. "It has been the subject of constant observation and study." Everyone laughed. Tracey seemed to warm to the attention. "I may not have raised horses, but I enjoy riding and did a lot of it in my younger days before I came East. I've been around horses and stables and trainers a good deal in one way or other."

"You have to be to make any kind of a decent showin' at the track," said Connor.

"Even the most knowledgeable among us don't always possess the luck, isn't that so, Mr. Tracey?" asked Mrs. Gage.

"Very true, ma'am, but making a study of it does increase one's chances."

"Love the smell of the turf then, eh?" asked Mr. Gage, as if savoring the aroma.

"I do, sir, I must confess."

"Must be a wonderful thing to have the leisure to follow such a pursuit," said Mr. Calloway, "and the capital. Horses can be an expensive business, whether raising them or racing them. No wonder it's called the Sport of Kings. I haven't ventured onto the turf much myself, though Mr. Jerome here tries to twist my arm on occasion."

"And I twist it back for him," said Mrs. Calloway, to which the party laughed.

"Own any horses, Mr. Tracey?"

"Not recently, no. As you say, it is an expensive undertaking. A trainer who knows his business is expensive and the training takes time."

"Yes, everything seems to come down to time and money. Some of us poor fellows have to work for a living," Mr. Gage continued amicably.

"I agree," said Tracey gravely as he raised his glass to his lips. "The pursuit of wealth can be a full-time job."

Blanche was mortified. How could Tracey dare to expose his feelings in such company? Each lady and gentleman stole an embarrassed look at Francesca. Scarlet spread across Francesca's chest and up through her neck and cheeks as she lowered her eyes to the plate in front of her. *How could he be so oblivious to his discourtesy?* thought Blanche. Tracey merely signaled to a waiter that his wineglass was empty.

"Sometimes a job can be mixed with pleasure," said Connor, barely skipping a beat. "Mrs. Alvarado has been after me to become more engaged in acquiring the paintings and other furnishings for the Excelsior. I feel a bit on shaky ground, what with the likes of the formidable Mrs. Worth and her excellent taste to compete with."

"Mr. O'Casey has a good natural eye," said Blanche, regaining her composure. "He only needs a little tutoring."

"Yes, I agree," said Mrs. Worth. "Besides, this isn't a competition. This is a hotel." *There you're wrong*, thought Blanche. *This is every bit a competition.*

"I've been trying to persuade Mr. O'Casey that a European tour might be in order," Blanche continued. "My sister and her husband live outside Milano, such an excellent cultural center. I'm hoping to visit them in the not-too-distant future and persuade Mr. O'Casey to join us there for a time, when his other business engagements permit. It would be an excellent opportunity for Mr. O'Casey to study some of the most famous art in the world in its own venues. I have yet to see the Galeria myself, which I understand is exquisite, and La Scala is incomparable. Of course Florence is splendid, as are so many cities in Italy. I adore it there. And if the Excelsior is to be stocked with art and antiquities, what better place to purchase them?"

"How thrilling, Mrs. Alvarado," said Mrs. Calloway. "I'm sure you would be an apt tutor."

"It's odd that you should be talking of travel, Mrs. Alvarado," said Francesca, whose color had regained its clarity and whose voice was even and sure. "I'm thinking of taking a little excursion myself." Blanche could have leapt for joy, had it not been for the surprise on Tracey's face. The Jeromes and the Worths exchanged looks. Tracey stared at Francesca.

"I don't recall your mentioning it, duchess," Tracey said.

"Did I not, dear?" she continued, meeting his gaze. "It occurred to me that the next time I have the opportunity for travel, it will be with you—which certainly has its attractions." The party chuckled. "But I thought to myself, What a pity I never took advantage of travel with a party of ladies. So many young women travel together and I've really seen so little of the world. I thought I might just work in such an excursion before we're married. I suppose I've merely been waiting for just the right place to capture my imagination. I think I've found it."

"In sunnier climes?" asked Blanche cautiously.

"No, Mrs. Alvarado. In another direction completely, as a matter of fact. It's that new place in the Canadian Rockies called Banff."

Blanche might have rejoiced had Francesca's pending departure not threatened to tip the balance of Tracey's fortunes and possibly her own and was, therefore, no cause for rejoicing. She watched as Connor's glass stopped in midair for a split second before continuing to his lips, his eyes on Francesca.

"Oh, how thrilling. How brave of you, dear, to choose the wilderness for your holiday," said Mrs. Calloway enthusiastically.

"I've heard of this Banff place," said Charlie Gage. "Quite exclusive, I understand. Hardly pitching a tent and cooking one's meals over a fire, though I hear that it's quite remote. Not thinking of following Nellie Bly's example and trekking across half the world, are you, Miss Lund?"

"It has its appeal," said Francesca pointedly.

"I understand it takes two weeks just to get there by train," said Mrs. Calloway.

"Only five days across Canada, as it happens," Francesca replied.

"That's not so bad then," responded the lady. "I do abhor long train journeys. How splendid for you, dear. When do you plan to leave?"

"I hope before the end of May. The arrangements haven't been fully made as yet."

"You don't mind the cooler weather and all that snow?" asked Blanche. "But of course, that cool Scandinavian blood makes you naturally immune." No one laughed and Blanche sensed that the party did not appreciate her attempt at humor.

"On the contrary, Mrs. Alvarado. One has to be quite warm-blooded to keep out the cold." Blanche was tired of being grateful for Francesca's grace. Francesca continued, "I love the mountains and the cooler climate, much more so than the hot weather. If the season started early enough, I'd enjoy catching the tail end of the winter, as well as the spring."

"Weddings don't plan themselves," said Maggie pointedly, looking from Francesca to Tracey and back again. "What with dresses and trousseaus and the church and all, you hardly have time to go traipsing off to the wilderness. You'll never be ready by Christmas, even if you don't go. I'm sure Edmund will have something to say about it."

"When I have the opportunity," said Tracey as he eyed Francesca.

"There's no point in being hasty," Jerry broke in. "I can understand the desire to have one last fling. Young men embark upon the Grand Tour before they settle down, don't they? No reason young ladies shouldn't, too. There's no reason some of the wedding plans can't be in the works while she's away. We do have modern communication, you know, or don't they have telegraph wires in Banff?" Jerry's tone was light but unconvincing.

"Ladies don't have fittings for dresses by telegraph, Jerry," retorted Maggie.

Blanche raised the linen napkin to her mouth and discreetly daubed the little beads of perspiration that had begun to collect on her upper lip. She directed a question to Francesca. "Whom have you chosen to accompany you, Miss Lund?"

"Two ladies. A dear friend of my mother's, Mrs. Esther Gray, my aunt Esther from Boston. You remember her, don't you, Mrs. Worth?"

"An excellent woman," said Mrs. Worth. "Very level-headed. Though I expect she will be the last to throw a wet blanket on your adventure."

"Yes, exactly. My other companion is Miss Lavinia Lawrence."

"Oh, what a splendid opportunity for her. She has had so few opportunities of this kind. Such a sweet young woman. What a splendid little threesome you will be."

"How very jolly," said Blanche with the barest edge of sarcasm.

"Yes, I've read about this Banff place," put in Mr. Calloway again. "You can't beat it for scenery, so they say. To my mind, outstanding scenery is as good as an old master any day. I expect to hear reports that these three ladies have taken Banff by storm. Banff should attract a good set of people. You should expand your horizons considerably there."

"Three women in the wilds of the Rockies. I can just see it," Connor said. "Black bear and white avalanches. Are you going armed with shotguns and pistols?"

"You don't have to worry about Miss Lund, Mr. O'Casey," said Blanche. "I'm sure she can fend off any trouble that comes her way. Besides, I'm sure there will be gentlemen willing enough to help a damsel in distress." Blanche could have shot herself for adding to Tracey's troubles, especially when she caught his angry eye. Jerry looked as though he could rear up over the table to grab Tracey by the throat. Connor's eyes smiled over the rim of his wineglass.

Mr. Worth's face was nearly purple with indignation under his wreath of white hair and his blue eyes flashed under the thick white brows, but his voice was gentle. "I hope this won't mean you're giving up all your charity work in favor of world travel."

"Oh, no. Not at all, Mr. Worth," Francesca said with faltering ease. "In fact you may be able to advise me regarding a little idea I have. I'm thinking of endowing some sort of music society that will encourage promising young artists and provide for their musical education. You recall my mentioning it to you, don't you, Edmund?"

"I don't recall the details. Perhaps you can enlighten all of us." Blanche felt the room squirm, all except Connor.

"A twofold plan," she continued. "The music society would be for the older students. I myself would like to help develop the musical interests of younger, school-aged pupils."

"I know some excellent private schools where you might find apt pupils, Miss Lund," said Mrs. Calloway.

"I'm sure, but I would prefer to help children who have fewer opportunities to discover whether they have any musical aptitude. In fact, I propose to offer piano lessons myself, for free, to schoolchildren. If they show interest and promise, I might sponsor them for the further study, and enable them to become eligible for support from the society."

"Very admirable, Francesca. Very enterprising—and very ambitious," replied Mr. Worth. "Indeed, you'll need much guidance with something as involved as you're proposing. Have you anyone in mind to work with you? Perhaps Mr. Tracey will join you in building this dream of yours, won't you, Mr. Tracey?"

"I'm afraid I haven't the musical aptitude that my fiancée so obviously possesses." Blanche could have stopped Tracey's mouth for his sullenness and lack of grace.

"But certainly your guidance will be invaluable when it comes to the financing."

"Finance rarely enters our conversation these days," said Tracey. Blanche felt she was watching his prospects and a future with him crumble before her.

"Some scoundrel'll see you coming a mile away if you're not careful, Miss Lund," said Connor. "You may as well be handing 'em your purse."

"Perhaps," said Francesca. "But I must try. Music interests me and helping people interests me. So, why not put the two together? Besides, it's my money, and I suppose I may lose it however I choose."

"A bold statement, however foolish," said Connor.

"Fools rush in, Mr. O'Casey."

Everyone laughed uneasily. Everyone but Edmund Tracey.

CHAPTER 30

An Utter Disregard

❧

There is a custom which is sometimes practiced both in the assembly room and at private parties, which cannot be too strongly reprehended: we allude to the habit of ridicule and ungenerous criticism of those who are ungraceful or otherwise obnoxious to censure, which is indulged in by the thoughtless, particularly among the dancers. Of its gross impropriety and vulgarity we need hardly express an opinion; but there is such an utter disregard for the feelings of others implied in this kind of negative censorship, that we cannot forbear to warn our young readers to avoid it.

—*Decorum*, page 115

The wait for carriages and cabs following the debacle at Sherry's was most unpleasant. Not until the Jeromes' brougham drew up did Jerry make it clear that Tracey would be going home alone, the latter fuming and abandoned to hail a cab. Maggie's injudicious remarks were met with Jerry's angry look and a crisp, "Not now." Francesca's good-byes were cool and unapologetic. Four years' habit dictated that she bear up under Maggie's tirade, but in the shadow of the evening's humiliating spectacle it was all she could do to keep from stumbling into the carriage.

"Never in my life have I seen such a display," Maggie said, as they pulled away. "I was ashamed and disgraced and I'm sure Edmund was too."

"I think we've had enough of Edmund Tracey for one evening," Jerry retorted.

"What on earth could have possessed you, Francesca? You certainly have come to think a lot of yourself and your ideas, haven't you?"

"Enough, Maggie," said Jerry.

"I blame you, Jerry," said Maggie, turning on him. "I blame you very much, you know I do. You egg her on and champion her cause at every turn."

"I said *enough.*"

"What on earth is all this business about going away?" Maggie continued. "Why did you say nothing to us before? Because you know we'd never have approved, that's why. I never heard of anything so ridiculous. An engaged young woman. Your place is here, seeing to your wedding, not gallivanting off to some godforsaken place with two women. And what about Edmund? What is he supposed to do while you're halfway across the world sitting on your mountaintop? Have you even considered how he might feel, being left here, alone, having to face all of New York society and explain your neglect?"

"*My* neglect?" said Francesca incredulously. She leaned against the corner of the carriage and raised a gloved hand to her head and massaged her temple. "*My* neglect?" she repeated softly to herself.

"God Almighty, woman," Jerry said to Maggie, "has that scoundrel managed to dupe you so? Can you honestly tell me you'd side with a man who has persistently embarrassed and disgraced someone as dear to you as your own flesh and blood? Edmund Tracey should be horsewhipped."

"How dare you—"

"Not another word, Maggie," Jerry shouted.

Francesca couldn't cry, not yet. She sat motionless with her eyes fixed on the seat next to Maggie that Edmund might have occupied. With each deep breath she felt dizzy, as if she were standing on a precipice, looking for a way down that would cause the least damage. She was slipping from herself, just like before when the Jeromes brought her to their home. Then as now, she had fought to wrest control of her life from them—from Maggie—to decide for herself what her life might be. She caught herself. Not their home, thank God, not this time—but my home, my sanctuary, my life. She could not wait to get home. They sat in miserable silence until they reached Sixty-third Street and Jerry left Maggie to stew while he saw Francesca into the house.

When they were well inside, Francesca stopped and began to tremble. Slowly at first, then faster, the tears came. Jerry stood in front of her and took her hand. John, waiting to take her wrap, faded into the background as Jerry gently motioned him away.

"There, there. You were splendid tonight. Splendid. I was proud of you, proud of you." He squeezed her hand. "You held your own and more. You can't ask any more of yourself than that. It'll be good practice for Banff. For anywhere. With anyone. After tonight you don't have to be afraid of anything or anybody."

"If it's like tonight, I shall hate it. I don't want to go. I shall hate every minute of it." She kept sucking in air in uncontrollable little gulps.

"No, you won't. Esther won't let you. Nor Vinnie. You did right, you know."

"I know. I know." Then suddenly she pushed out from the center of her being, "That bastard!"

Jerry chuckled. "That's the spirit. You just remember that." He dug for his handkerchief. "Have you written to Esther yet?"

"No, not yet. I hoped I wouldn't need to. I thought I was mistaken about Edmund. Maybe I am responsible for this horrid mess just as Maggie says."

"I don't believe that for a moment, and neither should you."

"You think I should make good on this jolly little holiday?" she said. "Won't that be a juicy little scandal—give people something to sink their teeth into."

"You sound like Vinnie," he chuckled again. "Let them sink their teeth into it. You'll be gone, away, out of New York."

"What happens when I come back?" Her brain was overtired and words were flailing in her mouth. "Or don't I have to come back? Maybe I'll build a cabin and shoot myself a black bear and learn to live like a mountain woman."

"Don't think about that now." Jerry put his arms around her in a bear hug. "Go upstairs, have a hot bath and a good sleep. Then tomorrow, you write to Esther and post that letter just as fast as you can. Have you asked Vinnie? Is she game? Shall I speak to her parents? I can write to Esther, too, if you like."

"No, let me write to Aunt Esther first. Then you and I can talk again."

"Fair enough. I'd better go, dear, before Maggie comes in after me. Don't worry. In a few weeks Esther will be here and before you know it you'll be off on a great adventure. You were right tonight, you know. You have seen so little. You can't restrict your view, when you've got the whole world before you."

May had been waiting, discreetly out of sight. She came forward now and helped Francesca with her wrap and guided her up the stairs to her room.

"I wish I were a drinking woman," said Francesca.

"No, you don't," said May. "And if you start I'll clear out the liquor cabinet and throw away the key. What you want is a nice, steaming bath and some chamomile tea. I'll give your hair a good, long brushing and I'll rub your shoulders a bit. Then we'll roll you into bed. You'll drop right off and I won't wake you till noon."

The storm of people and words had exhausted Francesca. The only storm that threatened now was the storm of words in her head. She walked out of her shoes at the bedroom door and stood in the middle of the room like a mannequin as May undraped her weary frame. The firelight flickered across Francesca's hair and skin and made May's white blouse nearly glow.

Layers of clothing accumulated in an elegant, perfumed heap on the bed where the orange tabby cat and his brown tabby brother nested as May removed Francesca's feminine armor. She unhooked the bodice of the blue-gray gown and peeled away the tight sleeves from Francesca's slender, white arms. The silk swag that hung like petals folded around her hips was unpinned from around her waist. The heavy skirt nearly stood supported by its own weight as May unbuttoned it and pushed it down around Francesca's feet. Layers of fine linen and lace petticoats that swathed her in a filmy chrysalis dropped away and May unhooked the corset, Francesca's freed breasts falling natural and voluptuous underneath the short chemise. She slipped a warm dressing gown over Francesca's shoulders and led her to the bathroom, where a fragrant bath was steaming. May held up the dressing gown to shield her eyes as Francesca shed the final layers of chemise, pantalettes, and silk stockings, and stepped into her bath.

Francesca stretched her full length in the enormous tub and relaxed her limbs one by one and cried and drenched her face and lay there till the water was cold. May helped her towel off and slip into her nightclothes and then guided her to the dressing table where she brushed Francesca's hair until the wet ends dried.

Francesca sipped the tea and looked into the mirror. A sad, familiar face looked back at her, like the first days of her grief, desolated, but calm. She had stepped back a few paces from the precipice, she thought. No explosions or ghostly images would disturb her sleep tonight. They were going to Banff—that was something at least. From this vantage, it seemed a monumental effort, like rolling a boulder up a mountain, but she had made up her mind. Once the preparations were begun, once the wheels were set in motion, she would not shrink from her decision, but own it.

"I'll only wake you if you sleep past noon," said May as she guided Francesca to bed. "Everything will be all right. You'll see. You'll be away soon and everything will be different." Clearly, May had overheard.

"Good night, May. Thank you."

"Good night, miss."

CHAPTER 31

A Proof of Good Breeding

❧

I think one can always tell a lady by her voice and laugh—neither of which will ever be loud or coarse, but soft, low, and nicely modulated. Shakespeare's unfailing taste tells us that—
"A low voice is an excellent thing in woman."
And we believe that the habit of never raising the voice would tend much to the comfort and happiness of many a home: as a proof of good breeding it is unfailing.

—*Decorum*, page 61

Connor was silent during the drive from Sherry's to Blanche's hotel. He didn't appear to be angry or even annoyed but had receded into a place she couldn't reach. His calm countenance would change in an instant to a barely perceptible look of sadness.

None of the guests had blamed Connor for the maelstrom that had all but swamped Edmund Tracey and Francesca Lund. The Worths, the Calloways, and the Gages had been more than civil as they took their leave, their handshakes warm and their parting looks sympathetic. Nonetheless, Blanche was troubled that she felt none of the flush of victory. Moreover, Connor was not crowing in triumph and producing from his pocket a glittering token of his gratitude.

"The Gages certainly seem worth cultivating," she began. "It's clear that Charlie Gage likes you very much. His wife is typical of so many society women, of course—not very original in her ideas, but none the worse for that. She's thought of as very reliable in social circles, I hear, which is all to the good. She was telling me that she feels it will be 'their turn' to host an event next and more than hinted that we should be on her guest list. It's tiresome not to have our own establishment, don't you think, darling? You really should begin to think of finding premises that would suit you or build something somewhere."

As the cab made its way through the lamp-lit streets, Blanche fidgeted with the silk fringe of her evening bag, opened and shut the black lace fan, and looked out at the darkened buildings. One by one the lights that proclaimed the havens of society and entertainment were being extinguished for the night. Here and there a solitary light glowed behind a curtained window.

"I believe Mrs. Calloway and I shall be great friends," Blanche continued. "Now there is a woman of taste, I daresay—clearly a superior person. I'm sure we shall have many things in common, particularly in the arts. She is familiar with a number of up-and-coming artists who are new to me. She so much as promised me to secure us introductions."

Out of the corner of her eye, she could see Connor's hands flex over the handle of his walking stick. So profound was his silence that she could hear the tiny squeak of the fine glove leather against the silver, even over hooves and wheels that clomped and ground against the pavement. He moved his head toward her only to look past her into the street. A lamp illuminated his countenance for a moment. His sober look brought an instant sting of tears to Blanche's eyes. The longer he waited to respond, the more rapidly her heart beat and a knot rose in her chest. She looked away and opened her eyes wide and hoped the tears would dry so that he might not see them fall.

"You were so right, darling, to place Mrs. Jerome opposite you at the end of the table," she said, and wondered if Connor could hear the tremor in her voice. "She seemed to appreciate such notice." In fact, the table's length had only spared Blanche the discomfort of sharing by proximity Maggie's vexation at the scene between Tracey and Francesca. Blanche wanted to blot out the memory of Tracey's ungentlemanly behavior and the disaster it might bring. The spring of her conversation began to run dry. They fell silent.

"It's no good, Blanche," he said finally. He spoke in a voice so low that she allowed herself to believe she hadn't heard him.

"What?"

"It's no good." The cab pulled up in front of the hotel.

"What do you mean?" But she knew. She knew it well. She suddenly felt like the struts had been knocked out from under her and she was falling down a deep chasm.

"I don't understand. It went so well tonight. You—we—made such a favorable impression, we—"

"It's no good," he said for a third time. He sat motionless, not looking at her. "We can't do this anymore. I can't do this anymore. It would never work between us, Blanche. Not over the long haul. I'm surprised we lasted this long. We're too alike, in all the worst ways. We'd wind up wretched and killing each other eventually. You need someone different from me, except just as rich or maybe richer. God only knows what I need, except a drink. It's not fair to either one of us to hang on. It's no use trying. It's over."

"Fair!" she said. "Fair! Since when has Connor O'Casey ever worried about being fair? Since when have you concerned yourself with anything or anybody who might put a hitch in your jolly little plans? You certainly dispatch people fast enough when it suits you. You lie, cheat, anything that will get you what you want. Grubby little cast-off guttersnipe."

Shock seemed to disengage her brain. The human part of her ceased to function as the essential part of Blanche telescoped to nothing and was overcome by the animal instinct to survive. Every fiber of her limbs fired to life and surged with energy that made her want to strike out. She grasped for words to hurl at him.

"You tog yourself up in rich men's clothes and make yourself out to be as good as the next man when you're nothing and nobody. You're nothing but the scum from the Belfast gutters. Filthy, no-good by-product of the docks. Bilge and scum, that's all you are." She was saying anything to get a rise out of him and make him strike back so that she would have something to strike against. He sat there, composed, his hands folded over the silver handle of his walking stick.

"You're right. For once, Blanche, you're right."

"It's that woman, isn't it? That Sunday-school teacher. That puritanical, do-gooding charity lady. She's got you sewn up good and proper. You've been watching her for months. What makes you think she'd have anything to do with the likes of you? She'd never let you touch her. Miss Plaster Saint. Miss Virgin Queen. Or do you think she yearns for some excitement and would fall for the dangerous type? You could wipe that innocence off her face in a hurry, given half a chance. For all I know you've been seeing her. What did she do, bare her ankle in your presence? Or has she been baring more than that?"

Connor grabbed her by the wrist. "Shut up, Blanche. You may find this hard to believe, but I've never hit a woman. I'd gladly start with you, if you don't watch your lying mouth." He threw her back against the seat.

Blanche's laugh held a sadistic edge. "A pretty piece of behavior to present to your goddess, your domina, your divinity. Has she ever seen you when you've lost your composure?"

"Why don't you shut up, Blanche. Face it. You don't care about me any more than I care about you. It's me cash you're madly in love with. Well, you shall have enough cash to get by and more. I'll see to it. You shall have enough to pay your expenses here and to get yourself to Italy to stay with your sister and keep yourself in Europe for a while till things here cool down." He got out of the cab and waited to help her down. Blanche hesitated, loathing to emerge from the cab. With effort, she pulled herself together and got out. He shut the door and walked toward the hotel. Blanche stood on the curb.

"Is this blackmail? Is there something in your dirty little past that you don't want her to know?"

"Such as what?" he asked. "There isn't anything that a hundred tongues from here to Denver wouldn't be happy to tell about me. Half of it's wound up in the newspapers anyway. Besides, there isn't a thing you could have on me that I couldn't match on you and more. The one amazing difference between us is that I have a hard time livin' up to the reputation I've got. It appears you'll never be able to live down the reputation you've got."

Shrieking like a wounded mountain lion, Blanche leapt toward his face and nearly sent him flying. Only her gloves prevented her from leaving deep gouges in his skin. Nevertheless, scratches seared across his face. He thrust himself against her and shook her off balance. Grabbing her arm before she could fall, he dragged her to her feet. Then he retrieved the hat and walking stick that had sailed across the pavement.

"No one walks out on me. No one."

He turned. "I'm doin' it, Blanche. I'll make the arrangements and let you know." He waited for her to move. She walked up to him and looked him in the face.

"She'll never take the likes of you. Never."

"Good-bye, Blanche."

Nothing, not even Alvarado's deceit nor his death nor her subsequent bankruptcy, had made Blanche as angry as this thorough dumping by Connor O'Casey. Alvarado may have deceived her in money, but he had never deceived her in love and his love and honor had extended to matrimony. How little she appreciated honor then, when he pursued her in Italy, the son of an Argentine *patron*, making his grand tour. It amused Blanche that Alvarado's honor had dictated that the liberties between them be followed rapidly by marriage. Experience had thus far taught her that such was not the case with all men and their professed devotion. She had greeted his first proposal with laughter, and his second. But as her relationship with Alvarado intensified she could picture herself with no one else. Their joy seemed complete the day he secured Blanche's consent and her father's permission to marry her. That she once possessed the power to make a man so happy seemed as if it were part of someone else's life. The prospect of another journey, another struggle to find yet another protector, was almost more than she could bear.

To her shock she realized that she was closer to Francesca's age when Alvarado died—and so much more resilient. She felt no such resilience now. The sinews of her being were taut and stretched to the limit. She had been pushed blindfolded into a rocky gorge to claw at the air and never be sure when she would hit bottom. All of what was once the proud Blanche Wilson de Alvarado would disintegrate into bloody and unrecognizable fragments.

She stood there on the pavement. Other cabs and carriages were pulling up to the curb, their merry patrons alighting and making for the warmth of the hotel, scarcely giving Blanche a second look. She pulled the hood of her wrap closer to her face and swept into the lobby, hesitating only long enough to ask for her key.

She slammed the door of her room behind her with a force that rattled the glass shades of the low-lit wall lamps. A fire crackled in the sitting-room hearth. She stood for a moment leaning back against the door. Rage shook her frame. She strode to the middle of the room and whirled around, looking for the first victim. A Chinese vase, Staffordshire dogs, a gilt mirror one by one were smashed into shards and dust. Faster and faster she hurled delicate objects against the marble fireplace. Fury mounted with each crash.

"O'Casey'll pay, O'Casey'll pay!" she shrieked with each missile. "Damn that bastard! He'll pay. He'll pay. If it's the last thing I ever do I'll make him pay!" Her arms flailed wildly as she recoiled from each throw. She heaved a ceramic urn up over her head and threw it with such force that she nearly toppled over with it. The tile hearth cracked under the weight. Small sticks of furniture were next—chairs reduced to kindling.

A violent knock at the door competed with the cataclysm visited upon the room.

"Open up! Open up!" called a gruff voice. "This is the management! Cease this instant and open up or I'll call the police!"

"Go to hell!" Blanche yelled back, hurling a side chair at the door.

"Make way! We're coming in!" called another voice. In a second the door was opened with the manager's passkey.

The two men stood in the doorway for a moment, horror spreading over their faces. Glass and porcelain ground into the carpet under their feet. The second man turned up the gas jets in the wall sconces. It was as if a tornado had ravaged the place, totally destroying some areas while leaving others virtually untouched. Blanche was reeling in the center of the room.

"What in blazes do you think you're doing?!" yelled the manager.

Unable to think or say or do anything, she started to laugh.

"I have never in all my years seen such wanton destruction as this, never in any establishment of mine. Have you any idea of the damage you have caused? Of the extreme inconvenience to other guests—and the damage to the reputation of this hotel?"

"Reputation," Blanche said and began to laugh uncontrollably. She threw her head back and howled at the absurdity of her predicament.

"Tomorrow, madam, you are out of this hotel. You have until noon. Every last penny of the damages will be paid or this establishment will not hesitate to file suit. Is that clear?!"

Still laughing and swaying like a drunkard, she motioned them toward the door. "O'Casey'll pay," she said. "Don't you worry, dearie. He'll pay all right." The men left.

Exhausted and sweating, she flung herself onto the settee. Her laughter gave way to sobs. She wept long, loud, and hard, not bothering to wipe the tears that washed across her face, into her hair and around her ears. She eased herself down on her back, one hand low over her forehead. Her face ached and her sides railed against her stays. Her head felt bulbous and swollen and her eyes burned and temples throbbed.

As the turbulent waters subsided, she lay there for a long time, breathing in, breathing out. She couldn't remember ever hating anyone as much as she hated Connor. Where others might count their blessings, Blanche counted the things she hated about him. His appearance. His brusqueness. His bravado. His self-importance. His arrogance.

Connor would be true to his word, of course. He would pay the damages to get her out of his hair. He would give her enough money to get her to Italy, and probably more than that. It wasn't the money that needled and nagged at her. It was Connor. What to do about Connor and whether it was worth the effort. After all, she didn't love him.

"Let her have him and all the trouble he'll bring her. Good riddance," she said to herself. "For every good thing he ever did for me, I did ten for him. Wretched ingrate."

Usurped, supplanted, betrayed, thrown over for another. These wreaked havoc with her pride just as she had wreaked havoc on the hotel room. Her life was a shambles just as the china and furniture lay cracked and splintered and ground into dust. The room would be dusted and swept, the furniture replaced, the new ornaments newly situated, but who would reassemble the broken pieces of Blanche's life? The room's new occupant would never know that one night a woman, in her misery, anger, and grief, took her emotions out on this room. It made her feel like a dead thing.

With effort she undid her bodice and corset, skirt and petticoats before she even took off her cape. Undone but not undressed, she flopped across the bed and fell asleep.

CHAPTER 32

Unwound

❧

When a ring happens to get tightly fixed on the finger, as it will sometimes do, a piece of common twine should be well soaped, and then be wound round the finger as tightly as possible or as can be borne. The twine should commence at the point of the finger and be continued till the ring is reached; the end of the twine must then be forced through the ring with the head of a needle, or anything else that may be at hand. If the string is unwound, the ring is almost sure to come off the finger with it.

—Decorum, page 404

Tracey wasted no time in visiting his displeasure upon Francesca. He was at her door before breakfast and would brook no opposition. The ruckus in the entryway with the servants was justified. The place was as good as his. They may as well get used to it.

He paced the drawing room, one hand in his pocket and the other running repeatedly through his hair and moustache. The energy his tall frame emitted was palpable. Francesca didn't greet him, nor did she shut the drawing-room doors behind her, but stood and waited. Edmund came quickly and angrily to the point.

"I've come for an explanation," he said.

"I might ask the same of you."

"You think I'm to blame for the spectacle you created last night?" The idea never occurred to him.

"I believe most people would call it self-defense."

"Self-defense against whom? Against me? For what?"

"For the mockery you made of our engagement, saying that the pursuit of wealth is a full-time job. How could you say, in front of all those people, that I was a job? You might as well have said I was a drudge, a torture to you. I've never in my life been so humiliated."

"It was an honest remark, wasn't it? After I pursued you, all the time that I waited while you . . ." Words failed him, for he had never bothered to understand what made her retire from society, what made her spend a year away from him in that appalling settlement. He never understood why Maggie Jerome had never been able to influence her to marry him sooner. He was past making any bones about his feelings.

"While I tried to make a life for myself?" she said.

"If that's what you call it. So now you want to exert your independence even further and go off without telling me? How long have you been plotting this little adventure?"

"I haven't been plotting anything."

"If you've been so dissatisfied, you could have discussed it with me privately."

"How can I? You fail to appear at events and appointments. You're gone for days and when you do appear you disregard everything I say and do. Then you insult me in public."

"My remark hardly warranted the kind of public retaliation you chose to display."

"If I don't defend myself, who will? Clearly you won't."

"Why should I?" He stood close and jabbed an index finger at her as he spoke. "You persistently disregard everything that is a man's right to expect of his fiancée—loyalty, honor, duty, respect—"

"*Respect?*" Francesca said, aghast. "I'm surprised you know the word. You certainly don't know what it means."

"You're the kind of woman who takes satisfaction in stripping a man of his pride."

"If you had any pride, any honor, any *respect*, you'd be conscious of the disgrace and dishonor you subject us to."

"*I* subject us to dishonor?" retorted Tracey. "What would you call that business about going away that you sprung on me so suddenly?"

"If you want the truth, I've been thinking about it for quite some time. Last night only confirmed my decision."

"That you want to get away from me? How do you think that made me look in front of all your friends?"

"They'd be friends to both of us by now if you'd bother to exert yourself. Obviously it's too much trouble to you to show some regard, to try to make them your friends, too. You have to show friendship to gain it, you know."

"What would I want with that pack of hypocrites?" Disdain swelled within him.

"If you feel that way about them, I take it you feel the same way about me."

"I did think you were a cut above that bunch of imposters. They talk about their money and their business and their art and haven't any idea—"

"If you disapprove so strongly of my friends then why, for heaven's sake, haven't you introduced me to yours? I presume you have friends, somewhere. You must be doing something with your time to spend so much of it away from me."

"Judging by your friends, I doubt that you'd approve of mine."

"I presume you're speaking of the track," Francesca said. At this he laughed. "Or are you speaking of Mrs. Alvarado?"

Tracey stopped dead. *She must be fishing,* he thought. *She can't possibly know about Blanche.*

"Do you think I'm stupid as well as—what did you call me, an imposter?"

"What do you mean?" Fury covered Tracey's face. Nell must be behind that remark. She must have decided to make good on her threat to betray him. It would be just like her.

He stood transfixed while she took her turn about the room, taking a few steps and stopping, rubbing her forehead. "How can you be so unbelievably transparent, Edmund? Do you think I don't see the looks that pass between you two? I can imagine where you were on New Year's. And what about Thanksgiving? With Mrs. Alvarado? My God, Edmund, how long has this been going on? Since the day we were engaged? Before?"

"Tell me who's perpetrating this slander!" Could he really have been so unguarded? Could she really have guessed all this from his behavior? Impossible. He'd been the perfect gentleman. If Nell had been behind it, surely his liaison with her would be exposed as well, unless Nell found a way to put Francesca on her guard without exposing herself. It was just like Nell to want to see him squirm, to keep him tied to her.

"You can't be suggesting that this is untrue," said Francesca. "At least give me a little credit for having eyes and ears."

"People will say anything out of jealousy."

"Jealousy? Jealous of whom? I hardly think any of my friends would stoop so low as to be jealous of my engagement to you. If they were, they'd have the decency to keep it to themselves." Tracey made no answer to this. "As for the men," she continued, hesitatingly, he thought, "I once entertained some small hope that there might be someone jealous of you, who might possibly count you lucky to have me. Instead, I find only embarrassment and shame—and pity."

"So, someone's been making up to you, throwing himself at you? That bloody Irishman, for instance? He's been interested in you from the first. What's he been saying?" *The perfect countermove,* he thought. He had no reason to doubt her fidelity, but Connor was sufficient to deflect suspicion from Nell.

Francesca opened her mouth to speak, then stopped as the light of revelation overspread her face. As if laid low by the thought, she walked to the settee and sat down hard. "No, that's not it, is it? How stupid of me. Of course. How many are there, Edmund? But of course, why should it matter whether there are two or two hundred."

"You are the consummate actress," he raged. "*Imposter* is a good word for you. Maybe *liar* is even better."

"People insinuate that I might do better, but I pretend not to hear. I'm finally beginning to believe them." She rose, trembling but controlled, and wrenched the opal and garnet ring from her finger and extended it toward him. "I used to believe that even a wrong choice was better than none. I was mistaken. You may consider yourself released."

"You damn bitch," was all he could say. He drew his arm across his body and with all the impact of his anger let fly with the back of his hand across her face. The ring flew from her hand. Francesca screamed as she hurtled backward against the end of the settee, which only broke her fall before she tumbled to the floor.

Tracey grabbed the ring from its landing place on the hearth and thrust it toward her in defiance. "You damn bitch!" he shouted and headed for the drawing-room door.

John reached the drawing room in time to be thrust out of the way as Tracey forced past him. "Stop him!" John shouted, as Harry came running down the hall. They tried to overcome Tracey, but an older man and a youth were no match for the wrath that electrified his whole being. May screamed and ran down the stairs. The glass shook in its frame as he slammed the heavy oak door after him. Fury propelled him up Sixty-third Street to catch a cab on Fifth Avenue and order the cabby, "Gramercy Park." He sat back, with regard for no one and nothing but his own seething anger. He would deal with Nell next.

A dull grayness smothered the house in Gramercy Park, which glowed its green and sickly glow within.

"Sir, you can't go in there, I have to announce you." The maid scurried to precede Tracey to the drawing room, but the force of his presence shoved her out of the way as if he had pushed her. He burst in and stood. The little maid made herself even smaller as she took up the dust rag where she had dropped it and resumed polishing the woodwork.

"Leave us," Tracey said, startling the maid and immobilizing her. *"I said leave us!"*

"It's all right, Daisy. I'll ring if I need you." The maid escaped and pulled the doors to. "What the hell do you think you're doing, barging in like this? You knew I was busy." Nell's tone was peevish. She was walking about the drawing room in a loose gown, a box of cigarettes in her hand, seeing that decanters and cigarette boxes were filled and glasses and ashtrays were plentiful. "I thought I told you to stay away for a few days. I'm having some new people in. You never know to whom they may be connected. For all I know this lot may be acquainted with your precious Jeromes." She drew on the stub of a cigarette that hung unattractively on her lips and walked over to the hearth to toss the end. Tracey stood, coat open, holding his hat by the brim. His face was red, as if he had run all the way from Sixty-third Street. His breathing was deep, willing the breath out of his body, and his anger with it. She doled out the cigarettes the way she doled out money—a bit here, a bit there. Nell walked to him and looked into his face. Her voice lacked emotion.

"Good God, Edmund, what's the matter? You look like someone's just taken away your favorite toy." She passed him to retrieve a lighter from a side table as she placed a fresh cigarette in her lips.

"What the hell did you think you were doing, Nell? You've ruined me."

She turned and faced him. "Ruined you? What are you talking about?"

"You've got a lot of gall to even think of playing dumb."

"I've been accused of many things in my life, but playing dumb was never one of them. I simply have no idea what you're talking about."

"After all the insufferable lectures? After all the threats?" He pulled the ring from his pocket and held it in front of Nell's face.

"Oh, God," she said with a droll smile. She took the ring from his hand. "She's thrown you over. Well, well. How did that happen?"

"I thought I knew you, Nell, how you like to control people, how you like to keep them on a string to see how much you can bleed out of them. You're like a cat—you want to keep your prey alive enough to play with, but not enough to let them escape. You like to play them along until you're sick of them, to intimidate and threaten, but I never thought you'd actually go through with this."

"Through with what?"

"Stop it, Nell! How else am I supposed to believe she learned about Blanche?"

"About Blanche? You think it was I?" She looked at him incredulously and put one hand on her chest. "Little me? You think I told your precious Chickadee about Blanche?" She began to laugh. "This is too choice for words." She crossed to her favorite chair. "Your golden goose, your golden Chickadee, has thrown you over because of Blanche—and I didn't have to lift a finger." She laughed and watched him pace the room. "Your little secrets are finding you out, darling. I'm surprised it took this long. You really must learn to be more careful. I hope you took it like a gentleman."

"I did what any gentleman would do."

"Which is what?"

"I left her in no doubt of my displeasure." The force of his voice was like a hand across the face.

Nell gave a shallow guffaw and looked at him as if she were scolding a child. "I hope you didn't do anything foolish. You really can be so stupid, Edmund. To be thrown over is one thing. At least you aren't to blame. But only an idiot would leave himself open to having charges pressed against him. What in God's name were you thinking? There's no permanent damage, I hope."

Her reprimand set him fidgeting. He moved to and fro and beat his hat against his leg as she sat there, her face inscrutable. How could she be so complacent, even amused by the utter ruin of his prospects? Though he himself considered the heart to be a useless organ, he expected his women to possess enough to never want to see him suffer poverty and disgrace. They owed him, didn't they? He gave pleasure to their miserable existence, didn't he? Women were all alike—feckless and fickle, easily charmed by their own designs and enamored of their own convictions, the worthless bitches. If they would not concede respect, he had every right to exact it.

What a liar. If ever there was an imposter, an actress, it was Nell. "You need me, Nell," he said, using his hat as a pointer and nearly shoving it in her face. She was unmoved. "All you ever wanted was to keep me tied to you, no matter what it took. You're the kind of woman who needs a man's attention but can't seem to get it on her own merit, so she pays for it. How much longer do you think you can lure men to their doom?"

"Don't waste your time trying to shame me. You don't think sentimentalism moves me, Edmund, do you? I'm a fair judge of what people are worth. I get what I pay for."

He strode to the chair. "I'm afraid you're living under a gross misapprehension." He grasped her around the jaw with two fingers and his thumb and cocked her head up awkwardly to look at him. Then with his thumb he caught the corner of her mouth and smeared the lip rouge down her chin. "Even money can't make that attractive." He pushed her face away.

"Don't flatter yourself, Edmund." Nell raised the back of her hand to the smear. "You're the one living under the misapprehension—that you're one of a kind, that your, what shall we call them, *talents*, render you indispensable. There are dozens like you to be had, darling, here or anywhere. One simply needs to know which rock to turn over."

"And you'd know, wouldn't you? You've probably turned over plenty in your time."

"I found you there, didn't I?"

In an instant Nell Ryder embodied every woman Edmund Tracey ever hated. In an instant he saw before him not the single face of fear and self-preservation, but the many faces of self-righteousness, self-love, and self-satisfaction who had failed in their duty of self-sacrifice for him and the restoration of dignity. As he pinned her body with his own against the chair and encircled her throat with his hands, a final rush of recompense and power surged through him. She pushed against him but could do nothing, her body wrenching, one hand struggling to reach his face, but to no avail. In seconds the struggling ceased. For a few seconds more he held her throat constricted, making sure that no insult, no degradation, no sound would ever pass Nell Ryder's lips again.

CHAPTER 33

Painful Correspondence

✦

On the mournful occasion when death takes place, the most proper course is to announce the decease in the newspaper. An intimation that friends will kindly accept such notice appended to the announcement saves a large amount of painful correspondence.

—*Decorum*, page 254

John had summoned Jerry from the bank. The news that the doctor had arrived worsened Jerry's alarm, in spite of John's assurance that only three stitches were required to close the wound on Francesca's cheek.

May brought up a tray of broth as the dogs followed her into the bedchamber and took up their posts by the bed. Francesca lay on her side, stroking the cats, waiting for the sleeping draught to do its work. A white patch of loose bandage sat high on Francesca's cheekbone.

"Shall I send up Mrs. Jerome?" asked the doctor as he put his instruments in his bag and snapped it shut.

"I'd rather you didn't," said Francesca. Even in her thickening fog she thought her words might have an edge. "It wouldn't be helpful just now. I'd rather she wait for Mr. Jerome. May can stay with me."

"I'll go down and see her then and let her know how you are, shall I?" asked the doctor. "I'll tell her I've given you something to make you sleep." Francesca nodded.

Jerry had telephoned Maggie from the bank and she had gone to Sixty-third Street at once and met the doctor alighting from his carriage—but Francesca had refused to see her. Without waiting to learn what had happened, Maggie had burst into Francesca's bedroom as John was showing the doctor through.

"Get out, Maggie!" Francesca cried, sitting at the dressing table as May held a wet compress to the wound.

"Dearie, you—"

"Get out! I want you out of here," shouted Francesca. "I want you out of my sight!"

"Mrs. Jerome, I think it would be best . . ." the doctor began, motioning toward the bedroom door.

"She's hysterical," said Maggie, undeterred. "What she needs is—"

"What I need is to have you out of my house, Maggie," shouted Francesca again.

"Mrs. Jerome, this will only aggravate the wound," the doctor began.

"Please, Mrs. Jerome," said John, taking Maggie by the arm, "perhaps you should wait in the drawing room."

"I beg your pardon," said Maggie to John. "Take your hands off me. How dare you speak to me—"

"Mrs. Jerome, please," said the doctor firmly. "Leave us."

John had promised to meet Jerry and tell him everything. John also was to tell him that Mrs. Jerome was not to be admitted under any circumstance.

Francesca was about to drift off when she felt her hair smoothed away from her bruising face.

"May I look?" Jerry asked. He lifted the patch. A welt of more than half an inch was swelling under the neat stitches.

"What did he hit you with?" he asked.

"It was Father's ring, of all things—the one with the crest carved into it. It caught just right."

"The doctor said she was lucky it wasn't higher," May whispered over his shoulder. "She could have lost an eye."

"Are you all right otherwise?" he asked. His fingers trembled as he replaced the bandage.

"I fell over the end of the settee. My ribs are sore and there'll be some bruising, but not too bad. I was more surprised and angry than hurt."

May pushed a chair next to the bed and he sat. The orange tabby dislodged himself from the cocoon of quilt and crawled onto Jerry's lap and began to purr. The house lay still.

"You don't know how sorry I am," he said softly. His words echoed as if she were falling down a well. She shook her head weakly. "I should have insisted—"

"Don't, Jerry," said Francesca. "Please . . ." Her tongue felt thick and clumsy.

"Well, it's over and done with now," he said. "God willing, you won't have to face Edmund again."

Every organ of the New York press ground out a version of the Nell Ryder murder case. The *Herald*, the *Times*, and the *Globe* presented at least a toehold on the truth. The old *Frank Leslie's Illustrated Newspaper* issued a special edition with engravings coupling the moment Tracey struck Francesca with an inset depicting the murder. The *New York World* reran the story of the Lunds' deaths, which had been buried in the musty archives of the news and society pages, embellishing on each juicy drop. On top of it all, a queue was forming of those who hoped to get their hands on Edmund Tracey. "And compared to what some of them want him for," the lawyer Mr. Grimly said, "Miss Lund's scar will look like chicken feed."

The Ryders' maid discovered the body almost as soon as Tracey had slammed the front door behind him. Premeditation only stretched the length of time it took to travel from Sixty-third Street to Gramercy Park, but it was enough to warrant hanging. On top of it all, the assailant failed to take away from the scene a vital piece of physical evidence—the ring Francesca had returned to

Tracey an hour before was discovered in the dead woman's hand. This sensational bungle linked Francesca directly to Nell and dashed the last hope of privacy.

Upon hearing that the moneyed class had interests in Tracey's fate, creditors began circling like vultures. Sadly for them, not one of the social elite would hear of covering Tracey's many debts. The vultures were left to circle the civil courts in hopes of picking his bones when the criminal courts were finished with him.

Then appeared a number of women to testify to Tracey's character—in the negative. The women were mostly of dubious character, breach of promise their complaints. The most plausible of these arrived at the district attorney's office armed with a baby.

Finally came a wire from Shillingford and McNee, promising extradition papers for crimes committed in Louisiana. With the bullet Philippe Letourneau's coffin had yielded and discovery of the doctor's body at Maywood, Henri Gerard began to bleat promises of help to convict Tracey if his own life was spared. The more that came to light, the clearer it became that should he pay the ultimate penalty no one would mourn him—except perhaps Blanche.

As the prosecution's star witness in the murder trial, Francesca had worries enough without pressing charges of her own for the physical and emotional injuries. Instead, Jerry and Mr. Grimly bent their energies toward preparing her for her ordeal upon the witness stand. The prosecution pinned its hopes on presenting Miss Lund as the linchpin that could bring the sordid details of Tracey's past to light. Her father's file and the detectives' testimonies, if admissible, might supply ample evidence regarding Tracey's activities in Louisiana and thus motives for his actions in New York. Privately, Jerry concurred with Mr. Grimly in hoping that Francesca's stitches would not come out before the trial.

McNee wasted no time in tracing the St. Louis telegraph office that had received the communications for Mrs. Helene Terrey, who called regularly and personally to collect them. With the tenacity of a bloodhound he went street by street until he located the modest boarding house whose landlady confessed to an occupant of the same name.

"But she's gone now," said the landlady.

"Gone?" asked McNee with a sinking feeling.

"Left yesterday in quite a hurry. She in some kind of trouble?"

"Do you know where she went?"

"No, can't say I do. She received some kind of message, then she packed everything she had and paid an extra week's rent—for my inconvenience, she said. Nice lady, Mrs. Terrey. Quiet. Always paid on time. Wish all my boarders were like that. Real reliable, you know. Sorry to see someone like that go. I was just about to clean up her room and put the sign up in the window."

"Before you do, may I take a look around?"

"Suit yourself, but I think she's pretty well cleared out."

The sunny room was indeed bare except for the plain furnishings provided by the house. McNee's eye caught the heap of ashes in the grate. Clearly a great deal of paper had been burned and the charred remains beaten into the tiniest fragments.

He sat on the quilt-covered bed and rubbed his eyes and face. Twenty-four hours lost. How could he have been so slow, he thought, kicking himself, yet how could he have been any faster? Having thus failed to clap a jar over the elusive butterfly, he wanted to stop altogether. He cast his weary eyes around the room. Nothing much to search. May as well do a thorough job and be done with it.

He looked under the mattress and in the chifferobe. Nothing. He opened the lady's desk and slid his hand into empty cubbyholes and pulled at the small drawers, one of which refused to budge. Nothing. He took down the one picture of a Biblical scene that hung on the wall above the bed and examined the back. He took up the wool rug and examined the floorboards, but even those concealed no treasure.

Again, he sat at the desk with his elbow upon it, with his head in his hand, looking around the room. Absently, he fiddled with the obstinate drawer, giving it a good yank. It released itself part way. He drew out his penknife. With much jiggling and coaxing the drawer surrendered and with it a letter that was crammed at the back.

McNee couldn't believe his eyes. The envelope was addressed to Mrs. Helene Terrey at the address of the house where he now sat. To anyone else, the back flap's scrawled words would have meant nothing, but to McNee, "New York, New York" meant everything. He opened the letter, dated 18th August 1886, and read:

>*My dearest,*
>
>*I hope this letter finds you well and that you are able to find respite from the summer heat. The summer here is most trying, what with all the people and little opportunity to escape. I hope that you are more fortunate and can persuade your friends to an outing in the country.*
>
>*The means of securing our future continues to elude me. I seem to have misjudged the influence of my patroness. Despite my exertions, her introductions yield little.*
>
>*However, I have one bright spot to relate. I have gained introduction to a much more fashionable set, in particular to a theatrical producer and his wife, who seem to be intimate with anyone who is anyone in society and may well lead to connections that may help to restore our fortunes.*
>
>*As yet all my connections here remain oblivious to my straitened circumstances, which is a mixed blessing. It affords me the ability to move easily among them, but it does nothing to relieve the humiliation I feel at my dependence and my longing to bring honor back to you and to my family. I must make the sacrifice now and find a way for us to live, though I am afraid by such means as are distasteful to you. Please believe that I find them equally distasteful.*
>
>*My one solace is that soon I may try my luck again*

in St. Louis or Natchez and thus may be able to spend time with you as man and wife. Please write and let me know how you get on. I hope that soon I may either reply and tell you of our improved fortunes, or present myself at your door.

  I am,
  Your devoted,
  Edmund

CHAPTER 34

As Self-Reliant as Possible

❧❀❧

A lady, in traveling alone, may accept services from her fellow-travelers, which she should always acknowledge graciously. Indeed, it is the business of a gentleman to see that the wants of an unescorted lady are attended to. . . . Still, women should learn to be as self-reliant as possible; and young women particularly should accept the proffered assistance from strangers, in all but the slightest offices, very rarely.

—*Decorum*, page 139

Ear-splitting blasts of the whistle announced the train's gradual, lurching arrival until the brakes finally screeched the black iron behemoth to a halt at the platform.

"Francesca! Francesca! Here, dear!" Esther Gray stood on the step of the first-class carriage and waved, a small handbag bouncing on her wrist. Out of the steam and smoke Francesca and Harry appeared like apparitions.

"Esther!"

The women caught each other in a hearty embrace, Francesca bending over to catch Esther around the waist, their hats colliding. They laughed. Half the platform's occupants were adjusting their clothing following exuberant greeting.

"I'm *so* glad you're finally here. What an uproar we've been in."

"Keep your voice down, dear," said Esther, threading her arm through Francesca's and pulling her close to emphasize the point. "Hello, Harry. How are you?"

"Very well, Mrs. Gray, thank you."

"Rosemary, help Harry locate the trunks. Harry, you remember Rosemary, don't you? I take it the carriage awaits."

"Of course, Mrs. Gray," said Harry, turning and doffing his hat to Esther's maid.

"Good. Rosemary, mind you see that the porter doesn't drop anything." Esther was all business, even in the midst of affection. She was a small package charged with energy, deceptively benign until the switch came on. "You, young lady, haven't bothered to tell me how wonderful I look after all this time. It's not as bad as all that, is it?"

"Don't be silly, Aunt Esther. Aside from looking generally wonderful, you can't imagine how glad I am to see you."

"That's better, though only slightly. Harry, this blue portmanteau is mine, too."

"Yes, Mrs. Gray."

Esther started forward, but was pulled back by the dead weight of Francesca, feet firmly planted, looking down into Esther's face. Francesca's smile mingled concern and amusement with gentle affection. Esther squeezed Francesca's arm.

"Everything will be all right," said Esther. "Now let's get along home."

"I know it will, one way or another," said Francesca. They strode down the platform toward the terminal.

"Do we dine alone tonight?"

"Yes. I managed to put off the Jeromes for a bit. Mr. and Mrs. Lawrence have invited us for tea tomorrow afternoon, so you'll see Vinnie. But you know Maggie. She may well breeze in at any hour."

"Well," said Esther. "We might have a little reprieve so you can fill me in."

They met the carriage at the curb. The hand luggage was hoisted aboard and the passengers deposited inside, a cart to follow with the trunks. Winter was yielding reluctantly to thaw. Snow was turning to slush and thence to free-flowing rivulets that splashed down gutters and pooled in puddles that sprayed up under hoof and wheel.

John's greeting was more like a suction pump that nearly sucked Esther into the front hallway. Dogs barked, penned up in the bowels of the house. The orange tabby cat appeared and quickly retreated. Coats and hats were taken as polite inquiries were made as to the general health of the household and the efficiency of the railroad. As the dust began to settle, the entire house seemed to heave a relieved sigh.

"You look well, John," said Esther.

"I'm very well, thank you, Mrs. Gray," said John. "Welcome to New York, madam. We're all very pleased to see you. Your room is ready, if you'll allow me . . ."

"In a minute, thank you, John. I'll give Rosemary a chance to sort things out and then Miss Lund can show me up. Shall we go into the drawing room, dear?"

"If you're tired—" Francesca began.

"Nonsense. I'm not as decrepit as all that, thank you," said Esther.

Esther Gray had been Sonia Lund's dear friend—a steady woman who had her share of heartache and the world's wisdom. She had married for love and never regretted it, despite the disapproval of her family. Widowed and childless, she had "retired" from society, until Francesca had drawn back the curtain of seclusion with a ferocious yank and proposed the journey to Banff.

Esther surveyed the drawing room and for a moment tried to conjure up the ghostly past of heavier furnishings and more somber hues. How many years had it been since she had last stood here? Six years? Seven? Since before Josiah's illness, it must have been. Sonia and Jurgen and the children had come to visit in Boston, but Josiah had been too ill and Esther too worn out from caregiving for the Grays to be much away from home. When Josiah died, the Lunds had come to be with her and then within the year they, too, were gone. She had been too overcome to offer Francesca solace or an escape from the Jeromes—a state of affairs Esther had always regretted. Then Francesca's appeal for help and proposal of travel roused her from hibernation and offered adventure with a double attraction—a chance to reengage with Francesca and to rejoin the world.

"You must be hungry, Aunt Esther. I've asked for sandwiches with our tea."

"In a moment," said Esther, warming her hands over the hearth. "First you can tell me anything you're dying to tell me." They sat together on the settee and Esther took Francesca's hand and searched her face—so like Sonia's fair beauty and equally inscrutable. "Tell me, how are you bearing up?"

Francesca looked away. Then came the tears. She pressed her hand to her mouth as if this might suppress them.

"I'm so sorry, Aunt Esther," she said in two small gasps. "I didn't mean for . . ."

Esther drew a handkerchief from her pocket and handed it to her.

"Nonsense," said Esther, putting her arm around Francesca. She understood well the Lund tendency to brace up under trying circumstances, to face out unpleasantness with a serene exterior while enduring torment and mortification within. From what Esther remembered of the Jeromes, they themselves could be classed as a trying circumstance, even beyond the tragedy that had befallen Francesca. With few safety valves at her disposal, was it any wonder that Francesca should break down? Esther felt glad—not for Francesca's distress, but for the respect and confidence this intimacy of tears showed. At last she might be of real use to her niece. Francesca blew her nose and dried her eyes.

"I can only guess what this has done to you," said Esther. "Have you been hounded very much?"

"Whenever something new comes to light the press seems to take up some sort of vigil around the house. It was horrible for about a month when the investigation ended and the trial began. I can't even tell you how to prepare for it. You can see now why I'm desperate to be gone. At first I only wanted to get away from Edmund, but now . . ."

"Yes, the sooner we're gone, the better for you. Shall we ring for tea and get a little sustenance?" asked Esther, rising and ringing the bell herself. She stood before Francesca for a moment before sitting again. "So tell me about the next few days."

"We've been invited to dine as the guests of Mr. Connor O'Casey on Saturday night, mostly as a courtesy to Jerry, I believe. I wasn't too keen, since the last dinner he hosted was a disaster—that horrible night at Louis Sherry's I wrote you about. But Jerry assures me that it will be a much smaller affair. I believe Mr. O'Casey may feel that he owes Jerry and Mr. Worth a proper dinner after Sherry's. They're all partners in the hotel business."

"Yes, I remember." She regarded Francesca for a moment. "You look none too happy about this. Why?"

"Mr. O'Casey is involved in this dreadful business with Edmund, though unwittingly. He—Mr. O'Casey—was on intimate terms with Mrs. Alvarado."

"Oh, yes, I certainly remember her name from the newspapers. I had no idea what association all these people had with you—Edmund with Mrs. Ryder, Mrs. Ryder with the Alvarado woman, she with Edmund. Now Mrs. Alvarado with this Mr. O'Casey, he with Jerry, and Jerry and Maggie back to you and Edmund. What a horrible web. Oh my dear, how did you manage to get yourself into this?"

"I really don't know. It just seems to have happened."

"I'm convinced there is no such thing as true coincidence. Everything happens for a purpose—for our edification or reproof. Let us hope in this case it's for the former."

"I do believe that Mr. O'Casey had no more idea than I that she was carrying on with Edmund," said Francesca. "I'd have more sympathy for the man if he weren't so insufferable. He appears at the most inopportune moments, presents himself as charming and funny, and seems determined to annoy and insult me."

"Might he be interested in you?"

"Good heavens, Aunt Esther, what a preposterous idea. You and Vinnie. What a pair you'll be in Banff. Yes, she thinks he's interested in me."

"But do *you* think he is?" asked Esther. "Men can be such odd creatures. He may be trying to endear himself to you."

"Endear himself? You'd think he would have the decency to hold his tongue. Besides, knowing what little I do of the man, I expect he would express himself quite bluntly if he were. I'll be as happy to leave New York on his account as on any."

John arrived with refreshment on a butler's tray and in one smooth motion released the spring to let down the four legs as he set it before them and departed. Esther poured.

"He has a way of looking at a woman that's very disconcerting," continued Francesca. "I imagine it would cow some women; it made me more determined to pay him no mind. You'll see what I mean when you meet him. I will give him one thing—he can't be a fortune hunter. Jerry and Mr. Worth had him thoroughly vetted on that score or they wouldn't have let him near their business dealings. Besides, if he showed any interest in me, Jerry would probably kill him."

"Nonsense. Jerry hasn't the fortitude to harm a fly. And speaking of Jerry, will we have an opportunity to speak with him—just the two of us?"

"I've thought of that," said Francesca. "I've asked him to take us to lunch one day."

"Well, that's something. I would like to have his opinion—unaided if possible—of the way things stand here, and what we might expect in Banff. We must have a clearer idea of what we may be exposing ourselves to, even at that distance."

"I suppose that's true," said Francesca. "Though honestly, if I understood fully, I probably wouldn't have the guts to try."

CHAPTER 35

An Interview with the Family

The arrangements for the funeral are usually left to the undertaker, who best knows how to proceed and who will save the family of the deceased all the cares and annoyances at the time they are least fitted to meet them. Such details as usually do not fall to the undertaker are entrusted to some relative or friend who is acquainted with business. This friend should have an interview with the family or some representative of it, and learn what their wishes may be and receive from them a limit of expenses.

—*Decorum*, page 255

Jerry knocked at the door of the reception room and came through without waiting for an invitation. The room was dark. The dim light of a single lamp illuminated the private inner office, where Shillingford was unloading the contents of his leather briefcase. The distinctive click of the hammer of a revolver stopped him.

"Mr. Shillingford?"

"Come in, Mr. Jerome."

The yellow lamplight pooled on top of the desk and played among the strata of files and papers and washed out dimly into the room, seeping into the folds and creases of two more figures. A tall man stood at Shillingford's shoulder, shielded from the light except for a reflection that melted into the lower contours of his face. In a leather chair in front of the desk sat a petite woman in traveling clothes, her face revealing youth and fear and fierce determination.

"Mr. Jerome," said Shillingford, "may I present Mrs. Edmund Tracey."

Jerry lowered himself into the other chair, not grasping what he heard. Shillingford went to an innocent-looking cabinet and swung open the little door, revealing bottles of liquor and glasses. He poured Jerry a brandy, standing by him while he took a large gulp, then poured another before returning the bottle to the cabinet and himself to his desk.

"This gentleman," said Shillingford, gesturing toward the other man, "is my associate, Mr. McNee." The men acknowledged each other with a nod. "Mr. McNee traced this lady to St. Louis, where she has been living since 1885. Pieces of this puzzle finally began to come together when my New York operative discovered that Mr. Tracey had removed to a cheap hotel, where he was living under the name Edward Terrey. He was paying a man at the Brevoort to take messages and collect mail for him. My operative had discovered that as Edward Terrey, Tracey regularly wired money to a Mrs. Helene Terrey in St. Louis."

"This, presumably, is why he wanted Miss Lund's money," said Jerry.

"And no doubt Mrs. Ryder's," said Shillingford. "Mr. McNee discovered Mrs. Tracey's lodgings at about the time the news broke of her husband's arrest for the murder of Nell Ryder. Unfortunately, when he arrived in St. Louis, she had already fled. Nevertheless, he obtained enough evidence to make the connection between Edmund Tracey, alias Edward Terrey, and the woman you see before you. He surmised that she was headed for New York and caught up with her en route. News had not yet reached her of our discovery of the bodies of Philippe Letourneau and a Dr. Warren and the implication of her brother Henri Gerard. She came to New York to see her husband, not knowing that she herself might be implicated in crimes perpetrated by her brother and possibly Mr. Tracey."

"My only thought was to see the wretch who is my husband," said the small but steady voice.

"I hardly think that matters now," said Jerry. "He's as good as hanged. There's nothing you can do to help him." He drained his glass and set it on the desk.

"You understand nothing, sir," Henriette continued. "Nothing would please me more than to see this man hang for his crimes. He has done nothing but bring disgrace to my family and to me."

"The evidence against Tracey is ample," said Shillingford without emotion. "Mrs. Tracey's appearance can only strengthen the public sympathies already against him."

"I knew we would never be able to maintain the lie. I wanted to make him pay and pay, but I knew it couldn't last."

"What lie?" asked Jerry. "Make him pay for what? And how could you"—he gestured toward Henriette's small frame—"make Tracey pay for anything? You have no idea of the kind of man Edmund Tracey is."

"I know him better than any of you ever will." She settled herself in the chair. "May I have something to drink?" Shillingford fetched a glass of water. She drank, then spoke.

"By now you have heard how my brother, Henri Gerard, introduced Edmund to our home when I was but a girl. Even though I was very young, I loved him instantly. More than just a childish infatuation. I wanted him body and soul. I believed he saw beyond the slip of a girl to someone who cared for him deeply, passionately. I was in agony whenever he came to the house, so much did I want to be in his company, but I could only steal a few words with him from time to time. Henri Gerard and Philippe used to taunt me about him, torment me, tell me that there were other women."

Jerry heaved a deep and painful sigh. Henriette ignored him.

"Well, I also know how to torment. I tormented my father until he let me have my coming-out ball. I wanted to show that I was a woman, just as good as any other, that I could do as I liked. What a fool I was. How could I, so small and so young, attract a man like

Edmund? What attracted him was Maywood and my father's money, money he knew I could get for him. One way or another I would get him the money and the land. He said he wanted to restore his family's honor, you see, honor that money and land could give him."

"And you fell for it?" asked Jerry.

"Yes!" she exclaimed. "He knew there was great enmity between my father and my brothers—the ruthless Henri Gerard and the spineless Philippe. My father loved me more than them and gave me anything I wanted. It made Henri Gerard and Philippe jealous and do stupid things, which made him hate them even more. Edmund knew I would have money someday. He protested his love for me and persuaded me to elope with him. Then everything that was mine would be his."

"Did your father approve of Tracey?" asked Jerry, almost for form's sake.

"Of an Anglo? He didn't."

"Then why risk his displeasure?"

"I could never remain out of my father's favor for long. He always forgave me. Besides, my father was not well and had not much time left. Then Edmund made sure there was a reason for my father to insist upon our marrying."

"The child."

"Yes, the child. It was not evident yet when we eloped, but I knew. I made sure that Edmund knew. And my old nurse. I told her the night we left and knew that she would arouse the household to follow us, find us, and force Edmund to marry me. They did find us, in New Orleans. My father forced us to marry and paid a handsome dowry for my hand."

For a moment, Henriette's voice wavered and a look of pain clouded her face. "It was the shock of it all that killed my father. He took to his bed almost as soon as the ceremony was performed. He lay in agony for several months, unable to care for himself. The doctor attended him constantly."

"Dr. Warren?"

"Yes. My father would have lapses in memory and bouts of pain. Dr. Warren administered laudanum to give him rest, but I knew he was miserable. I truly believe my brothers tormented my father to hasten his end. They expected to inherit, you see, and the sooner the better for they had many debts.

"Then in the last month, my father's health declined rapidly. The house was in chaos. Edmund and my brothers fought constantly. I don't know how the priest was finally sent for. I only remember that I beat upon the chamber door, calling for my father, but they would not admit me. The doctor said I should not be in a room of death with a child in my womb. I could hear my father cry in his delirium, '*Mon papillon, mon papillon,*' above the sound of the prayers as the priest performed the anointing. My father could barely kiss the cross. Edmund only shouted at me but I was inconsolable and fought him with all my strength. Philippe came out to drag me to my room, but Edmund prevented him and took me away himself. I wept and wept until finally the doctor came and told me that my father was dead.

"A day later, Monsieur LeGros came. My brothers fully expected a male heir to inherit Maywood, despite the bad blood between them. But I had known all along that Maywood had been left to me. My brothers were furious. And I? I laughed and Edmund with me, for he knew what was mine would be his. Henri Gerard told LeGros his business with the Letourneaus was finished."

"So if you had inherited, why didn't you and Tracey throw them out and bid them good riddance and be done with it?" Jerry asked.

Henriette took another sip of water and sat quietly for a moment, as if willing herself to continue.

"As soon as LeGros quitted the place, Philippe turned on me. He began to beat me and tried to strangle me. Henri Gerard shouted at him to stop, but never laid a hand on him. Edmund attacked him, but Philippe threw him off. Edmund ran from the room. I nearly fainted when I heard a shot and Philippe released his hold on me and I fell to the floor. Edmund had shot him dead.

"The child began to come, too many weeks before his time. The pain was horrible. Edmund and Henri Gerard again sent for Dr. Warren. There was nothing the doctor could do. When the child finally came, he was dead. *Mon petit.* So much death in that house. I only wanted to get away, to die, too." The tears came, but Henriette persevered. "Everything Edmund Tracey touched came to ruin. I had had enough of him, and yet was tethered to him for life. I nearly went mad with the prospect of a life with this monster.

"They hid Philippe's body and told the doctor that he had gone to France upon the death of our father, but the doctor was suspicious. He threatened to expose everything that had happened at Maywood unless he was paid. He threatened to have Edmund arrested and the weasel Henri Gerard joined him in this threat—and in my heart, so did I. So it was I who came up with the plan. The doctor would pronounce me dead in childbirth. Then I would be out of the way. The property would pass to Edmund and he would sign it over to Henri Gerard. Henri Gerard would pay the doctor. Then Edmund would be free—on one condition. I had no money other than my dowry and what jewels and clothes I could carry away. So Edmund was to set me up in a household of my own and send me money for my keep. As long as he kept paying, I would say nothing about his involvement in the death of my brother or his attempt to swindle the Letourneaus out of their property by using me. He could lead whatever life he liked."

"Why did Henri Gerard abandon you?"

"He hated me for the favor my father showed me. Any plan that got rid of me was favorable to him. Besides, the Letourneaus' money was tied up in the property, not in cash, so he couldn't help me if he had wanted to. Edmund wanted to go abroad—to the West Indies or to Europe. Even if he had to marry your mademoiselle and then leave her—to get enough money to keep me and enough to leave the country."

"But how could you stand the thought of his pursuing other women?" Jerry found the acceptability of such a plan incomprehensible.

"Because I knew they meant nothing to him. He hated them—all of them. They stripped him of his dignity. They barely kept him alive. He used to write to me about how he hated them all, even your precious Miss Lund. He hated them just as passionately as I had once loved and now hated Edmund."

"But what about this letter," interrupted McNee. "It doesn't speak of hatred."

"What letter?" asked Henriette.

McNee drew from his pocket the letter he had found in the St. Louis boarding house and handed it to her. She opened it, and after a furtive glance across the page, crammed it back in its envelope.

"You can't see his cruelty?" she asked, thrusting the letter toward the detective. "I was only dear to him when he believed more money was coming, when he thought he was safe. He thought your mademoiselle would make him safe, that he could settle a sum on me and be done with it—done with me."

Jerry could stand no more. He was sick at heart. He rose to leave. He looked at Shillingford. "What do we do now?"

"Inform the authorities," Shillingford answered.

"Thank you," said Jerry to Shillingford, "for letting me hear the conclusion of this business before, before . . ." Jerry could think of nothing to say. Before the police beat down the door? Before the press sensationalizes the story? He turned to go, but Henriette grabbed his arm and held him there a moment longer.

"I did love him once, monsieur, just as I imagine your mademoiselle once did. God spare her the hatred for any person that I now feel for Edmund Tracey."

"God grant your prayer, Mrs. Tracey," said Jerry. "I've heard enough, Mr. Shillingford. Good night."

CHAPTER 36

The Sound of Feasting

Guests should not return to the house of mourning after the funeral. "In some sections it is customary to conclude the ceremonies of the day with a dinner or banquet, but this is grossly out of place and not to be tolerated by any one of common sense and refinement. . . . It is the cruelest blow which can be given bereaved friends to fill the house with strangers or indifferent acquaintances and the sound of feasting at a time when they desire of all things to be left alone with their sorrow."

—Decorum, page 259

"They've already been checked," said Blanche with indignation, as the policeman on duty inspected the basket. She stood outside Edmund Tracey's cell—a relatively posh cell for the relatively posh prisoners of high society. "You should know me by now."

"Can't help it, lady," said the policeman as he pawed through the clean clothes, soap, a book of poetry, and baked goods. "Rules is rules. You could come a hundred times—"

"Which I have—"

"—and this might be the very time you'd bring an extra special surprise for your friend here." The gauntlet of authorities had already broken the soap into pieces and reduced baked goods to crumbs before being satisfied that they contained nothing beyond a little comfort the Tombs had failed to provide. "Okay, lady. You're all clear." He unlocked the cell and let Blanche enter, then slammed the door behind her and rooted himself outside the door, where he watched them through the bars.

"I brought you a clean shirt and underthings," she began, trying to keep a light tone. "When I come tomorrow you can give me your laundry . . ."

"You don't have to keep doing this," said Tracey.

"Nonsense," Blanche said as she crossed to the small table, placed where it had caught the last of the day's sunlight, and made room for the basket's contents among the books and papers resident there. "I'm afraid the tin of sweet bread got the worst of it this time." She lowered her voice and tried to offer a sheepish smile. "I saw to it there was a little extra rum." She opened the tin and the fragrance of the sweet bread drifted genie-like into the cell, which was already warming in the dim morning light of late May. She sat down on a wooden chair adorned with a cushion of once-bright tapestry in gold and blue.

Edmund absently lifted the cover of the book and ran his thumb up the side of the pages, breaking the awkward silence with gentle fluttering. He put a large crumb of bread in his mouth and then looked as if he thought better of it but dared not offend her by spitting it out. Blanche had never seen him look so thin and pale. The whiteness of his collarless shirt and wan complexion made him appear nearly luminous against the cell's dingy whitewash. The auburn hair and moustache and the freckled face were ashen. The bed looked like he hadn't slept in it, so taut was the quilt and pristine the pillow. He fingered the clean shirt—gingerly, she thought—as if thinking of the linen shroud that awaited him. She shuddered and searched for something to say.

"I was sorry I couldn't come yesterday. It took all day to see to these things." She nodded toward the table.

In truth, the strain of almost daily visits, tamping down her fear and willing herself not to break down in Tracey's presence, had become a monumental effort. Each time she stepped across the threshold of the Centre Street entrance, sorrow and hopelessness weighed her down. The reckless speed with which Tracey's case came to trial frightened her, portending a swift and merciless verdict. As she passed like an automaton through the lobby and the hallways with their offices and courts, through the checkpoints, and so up the stairs to the cells, she was torn between abandoning her vigil for the sake of her own sanity and offering comfort to the only man she had ever loved.

"Did anyone come to see you yesterday?" she asked.

"My lawyer, of course." He drew up a stool and sat down at the table opposite her.

"What did he say?" She pushed out the words. "Will there be another appeal?"

"There's no new evidence in my favor to make that possible. With the Louisiana business looming it's unlikely there'll be anything."

Louisiana, where they had seen their happiest days together before life had intervened. New Orleans, with the lacy loveliness of its gritty gentility, the refined culture alongside primal superstition. They had soaked up experience moment by moment many a moonlit evening and many a steamy afternoon. Now it was all gone. She wondered if she should bring up the happy past to divert him. She couldn't, she thought. If he had half the feeling for her that she had for him, the remembrance would only bring pain. That there would ever be a time to come when she could look back on these memories with fondness seemed an utter impossibility.

"Has she come to see you?" Blanche asked.

"To which 'she' are you referring?" Tracey smirked. "My wife? My fiancée?"

"Anyone," Blanche said.

"They'll let me have no contact with my wife." Tracey sighed. "It's just as well. She is also a guest of the City of New York, over in the Women's Prison. Ironic, isn't it? This is the closest we've lived together in years, but not for long. She faces trial in Louisiana with her brother, as soon as the extradition has gone through. It seems there's to be quite a family reunion, since I may be joining them. I'm quite popular, you know. Louisiana is haggling with

New York State over who will have the pleasure of dispatching me. Louisiana wants its chance to hang me before New York can send me to Auburn and allow me the honor of being among the first to test their electric chair. I don't know which is more appealing—to hang like a gentleman in my native land or to fry among the imposters like a foreigner."

"Oh, Edmund, don't." Blanche hated the acid tone that crept into his languid voice.

"The Chickadee and the Magpie," he said disdainfully. "They both have written—frequently."

"What do they say?"

"I have no idea. The prison authorities know them intimately, of course, having perused my correspondence with interest. I'm sure they found them entertaining. Would you like to read them?" He picked up a little stack of opened letters and held them out to her. "You may as well. I've not been able to bring myself to do it. The Magpie would either say that I had been cruelly misunderstood or rail upon me as a villain for having deceived everyone for so long and condemn me to perdition."

"Might she offer some help?"

"She might."

"Isn't it worth finding out?"

"I think Jerome may see that as a conflict of interest, since he is doing everything he can to act in the interest of the Chickadee. As to the Chickadee herself, she has sent me three. I can almost predict what they contain." He did not look at her, but looked toward the barred window. "The first is an appeal to unburden myself as to what drove me down this path—a desire to understand me in a way she had hitherto not bothered. One contains a self-examination and asks me to forgive her for anything she might have done to hurt me. The final one, if I know her at all, requests an interview that we may exchange our mutual forgiveness. I find it revolting and hypocritical—a reminder of everything I hated about New York and her class of people. Had the scheme come off and we had . . ." His voice trailed off. He looked down at the table. "It doesn't matter. I'm not the man I was when we were both free and knew each other well, when we loved each other in New Orleans."

"But I still see in you the man I knew."

"And that's the man I want you to remember, not the one you see before you." He raised his eyes to hers. She wondered for a moment whether she had lied, to him and to herself—that this was not the man she had known, but a stranger.

"I don't want you to come anymore, Blanche," he said softly.

His statement shocked her. In one instant she felt the fear of being cut off from him and the shame of relief at being released. The distress must have shown plainly on her face, for he continued quickly.

"Don't think I haven't appreciated your faithfulness," he said, almost comfortingly. "No one has ever shown me this kind of fidelity—especially now. If there is such a thing as Christian charity, you at least haven't been ashamed to visit the prisoner.

"I don't want you to come because I want to spare us both. I am selfish in this, I admit, but I want to remember you at your loveliest and happiest. I know you've tried to cheer me, to look your best and not like some woebegone widow. I also see how visiting me has worn you down. You have seen me waste away day after day. I don't want to be remembered like that—not by you of all people. Will you please honor my request?"

Blanche could no longer hold back the sadness that welled up in her. She began to cry. He reached across and took her hand. She had feared that the warmth of his touch would stir painful memories. But the cold she felt through her lace glove nearly repelled her. She was glad, but the gladness did nothing to suppress the tears.

"Please listen, Blanche. I have a request to make of you. After everything is over, I have directed my lawyer to find you and send you all my personal effects."

She shut her eyes and put her hand tightly over her mouth to keep herself from sobbing. He continued.

"Among these you will find a large ring with a crest in it. It belonged to my fiancée's father. It's the only thing among my few possessions that is not mine. She gave it to me upon our engagement. Please see that it is returned to her. I leave her to wrestle with its associations. Anything else that's left, you may keep or do with as you see fit."

She could not help the sobbing now. He waited for the flood to subside.

"If they send you to Louisiana, shall I follow you?" she offered, knowing—or rather hoping—his answer would be negative.

"No. Leave it alone, Blanche. Leave our good memories there. Don't scar them." She nodded her assent. The warmth from her fingers slowly gave his cold hand life.

"You must go now," he said.

"Can't I stay a little longer?"

He shook his head. "No. There's no point. Let's say our farewells now."

"May I send you some things—anything you might need?" she asked, nodding toward the basket.

"As you wish. Yes, it does help. But please don't bring them yourself." She nodded.

She looked toward the door at the policeman standing there.

"Officer, I'm about to leave. I'm not coming back. May I say my good-byes?"

The policeman sighed and looked to his right and to his left. He made no move to turn away, but averted his eyes.

Blanche and Tracey rose. In their embrace she felt how thin he had grown, the ripple of ribs beneath his shirt and the sharp collarbone against her cheek, but it didn't matter. She was comforted that he held her for so long, that he might regret releasing her. Then she raised her face to his and her hand to the back of his head and kissed him, not with the passion of a lover, but with an ardent esteem she felt for him now. She held the kiss for a moment and afterward leaned her forehead against his mouth and felt the auburn moustache brush her brow.

"Say my name once more," she said.

He put his hand under her chin and pulled it up gently until their eyes met.

"Go quickly now," he said. "Farewell, my dearest Blanche."

She did not resist as he urged her toward the door. The policeman unlocked it for her and closed it again with a dead clang. She did not look back, but hurried down the hallway and descended the stairs.

She was halfway to the entrance when she saw a tall veiled figure coming through the door. Blanche stopped and waited till the figure saw her. The woman approached and stood before her. Francesca lifted her veil.

"He said you'd want to come," said Blanche. She felt almost triumphant, as if she owned something this privileged woman never would. Yet this was no triumphant time. There was pain enough without heaping it upon a woman who merely wanted to make her peace. Blanche could not begrudge her that. "He doesn't want to see you."

"No. I suppose he doesn't."

"Then why come?"

"You think I shouldn't?"

"I suppose you have a right to try." Blanche sighed. "No, I suppose I can't blame you."

"You're sure he—"

"Yes, I'm sure," said Blanche. "He said he doesn't want to see you."

"He actually said as much?"

"Yes. Just now when I was there."

Tears welled up in the woman's eyes, but her voice was steady. "That's that, then," she said. "I'm actually glad to have seen you. I'd rather hear it from you than hear it from some official or embarrass Edmund with a scene that neither of us wants."

Blanche nodded.

"I'll go then," said Francesca.

Both women hesitated.

"I'm so sorry about all this—" Francesca began.

"Don't," said Blanche. "Please don't bother."

"No. No, I'm sorry."

Neither woman moved. Blanche thought the other looked a little awkward and was surprised at herself for feeling completely at her ease.

Then Francesca turned and added, "May I drop you somewhere? I have a carriage outside. . . ."

"Thank you. No," said Blanche. "Don't worry about me. I'll find my own way."

CHAPTER 37

Gallantries

❦

It is a still greater crime when a man conveys the impression that he is in love, by actions, gallantries, looks, attentions, all—except that he never commits himself—and finally withdraws his devotions, exulting in the thought that he has said or written nothing which can legally bind him.

—*Decorum,* page 184

The manservant showed no emotion as he admitted a soberly dressed, dark-haired, pale man with dark, morose eyes. The news that Edmund Tracey would be executed by a method both modern and horrific made a call on Francesca tricky at best. To present a small tribute might be appropriate or it might be thrown out after him. Resisting his homing-pigeon urge to take in Tiffany's on the way, he settled on a nosegay of hothouse roses, African violets, and ivy whose only significance lay in sentiment. Connor produced his card.

"Is Miss Lund receiving visitors this afternoon?" asked Connor.

"I will inquire, sir. Won't you step in? Shall I take those for you, sir?" the manservant said, indicating the flowers.

"No, I'll hang on to them."

The manservant gave two quick raps at the drawing-room door, pushed it open, and announced, "Mr. O'Casey, ma'am."

Momentary silence greeted this news. Braced for dismissal, Connor breathed again at the announcement, "This way, sir."

Connor surveyed the room. It was not so crammed and cluttered as in many of the houses of their peers, the walls decorated in a plainer paper with a few well-executed paintings in ornate gilt frames. He recognized the vase of flowers from that day at Venables', situated next to the fireplace. The settees, though severe, were upholstered in green. Belgian lace or tatted doilies covered the piano, tables, sideboard, chairs, and settees. Francesca's doing, no doubt.

"Mrs. Gray, Miss Lund, Miss Lawrence," said Connor with a nod to each in turn.

Esther rose, her needlework still in her hand. Vinnie, her surprise evident, remained seated. Francesca was standing with one hand on a mantelshelf crammed with photographs in silver frames. In her pale rose dress and a high neck of cream lace that blended with her hair, she nearly matched the decor of the room. The small cut high on her cheekbone, the one flaw in the otherwise perfect picture, was red and taut and made her look more vulnerable, and more defiant. He would remember this look of her forever.

"Oh, God. What do you want?" Francesca said, in a foul-humored tone Connor didn't recognize.

"I beg your pardon if I'm intruding," he began.

"We weren't expecting you, Mr. O'Casey. I apologize for my niece—"

"Don't bother apologizing, Aunt Esther," said Francesca.

"—but I agree with her that this may not be the most opportune moment for a visit."

"I realize that. It was all in the morning editions," said Connor. He extended the nosegay to Francesca. "A small balm."

"Thank you," said she, taking them from him. "Yes, every gaudy detail," she said, speaking of the papers, a trickle of venom in her voice. "I thought I had heard everything. It seems I was mistaken. Bloodhounds and leeches, all of them."

"There's nothing to be done, it seems," said Connor.

"No, there's nothing," said Francesca. She fixed her gaze on the flowers and crossed to the piano and set them upon it.

"My niece isn't well, as you can understand, Mr. O'Casey," said

Esther as she stepped forward—like the female Marquess of Queensbury laying down the rules for two pugilists. "Perhaps if you would have the decency to wait a few days before you call again."

Vinnie preempted her and rose and extended her hand. "I, for one, am glad to see you, Mr. O'Casey. I think it's very kind of you to give us a little diversion."

"Thank you, Miss Lawrence." *Bully for the referee,* thought Connor.

"Francesca tried to see him, you know," continued Vinnie.

"Lavinia," said Esther firmly. "I don't think we need burden Mr. O'Casey—"

"On the contrary, ma'am, I'm here to see if there was anything I could do, don't you know," said Connor, closing the drawing-room door behind him. Though he hated that she had made such a gesture to a man he considered a blight on humanity, he recognized that Francesca's generosity of spirit toward Edmund Tracey was the same generosity he hoped for himself. As long as this was her attitude, he couldn't very well gainsay it.

"He wouldn't have anything to do with her, I'm afraid," continued Vinnie quietly, as she cast a glance over her shoulder at Francesca.

"I'm not surprised that Miss Lund would try to see him. I'm even less surprised that he wouldn't want to see her." All three ladies reacted to his words with gestures of dismay and looks of astonishment.

"I'm afraid I have to agree with you," said Esther. "I told her it was unwise, especially now."

"But why?" protested Vinnie. "I should think he would have something to say to her after all this time."

"What would that be?" asked Connor. "To ask her forgiveness?" Vinnie's look told him he had guessed right.

"To at least express some remorse—something," Vinnie said.

"I'm afraid if a man is unaccustomed to asking for forgiveness under the best of circumstances he's not likely to ask for it when circumstances are at their worst."

Vinnie opened her mouth to protest again, but Connor continued.

"Think of it from his point of view—a man's point of view, if I may so put it. He may not have wanted her to see him that way, when all the world appears to be against him, when every hope is gone. He could be torn between wantin' to see a loved one and wantin' to spare her—and himself." Awkward that he was trying to make the man look less like a cad, now that he was as good as dead. He paused and let silence fill up the room, as if the moment had a reverence about it. "I confess I would feel that way—torn, I mean. For instance, I wish I could take back everything I ever did or said in the last few months that may have hurt or offended you. I'm me own worst enemy most of the time. I talk a lot and put off those I care about most. As for Mr. Tracey, he may feel this is the one thing left that he can still control—whether to see you or not. He's chosen to exercise that control."

"Control was certainly something he wanted—and never got," said Francesca, nearly inaudibly. *She's not crying,* Connor thought, *she's simply played out.*

"I don't mean to be unkind, Mr. O'Casey, but I really do think it would be best—" Esther began again.

"Would you like some tea, Mr. O'Casey?" interrupted Vinnie. "Won't you please sit down?"

"If you're sure I'm not intruding—" said Connor, though he remained on his feet.

"I believe you are, Mr. O'Casey."

"I think he should stay, Mrs. Gray," said Vinnie. "Mr. O'Casey means well. What do you think, Francesca? Milk and sugar, Mr. O'Casey?"

"You can't have come solely to inquire after my health," said Francesca, turning to face him. "What other subject could have caused you to make such a tasteless and unfeeling gesture as to come here at this moment? You could have had the decency—"

"Beg pardon, Frankie," said Connor. The name slipped out, easy and natural. It brought her up short. She stood still and threw him a look of—what was it? Astonishment? Puzzlement? Pain? Another moment, and the look was gone. "Decency wastes time, which I can't afford. I'd like a few moments alone with you, if I may."

"Really, Mr. O'Casey," said Esther. "I hardly think—"

"Mr. O'Casey might be a tonic—" Vinnie began.

"A tonic?" cried Esther.

"As a matter of fact, your health does concern me," said Connor to Francesca, paying Esther no mind. "I'm relieved to find you've not taken to your bed. That's a good sign."

"Is it? I wonder." Francesca dragged herself to a low overstuffed chair on the opposite side of the room and sank into it.

"Of course it is," said Connor. "You're up and about. That can only be good."

"You're not disappointed that I haven't suddenly sought consolation upon your manly breast? That I haven't swooned so that you can minister to me, wretched invalid that I am?"

"Don't talk nonsense," said Connor. "You'd prefer, I suppose, that I make you ten times the invalid you are. I don't believe that for a moment and neither do you."

"Francesca, don't make things worse with these histrionics," said Esther.

"Exactly," said Connor.

"I thought you wanted him to leave, Aunt Esther."

"I never said I thought you should be coddled," retorted Esther. "It may be the one point upon which Mr. O'Casey and I agree."

Connor relaxed and looked at Francesca.

"I do want to talk to you—" he began.

"Did you really expect a private interview, Mr. O'Casey?" asked Esther.

"Of all the barefaced impertinence," said Francesca. "All the unfeeling, stupid—"

"I do understand where this is going," said Connor.

"—unsympathetic, selfish, arrogant, insensible—"

"All right, all right, I do get your drift. But I'm not leavin' till you hear me out so you may as well simmer down. A private interview would have been preferable, but there's nothing I have to say that can't be said in company." He paused and sighed and collected his thoughts. "I want a chance with you. I'm proposing a way to find out if you can stand me. I'm proposing that I go to Banff with you."

"*What?*" said all three ladies.

"Hold on. It's not what you're thinking. I'm proposing that we travel separate-like, and that you go on and be chaperoned by your lady friends, but we'd end up in the same place. I'd get to see you. We could spend time in each other's company without all of New York breathin' down our necks."

"You must be mad." Her look at him was not unlike the look she gave him that night at the Jeromes', a knowing look—not disapproving necessarily, but calling a spade a spade.

"I know it may appear that way—"

"Appear that way, yes," she said.

"But it's the sanest thing I've ever proposed to anyone. Don't you see? Would the Jeromes ever stand to let you see me unless we had an understandin' between us? At least if I could see you in Banff we could spend some regular time together. Then, at the end of two or three months, if you think we can't make a go of it, I promise I'll leave you alone."

"Just what do you mean by 'make a go of it'?" she said.

He squared his shoulders. "Marriage."

She got up and walked to the piano, picked up the nosegay, and held it to her face, breathing deeply, unable—or perhaps unwilling—to speak. She circled the room and came back to the piano, not looking at him.

"I'm afraid my honesty hasn't gotten me very far with you up to now," he said.

"No, it hasn't, thank you very much."

"That's why I wanted to see you. To apologize—and to propose to be at Banff together, to let us start out again on a different footing. Don't you see? It really is the perfect answer." He was working up a head of steam.

"Oh, yes? For whom, you or me?"

"For both of us. We can see other daily—"

"I don't know if I can stand you daily," she cried, returning to her chair. "My entire purpose in going is to get away from everyone—which includes you, I might add. Every time I see you the encounter turns to absolute bedlam."

"Now, hold on—"

"They may as well meet me in Calgary with a straitjacket. How am I supposed to find rest? How am I supposed to find peace? You can't possibly think I can find peace with you?"

"Now, hold on there. Why not? Why not with me any less than anyone else? Not everything between us comes to ruin. We've had some good times, have we not? Well, here's the perfect way to find out whether we can have them more regular-like."

"I cannot believe what I'm hearing. Your sense of timing is positively breathtaking." Francesca's eyes were red and hard. The little furrow tightened between her brows. She leaned back in the chair, feet planted on the floor, a handkerchief clasped in one hand. She had something of the cornered animal in her. "You are the very limit. Here I am at the age of twenty-eight, standing amid the wreckage of my own life, watching as everything I ever cared about or hoped for crumbles under the weight of scandal, not knowing whom I can call friend—and you have the gall to come to me about marriage? What do you think this is, a rescue mission?" She laughed. "Or do you think that my marrying you will make up for two deaths and the misery around them?" she said distractedly. "Or is it three or four deaths? I've lost count."

"You certainly think highly of yourself, don't you, Mr. O'Casey?" said Esther.

"No, ma'am," Connor said. "It may surprise you to learn that I don't think particularly highly of any of it, nor of myself. Don't you think I wish that none of this awful business had happened to her? Don't you think that I, above all people, wish that things could have been different? That I could have come to Frankie—to Francesca, Miss Lund—as a plain, honest man from the start? That I could have offered her a reputable, honest name and a life full of beauty and culture and good works and religion and all things that she holds most dear, without the stain or blemish of scandal? Do you think I've known her all these months only to know so little about her and how little I measure up?" He turned to Francesca.

"I am what I am, Frankie. I can't help it. I wish things were different. I wish I were a better man. But that doesn't stop me from knowing I'm the best man for you."

She glared at him.

"You are the absolute limit, aren't you?"

"So I understand."

"So," said Francesca, "you have no decency, you're arrogant, insufferable—"

"Yes, you needn't cover that ground again."

"You have no sense of romance, have you, Mr. O'Casey?" Vinnie chimed in.

"Romance? What the hell has romance got to do with anything? Holy Mother of God, woman, what I'm offering your friend is a perfectly good, reasonable proposition—"

"*Proposition?*" all three women said in chorus.

"Will you please do me the courtesy of hearing me out?" They were silent.

"Look at your choices, Frankie. You are, as you say, fairly swimmin' in a sea of scandal. You've been taken in by a man who's a crook and a murderer, which proves to all the world that you are an ignorant, vulnerable female—"

"But Mr. O'Casey—" Vinnie broke in. He raised a hand against the onslaught.

"Do you think no one will talk about you while you're away frolicking in the Rockies? You'll be a social pariah when you get back to New York, not to put too fine a point on it. If the Jeromes haven't died of apoplexy, you'll likely get the tongue-lashing of your life before society snubs you altogether, they and all their church-going friends."

"Really, Mr. O'Casey, I must protest," objected Esther.

"And don't bother to tell me how they'll stand by you in your time of need. I've seen needier and worthier than you dropped like hot potatoes by better people than the Jeromes."

"Of all the barefaced—" said Francesca.

"You'll either end up an old maid or fall prey to a marriage to any one of a dozen thrill-seekers who thrive on scandal and aren't worth a bean. Even genuine lords, no matter how poor, won't give you the time of day. So what'll you do? Slink back to the settlement to live out your days in endless charity?"

"What's wrong with that?" Francesca said.

"Not a thing—for ordinary women," said Connor with enthusiasm. "But it's not good enough for you. Why not come back to New York with a bang? Nobody'd expect you to come back married, or even engaged. If you're going to scandalize your precious society, do a proper job of it. Marriage to me would be the best shock of all. The murder of Nell Ryder would be chicken feed compared to the bodies of swooning women lining the streets of New York over that one. People can talk behind their hands all they want, but they wouldn't dare say anything to your face. Things might be a bit warm for a while—"

"*A bit warm?*" Esther interjected.

Again, Connor raised arresting hands.

"They'll cool off fast enough, once we get back from the honeymoon and you start your music charity and picking up your life. I can help you with that. We can come in together, fighting. The miscreant and the madwoman. You can be a scrappy thing, when you set your mind to it. We can brazen it out together and choose a place for ourselves that suits us. And as to the romance?" said Connor with a nod to Vinnie. "If romance is what you want, Francesca Lund, I'll romance you the likes of which you can't begin to imagine."

Vinnie raised a hand to her lips as if to suppress delight. Esther was silent. Francesca managed a smile. She shook her head. Then a little puff of laughter burst from her lips.

"Now what's so funny about that? You don't think I can do it, do you? Well, I assure you, woman, that Connor O'Casey will be unmatched in the romance department."

"You think so?"

"I know so."

"I think so, too," said Vinnie with a smile. Then catching the eyes of the other two ladies, she amended her remark. "Francesca's right. You are the very limit."

Connor strode across to Francesca's chair and knelt in front of her, pinning her down, his hip against her knee, his arms resting on hers, his face thrust toward her face.

"What would *you* rather be? Strong and good and brave, or an object of pity?"

"They'd pity me with you."

"Perhaps so," he sighed. "But they'd pity you all the more for never having had, never having experienced, never having known. Or maybe by now they think you know all there is to know anyway. So, to hell with it.

"And what of yourself? Will you not pity yourself in the end? Will you not regret? Have done with regrets, Frankie, and move on. Do you want your mountaintops? Have them, I'll not stand in your way—and your music and art and ideals, and children and a home. I want those, too."

Francesca pushed him away. "Stop bullying me. Do you think I want a lifetime of bullying? I'm too tired to think. I'm weary to the bone. Why come here now? I can't stop you from doing what you want to and haunting me in Banff. I don't know what I want anymore—except that I want to be left alone."

No legal mind could have parsed an answer so skillfully, thought Connor. She had not rejected him outright, but left him an opening that preserved all sense of decorum. Through that tiny opening he would drive a westward train to Banff.

"So I must wait? How long?"

"I don't know."

"I can't wait forever, Frankie, and neither can you. Time's awasting for us both. So, let me give you a little something to ponder: Would you prefer to spend your life known as the Poor Miss Lund, to wend your way to a decorous and respectable old age, to be pitied by all? Or would you rather revel in the grand and glorious splendor of being known as the Notorious Mrs. O'Casey?"

CHAPTER 38

An Habitual Self-Control

༄྅ৎ

Cautiousness, and the check of an habitual self-control, should accompany the mind of every one who launches out in animated conversation. When the fancy is heated, and the tongue has become restless through exercise, and there is either a single listener or a circle, to reward display, nothing but resolute self-recollection can prevent the utterance of much that had better been left unsaid.

—*Decorum*, page 230

The shock of Connor's declaration, coupled with days of inactivity forced by blustery weather, drove Francesca out of doors on the pretext of a walk for Chalk and Coal.

"You'd best go out the back, miss," said John, helping her on with her coat. "There've been a couple of reporter fellows hanging around the front most of the day."

She was redirecting the dogs to the back of the house when the bell rang. The riot of barking ensued as John opened the door to find Maggie Jerome.

"How are you, John?"

"Very well, Mrs. Jerome, thank you."

An encounter with the press would have been more inviting

than a call from Maggie. She had bothered Francesca very little since Edmund's arrest, sending messages through Jerry or by hand.

"How are you, dearie? I didn't sleep a wink last night—for the past several nights really. I thought perhaps we might have a little chat," Maggie offered tentatively as she took off her gloves. "But don't let me interrupt if you and Esther have plans."

"She's gone up for a little nap, as a matter of fact."

"Oh, I'm sorry, dearie, were you going out?"

"Just to take the dogs for some exercise."

"I'll stay and supervise tea. I can have it ready when Esther wakes up. It'll be nice for a change, just like I used to do for you." She unpinned her hat.

"Yes, why don't you. I won't be long."

What unbelievable timing, thought Francesca as the door closed behind her. God was punishing her by sending an angel of retribution for even contemplating involving herself with Connor O'Casey. There they would be, she and Esther and Maggie, drinking tea and talking—Francesca in agony lest she spill the news, relying heavily on Esther's calm demeanor and diplomacy. Unless they could direct the conversation, Francesca would have to prepare to meet the terrible swift sword of Maggie Jerome. Well, so be it.

Lost in thought, Francesca lingered while Coal and Chalk investigated every wall, fence, tree, and shrub, not realizing how much ground they had covered. When she came to herself, she realized she was headed in the direction of Jerry's office. What time was it? Jerry might still be there. She picked up her pace, the dogs happily panting at her side. Without thinking, she transferred both leashes to one hand and with the other hailed a cab. A moment later, Francesca and Coal and Chalk were piled into a hansom and whisked away to the Merchants and Mechanics Bank.

It was bad enough to explain how a lady with two large dogs had bolted past every line of the bank's defenses, disrupted transactions at teller windows, and arrived, all three panting, at the desk of Jerry's secretary and demanded to see him. How she would explain the arrangement with Connor O'Casey was another matter.

"You've *what?*"

"I know. I know." Francesca sank into a chair, the dogs lying at her feet. "I can't very well stop him from going where he wants."

"Have you lost your senses completely?! How on earth could you agree to this harebrained scheme? Do you know what kind of man he is—what kind of reputation he has?"

"Apparently good enough for you to engage him as a business partner."

"That's beside the point and you know it, Francesca. What about that Alvarado woman?"

"He's assured me that it's over between them."

"And you believe him?"

"I have no reason not to."

"You have several million reasons. I didn't even know he was interested in you."

"Nor did I. Not really. I believe he wants to see if we can make a go of it." The whole thing sounded ridiculous, even to her own ears.

"Make a go of it? Go of what? Is that his idea of a proposal?"

"Apparently," said Francesca. Jerry began to protest. "Yes, Jerry, it was his way of proposing. And before you ask, yes, he did use the word *marriage*." She couldn't remember having actually uttered the word *yes* in answer. Could she really have consented to such a thing? Perhaps she was mad after all. Her head was beginning to throb.

"Do you have any idea how this looks—for either of you? Here is a very worldly man who has just shed himself of a, a, a strumpet. Here you are, having just been taken in by a man who turns out to be a gigolo and a murderer, and you think that the two of you can simply sail off into the sunset—"

"We're going by railroad." She cracked a smile.

"Don't be impertinent. You think you can leave all the cares and opinions of the world behind and never have to face society again? You think you won't be vilified up one side and down the other?"

"I know it looks dreadful."

"*Dreadful?* Is that all you can say?"

"I could say more if I could get a word in." She felt oddly at peace in the eye of Jerry's storm. The plain language and concern for her welfare were comforting somehow—so unlike what she might expect from Maggie and her formulaic approach to decorum. After the initial tirade, he went to the window, unlatched the shutter and pulled it back, and looked out into the street.

"Yes, I know how it looks," said Francesca. "I can't say why I have the least bit of faith in him, except that he didn't seem to be making promises he wasn't willing to keep. He didn't say he loves me. And while we're on the subject, no, I don't love him. Don't you think his intentions would be far more suspicious if he came to me protesting love? I know full well a man like that doesn't change overnight—if at all. There may be something in what he says about our wanting many of the same things. It seems I might have a better chance of being happy with someone who can be honest about it, with or without love."

"I wanted better for you," said Jerry, still staring out the window.

"Better isn't good enough, Jerry. I want the best. Who, of all the men you know, is best for me? Name three. No, no, name two, or even one. You can't, can you? Who is to say that in the end Connor O'Casey might not be the best? He wants a chance. So do I. He's the only man I've ever known to be forthright about it and to respect my feelings, in his own bluff way, and to offer me a respectable way out."

Jerry was calmer now. "You sound resolved to do this."

"Let's simply say that I believe I have the right to change my mind, though I think it would be much easier, much better, to take the chance and let God direct things. Human interference has certainly availed me nothing up to now."

"Do you want me to go with you?"

Nothing Jerry could have offered would have sounded more appalling than Banff with the Jeromes.

"Don't be silly. Esther and Vinnie will be enough. If I need you I can wire."

"What'll we do about Maggie?" Jerry asked, sounding weary.

"Well, you'll have the perfect chance to find out. How would you like to take me home to tea?"

* * *

"I wondered how long it'd be before you showed up," said Connor, standing in the doorway. "Come in."

Jerry decided to forgo tea and Maggie and headed for Connor's hotel. Francesca's revelation—and her consent, however passive—had left him stunned and perplexed. He liked Connor, the way one likes an underdog. Often Jerry spoke up for him, urging and cajoling others into giving the poor blighter a chance. Connor's admirable persistence and guts had enabled him to rise from nothing to a position that accorded him, if not respect, at least envy. He understood Connor's aspiration to shrug off the mantle of an outcast and acquire the tastes and refinements of the social set to which he aspired. Above all, he understood Connor's desire to ally himself with a woman of intelligence, talent, beauty, and wealth who could help him move easily in society. When the object of that desire was Francesca, however, all Jerry's noble biases flew out the window and Connor was reduced to the image of the brash, uneducated, unrefined, papist hooligan his friend was trying so desperately to shake off.

Jerry's own hypocrisy alarmed him. His father had come from stock no more refined than Connor's, and his father hadn't Connor's desire to become self-taught. He was proud of the rugged individualism, however coarse, that made his father self-made. The harangues with Maggie over occasions where his father might embarrass had hurt Jerry deeply.

Oh, God—Maggie. Maggie, who had protected the family honor for their thirty years together, would make life hell for Francesca over this arrangement with Connor. Until this moment he hadn't understood her revulsion toward his father, pulling Jerry further and further away from his influence—and his love. Jerry now felt a similar revulsion at the idea of Francesca's marrying this man who drank, swore, fought, cheated, and was far too wealthy for his own good, who had no religion, principles, or scruples. He was ashamed to discover that he couldn't decide which of the two of them, Jerry or Maggie, was the more noble—Jerry, with his high-minded favoritism of the underdog, who found that his principles couldn't hold water, or Maggie, who was so damnably consistent.

Connor left Jerry to shut the door while he walked to the side-board to pour himself a drink. He held out the decanter and raised his eyebrows.

"No, thanks," said Jerry. He started to make for the settee, then turned. "On second thought, make it a double."

"So," said Connor. "Out with it."

Jerry sat, still wearing his coat and hat. "I don't know what to say. I couldn't believe my ears when Francesca told me. What the hell are you thinking of, proposing to expose a woman whom you profess to want to marry to the kind of scheme that could ruin her?" He took off the hat and plopped it on the settee. "Have I failed to grasp the situation? Did you not go to Francesca and suggest that you follow her to Banff so that you and she can 'get to know one another' to find out whether she could stand you enough to marry you?" Jerry was on his feet. "Whom do you think you're dealing with, man? Do you think she's the kind of woman who indulges in sordid intrigues? What can you think will happen to her reputation while you and she are 'getting to know one another'? Do you think I'd let her do a thing like that? And Maggie—oh, my God—would probably have you shot. And what about this Alvarado woman? Do you expect me to believe that after all that show and all that talk about Italy and that indecent, yes, indecent, way that she so obviously laid claim to you, that any of us can possibly believe that you and she are through?"

Connor, who was still standing at the sideboard, now and then taking a drink, turned quietly and faced Jerry.

"Might I answer some of these charges?"

Jerry took the whiskey that had been poured for him and took a long drink.

"Did I make such a request of her? Yes. Did I propose to marry her if she could stand me? Yes. Do I understand the position I'm puttin' her in all the way round? Of course I do." He set the whiskey decanter back on the sideboard and paused and blew out an exasperated sigh. "Why do you think I proposed marriage outright? So's she'd have some assurance that marriage is a choice for her if the opinion of the society that you're so pitifully tied to should go against her. So's she wouldn't be left high and dry."

"Why Francesca in the first place?"

"Why not Francesca?" demanded Connor. "Why should I not aspire to someone of her quality? Why am I not entitled to the same desires for a respectable home presided over by a woman that a man would be proud to have as queen of his castle?" Connor set down his glass and leaned upon the sideboard. "What the hell am I talking to you for? You and your pious—you know, Blanche was right about you. You're a sanctimonious bunch of bastards." Connor downed the contents of the glass.

"Do you have any idea what it's like to be on the outside lookin' in? Do you know what it's like to peep through the keyhole, and to watch people feastin' and fattenin' themselves, and know that you don't have the key that will let you in? Do you have any idea what it's like to spend your whole life hammering on the door and to not have anyone who'll answer? And what about Francesca? She's no better off than I am."

"Just what the hell do you mean by that?"

"You've got her trussed up good and proper. She can't move without your permission or approval. I'll wager this Banff business is just as much to get away from you and your wife as it is for a pleasure tour. You dandle her in front of people like a Christmas ornament. You wind her up and set her out to perform, then carefully wrap her in tissue or put her under a bell jar for everyone to admire. You don't really give a damn about her except to find her a husband that you pious lot can approve of."

"That's not true and you know—"

"What the hell were you pushing her off on that bastard Tracey for then?"

"That was Maggie's doing, not mine." Jerry was in no mood to defend Maggie. A pang of guilt gripped him as he wondered if things might have been different had he shared Shillingford's discoveries. No, Maggie wouldn't have believed him anyway.

"Or maybe a bastard great-grandson of an English lord, God help us," continued Connor, "who'd have swept her off and left her bankrupt. Or some damn rich fool whose whole family hasn't a worthwhile thought among 'em, who'd bore her senseless. None of them would ever understand what she's made of."

"And you do, I suppose."

"Yes, I do," Connor said emphatically. "I understand her better than the whole lot of you—and do you know why? Because in the end, we want the same things—to build something that lasts. A name, a family, a reputation. Not just a business or your damned luxury hotel. Businesses can be bought and sold and hotels can be torn down."

"Reputations can be bought and sold—and torn down," said Jerry.

"But family and name and doin' something good that lasts can't. If you've got that, you can keep your damned feasts. You can bolt the door for all I care—but the door is bolted for her just as surely as it's bolted for me. Maybe not for the same reasons. She has things I'll never have and I've gotten things she'll never be able to get on her own. But the door is bolted for her all the same. Maybe we can unbolt it—or beat it down together."

"Why do you want to be one of us if we're such pious, pompous asses?"

"Sometimes I ask myself that very question. I see how you squeeze people dry, or crush them under your feet, or worse, pretend they're not there. For all their faults poor people can be nobler than you'll ever be."

"I know," said Jerry, looking into the bottom of his glass. "If you want Francesca so badly, why not court her openly here?"

"If we conduct even the properest courtship here, we're doomed before we start. You people smother her and treat her like a child. She's trying to use the brains she was born with, to experience something of life—"

"That's what I'm afraid of."

"What would you have me do, show up unannounced and say, 'Excuse me, ma'am, but I was just in the neighborhood and thought I'd pop in for a spot of scandal?'—which I could have done, by the way. Look, I've made her an honest offer of marriage. She can accept me or reject me. All I've asked is that she not reject me out of hand without our getting to know each other. This Banff business is the perfect way to do the least damage to her reputation. At least if we're engaged by the time we get back to New

York, nobody'll have the pleasure of gossiping without a ring on Francesca's finger."

"You still haven't answered my question about Mrs. Alvarado."

"Do you think I put the two of them in the same class? Blanche isn't fit to polish Francesca's boots. Yes, it's over with Blanche. I sent her packing the night of the dinner at Sherry's. I've bought her passage to Italy and supplied her with money so she can go and leech off her sister."

"Oh, God," said Jerry. He drained his glass. "How do I know—how does Francesca know—that that kind of business is over?"

"She doesn't. Nor does any woman when she gets married—or any man, come to that." Connor poured himself another drink, then crossed to Jerry with the decanter. "Would you like to know where half the married men in this town go of an evenin'?" Connor poured. "It might prove quite informative for you to accompany me some night and watch outside selected small hotels and see who the clientele might be."

"I don't want that for Francesca."

"Nor do I. Nor do I want it for myself. I'm tired. I've had enough. I just want *her.*"

"What on earth do you expect her to see in you?"

"I don't know. Maybe nothing. Maybe everything. Maybe I'm not what she wants, but maybe I'm what she needs. Just like she's what I need."

Jerry hesitated. "You haven't said that you love her."

"I'm not sure I know what 'love' means—and I wouldn't profane the word by using it amiss with Francesca." He drank. "Do I appreciate her for her intelligence, her ideas? Yes. Do I appreciate her for her talents? Yes. Do I appreciate her for her gentleness and her heart and her soul? Yes. Do I agree with her religion and her mountaintops and her miracles? Probably not, at least not the religion and I don't understand her mountaintops. But I hope I'm not so stupid that I don't realize that without those things Francesca wouldn't be Francesca."

Jerry didn't know what to say or think. To give his blessing was out of the question and he had no power to say no. A negative answer would only add fuel to Connor's fire.

"I don't know what I'll tell Maggie."

"Why tell her anything?"

"She'll find out sooner or later. And she'll give Francesca hell before she leaves."

Not knowing what else to do, Jerry prepared to depart. He stood for a moment, running his hand around the brim of his hat, thinking. He looked Connor in the eye. "If you ruin her, if you leave her to face a damaged reputation alone, if you make one false promise or one false move, if you harm one hair on her head, as God is my witness, Connor, I will hunt you down, I will find you, and I will kill you. So help me God, I'll kill you."

CHAPTER 39

Charades

◈

*There is no game that can afford so much amusement to
a circle of friends as that of acting charades. It affords a
scope for the exercise of both wit and ingenuity.*

—*Decorum*, page 357

"Our researches haven't been as thorough as they might be," ventured Connor one day after an investors' meeting. Everyone had left but Jerry Jerome and John Ashton Worth.

"How do you mean?" asked Worth. Jerry shot Connor a quizzical look.

"I mean, we haven't really looked at the competition properly, have we?" He drew his notebook from his breast pocket and began to thumb through the pages.

"The competition?" asked Jerry. "I think we're quite familiar with most of the best hotels in New York—best for the moment, that is. We're familiar with their service and amenities. There's the omnipresent notebook"—he gestured toward Connor—"that gives us plenty of particulars on that score. By the way, how many notebooks does this make it? Five?"

"Seven," said Connor, unperturbed.

"Seven. Precisely. We've certainly found out as much as is humanly possible about what the Vanderbilts are up to—and whom they're scared of and why. And we know what we're after—simply the best apartment hotel New York has to offer. You've been the biggest proponent of the Louis XV business, the decoration and all."

"Yes, yes," said Connor. "But have we really looked into how a truly modern hotel is run nowadays? Since we have the luxury of startin' at scratch as we are."

"I suppose you have a point there," agreed Mr. Worth. "We won't have had to wire an existing building for electricity, if that's the kind of thing you mean. We'll have the advantage of the latest plumbing and elevators and such."

"But don't you think it goes a bit beyond elevators and plumbing? Don't you think we should scout out some of the newer places, see what they've got goin' that the payin' public is excited about and see if we can improve upon it?"

"Surely, it's only wise to expand our horizons," Jerry agreed. "The Sacher in Vienna is magnificent, I understand. It's new and has everything a man could hope for or knows where to get it."

"Isabel would love it, but I confess we'd easily become bogged down, what with her passion for collecting."

"We still must look for those Louis XV rooms," said Jerry.

"Vienna's all well and good," retorted Connor, "and certainly the Sacher would cater to the same kind of clientele we mean to attract. But Louis XV or no Louis XV, we should offer a hotel that's distinctly American in service and modern convenience with the comforts of an established European hotel."

"So we should be looking on this continent for our inspiration?" asked Jerry.

"It bears investigating. It seems to me that the uniqueness of a grand American hotel should be the draw—no matter where the clientele may come from. If we don't go further afield in this country, we may be overlookin' something that could be just what people are lookin' for. I'm sure we can improve on what somebody else has thought of."

"Hmm," said Mr. Worth, beginning to gleam. "You mean perhaps we should choose a few select places on this side of the Atlantic and pay a visit? Check in as guests and put their service to the test? That's certainly an idea."

"San Francisco is booming in construction with somethin' new goin' up all the time," said Connor.

"I myself wouldn't mind seeing what Flagler's been up to in Florida," put in Jerry. "Sounds like he means to take a god-forsaken place and turn it into a paradise and not unlike what you describe."

This was the opening Connor was looking for. "Now you're talkin'," he said, sitting up straight and inching to the edge of his leather chair. "A paradise in the wilderness, an oasis in the desert. Perhaps that's the way we should be lookin' at this hotel."

"I'd hardly call New York a desert," Mr. Worth observed.

"You might, if you're looking for an exclusive place to call home for a few weeks."

"Is there someplace in particular you were thinking of?" said Mr. Worth.

"There are a handful of excellent possibilities. Jerome's suggestion of Florida's a good one—and San Francisco. There's that place in Michigan, up on an island somewhere, a really grand place, or so they say. That's it—the Grand Hotel."

"San Francisco is hardly a wasteland either," said Jerry.

"And therefore a good prospect," Connor agreed, to smooth the way, "being much like our situation here in New York. There's St. Louis. St. Louis may not be New York, but being a major cross-roads it sees a lot of hotel trade, though maybe not of the apartment variety we're talking of. It bears lookin' into."

"And?" asked Jerry, awakening to Connor's drift.

"Well, Canada is in much the same fix as we," said Connor, avoiding Jerry's glare. "They've got their big cities in Toronto and Montreal. Upper-class people must sleep somewhere when they pay a visit. The Canadian Pacific Railroad is sinkin' a lot of money into makin' the hotels on the line some of the best. Take this Banff place that Miss Lund is headin' for."

Jerry looked ready to shoot Connor.

"I know I made fun of the place when she first introduced the subject, but I've been lookin' into it and her choice may not be so far-fetched as I thought."

"You mean you're admitting error?" teased Mr. Worth. "Mark this down, Jerry. A red-letter day."

"I certainly will," said Jerry, none too happy.

Connor ignored them both. "Cornelius Van Horn's been able to make that place the envy of any Continental hotel. The Banff Springs is drawing clientele from all over the world—and doin' it in the middle of the wilderness, I might add. Makin' the wilderness itself an attraction from what I hear, the town not having much to speak of as yet. Chargin' three dollars and fifty cents a room *per day*—and gettin' it, too." Jerry and Mr. Worth exchanged glances. "At those prices they must have something to offer. Same idea with Flagler in Florida. Florida'd be just the place for you and Maggie, Jerome." Connor smiled at Jerry. Jerry glared back. "The perfect place for you to investigate."

"I don't know if I could persuade Isabel to a trip to San Francisco," Mr. Worth went on innocently. "Her biases are so strongly European. Mediterranean, to be precise. Then again, she is the adventurous type. She may surprise me."

"Then the three of us have chosen the far corners of the continent. If we can persuade Calloway, Gage, and Monroe to pursue three other places, we should have an excellent feel for what we're after."

"Perhaps I should be the one heading to Canada," said Jerry.

"You've already expressed an interest in Florida," Connor retorted.

"Canada would have no appeal for Isabel. You can have San Francisco if you want, Jerry," said Mr. Worth, musing. "Maggie may enjoy it more. You do mean to take Maggie, don't you? I can't see leaving Isabel at home. She might be persuaded to go to Florida."

"She'd be an asset in any case," said Connor. "She's good at pouring oil on troubled social waters, not to mention her eye for decoration."

"I'll tell her you said so. She'll appreciate that."

"Nothing's settled, John." Jerry's voice was gaining an unusual edge. "Connor just foisted this scheme on us and you practically have us packed and on the next train."

"Foisted? That's a bit strong. I suppose I have been carried away by your enthusiasm, O'Casey. It is a sound idea, though. No one ever said that hotel building had to be dull. I think we're free to choose our own perquisites. Personally, I think we can all do with a little fun. These last few months have been trying, especially for you and Maggie. It would do you good to get away."

"I'm not disagreeing. I was merely suggesting that because I practically have family going to Banff that I might make the sacrifice and go along."

"It might do you and Maggie some good to be going in a different direction from Miss Lund," said Mr. Worth. "You've practically been living on top of each other since February."

Thank God that remark came from a more disinterested quarter, thought Connor.

"Whose side are you on, John?" Jerry was growing testy.

"Call it enlightened self-interest. You could do with a break. This kind of break would be productive for the hotel and relaxing for you and Maggie."

"I'd be happy to look after the ladies while I'm there, Jerome." Again Connor smiled. "Just as you might yourself. You needn't worry."

"That's easier said than done," Jerry mumbled as he passed Connor.

"There, you see, Jerry. What could be easier?" said Mr. Worth.

CHAPTER 40

Small Concessions

❦

Before dismissing this part of our subject, we beseech you to avoid all bickering. What does it signify where a picture hangs, or whether a rose or a pink looks best on the drawing-room table? There is something inexpressibly endearing in small concessions, in gracefully giving up a favorite opinion, or in yielding to the will of another; and equally painful is the reverse. The mightiest rivers have their source in streams; the bitterest domestic misery has often arisen from some trifling difference of opinion.

—*Decorum*, page 204

"Mr. Jerome's party," said Esther to the maître d' as a small string ensemble struck up an air. The Café Savarin glowed in welcoming honey tones of white mahogany woodwork. Marble-top tables were crowned with shallow dishes of yellow crocuses that breathed spring into the light-filled main café. The somber winter fashions were giving way to green, violet, and blue with ornaments of flowers, feathers, and ribbons.

"I don't remember Jerry ever possessing such a sheepish look," she whispered to Francesca as Jerry saw them and waved.

"Good gracious, there's Maggie," Francesca said as Maggie turned and acknowledged them with a nod. "I thought we were lunching alone with Jerry. Neither of them looks very happy. It could very well be that she knows."

"So she should," said Esther. "I don't approve of secrets between husbands and wives. Jerry has a perfect right to preserve his domestic life above any consideration he has for you, you know." Francesca merely sighed. "Nevertheless, we should assume nothing and follow Jerry's lead. Since there has never been any love lost between Maggie and me, that look of disapproval may be entirely for my benefit."

The maître d' gathered up the leather-bound menus and led the ladies through the labyrinth of tables as if parading violet and lavender flowers toward the far side of the room. The tap of Esther's walking stick upon the marble floor awakened the curiosity of a succession of onlookers.

Jerry rose, looking more like his amiable self, his smile spreading. He extended a hand to Esther and gave her a family kiss on the cheek before pulling out her chair for her while the maître d' seated Francesca and handed them menus. Maggie merely nodded.

"How are you, Maggie?" said Esther, when no further greeting was forthcoming.

"As well as can be expected, thank you, Esther," said Maggie, perusing the open menu before her.

Francesca cast a furtive look across the table at Esther, whose attention was directed toward soups, hors d'oeuvres, and fish.

"Oh?" said Esther. "I thought perhaps you looked a little peaky. I hope the dinner party didn't upset you. I thought it was rather fine myself, didn't you, Jerry?"

"Yes, indeed," he said.

"We were sorry we couldn't join you for a nightcap afterward, weren't we, Francesca?" Esther said. "But I'm afraid I'm still not quite used to such a press of social engagements."

"I should think it will be a little easier at the Banff Springs," said Francesca. "With the convenience of social engagements and recreation in and about the Springs and being able to retire at any time."

"I certainly hope so, dear. How's the beef Marseillaise, Jerry?"

"You missed a very enlightening time, didn't they, Jerry?" said Maggie. "I'm sure I wouldn't have missed it for the world."

"Excellent," said Jerry to Esther.

"Oh, how so?" asked Esther.

"I believe it's the way the pan is seasoned," said Jerry.

"I'm sorry, Jerry. I meant the enlightening time that Maggie referred to." Francesca caught Esther's eye this time, but the latter placidly ignored the distress signals Francesca exchanged with Jerry.

"It seems you'll have your hands full, Esther," retorted Maggie. "Mr. O'Casey has decided to take himself off to Banff—just like that. I can't imagine what could have given him the idea, especially since he made such fun of it only a few months ago."

"I suppose the man may amuse himself wherever he chooses," said Esther.

"He certainly could have been more considerate by choosing to go somewhere else for his amusements, as you call them," said Maggie.

"He is going for the sake of the Excelsior," interjected Jerry. "It doesn't follow that all business has to be hard labor."

"Perhaps not. But anyone, however loosely connected with our family affairs, should not be imposing himself upon Esther and Francesca—especially Francesca."

"Can you recommend a Bordeaux to go with the beef, Jerry?" asked Esther. "You act as if you think a powder keg is about to detonate beneath us, Maggie," she continued. "I'm sure there will be plenty of other people in Banff to occupy his attention and ours."

"He will only be a problem if we allow him to become one," said Francesca.

"Well, Jerry, perhaps for safety's sake you and I should join the ladies," said Maggie.

"To do what? Police the corridors?" asked Francesca with a touch of sarcasm.

"Calm yourself, dear," said Esther, "and please lower your voice. If we all keep our heads and mind our own business, everything should come off well. Transplanting the entire family three thousand miles to occupy closer quarters than Manhattan Island might well be a greater folly. What on earth should we do to keep from living in each other's pockets while we're all in a single hotel in the Canadian Rockies? Pitch tents by the Bow River?"

"Really," returned Maggie, indignant.

"How well I remember your ability to get straight to the point, Esther," said Jerry. "Not that I object, you understand. I certainly get enough of it around the women I know"—here he looked at Maggie and Francesca—"so you might say I'm used to it. The degree of tact varies considerably—something I know I don't have to worry about with you."

"That was a tactful move in itself, Jerry." Esther unfolded the linen napkin and placed it in her lap. "Besides, it isn't as if he's going to marry my niece, is it?" Both Jerry and Francesca looked daggers at Esther. "I could do with an aperitif. How about you?"

CHAPTER 41

Reserve and Discretion

❦

It is impossible to dwell too strongly upon the importance of reserve and discretion on the part of ladies traveling alone. They may, as has been already said, accept slight services courteously proffered by strangers, but any attempt at familiarity must be checked, and this with all the less hesitation that no gentleman will be guilty of such familiarity; and a lady wants only gentlemen for her acquaintances.

—*Decorum*, page 142

"They're here," cried Vinnie, peering out the front-parlor window as she pinned her plain hat of Panama straw with its zigzag ribbon and smoothed the front of her smart new traveling suit. The parlor was aflutter. Anne and Mrs. Lawrence tallied the last of the hand luggage in the front hallway as Michael carried it down from Vinnie's room.

As the carriages pulled up in front of the parsonage, Mr. Lawrence walked down the front steps to greet them. Two carriages and a cab there were to take them to Grand Central Terminal. Francesca and Esther alighted from the first carriage and May and Rosemary from the cab and accompanied him into the house.

"I have such butterflies," said Vinnie as she greeted Francesca.

"I can't believe the day has actually come. You both look so elegant. Goodness. We shall be ever so grand." Francesca's smart steely blue-gray suit, Esther's Copenhagen blue, and her own soft light brown would surely make them the most noticeable—and envied—trio on the platform.

"You're not nervous, are you, dear?" asked Esther as she kissed Vinnie on the cheek.

"Good gracious, you're flushed. Are you quite all right?" Francesca removed a glove and touched the back of her hand to Vinnie's forehead and then her cheek.

"She's perfectly fine," chided Mrs. Lawrence cheerfully. "She's only worked herself into her usual stew. Gracious, she hasn't stopped chattering since dawn—and this after being up half the night packing and repacking and frightening us half to death that she had forgotten something."

"I should think that's a good sign, then," said Esther.

"Yes," chimed in Michael. "If you should ever get total silence from Vin, you'd better send for the doctor."

"I should think with all the lists you've made you should have been able to keep track of *something*," chided Anne with a smile.

"Yes, but I kept crossing things out and adding things in until I couldn't read the lists and then I'd make new lists and not be able to remember why I had crossed things off the old lists. Then I had to pull everything out of the trunks to remind me of what I thought I was taking in the first place and had to start over."

"Did you bring your—" began Esther.

"Don't mention a thing, please, Mrs. Gray," interrupted Mrs. Lawrence, "even in jest. I was never so glad to see Harry take those trunks to the station where she can't touch them. It was all I could do to restrain her from going with May and Rosemary to Mr. Worth's private car yesterday to make sure everything was in order."

"It isn't as if I do this every day," said Vinnie. "Once we get past Winnipeg there really won't be anyplace to get something I may have forgotten."

"Let's make haste, Lavinia," said Mr. Lawrence. "We can't keep Francesca and Mrs. Gray waiting."

"Would you give us a blessing, please, Mr. Lawrence?" asked Francesca, catching May before she could go out the door with Vinnie's last bag.

"Of course," he said. "I would have proposed it if you had not."

The anticipation was palpable as the entire party assembled in the parlor. The early June sun streamed warm and comforting through the lace curtains of the front picture window and brightened even the somber black horsehair and dark oak of the Lawrences' parlor. Peace equal to the anticipation descended as Mr. Lawrence enjoined them to bow their heads.

"Almighty and everlasting God," he began, "we thank Thee for the great love shown to us through Thy many blessings of health, home, friendship, and family. We ask that we would be ever mindful of Thy great love and care for us wherever we may be and of Thy great call that we extend Thy love and care to others. We ask that Thou wouldst bless these Thy servants—Esther, Francesca, Lavinia, May, and Rosemary—on this long sojourn. Protect and keep them, we pray, that they may be gentle as lambs and wise as serpents and may return to us whole and happy. In the name of our Lord and Savior Jesus Christ."

A collective "amen" broke the stillness.

"Maybe I should check my room one last time," said Vinnie, making for the stairs.

"Enough, Lavinia." Mrs. Lawrence blocked her path. Vinnie smiled at her mother's hasty glance around the parlor in spite of herself.

The party sorted itself into the two carriages—Esther, Michael, and Anne in the first carriage, and Francesca, Vinnie, and her parents in the second.

"I must admit," said Mr. Lawrence when they were settled, "I feel quite as if I were going to Banff myself. Always exciting to see people off to interesting places."

"I can't wait for you to see Mr. Worth's varnish," said Vinnie. "It's stunning. Our own little luxury home on the rail for five days."

"You won't want to come home to us, I fear," said Mrs. Lawrence. "We shall have to come and visit you on the siding at Grand Central."

"Mr. Worth has shown you a great kindness," Mr. Lawrence said to Francesca, "and a great consideration for the safety of three ladies"—a point to which his wife assented with a nod. "Will you take your meals in your carriage, or will you eat in the dining car?"

"We may do either," said Francesca. "I suppose it will depend on how much we will be in need of company other than ourselves over five days."

"Or what we look like first thing in the morning," said Vinnie with a laugh.

"I hope you won't give up a civilized toilette altogether, Lavinia," said her mother in mocking dismay. "I realize there is such a thing as letting one's hair down, but have a little mercy on people, for goodness' sake."

"We're going hiking and driving and taking in ever such a lot of activity out of doors, aren't we, Francesca?" Vinnie retorted.

"I hope so," said Francesca. "I'm looking forward to wearing holes in my boots from the long walks."

"Well, for everyone's sake I hope the Banff Springs Hotel has ample hot water," said Mr. Lawrence.

When the carriages finally set down their charges, Francesca, Esther, the Lawrences, and the maids threaded their way through the travelers, porters, railway workers, fruit and flower sellers, newsboys, and handcarts. As they approached the platform, the slick, immense Prussian blue varnish came into view with its gleaming black trim and the gold and black lettering of the Worths' crest and the private car's moniker CAPRICE. Just at the steps of the varnish's doorway stood Mr. and Mrs. Worth, smiling broadly and waving welcome, an attendant with his passenger list standing with them.

"How very dear of you to come and see the ladies off," said Mrs. Lawrence, extending her hand to Mr. and Mrs. Worth in turn. "We must say again how grateful we are for your kindness."

Esther, Francesca, and Vinnie pulled from their handbags their travel documents, which the attendant duly checked off as he greeted them.

"It's our great pleasure. We could hardly let you depart without seeing you safely aboard and making sure you have all you need," said Mrs. Worth. "Shall we give you all a brief tour?" She motioned Vinnie's parents toward the door.

"Oh yes," said Vinnie. "Then you can picture us all on our way."

Mr. Worth led them up the steps and onto a small platform bounded by wrought-iron grillwork. Through the door and past storage closets, they came to a small entryway, which opened into a spacious observation room of satinwood and blond mahogany. The Lawrences gaped at the hand-painted ceiling framed in carved gilt and Prussian blue, and the Prussian blue carpet with its ropes of gold flowers. Fine landscape and still-life paintings in gilt frames made cool spots of bright color on the walls.

"This couch," said Mr. Worth, indicating a long tufted sofa, "can form into an upper and lower set of beds at a pinch. Very handy for when the children and grandchildren are aboard, you know." He strode to the center of the room and pulled down the chandelier so that the cut glass globes were within reach. "I had fully intended to have the carriage electrified by now. I'm afraid you ladies will have to put up with gas."

"I'm sure we'll manage," said Francesca with a wry smile.

"If you'll follow me," he said, raising the chandelier into place and moving past a mahogany sideboard and gilt mirror toward a windowed hallway, "we come to the first of the staterooms." He opened the door to a sunlit room with a comfortable daybed topped with crimson tapestry pillows. A small table and chair were next to the bed and behind them, a mahogany closet. A mosaic tile wash-basin with gilt taps, a gilt mirror, and a pair of lamps occupied the near corner. Above the bed on the luggage rack was Vinnie's valise.

"This is my room then," said Vinnie. "Isn't it lovely?" Her few belongings, however neatly stowed, seemed to take up every available space.

The family snaked its way through Vinnie's room and out again, and through Francesca's stateroom, similarly furnished in blue, admiring all the latest conveniences.

A door to the water closet was discreetly indicated. "Water tanks for nearly five hundred gallons of clean water are situated under this carriage. Quite the latest thing," Mr. Worth noted. "Ample for drinking and bathing and cooking and other necessities on the journey." He opened the door to the bathroom with its claw-footed tub, a small chest, a mirror, a set of brass dress hooks, and an oak side chair.

The next stateroom was where Esther's belongings were set out—Mrs. Worth's usual stateroom of purples, mauves, and gold.

"You must excuse the dining room," said Mrs. Worth as the hallway opened up to the car's full width. "John uses it for business meetings and his office as well as for our family dining." She indicated the carved tiger oak table, eight chairs, and china cabinet.

"My wife always complains that the big boys can be as hard on the furniture as little boys," said Mr. Worth with a laugh. "We're nearly at the end. Allow me."

Mr. Worth knocked at the last bedroom door. Upon being admitted they peered in and found May unpacking and hanging a few clothes in the closet and on hooks. The upper berth was stowed away. Rosemary was arranging her belongings around the plain porcelain washbasin. Vinnie was abundantly thankful for her own small space.

"Don't let the small size deceive you," said Mrs. Worth, as they finally came to the kitchen. "Our chef has managed quite sumptuous meals here, hasn't he, dear? I'm sure you will find it adequate for the journey."

"We've even laid in a few stores for you ladies," said Mr. Worth, opening the doors to cupboards and the icebox. "Though I'm sure the Canadian Pacific will have made some provision along the way."

As they descended the steps and the ladies walked the Lawrences to the front of the *Caprice*, the conductor gave a piercing blast on his whistle. "All aboard! All aboard! Last call, ladies and gents!" Steam began to cloud the platform.

Vinnie's muddled emotions welled up in her throat. Eager to leave yet loath to go, she seized her mother around the waist and kissed her hard upon the cheek. She could barely hear the words of parting offered her, for all the clanging bells and slamming doors and sharp whistles. She quickly hugged her brother and Anne as Francesca and Esther made their farewells to the Worths and the

Lawrences. With tears in her eyes, Vinnie threw her arms around her father's neck, shouted, "I love you, Papa," in his ear, and kissed him good-bye. He handed her up the steps and she raced to join Francesca and Esther at the open window of the observation room before her courage failed her. She drew out her handkerchief and leaned on the windowsill.

In that moment of noise and hurry, Vinnie was overcome by an enormous sense of well-being. As she looked upon those she loved most in the world, she knew it was going to be all right. She didn't know how, or why, or who would cause it to happen, but that didn't matter. Her heart soared.

"Good-bye! Good-bye! I love you!" she shouted and kissed her hands toward them as they kissed their hands toward her. "I love you!"

Good-byes resounded up and down the platform. Handkerchiefs waved from every window and door.

"Good-bye! I love you," Vinnie repeated as the engine began its great chug forward and the successive pull of each car brought the mammoth train to attention. With each belch of steam the train drew them farther and farther apart till she could hardly hear them over the clamor. Then, to her joy, her father's voice rang out clear and sweet.

"Good-bye, my dears," shouted Mr. Lawrence, waving. "Good-bye, my dears, and God bless you."

CHAPTER 42

A Little Inconvenience

When you are traveling, it is no excuse that because others outrage decency and propriety you should follow their example, and fight them with their own weapons. A rush and scramble at the ticket office is always unnecessary. The cars will not leave until every passenger is aboard, and if you have ladies with you, you can easily secure your seats and afterward procure the tickets at leisure. But suppose you do lose a favorite seat by your moderation! Is it not better to suffer a little inconvenience than to show yourself decidedly vulgar? Go to the cars half an hour before they start, and you will avoid all trouble of this kind.

—Decorum, page 138

Connor stood on the platform at Grand Central Terminal with Jerry Jerome and Charlie Gage, who had come to see him off. Charlie's offer to bring a carriage to take Connor and Jamie to the station had saved Connor no end of trouble, especially by sparing him the parting words of disapproval Jerry surely would have lavished on him had the two of them been alone.

"You'll escape the city just in time," Charlie shouted over the platform's uproar. He adjusted his brown bowler hat and squinted up at the taller men and shifted so that Connor gave him shade in the bright sunlight. "I envy you that cool mountain air already. Have you heard from the ladies, Jerome?"

Ten days had passed since Francesca, Vinnie, and Esther Gray had left New York. To be honest, Connor was glad of the respite from daily wonder about whether he should call at Sixty-third Street. His own preparations, though simple, had kept him busy. He had secured a first-class stateroom for himself and would make do with the first-class fare the restaurant car offered. Nonetheless there were travel details, last-minute purchases, and what seemed to him like relentless packing to attend to. More than once he had caught the patient and efficient Jamie muttering to himself about needless worry and undue haste.

Now, on the railway platform, Connor's spirits were buoyant. He was leaving the scrutiny of New York to pursue the last goal on the quest that had brought him here nearly a year before. Business and society had embraced him, however cautiously. Francesca had not said yes to his proposal, but neither had she rejected him outright—a chink in the wall that Connor felt sooner or later he might just squeeze through. He was gambling his future on this venture in Banff, exposing her not only to his amiability, but also to his temper, his stubbornness, and all his other faults. Yet living with a woman and being able to please her, in spite of that outcome, gave him hope that he would not fare so poorly.

"Oh, yes," said Jerry without enthusiasm. "Francesca wired from Toronto to say they had arrived there safely and the varnish had transferred to the Canadian Pacific line without mishap. They planned to see something of the city before leaving for Banff."

"I'm surprised they didn't try to make at least half the journey cross-country here," said Charlie. "Maybe head north at Minneapolis or somewhere."

"I had suggested something of the sort, but having determined to see Canada, they decided to see it from stem to stern."

"I can't say as I blame them," said Charlie. "You decided to follow suit, I see, O'Casey."

"Indeed," said Connor. "I'm unfamiliar with that part of the world, so as the ladies have done, I intend to make a good job of seeing it. The ladies should be there by now, I should think."

"I expect so," said Jerry, looking up and down the platform.

"What's eating you, Jerome?" asked Charlie. "You look positively dyspeptic. Something not agree with you?"

Connor laughed. "He's just jealous he's not going. I said that he and Maggie should be heading for Florida. When are you off, Charlie?"

"I can't get Cora to make up her mind where she'd like to go—unless it's the courts of Europe," he chuckled. "I told her we're not moving a muscle until she's decided between the Grand Hotel in Michigan and that place in New Brunswick. This is not a pleasure trip, I told her—not strictly speaking."

The conductor gave a blast of the whistle and called passengers to board.

"All aboard, gentlemen, please," he said as he passed them. He consulted his railway pocket watch. "The train'll be leaving in two minutes. All aboard." He sauntered the length of the platform admonishing stragglers.

Connor shook the men's hands, accepted their good wishes of safe journey, mounted the steps of the first-class carriage, and turned to face them.

"All secured and correct, Mr. O'Casey, sir," said Jamie in his ear as he came up behind him. Connor nodded and Jamie disappeared into the depths of the carriage.

"I wish you weren't abandoning the Excelsior like this," said Jerry—much less than he wanted to say, Connor suspected—"just when we need you most."

"Nonsense. I won't be out of touch," said Connor. "What do you think modern communications are for, man? I'm told that telegraph wires extend to Calgary at least, and no doubt to Banff itself. You'll find me right enough." Connor was jubilant. "And don't worry, I'll find *you*."

"What about Europe?" shouted Jerry. "What about all this talk of furnishings and searching out fifteenth-century rooms?"

"Don't worry," called Connor as the train slowly pulled away from the platform. "With any luck, I'll be going there on my honeymoon."

"May I help you, madam?" The gentleman stood up from his desk and came forward.

"Yes," said Blanche. "I have a reservation on the *Etruria* and wanted to inquire as to whether it is too late to cancel it."

The attention of two other booking office clerks, who were assisting customers, was diverted long enough to note the striking woman standing at the counter. Posters adorned every inch of wall space, announcing special fares and limited-time offers, including a ten-day package tour of the Caribbean for the bargain price of forty-seven dollars.

"Of course, madam. Won't you please come through." The man opened the low swinging gate for her to enter. She took her seat in front of the desk.

"Now, madam, how may I be of assistance?"

"I have a passage booked on the *Etruria* on June twenty-fifth to Liverpool via Queenstown and from thence to London, where I shall stay for a few days, from whence I should be traveling by the boat train for the Continent."

"Yes, madam. Did this agency handle the booking?" The man peered at her over his spectacles.

"Yes, I believe so," said Blanche. "The matter was put into the hands of a friend who handled the booking for me."

"A single passage, madam?"

"And my maid, of course."

"And your name, please, madam."

"Mrs. Blanche Wilson de Alvarado."

"Wilson?"

"Most likely under Alvarado."

"A-l-v . . ."

"A-r-a-d-o."

"Thank you. One moment, madam." The man consulted a card

file, a register, and a passenger list before returning to his customer.

"Yes, madam, we have you listed for a first-class stateroom on the *Etruria* departing on twenty-fifth June. The booking came to one hundred dollars."

"Yes, well, unfortunately, I have experienced a rather drastic turn of events and find that I am prevented, sadly, from traveling to Italy. I'm heartbroken, of course, but I'm afraid the change simply cannot be avoided. Would it be possible to cancel the reservation and have my money refunded?"

"Well, I'm very sorry, madam," the man said, feigning embarrassment, "but I have a note here that indicates that the booking was paid for by a check from the other party. So I'm afraid that unless that party wishes to cancel the reservation and claim the refund, we shall not be able to accommodate you."

Blanche tried to hide her displeasure. Connor had bought the ticket himself, no doubt to make sure she left the country. "But you see, I gave my friend the money with which to buy the ticket. The silly man must have deposited the money to his own account and then wrote a check against it." Her smile was as seductive as her annoyance would permit.

"Yes, madam, but I'm afraid that we are powerless to deal with anyone but the signatory."

"Even though the reservation itself is in my name."

"I'm afraid so, madam."

Blanche was silent for a moment, her brow furrowed. "Dear me. Surely, I don't want to inconvenience my friend."

"Of course not, madam." The man looked at her, clearly prepared to wait as long as necessary.

"This is rather trying." She bit her lip and tried to look helpless, not an attitude that came naturally. "You see, my friend has already left the city and is therefore unable to conclude the business himself."

"Is it possible to send your friend a telegram and apprise him of your change in plans? If we could obtain instructions from him as to where to deposit the money—which I'm sure would be to your own account, madam—we may be able to conclude the business for you satisfactorily."

"Oh, no, no. He is quite out of reach at the moment—on a hunting expedition."

"Indeed. I'm so sorry, madam." The man continued his blank and unhelpful expression. He evidently was not moved by an attractive woman in peril.

The cash Connor had left should have supported her for months, but these resources were so drained from the trial that she had little left for a good showing before her sister. The well would soon run dry. To arrive at her sister's home with a rich man on her arm was one thing. To arrive with no prospects and no money was quite another.

"Well, I suppose that is that." She rose and prepared to leave.

"Unless you have alternative arrangements you wish to make."

"What?"

"Alternative arrangements. If your change in plans calls for alternative arrangements for travel, I see no reason not to use the sum already committed toward the alternative." The man looked at her with a more hopeful expression. She thought for a moment.

"Why, yes. Yes," she said slowly, settling back on her chair, "as a matter of fact, I must make alternative arrangements. How kind of you to remind me."

"Indeed, madam."

"Would it be possible, can you tell me, to cancel my sea voyage and book a railway journey to Banff?"

CHAPTER 43

Politeness, Ease, and Dignity

༄

If, in traveling, any one introduces himself to you and does it in a proper and respectful manner, conduct yourself towards him with politeness, ease, and dignity; if he is a gentleman, he will appreciate your behavior—and if not a gentleman will be deterred from annoying you; but acquaintanceships thus formed must cease where they began.

—*Decorum*, page 31

Francesca stood on the steps of the *Caprice* and inhaled deeply. The opiate of fresh air, crisp as a starched pleat, filled her lungs with the heady scent of earth and pine. As the train made its way across the seemingly unending sweep of Canadian plains, she could feel the pull of the mountains. Like gravity, once in the Rockies' grasp, Francesca's spirit was helpless to resist.

With each westward mile her wonder grew at how the tiny fragment of earth that was New York could chain her to so restricted an orbit of a single set of people. Even in Toronto she still felt the tug of the American East and struggled daily to break free of its associations. She could not bring herself to jot but a few words in the journal Vinnie had bought her, confining her remarks to "weather hot" and "roast pork fine" while Vinnie flooded the Lawrences with notes and postcards and chronicled each day's minutia. New York held no one with whom Francesca wished to share her thoughts. She left to Esther the decorum of keeping the Jeromes apprised of their journey's progress. Besides, she told herself, she had brought her childhood friend with her; no need to confide her feelings to a bit of paper. Amused and a little envious, she looked on as Vinnie sent the Lawrences a telegram on their last day in Toronto, her eagerness spilling out over a dozen words.

Now, with the Rockies within reach, she was impatient to shed the remaining vestige of New York. In Banff, the *Caprice* would be uncoupled from the other cars and moved to a siding to await the next eastbound train back to New York. The train was at the last of the Canadian Pacific Railway's dining stops before the final dash to Banff.

"I must admit," said Esther's voice behind her, "I shall be sad to lose the *Caprice*. Apart from its amenities, one doesn't appreciate one's privacy until it's gone."

"Oh, I don't know," Francesca mused aloud. "We'll be in the mountains after all. What more does one need, really, besides a decent bed, decent food, and a bit of hot water now and then? I might even give up the food—not all of it, but you know what I mean, the *cordon bleu* business—if I could be surrounded by a landscape unlike any other as part of a steady diet. The solitude—that's what is so powerful."

"Solitude and privacy are vastly different things," said Esther.

"You're quite right, of course," Francesca continued, "but to be in a place where one can achieve some inner solitude. That's what I hope I can carry with me."

Francesca could not bring herself to add, "to New York," and all it represented.

"I take your point, my dear," said Esther. "There is much to be said for a still center in oneself, but for the moment I will leave the philosophical side of our journey to your care and settle for a little privacy."

"Privacy is all well and good," said Vinnie as she joined them, "but I for one can't wait to see who else might be traveling to Banff. With all the comings and goings at each stop it's hard to tell who might be going as far as we are."

The three ladies alighted and began to walk down the platform toward the substantial log structure that comprised the dining room and kitchen, with guest rooms on the second floor and construction underway on a new wing. Another varnish was moored on a nearby siding, nearly as large as the *Caprice*, with a green-and-black lacquered finish trimmed in gold. It bore no frivolous moniker, but a coat of arms with an inscription—*Nec spe, nec metu*. Without hope, without fear. A dark, well-built young man of medium height, presumably a servant, was gathering sundry sporting gear on the vestibule.

"Well," said Vinnie in a low voice to Francesca as another man emerged carrying a collection of hunting gear.

He was somewhat older than the first, in his forties perhaps, but striking in appearance and command, with olive skin and black eyes. His hair was close-cut about the ears and neck, nearly all silver gray save for a thick wave of dark brown across the crown, which he was covering with a Tyrolean-style hat. The loden-colored European tweeds clothed a slim, muscular form and the knitted stockings below the buckled knickerbockers showed legs well used to exercise. Francesca, whose ear for languages was good, placed their speech in the eastern part of Europe—a Slavic language perhaps or a German dialect she did not recognize. As the two men descended the steps and made their way toward the platform, Francesca saw the same crest emblazoned in some fashion on cases and gear they carried. Stopping to let the ladies pass, the tweedy gentleman gave them a brief, courteous inclination of the head and his servant gave a slight bow. Was it her imagination, or did the gentleman's eye seem to single out Francesca? What an attractive man.

"Mmm, what a nice-looking man," whispered Vinnie nearly in her ear. "I wonder who he is. Maybe he's going to Banff too."

To have her own thoughts come out of Vinnie's mouth, and with an inflection Francesca herself would not dream of, gave the words an almost risqué quality that startled her. All ideas of attraction had been tucked away behind a convenient barricade of remorse and grief. All thoughts of Banff had been of escape and rest, never the possibility that so remote a place could offer diversions other than fresh air and exercise.

What of Connor? The friction of their encounters, in spite of their buried compliment to her, threw a wrench of consternation into her feelings at the same moment when his wit and intelligence made him fascinating. He might trouble himself to romance her, Francesca thought, a skill that remained to be seen. That the fleeting regard of a total stranger could set her thoughts dancing caused her to wonder what kind of complete fool she could make of herself and whether she really even cared. By the time she had arrived at this disconcerting notion, they had reached the dining room.

The room of rough-hewn beams and rustic paneling was filling up with passengers eager to feast on fresh local game. Vinnie made for a table for four and stood with her hands upon the back of the chair as she waited for Francesca and Esther. With Vinnie's back to the corner, her position commanded the room. Torn between scenery and satisfying her natural curiosity, Francesca faced Vinnie, content with a view out the nearest window. Esther drew up between them and, with a nod of approval, sat on Francesca's right. With these two ladies as her eyes and ears—and the balance between sensationalism and sense—Francesca would miss nothing. No sooner had they ordered the soup than a voluble lady of middle age could be heard approaching.

"Silly girl," said the voice with a flat twang that grew louder with each tap of a walking stick. "I thought I asked you to save a table for me. Now they're almost all full up."

The reply came in a whisper that arrested movement. The room strained to hear.

"But madame rekested zee tapestry reticule and a fresh handkerchief before proceeding, which rekired a search sroo madame's luggage." The voice was refined but with an edge that suggested familiarity with confrontation and a disinclination to back down.

"Zere is a seat at zat table," she continued. "I am sure zoz ladies will not mind so much to share. It appears to be zee custom, no?"

Realizing at once that they were the target of "zee custom," the three ladies froze—Esther with eyes fixed on the sugar sifter, and Francesca with a reproving eye on Vinnie's suppressed smile. The walking stick gave a tap of finality behind the empty chair. Francesca was surprised to find that the Amazonian voice belonged to a diminutive, buxom middle-aged woman, wearing a gray woolen traveling suit and a black hat with a short feather held in place with a cameo brooch. A three-strand pearl necklace fought with the ruffled blouse collar around the short neck. The reticule in question was of fine petit point and hung from her wrist by a silver chain.

"I'm sorry to trouble you ladies," she said with a smile and more grace than Francesca expected, "but I seem to have been a bit slow out of the starting gate, so to speak. Would you mind so terribly if I shared your table?"

"Not at all," said Esther, gesturing toward the empty chair. "Please join us."

"Thank you kindly," she returned, waving a hand of dismissal at the maid, who gave the briefest curtsey before vanishing.

In an instant, a waitress was at her elbow, proffered a menu, and waited for instructions. The woman hooked the ivory handle of her walking stick on the table, laid the reticule and gloves in her lap, produced a pair of pince-nez from her breast pocket, and glanced through the menu.

"Is the fish fresh?" she inquired of the waitress.

"Of course, madam."

"The soup of the day?"

"Bean soup, madam."

"Very well," she said, handing back the menu and replacing the pince-nez. "That's what I'll have."

"To drink, madam?"

"Well," said the woman, looking at the water pitcher and three glasses on the table and frowning. "I guess it'll be water then." The waitress took the empty pitcher away. The woman folded her hands on the table, as if prepared to mind her own business.

"Please continue with your meal, ladies," she said. "Don't let it get cold on my account." The three took up their soupspoons.

A few moments passed. The waitress appeared with a large tray and deposited the water pitcher and the soup and a glass. Francesca looked at Esther, to gauge between them whether to offer conversation. This stranger, despite the bluff manner and incongruous costume, seemed eager not to offend. Esther cleared her throat.

"Is this your first journey to the Rockies?" she asked.

"Land sakes, no," said the woman, appearing relieved to be addressed. "Sometimes I ask myself why I've come, exchanging one end of the Rocky Mountains for another. Denver is my home—Denver, Colorado. So you see, I already have the Rocky Mountains on my back doorstep, as you might say."

"That must be very pleasant," offered Francesca.

"It is," replied the stranger, "though I'm afraid a person gets used to his surroundings wherever he might be and might not appreciate them as much as when they were new to him."

"That's probably true," said Francesca.

"I suppose that's one of the virtues of travel among folks who are strangers to a place," the woman continued. "They help a person to see things fresh and new, as you might say. I'm sure when I was in Europe last year I noticed ever so many interesting things that the Europeans themselves took for granted. So much more history than we have, of course, and art and music and so many refined and beautiful things to see and hear." The woman sighed. "It was almost more than a person could take in."

"Were you there long?" asked Vinnie.

"Yes, indeed. Nearly a year. My daughter was being married in England and we had many arrangements to attend to." Her plain speech was modest and perhaps even a little embarrassed. They lapsed into silence at the arrival of the main course.

"I declare, one does miss home, though," said the woman at last, her tone softened by a touch of wistfulness, "traveling for such a long time. The Alps were certainly splendid, I'm not saying they weren't, but they were different. They did make a person homesick."

A widow, thought Francesca, *who has just married her daughter to a penniless European, perhaps with a title—a vagabond of the nouveau riche whose work is done, now that her daughter is well settled.* The woman seemed to gather her wits and posed a polite question in return.

"Have you ladies seen the Rockies before?"

"No," said Francesca. "This will be our first encounter with them."

"You say that as if the Rocky Mountains were people," said the woman with a little more animation. "Well, I daresay you're right, if you'll allow me to say so. The mountains—and the trees and the rivers—each has a character of its own, if we could just appreciate it. Some say, 'You've seen one mountain, you've seen 'em all,' but if that's so, you may as well say, 'You've seen one cathedral, you've seen 'em all,' or one palace or one fountain, but I never found that to be the case myself. Every peak is as different as people can be."

"I'm sure that's true," said Francesca, glad to see this glimmer of sentiment. "Are you traveling far—if you'll forgive my inquiry?" Esther threw her a cautionary glance.

"Why, land sakes, of course. I'm stopping off for a time at Banff, but I may go as far as Vancouver if the mood takes me."

"How interesting," said Esther.

The first shift of luncheon diners was beginning to leave. A waitress, brandishing an enormous tray and a damp cloth, cleared and wiped a small nearby table and returned the condiments to their proper order.

"We're going to Banff . . ." said Vinnie, cutting herself off in mid-sentence. The other three ladies followed her gaze, which had lighted on the sporting gentleman in tweeds making his way across the room. Before he sat, his eye caught that of the stranger at their table, to whom he gave a slight bow. This she returned with a smile and an upraised hand.

Amazed at this new factor in their acquaintance with this un-known woman, the ladies gave up all decorum, exchanged glances, and fixed their collective gaze upon her.

"Yes," she chuckled, raising her napkin and daubing her lips. She lowered her voice and bent toward them a little. "Handsome fellow, isn't he? His name is Sándor Krisztián Filip Király. A count, a member of the Hungarian nobility—a second cousin so-many-times removed to someone. He told me who it was, but I do so like to learn to pronounce a name properly, and I'm afraid I didn't quite master it this time."

"You've met him, then?" asked Francesca.

"Oh, yes," said the woman. "You probably saw his varnish on the siding. He and his manservant have been here for a few days, hiking and hunting and such. I stopped off here for two days to break my journey and stretch my limbs. He's keen on all sports. He used his varnish but came in here to take his meals. He was kind enough to take coffee with me one evening and we got to chatting."

"How very interesting," said Vinnie.

"Will he be staying on here for very much longer?" asked Esther.

"It looked like they were preparing to hitch his varnish," added Francesca.

"That's right. They're joining this train and will travel to Banff for the sport. I understand from him that he's climbed almost everything there is to climb in his native land and thereabouts, so he means to begin on the Rockies." She chuckled again.

"It sounds as if we shall all be in Banff," said Vinnie.

"It does indeed," said Francesca with a raised eyebrow and a look at Esther.

"In that case, it would only do to introduce ourselves," said Esther on cue. "My name is Mrs. Gray, and these are my companions—Miss Lund and Miss Lawrence."

"Thank you kindly," said the new acquaintance. "I'm very pleased to meet you, I'm sure. I'm Mrs. West—Mrs. Ida West."

CHAPTER 44

No Inducement

❦

If you wish to avoid the company of any one that has been properly introduced, satisfy your own mind that your reasons are correct; and then let no inducement cause you to shrink from treating him with respect, at the same time shunning his company. No gentleman will thus be able either to blame or mistake you.

—*Decorum*, page 31

Francesca had suggested that Mrs. West dine with them in the main restaurant of the Springs. The ladies had been coolly polite to Ida West at first, not wishing to foster an acquaintance that might prove to be a nuisance. Mrs. West, however, did not assume a single meal at a remote dining stop was the basis for fast friendship. Her plain speech and ensemble of tweeds and pearls may have caused a smile, but she was kind to all and appeared to be sensible and discreet, of which the sensible Esther could only approve. Sándor Király had dined with Mrs. West the first evening, and through his introductions she had made desirable connections. Indeed, it began to appear that better acquaintance with Mrs. West might be advantageous. After three days in Banff with no alarming incidents, Francesca thought it would be churlish to exclude Mrs. West.

By nine o'clock, the four ladies were well settled and waiting for the main course, having feasted on an aperitif, soup, fish, salad, and wine. A new crop of visitors had arrived that afternoon, the Banff Springs' tallyho having transported the guests while wagons followed, laboring under trunks, valises, portmanteaux, and sporting goods. Like the first night aboard ship, the newcomers wore their Sunday best, not full evening dress, their servants working at full throttle to unpack and prepare silks and jewels for the following evening.

"Why, I never," said Mrs. West in some surprise. She sat upright, both hands on the table, staring across the room.

"What is it?" asked Esther, following her gaze to the entrance, where the maître d' had just engaged a familiar figure.

"I can't believe it. Connor O'Casey. As I live and breathe."

"You mean you know him?" asked Francesca, with astonishment shared by Esther and Vinnie.

"Land, yes," Mrs. West replied in a low voice, clearly preoccupied with the sight before her and the memory he stirred. "Though I haven't seen him since . . . land sakes, I don't know when. Must be three years now—going on four maybe. He and my late husband were business partners together in Leadville. Connor was in the mine disaster that killed my husband."

"Oh, my heavens," said Francesca, still fixed on the thought of a mutual acquaintance in the person of Connor O'Casey. A thousand contradictions passed through her mind. What sort of disaster was it—physical or financial or something else she couldn't grasp? Was Connor a cause or a remedy applied too late? Did he possess virtues with which Esther had been loath to credit him, or was she justified in thinking him a fiend?

"I'm so sorry, my dear," said Esther with genuine feeling, as she laid a tentative hand on Ida's wrist.

"Connor nearly died, too," said Ida. "He was laid up for months, poor soul."

The three ladies looked at each other in alarm.

"Connor? Nearly died?" echoed Francesca. "I can hardly believe it. He's never said a word."

"Do you think he would?" asked Ida. "How does a man talk

about a thing like that, lives taken before his eyes, and knowing he was nearly one of them?"

As Connor was shown to his table, he spied them at their table by the window. It was as if Francesca, Esther, and Vinnie didn't exist, his eyes were so clearly on Ida with a look—of compassion? Francesca wondered. He diverted his steps as the maître d' continued to his table and waited there to seat him.

As he approached, Ida raised a hand and he took it in both of his and held it as he stood close by her and looked into her face. Before he uttered a word, he bent down and kissed her on the cheek. His open demonstration of regard took Francesca by surprise. She looked at the other ladies as if she mistrusted her own heart and hoped to gauge by their faces how she herself should feel. Esther's face was serene and betrayed no indignation, no sidelong look or hint at impropriety. Vinnie, too, looked on in wonder, oblivious to the attention the display had drawn.

"Hello, Connor."

"Hello, Ida," he said. "You're looking well."

He squeezed her hand and a smile of old friendship passed between them.

"You too."

She clasped his hand and shook it, and, as if remembering herself, released him.

"I believe you know these ladies," Ida said, motioning around the table.

"I do indeed. Mrs. Gray. Miss Lund. Miss Lawrence," said Connor, nodding to each lady in turn. "It's good to see you, Ida. It's been far too long—and entirely my fault."

"No matter," said Ida, shaking her head. "We were each living our own lives."

"And Mary, is she well?"

"Married off, you scoundrel."

"No, not really," said Connor in mild surprise. "A good match, I hope."

"I think so. I hope so. It should have been you, you know. I always said so."

"Well then, my loss," said Connor graciously. "I see they're holding my table. Don't let me disturb you. We'll catch up by and by. Ladies."

He bowed and left them. Francesca felt as if the wind had been knocked out of her.

"How long do you intend to be with us?" said the pleasant but professional clerk.

"As long as necessary," Blanche said as she stood at the registration desk, her pen poised over the guest book. She wrote her name— Mrs. Blanche Wilson. The clerk looked puzzled behind his professional reserve. The letter of credit she bore for two thousand dollars would guarantee her admittance to the Banff Springs Hotel; it would remain to be seen whether it would cover a prolonged stay.

The clerk didn't challenge her. Financial matters required delicate handling—and social matters no less so.

"Excuse me while I call the manager, madam. He may wish to assist you personally."

"Certainly." Blanche expected no less. She turned and looked at the spacious and lofty lobby, with its tiers of balconies from which guests were observing the hotel's activities. Others were seated in comfortable chairs or clustered about making plans or recounting the day's exhausting occupations. She pulled a small mirror from her handbag. First-class sleep in a first-class train carriage and a brisk tallyho drive to the hotel had left her spirits refreshed and her skin clear. She half-expected to see O'Casey himself saunter through the lobby. Indeed, she had fantasized about their first encounter and her delight at the shock her presence would administer.

Among the seekers after fresh air and exercise was a small, chestnut-haired young woman who walked into the lobby, drawing off her gloves and unbuttoning her jacket. Blanche knew this woman instantly—the little Busy-Body from the milliner's who was attached to the source of all her problems. If the Busy-Body was here, the Iceberg wasn't far behind. She turned to chasten her companion, and in so doing turned toward the registration desk. In the same moment, Blanche turned away, raised the mirror high, and pushed a black wave under the brim of her hat. At the movement of the electric blue of her traveling suit, the Busy-Body stood stock still and looked. By the time she remembered herself, two companions had joined her. The Iceberg's look drifted to the registration desk. A quick whisper apprised a third lady of the object of their attention. This lady hastened the younger women through the lobby and up the stairs, circling the balcony before disappearing. Through the mirror she saw the clerk approach with the manager. She turned.

"Welcome to the Banff Springs," said the manager. Blanche had encountered plenty of men of this type—diplomatic and cordial but no nonsense. He held her letter of credit in his hand. She smiled. He continued, "I am Mr. Mathews. My associate, here, tells me that you have no fixed plans as to the duration of your stay with us. Is that correct?"

"Yes," she said, replacing the mirror in her handbag and clasping it with a snap. "I understood from your wire that there was sufficient accommodation for myself and my maid for the duration of the season, if I should decide to stay that long."

"That is so, madam. Would you care to step into my office for a moment? I should hate to give unnecessary publicity to this little mix-up."

"With pleasure."

Ah yes, publicity—a term to strike fear in the most discreet bosom. If the publicity and the notoriety it nurtured were of the right sort, it could open doors, not close them. If the Banff Springs Hotel was indeed becoming the world's crossroad that publicity portended, it would suit her purposes admirably. If there was one thing publicity had done for her, it was to inoculate her against discretion.

When the office door was closed, he spoke first.

"You realize it is customary that an excess of funds be made available to guarantee your stay."

Of course she realized it. What did he think she was, a fool? O'Casey's money may be gone, but she would see to it that the *New York World*'s small investment would reap dividends.

"I should think the two thousand that this letter indicates that my paper guarantees, plus the three hundred and fifty I have in hand, should be sufficient for the time being." Her eye was fixed as steadily on him as his was on her and her smile just as fatuous.

"I hardly need say, madam, that the Springs is attracting a very select clientele, which I'm sure was why it appealed to a lady such as yourself." He gave the last three words the barest emphasis. "The usual letter of credit for our guests can be many times this sum. Though I don't deny that the Springs holds many attractions for a wide range of enthusiasts with a wide range of means, I'm sure that you, as well as we, would find the stay much more enjoyable knowing that all eventualities were provided for."

"I couldn't agree more. That is why I said to your associate that my editor, Mr. Julius Chambers at the *New York World*, will see me guaranteed." Her gaze was steady. "Of course, if an additional reference would ease your mind, I believe Mr. Connor O'Casey is a guest here. You may ask him."

"The comfort and enjoyment of our guests are the Springs' foremost concerns. To that end, you will understand that we make it our business to ensure that our clients are spared any inconvenient associations that might put them under unwelcome obligations."

The smile was disappearing from his lips, but not from hers.

"Oh, I assure you, Mr. Mathews, that Mr. O'Casey and I are very old, and I might even add, intimate friends." It was she who gave emphasis to the last words this time and added a carefree shrug. "I am positive that he will be only too glad to relieve all parties of any unnecessary embarrassment."

"If that is the case, you won't object if I have Mr. O'Casey paged, will you? I'm sure we can clear up this matter in no time."

"I welcome the opportunity." She smiled again.

He opened the door and called to a nearby bellboy, "Please run and find Mr. O'Casey and give him this note"—he jotted it hastily, blotted it, and sealed it in an envelope—"and ask him, with my compliments, if he would come and see me as soon as possible. Now," he said, turning back to her, "won't you sit down, Mrs. Wilson." They waited.

Blanche rose as Connor entered the room.

"Connor, darling." She touched his arm gently as she tilted her head up to kiss him on the cheek. "Why, what's the matter, darling?

You look like you're about to burst a blood vessel." She brushed a bit of fluff off his lapel, glided over to the settee, sat down, and patted the empty space next to her. "Why don't you come and sit a little?"

Connor stood ramrod straight and looked like black powder before the explosion. The manager's note was crushed in one hand. With the other he pointed to Blanche, but he looked only at Mr. Mathews.

"I want this woman thrown out."

"Oh, darling, don't be silly. You'll get yourself all worked up for nothing. Mr. Mathews, do you think we might have some drinks?"

Connor stared at her. She took her time and drew off her gloves.

"I think Mr. O'Casey needs one and I certainly wouldn't take the offer of a drink amiss. In fact champagne might just suit the occasion."

"Have you gone mad?" said Connor in a low growl.

"Oh, Connor," she said in mock reproach. "He's such a kidder, Mr. Mathews, don't take any notice of him. He always begins this way when he's a little put out."

"Put out?" Connor walked to the settee and stood over her. "Put out? I'll have you put out, Blanche! I don't know what you're playin' at, but I've had enough already. I want you out of here, *now*."

"Oh, but darling," she cooed. "To begin with, I have more than two thousand dollars that says I can stay, isn't that so, Mr. Mathews?"

"Two thousand dollars wouldn't keep you in shoe leather for a week," said Connor.

"Only if your stay were calculated to fit within your means, madam," the manager began.

"There, you see?" she said.

"And," he continued, "if your presence does not create a nuisance—"

"I want her out," said Connor, turning to the manager and continuing to point at Blanche. "She's a nuisance just being here—and I'm not the only party who would find her so. The sooner she's gone the less likely anyone will know she's ever been here."

"They know already." Blanche felt ten feet tall. "Will you ring for the drinks, Mr. Mathews, or shall I?"

Connor turned. "What?"

"They know already," said Blanche, trying to contain her immense satisfaction. "I saw them in the lobby, while this gentleman was fetching Mr. Mathews. And they saw me, which I fear is more to the point. One attempted to look dignified, one looked completely reserved and unmoved as one might expect, and the other looked almost amused. Yes, darling, you'll have a little explaining to do, I'm afraid."

"Oh, hell."

"Oh my, have I committed a little faux pas? Now then. Why don't you come over here and sit down and we'll have a nice little chat."

The manager asserted himself.

"Mr. O'Casey, I cannot allow this type of incident to disrupt the management of this hotel or disturb the comfort of our guests. If this can't be resolved reasonably, I'm afraid I must ask you . . ."

Connor stayed on his feet.

"Would you leave us, please, Mr. Mathews?" he said, regaining a measure of composure. "We'll soon get this sorted."

It was really all Blanche wanted in the first place.

"Now what's this all about?" demanded Connor when the manager and the clerk had withdrawn.

"I'm surprised you have the audacity to ask," said Blanche. Her tone had lost its gaiety, but retained a grating satisfaction. "Ever since you left me at midnight, standing on the pavement in front of the Fifth Avenue Hotel, alone and friendless, I've been trying to think how you could assist me in getting back on my feet again."

"I left you with plenty of cash, Blanche. You were supposed to go off to Italy to your sister's."

"Fate intervened, it seems."

"I can't help that," said Connor. "If you had minded your own business instead of going off with the wrong crowd and getting yourself tangled up—"

"Yes, and what was I supposed to do, sit in the hotel all day and wait for you to throw me a few crumbs? You never lifted a finger to help me, to win me the approval of your friends. You didn't even try."

"Why go raking all this up? What in God's name did you do with all that money? No, no, don't tell me. Obviously it's gone. I don't want to know where. But what did you think you'd gain by following me here? If you think I'd marry you—"

"Marry?" Blanche started to laugh. "*Me?* Marry *you?* That's very funny. I admit that at one time I wanted exactly that. No, you can rest easy on that score, I don't want to marry you. The Lund creature is welcome to you, if you think she'll have you. What I want from you now is quite different from what I wanted then."

"Meaning what?" Connor said.

"I want the help you wouldn't give me in New York. You can introduce me around to the friends you're cultivating here. You introduce me and I'll do the rest. In return I promise I'll stay out of your hair. I mean to come out well, O'Casey. The fact is I can't do it alone."

"And if I refuse?"

"More than two thousand dollars buys me enough time and credibility to be of use to those New York reporter johnnies I've become friendly with. Chambers and the *New York World* are paying handsomely for exclusive stories for the society pages about the wonders of the Banff Springs Hotel and its exclusive clientele and the scandal it's supporting under its very roof."

"You're bluffing, Blanche."

"Oh am I? After the stunts Pulitzer paid Nellie Bly to perform for them? If she can telegraph them from Hong Kong, what's to stop me telegraphing from Banff? Five days across country and two more for the mail to reach New York for an interview or a colorful feature—what's that to Chambers or to me when I can be feeding them a story every week? It's a simple proposition—I send them stories, they send me money. Even if I had to set up camp by the Bow River I fancy I could gin up enough to keep them interested and my name in the papers. All that peace and quiet you were seeking away from the omniscient New York society will be for naught. Don't you see? The sooner you help me, the sooner I'll be off your hands—and so much the better for both of us."

She sighed deeply and relaxed.

"Now, I think we should ask Mr. Mathews to come back in. What about that champagne?"

CHAPTER 45

Condescension

❦

If you are a gentleman, never lower the intellectual standard of your conversation in addressing ladies. Pay them the compliment of seeming to consider them capable of an equal understanding with gentlemen. . . . When you "come down" to commonplace or small-talk with an intelligent lady, one of the two things is the consequence, she either recognizes the condescension and despises you, or else she accepts it as the highest intellectual effort of which you are capable, and rates you accordingly.

—*Decorum*, page 68

"So, that was the lady," said Esther. "What has happened, Francesca?" Esther sat on the settee in front of the fire, her face impassive but for an almost imperceptible animation in her eyes. "I can't imagine that he could be completely ignorant of her intentions."

"I don't know. This must be some contrivance on her part, Aunt Esther."

By the time the ladies had retired to Francesca's suite she was in no mood to deal with Connor and Blanche. It was as if she and Connor and Blanche were wind-up toys that had developed an annoying habit of walking in circles and bumping into each other.

A knock came at the door. Francesca opened it to the outstretched hand of Jamie, proffering a note and saying, "For you, if you please, ma'am." She received it with thanks and closed the door, opening the small envelope and drawing out the sheet of thick paper emblazoned with the hotel's crest. She walked to the window and read.

"He's prompt, I'll give him that," said Esther. "Let's hope he's truthful as well."

"He wants me to meet him in the little parlor in ten minutes," Francesca reported and looked at the clock on the mantelshelf.

"Certainly not alone," said Esther.

"I think we should go with you. Bother propriety. Her presence affects all of us," said Vinnie. "Besides, Aunt Esther and I can't sit here and leave all the unpleasantness to you."

"The parlor is public territory," said Francesca. "Does anyone honestly think we'd go there to misbehave ourselves when there are plenty of private rooms?"

"Well, I think we should all go anyway," said Vinnie, making for the door. "Are you coming with me? Or will I be the one facing Mr. O'Casey alone?"

A bellman directed them to one of several small parlors for the private use of hotel guests. Connor was waiting. Francesca opened her mouth to speak, but he paid no heed.

"I'll thank you not to start," he said, leaving her agape and frowning.

"I don't like your tone, Mr. O'Casey," Esther retorted.

"Let's not begin like this," said Francesca, determined not to let tempers run unchecked while fearing hers might be the first to go. "Let's give Connor the courtesy of a hearing first."

Esther and Vinnie retired to a settee, but Francesca remained on her feet.

"Thank you, Frankie." He drew a deep breath and began. "I know you saw Blanche. I just saw her myself a few minutes ago."

"Quite a fast worker, isn't she?" Esther said to no one in particular.

"Goodness, already?" blurted Vinnie.

"She sought you out?" asked Francesca.

"She caused a ruckus about money and the management called me in to get it sorted," said Connor.

"What does she want exactly?" asked Esther. "We understood that she intended to go to Italy."

"So did I," Connor replied. "Unfortunately she's managed to get herself attached to the *New York World* as a reporter. She's here covering society in Banff for the newspaper."

Variations on, *Oh, for heaven's sake,* were spoken by all three ladies at once while Esther threw Francesca a look with a glint of *I told you so.*

"I can understand why she didn't go to Italy," said Francesca. "If I were in her place I wouldn't want to admit defeat in front of family."

"You're not serious," said Connor.

"But with the kind of life she's led . . ." began Esther.

"Yes, exactly because of the kind of life she's led," Francesca continued, a little uncomfortable that Blanche's ally in infamy was standing in the same room, but having begun she went on. "With her last prospect for a respectable marriage gone, whom can she face or to whom can she turn for help? She probably thinks you owe it to her."

"I don't owe her a thing."

"Oh, really?" said Francesca, the heat rising. "I'm not sure I agree. She certainly put up with *you* for a goodish while and I suppose one is justified in arguing to whose advantage. A woman always pays more heavily than a man."

"I've paid her plenty."

"That makes it right? A simple cash transaction? I'll bear it in mind in the future."

"Frankie, that's not fair and you know it," exclaimed Connor angrily.

"Kindly refrain from telling me what I do and do not know."

"I'm sorry," he said with a gesture of frustration. "I'm sorry. I just can't see how she managed to get you on her side."

"I'm not on anybody's side," said Francesca, trying to regain her control. "Just because I don't care for the woman doesn't mean I wish her ill. I'm simply saying that I can understand why she might feel this way and why she might come to you, that's all. It's a shame that she should choose you, but she has."

"Charity aside," said Esther, turning to Connor, "if you feel no obligations to her why didn't you simply send her packing?"

"You think I didn't try? You think I stood there and let her run roughshod over me?"

All three ladies looked at him.

"All right, all right." He sighed and collected himself. "She threatened me."

"*She* threatened *you?*" asked Vinnie. "How on earth—"

"With publicity. She wants introductions, help in navigating through society at Banff so's she can get her stories to send back to the *World*. If I—or we, most likely—if we fail to help her, or even try to freeze her out, she'll spill the whole story about our connections in New York. There'll be a storm of publicity that'll completely undo our stay here."

"Unfortunately, she's very good at publicity, if you'll recall," said Vinnie. "She certainly isn't afraid to get her name in the papers—and now that it's in her professional interest—"

"That's monstrous," retorted Esther.

"Oh, Esther," said Francesca, "publicity is at once the fair-haired child and the dark demon of all society. Half the society matrons of New York know too well how to set the publicity pump going, a skill for which I have no facility."

"You've had your share of publicity," said Vinnie.

"Not of my own making. None of my family ever sought it. I don't know whom Jerry had to pay off to see that the press treated me sympathetically over Mother and Father and Oskar, and to treat me well through—through all the recent business."

"That's not so hard when you're the victim," Vinnie said, then caught herself. "I'm sorry, Francesca, I didn't mean . . ."

"I know, dear, don't worry. Vinnie's perfectly right. 'Victim' is certainly one way to portray someone—or oneself—when seeking favorable publicity. Mrs. Alvarado is only doing what hundreds of others do. She intends to bring everything we're trying to escape from in New York to Banff if Connor doesn't cooperate."

"Yes," admitted Connor.

"But I don't understand. She'd only be hurting herself," said Vinnie. "Why draw attention to her own past by making trouble for Mr. O'Casey and for us?"

"She's not a complete fool," said Connor. "She is trying to distance herself from recent events. She's taken on her maiden name and has styled herself Mrs. Blanche Wilson. I've no doubt that she'll not scruple about doing what'll suit her purposes."

"She has nothing to lose," said Francesca. "She couldn't make things worse for herself than they are already."

"You've done too much settlement work," said Vinnie. "You're always taking other people's sides and seeing their points of view. You're too good by half—and it's very trying of you."

"I couldn't agree more, Miss Lawrence," said Connor with a smirk.

"All right," Esther interrupted, "enough of this. What are we to do about it?"

"I think we should help her," said Francesca, and waited for the outbreak.

"You can't possibly mean—" began Vinnie, suppressing her relish.

"I knew that's where this was going," retorted Connor.

"Wait just a moment and let me explain," Francesca said, her voice firm. "I'm not suggesting that we become her bosom friends. On the other hand we can't hope to avoid her, at least not without consequence. The Springs is like its own small town. Everybody will know everybody's business. Though she may have achieved a certain notoriety, which may be acceptable to the *World*, she still can't afford to become persona non grata. This may be enough to keep a certain pressure upon her."

"I can't understand why you should want to give legitimacy to this woman's claims by giving in to her demands in such a way," said Esther. "I don't think we should be encouraging her in the least."

"It's not a matter of giving her legitimacy or encouragement. I simply don't see how we can avoid her in so small a place as Banff. We may as well exert what control we can."

"We could try to call her bluff and freeze her out," said Vinnie. "She may give up and leave."

"I don't think it would turn a hair. She has something to prove, now that she's with the *World*. I think that's exactly what she's prepared to meet."

"I'm afraid I agree," said Connor. "So, Frankie, you think we should brazen it out?"

Francesca's speech was measured. "I suggest that we be civil, stay out of her way for the most part, lend a hand with the odd introduction. Perhaps we ladies can divert people's attention from associating her too closely with you," she said to him. "If she makes a nuisance of herself or engages in unacceptable behavior, the hotel will intervene and save us the trouble. As I said, I don't wish her ill. I'm afraid with that we must all be content."

"Let's go outside," said Blanche, notebook in hand, "so we can both smoke."

Her reluctant quarry did his best not to show his displeasure at being collared for an interview. Connor usually welcomed the opportunity to talk about the Excelsior—the alleged topic of the afternoon. Not wishing to sabotage her chances at gaining interviews with others, he realized that a good public performance might aid in getting her off his hands.

"Sunshine or shade?" she asked.

"You have no parasol," he said gallantly.

"I can sit with my back to the sun," she replied. "It will feel good on such a cool day. Would you like drinks to be brought out?"

He motioned her to precede him out the door and onto the terrace. The great bowl of the Bow Valley swept out before them, where the Bow and the Spray sliced through the thick, spiky green spruce that lined the bowl's bottom. The trees marched in legions up the sides of the mountains until stymied by the unrelenting, snowcapped sandstone and limestone peaks that sashayed around the bowl's rim through an eternity of vista.

"No," he said. "Thanks anyway. I'm happy to attend to the business at hand." He thought better of it. "Would it look better for you—more congenial like?" he asked, his voice lowered. "We could have tea brought out—or a drink if you prefer."

She looked at him in some surprise.

"As a matter of fact, it would look better. Thank you. A drink would be lovely."

No sooner had they found seats where neither the hotel nor the mountain nor the terrace's roof impeded the sunshine, when a waiter appeared and took their orders.

"So," said Connor, offering his opened cigarette case to Blanche, "since you can write your article just as well without me, what did you really want to talk to me about?"

"I do need a favor, yes," she said as she held the cigarette between her fingers and with her other hand searched in her bag and produced a little silver pencil set.

"Naturally," said Connor as he drew out a small box of matches and struck one from which he lit her cigarette and his.

"Mr. O'Casey," she said with overdone emphasis and in a voice raised just enough to make the conversation less than private, "my readers back in New York will be positively agog to learn of the progress of the Excelsior."

"Thank you, Mrs. . . . ." Connor hesitated, feigning a smile at her under the furtive glances of other guests who milled about the terrace.

"My maiden name, thanks," said Blanche, smiling at him, her lips barely moving.

"And it is Mrs.?" he asked as he drew on his cigarette.

"Of course." She pretended to make a note. "As to the hotel's progress, would you care to comment?"

"Certainly, Mrs. Wilson," Connor said aloud. "The investors in the Excelsior Hotel Company of New York are engaged in several activities aimed at bringing luxury apartment hotel accommodation to New York City. At present, we are in the midst of acquiring suitable premises in what we believe will become the very heart of social and cultural life."

The drinks arrived. Connor gave his room number. Blanche's pencil scratched across the page.

"So, the Excelsior is to cater to an exclusive clientele," she said. "Not unlike here at the Banff Springs? And what brings you personally here to the Springs," she asked through clenched teeth, "that's fit for the New York press?"

"I'm sure the press won't miss much with you about," Connor said under his breath. "The investors have a little scheme on, as a matter of fact," he said, recovering himself. "Each of us is visiting some of the best hotels we can find, all across the continent."

"Ah, a spy mission," said Blanche.

"Yes, if you like. We're looking for inspiration, you might say. We aim to make the Excelsior a distinctively American hotel, but we're going to the ends of the earth, quite literally, to find out what the people want, what appeals to the tastes of the elite clientele we aim to serve, as well as what's new, what's modern, what will make their stay a pleasant one—and of course, will make them want to come back when they're in New York City."

Connor flicked the cigarette ash across the valley, took a sip of whiskey, and considered her as she jotted her notes. She looked well enough, he thought—perhaps a little strained about the eyes, or was it his imagination? Her frame, even beneath the woolen jacket, might have been a little thinner, though she had always been slim. He knew from experience how well she could hide her feelings just as he knew how vehemently she could express them. That she should want to hide her feelings when they were no longer his business was understandable, but he could not help wondering whether she was really all right. Though he wanted no truck with Blanche, he was acutely aware that this God in whom Francesca had so much confidence had probably set Blanche there because she was in some measure unfinished business. When she looked up at him, her expression was of surprise, as if his face betrayed his thoughts.

"Now what's this favor you want?" he asked.

"I'd like an introduction to my next big story, darling," she said. "I want to meet Sándor Király. Have you met him yet?"

"I have, as a matter of fact," he said. "Mrs. West introduced me. Have you met her? She could probably get you some useful introductions. She hasn't the usual qualms about making people's acquaintance, if she wants to know someone. Whatever you may have heard, she is tactful and a good friend, so I'd appreciate your playing fair with her."

"Yes, that would be splendid," said Blanche loudly, and scratched a few words on the pad. "I'd be happy to meet Mrs. West. I think I should prefer the introduction to Király to come from you, though."

"Very well," said Connor.

He hesitated again and then decided to put the question to her.

"Are you all right, Blanche?" he asked with voice lowered. "I mean, really? I know it must sound like damnable gall to you, but I do want to know."

"Why, certainly, darling," she said, her air flippant as she drew on her cigarette. "Who wouldn't be when one has spent every last penny on coming to this godforsaken place to wait while one's lover—who doesn't want to see her—is sent to the gallows?"

Blanche tossed her head as if tossing back tears and took a sip of whiskey.

"Is this guilt speaking?" she asked, looking him in the eye, but with a subdued voice.

"What I did was beneath me," he said, "or at least beneath what I thought I was. I'm sorry, Blanche. I'm no good at parting."

"No one is," said Blanche. "Parting is always inconvenient to somebody."

Clearly, Blanche was shaken. She looked as if she wished she were anywhere other than the terrace of a busy hotel. Her handbag lay in her lap. She clutched it like a life preserver. Connor wished he could have handed her his handkerchief, supposing her reluctant to retrieve her own. Her voice caught.

"Look, let's change the subject, shall we?"

"I am sorry," he said again. "Of course, I'll help you with introductions. If it's Király you want, I'll produce him for you—and Ida, too."

CHAPTER 46

A Lesson for Your Own Improvement

❧

Observe your own feelings when you happen to be the guest of a person who, though he may be very much your friend, and really glad to see you, seems not to know what to do either with you or himself; and again, when in the house of another you feel as much at ease as in your own. Mark the difference, more easily felt than described, between the manner of the two, and deduce therefrom a lesson for your own improvement.

—Decorum, page 87

Cue balls clacked and scudded across the green baize. Glass-shaded lamps pooled their light over the tables. The dark wood-work deflected the low conversation as the players calculated their next shots.

Now at ten o'clock, the gentlemen stood, some with pool cues shouldered, to the nightly strains of "God Save the Queen" that echoed through the hotel. The sun dipped behind the mountains, leaving its rose and orange beams to mock the twilight with the promise of an early dawn. The temperate June air freshened the basement billiard room and carried off the sweet-and-sour cigar smoke. A manservant entered and closed the windows to a healthful crack and stirred the fire in the hearth.

Gentlemen were reduced to shirtsleeves, their tailcoats arrayed on hooks like ravens roosting in a tree. They bent over their cue sticks, an errant cigar stub poised between their teeth or held by two fingers with the cue resting in the crook of the thumb. A few men watched on the fringes, whiskey glasses and cigars in hand. Billiards afforded the chance to be seen mixing, to acquire nodding acquaintances, and having weeded out the social nuisances, to seek introductions.

"Sporting man?" asked Sándor Király of Connor, as the former shot the cue ball toward its target.

A cordial dinner with Király and Ida West had acquainted Connor with the Hungarian well enough to suggest billiards after coffee. Connor had as yet been unable to fulfill his pledge to Blanche, but hoped that with a friendly game and a drink or two an opportunity might suggest itself.

"Depends," Connor replied, picking up the cube from the rail and chalking his cue stick. "I s'ppose you could say I was a gaming man rather than a sporting one."

"Is there a distinction?" asked Sándor.

"A fine one, perhaps, for those who enjoy both," said Connor. "One implies strategy. The other implies strength. I grant you that they do often occur together."

"Ah, but there, do we not also venture into the realm of ingenuity and education?" asked an elderly gentleman bending to his cue stick.

The two men had offered a place in their game for this stranger— a minor English nobleman who had not been introduced nor introduced himself and who seemed in no hurry to discover who his companions might be. Connor wondered how this gentleman would react if Ida West were set upon him and how shocked Esther Gray would be.

"And luck perhaps," said Connor.

"But a man has to be ready when the opportunity—luck if you like—presents itself," retorted the gentleman and then made his shot. He took up his cigar from the rail and drew on it. "Was it not the philosopher Seneca who said that luck is simply where opportunity and preparation meet? A man can spend his whole life preparing for the one moment when he realizes what he's done and what he's worked towards and what it all means, and finally is ready to seize the opportunity that is placed before him."

"That's very true, sir," said Connor. "Many years of backbreaking work go into many a lucky break. The trouble is many men today want the lucky break without doing the work beforehand." Connor paused to take his shot.

"Still, as you say, the two principles so often meet together," said Sándor. "Climbing and mountaineering certainly rely on strength, especially when one has misread twenty centimeters of cliff in front of one. Ideally, though, a more accurate reading—and a convenient cleft or outcropping—can make actual strength a less formidable consideration. Leverage, when properly applied, can be more important."

"Ah," said the elderly gentleman, standing as the designated ball dropped into the pocket. "Leverage is an important consideration, especially when applied strategically, if I may say so. Leverage requires one to know the precise nature of one's own strength and to use it to best advantage."

"Exactly, very well put, sir," continued Sándor. "In fact, when one considers the importance of leverage, I believe, if trained properly, ladies may even become good climbers."

"Hmph," grumbled the elderly gentleman. "I can believe anything of ladies these days."

"I can think of one or two who might try it," said Connor, smiling to himself.

"Exactly," said Sándor. "One sees many ladies here in Banff taking long hikes and being guided over rough terrain, even mountaineering in a small way. In Europe, many ladies of beauty and accomplishment have a taste for vigorous exercise in the mountain air—and of course an appreciation for the beauty of their surroundings. Their only real encumbrance in moving from hiking to serious mountaineering is their clothing."

"What would you do, sir," asked the old gentleman, "put 'em in jodhpurs or plus fours and hobnailed boots? Gaiters, too, I suppose. Damned silly business for ladies, if you ask me."

"Why not?" said Sándor with a smile. "They wear the hobnails already and the plus fours would not bother me, especially if it is safer for them, rather than to become entangled in long skirts. I should prefer them in plus fours if it prevented the need for carrying them down a mountain with a broken ankle or scraping them off the bottom of a ravine where there is no sign of civilization. God knows we men run the risk enough even with the proper attire and gear. Yes, I should much prefer the ladies to climb in plus fours."

"Damned progressive way of thinking, sir," complained the gentleman. "Popular with the ladies, are you? Women are always wanting some damned thing or other, even if they know it's not good for 'em."

"Who is to tell them what is good for them, if not themselves?" asked Sándor with a grin. "You, sir?"

"It'd be an improvement," muttered the gentleman.

Ah yes, thought Connor. Logic, leverage, and knowing what was in one's own best interest. If only women understood a good thing when presented to them in a forthright, logical fashion. If only Frankie could accept what was so plainly reasonable from his point of view—the unimpeachable logic of a match with himself. He tried to picture her in plus fours and hobnail boots but found it an effort. He was a little dismayed that the effort was not so great when applied to Blanche.

"Maybe *instinct* is a better word than *strategy*," Connor offered with a chuckle.

"What do you find so amusing about instinct, sir?" asked Sándor. "It is a vital ingredient in so many of men's pursuits."

"I couldn't agree more. Only I can hear certain ladies chide me that what might be called 'instinct,' so revered in men, is called 'intuition' and reviled in women. They, poor females, generally receive precious little credit for intuition, while we, poor mutts, rely on instinct when we have precious little else."

"Well said, sir," Sándor replied.

"Utter bosh," the elderly man said, addressing Connor. "You must be popular with the ladies, too."

"I only wish it were so, sir," said Connor.

"Speaking of ladies and their pursuits," said the gentleman as he replaced his cigar on the rail and prepared his shot, "has anyone had any dealings with this lady reporter?"

Grateful that the subject had introduced itself, Connor nonetheless was cautious. Such an introduction might lead anywhere and might well turn from opportunity to disaster.

"What makes you ask?" Connor ventured.

"Has she been making herself a nuisance?" asked Sándor.

"As a matter of fact," said the gentleman. Connor held his breath. "No. I shouldn't say she was a nuisance—exactly. Damned if I can catch her eye half the time."

Connor smiled and shot a look at Sándor, who returned it with amusement.

"Thought I might be able to help, don't you know. Offer her introductions, that sort of thing. Seems determined to do it all on her own—like so many of these damned females who don't want a man to give them a helping hand. Think they can do it without proper introduction these days. They'll soon find out."

"I'm acquainted with her," said Connor. "Certainly she's a determined lady and wants to get on and make a good job of this reporting, but I think you'll find, sir, that she would welcome any introductions you might offer." *If this gentleman offers her anything else, Blanche can take care of herself,* he thought.

"If she has any sense of decorum," said Sándor, "she may be somewhat reluctant because no one has introduced her to you."

"I can assure you," said Connor, "she is keenly aware of social boundaries and would hardly sacrifice her professional reputation by barging in where she isn't wanted. If I can help in any way, sir, I would be happy to effect an introduction myself."

"Damned fine-looking woman," said the gentleman as he bent to his cue, took his shot, and stood straight. "And who might you be, sir, if I may ask?"

Connor introduced himself and proceeded to recite a catalogue of reasons the gentleman should consider him an appropriate go-between. Had he not promised Blanche assistance, the man's cross-questioning might have rankled him. Instead he regarded the man as Blanche's avenging angel and bore the interrogation with more patience than was normally his wont. By the time the examination was over, the gentleman had consented to allow Mr. O'Casey the honor of presenting him to Mrs. Wilson. The question was, how to transfer this evident enthusiasm for Mrs. Wilson from the Englishman to Sándor Király.

"You understand," said the gentleman, "I abhor publicity. Shocking business, generally speaking."

"I couldn't agree with you more," said Sándor. "Reporters are so often such low people, scrounging for crumbs from which they make a soufflé to feed the public—all air and no substance."

"On the other hand," said the gentleman, backpedaling vigorously but with perfect dignity, "one can be overly scrupulous in these matters. Seeing one's name in the papers on occasion—under the right circumstances, of course—does no harm."

"I can assure you, Mrs. Wilson is a well-educated, knowledgeable sort of lady," said Connor. "I believe she has relations in Italy and has lived and traveled abroad a good deal. I think I can safely say that she would conduct an intelligent interview." More than that, Connor dared not promise.

"What about you, Király?" Connor continued. "Why don't you let me introduce you?"

"I can hardly imagine a lady reporter, however knowledgeable, would find climbing and outdoorsmanship the least bit interesting. Besides, if I want publicity I can generally find it on my own—or, I should say, it generally finds me."

"Ah. So all this liberal talk of ladies and their interests and abilities is just that—all talk, eh?" jibed the gentleman. "Can't actually stick it when it comes to the point, eh?"

"Not at all, sir—" Sándor began, a little defensively.

"Wouldn't actually take a woman out on that mountaineering of yours, eh?"

"I'm sorry, sir, but I really cannot tolerate—"

"Wouldn't care to have a small wager? That is, if she's as good a reporter as O'Casey here makes out."

At the word *wager* the billiard room stood still. The players brought their cues to rest as their attention migrated from their own tables to Connor's.

"I beg your pardon?" asked Sándor. He looked as if this sudden scrutiny were an inconvenience to maintaining his normal cool reserve.

"I'm intrigued," said Connor, as nonchalantly as he could manage. Until this moment, he thought he knew Blanche well, particularly where men were concerned. In fact, he realized he had no idea how she would react when a roomful of gentlemen of "the right sort" were fixed upon her or what her wishes would be. It surprised—and to some extent comforted—him that his instinct was to protect her as he would want to protect any woman from attentions that might prove a nuisance. On the other hand, he thought, this was Blanche, a woman who knew well men's intentions and whose new profession would bring her all manner of attention that she would have to manage herself. In fact, she might regard his solicitude as interference. Women could be so difficult.

"Just what do you propose, sir?" asked Connor, trying not to jump two steps ahead when only one was required.

"Now, now, don't interfere, O'Casey," said the gentleman, as if reading Connor's thoughts. "I'll bet you any sum you like, Király, that if you let O'Casey here introduce this Mrs. Wilson to you, you can't get her to report on more than your trifling social interests rather than your sporting interests."

"I have no particular social interests worth reporting," said Sándor, preparing to take his shot. "So there is no point in introducing me."

"Precisely my point," persisted the gentleman. "Your lack of social interests forces the issue, don't you know. It's the sporting interests or nothing, don't you see."

"What do you think of my chances, O'Casey?" asked Sándor.

"I can't say for certain that she wouldn't try the social angle first, especially if that's what her paper has sent her here to report," said Connor, trying to leave Blanche a sufficiently wide opening. "Mrs. Wilson certainly knows her own mind, however, and I wouldn't put it past her if she were to come round to your way of thinking. I think it's a fair bet."

"There, you see," said the gentleman in triumph. "So what will it be? What will you consider *sporting?*"

The Hungarian frowned at Connor and considered for a moment.

"If I win, you shall outfit my next expedition. I can provide you with a rough sum for two guides, my man, a packer, horses, gear, and possibly one or two other persons."

"Sounds fair," said the gentleman. "And *when I* win, you must come for two months and stay with me at my house in London and must make the rounds of every ball, banquet, and social event the season has on offer."

The room was still. All eyes moved from Sándor to the gentleman to Connor and back again.

"You will make the introductions," said Sándor to Connor, "purely as a disinterested party, of course."

"Of course," said Connor, relieved at being accorded no greater role.

Finally, Sándor stretched across the table and offered his hand.

"Done," he said as their hands clasped.

"And done," said the gentleman.

Francesca had avoided all company since breakfast, when the telegram arrived, and had not even taken Vinnie and Esther into her confidence. The better part of the morning was gone before she realized that all her energy had been expended in private tears while Blanche knew nothing. She summoned strength to scribble the note and ring for a boy. He had not come back. He must have found her. Blotchy redness looked back at Francesca in the mirror, but she bathed her face and arranged her hair.

Francesca and Blanche had been saved the angst and embarrassment of direct confrontation and had negotiated public meetings with civility. Their common past held them together in a vise grip while it slashed an enormous chasm between them. Yet Francesca had never really known Blanche. Since Edmund Tracey's arrest, everyone had been anxious that they should never meet until the law's proceedings had reached their dismal end. Judging by the newspapers' near beatification of Francesca, she could only assume that their sensationalist portrayal of Blanche was equally fantastic. In spite of all they shared—or perhaps because of it—Francesca felt compassion toward Blanche while being sensible that compassion can easily humiliate and render best intentions pitiable.

Blanche arrived at the appointed time. Her brisk knock at the door seemed impatient, eager to be done with whatever it might be. Francesca let May answer. Blanche watched as the maid left the suite on some errand, a signal that this interview would indeed be private. Her eyes betrayed a touch of amusement as she relaxed into an easy stance.

"Mrs. Wilson," said Francesca. "Won't you sit down?"

Francesca gestured toward the settee. Blanche glanced around a room void of hospitality. The civility of tea had seemed somehow out of place, and stronger refreshment, were it needed, was well within reach.

"Thank you."

Blanche took a thousand years to cross the room and a hundred more to sit down. She fumbled in her pocket and pulled from it a small gold cigarette case, opened it, and offered it to Francesca.

"No, thank you. I don't smoke."

"Pity," said Blanche as she drew out a cigarette. She looked around for a lighter.

"Allow me," said Francesca, retrieving matches from the mantelshelf. She drew one out, struck it, and held it while Blanche put the cigarette to her lips and leaned forward to light it. She drew heavily and threw her head back. A jet of smoke shot from the corner of her lips and over her shoulder.

"I'll come to the point, if I may," said Francesca.

Blanche considered Francesca before she answered, and then said, "By all means."

"I'm so sorry there is no easier way to do this." Francesca returned to the mantelshelf, took a telegram that was leaning against a little porcelain vase of mountain wildflowers, and stood for a moment, holding it and looking at Blanche.

"This came this morning from New York." She held the telegram toward Blanche. "I wanted you to know as soon as possible. I didn't want you to hear it from someone else. I'm sorry I couldn't think of a better way."

Blanche took the telegram and stared at the addressee, as if the gift of penetrating sight could burn her vision through the paper and draw out its contents without opening it. She dropped her hand that held the unopened telegram to her lap.

"I have yet to communicate the contents to anyone else. I'll leave you alone. Please take as much time as you need. It's no trouble."

As she opened the door, she glanced back long enough to see Blanche's face drain of color as she turned her gaze from Francesca to the telegram.

Connor was having coffee on the terrace with Mrs. West when a hotel messenger interrupted them and handed him a note summoning him at once to meet Francesca in a private parlor. Never in their communications had Francesca used the word *urgently*. He excused himself to Ida. As he crossed the lobby he glimpsed Francesca and quickened his step so that he followed her into the parlor almost before she could shut the door.

"Thank you for coming," she said in a low voice.

The look of her frightened him. He thought he had seen all her moods—anger, despondency, grace, and calm—though somewhere in the back of his mind he could not recall a hearty laugh. He chided himself for thinking of laughter when she looked so pale and was clearly in some perturbation of spirit. Maybe the extreme made him think of laughter. Now that he was seeing her extreme grief, he hoped that laughter was not far off.

"What's happened?" he replied without ceremony. "Have you been crying?"

Her eyes pleaded with his for a moment, then she looked away. "Edmund's gone."

Before he could think what to say, her knees gave way and she crumpled against him. As she gave a little cry, he pulled her to her feet and guided her to the settee, where he set her down and himself next to her and held her. He leaned against the back and felt her whole weight rest against him. Her frame contracted with every sob.

Her crying gave him time to think. So, why him? Why was she not alone in her room, or pouring out her feelings to Vinnie or Esther? Perhaps it was not sympathy she sought. Sympathy could be damnable. That she could be so thoughtless as to choose him at this particular crisis only drove home to him her distress. Francesca would be mortified to think she had caused anyone discomfort. Besides, if they were to have any kind of life together, he should wish that she could come to him for any reason. He may not have chosen this one, but he acknowledged that in choosing Francesca he was relinquishing his right to choose for what reason she might come to him. Her grief was the issue, not its cause. If detachment and not sympathy was what she needed, he would supply it.

Preoccupied with these thoughts, he hardly noticed when her sobs subsided and her breathing had become calm. She lay against him, her ear to his chest, her hair brushing his face. His deep sigh seemed to bring her to herself and she sat up and without looking at him blotted her face with the thick folded handkerchief he offered her. He waited.

"Jerry sent a telegram this morning—it arrived at breakfast time." She blew her nose. "I'm sorry to be making such a fuss."

"It's all right," he said. "What did it say?"

"Something about 'No appeal. Auburn business concluded. Letter to follow. I'm sorry.' Auburn was where it was to take place."

"Have you told anyone else?"

"Only Blanche."

"Blanche?" He frowned. "Oh, yes. Of course. Blanche had to be told."

"I was afraid one of her New York connections might tell her in some ghastly way. I wanted her to have some privacy at least. She's in my room now—or was. I left her there with the telegram and came to find you. Are you sorry I did?"

"That you told Blanche? Or that you found me?" He sat forward, took her hand, held it briefly, and with a squeeze he let it go. "Never mind, I'm glad of both."

He sensed that she was not finished. He waited for her to signal in some way that their interview was over.

"Connor, I'm sorry about this—all of it."

"All of what?"

"I feel as if I'm the cause of so much unhappiness—"

"Nonsense."

"No, please listen. Please understand that it isn't just regret over Edmund." She gazed at her own hands and worked the handkerchief between them. "It's that all this unhappiness, all this desperation was so unnecessary, so wasteful. I'm as culpable as any-one. I go over and over in my head how I might have said or done something differently, how I might have chosen a path that might have had a different outcome."

She paused. He wanted to speak, but checked himself and watched her face. She swallowed hard and he thought another tor-rent might be coming, but she was calm.

"I also think about what you said about having no regrets. I don't know if I can do that. At least not now, not for a while. I don't want regret to haunt me, to follow me into whatever decisions I should make in the future, Connor. But I'd be lying to you if I said that I expect the future to be easy, that I could simply show regret the door."

When she finally looked up into his face, he realized how greatly he had been caught off guard. "Do you understand what I'm saying to you, Connor?"

Though he had never known her eyes to be anything but frank and open, they now bore through him as if to grasp some part of his being and hold it firmly. It dawned on him that in holding him thus, he was glimpsing what a life of commitment to her would mean. At its heart this was not about Edmund Tracey at all. She was not simply asking him to be honest with her, but to be honest with himself.

"Deceit and selfishness have wrought all this misery. Until de-ceit and selfishness are shown the door, regret can't follow—and forgiveness can't enter. Do you understand?"

He took his time and let himself feel her uncomfortable scrutiny.

"Yes, Frankie, I believe I'm beginning to."

Francesca sighed and sat up straight. She reached a hand up to her hair and felt for hairpins and combs, more from habit than necessity, he thought.

"I'd better go and find Blanche," she said.

"She may not want to see you."

"Then I'll let her tell me. I'd rather let her know that she doesn't have to be alone if she doesn't want to be."

"Do as you wish," he said. "I must go and find Ida. She'll be wondering what's happened to me."

Connor stood and offered his hand to help her to her feet.

"I'll treat this confidentially, of course," he said as they made for the door.

"I doubt that Mrs. West will have heard about Edmund in any case."

"I wouldn't be so sure," said Connor. "It's surprising what she manages to glean along the way. She's not a busybody but she does like to know things."

"I leave that to your discretion," said Francesca.

"Will you come to luncheon with us?" he asked in a tone that suggested he expected a negative.

She hesitated. "I think not, if you don't mind."

"Of course," he said. "I'm glad you sent for me. Truly. I hope you know I'm at your disposal at any time."

"Yes, I do know that. Thank you."

Blanche had indeed left Francesca's suite. The telegram was on the settee. May was at work in the bedchamber. A fire was burning in the grate. Francesca took the telegram, tossed it into the fire, and watched the letters of the script turn deep black and then glow white against the graying paper before it broke into ashes and died. She shuddered.

She undertook a modest toilette and changed her blouse before she sought out Blanche and tried to think what she would say upon finding her. An automaton in Francesca's form walked down three corridors before she came to Blanche's room and knocked on the door. A reluctant step approached, then seemed to turn and walk away.

"Blanche," said Francesca through the door. "Blanche, please. It's Francesca."

The steps came back and the door opened a hand's breadth.

"Please, Blanche, let me in for just a moment. Then I'll leave you alone if you want."

Blanche said nothing, but opened the door wide and stepped aside to let Francesca pass, but she stayed planted at the door and left it ajar, her hand still on the knob. Francesca saw her own grief mirrored in Blanche's face.

"I won't insult you by asking how you are," Francesca began. "I came to see if you'd like to have some lunch with me in my suite," she said, taking Connor's last offer as a cue. "No doubt that sounds like utter gall to you, but there it is."

"I don't think I cou . . ." Blanche began, looking at the floor.

"Don't be silly. Neither of us should be alone and both of us should eat. We needn't say anything to each other if we don't feel like it. Besides, it causes gossip to drink alone."

"I'm afraid I'm already ahead of you," said Blanche, nodding toward the decanter and glass on a side table.

"I didn't mean you," said Francesca. "I meant me. Let's get something to eat."

CHAPTER 47

Flagrantly Indecorous

❧

If you are walking with a woman in the country—
ascending a mountain or strolling by a bank of a river—
and your companion being fatigued, should choose to sit
upon the ground, on no account allow yourself to do the
same, but remain rigorously standing. To do otherwise
would be flagrantly indecorous and she would probably
resent it as the greatest insult.

—*Decorum*, page 127

The brilliant late morning sunshine flooded the Bow Valley in a golden glow. Wildflowers tossed in the light breeze as if turning each side to luxuriate in the strong rays. The crystalline river bubbled and rushed and surged through its rocky trough.

To distract herself, Blanche bent her energies to her work and had persuaded Sándor Király to walk with her down to the town. How a man with such a small frame could achieve such long strides she attributed to the hiking and climbing that dominated his waking hours. He strode out about a half a pace ahead of her and, to her great annoyance, carried on their conversation over his shoulder.

"Why won't you let me record your exploits here in Banff?" she asked, trying to control her exasperation. "I'm sure my readers in New York would adore learning about mountaineering."

A story—better yet a series—on exploration of any kind would go far in stemming the flood of telegrams from New York demanding a story with guts. With exploration and the conquest of unknown parts the current rage, Sándor Krisztián Filip Király seemed heaven-sent. Though he loved to talk about climbing with those who shared his passion, she was doubtful whether his patience could withstand the pumping for minutiae her stories would require. With scenery aplenty to fill in the blank spaces of her mountaineering knowledge she might captivate an ordinary reader's attention, but scenery soon would wear thin with her editor. Hitherto Király's conversations with her had been less than enthusiastic—though whether from her lack of knowledge, her true lack of interest, or the fact that she was a woman, she could not tell. He always seemed to taunt her—no, not taunt her. He challenged her, as if he knew what fears lay behind her defenses and was happy to use a walking stick or an ice axe to batter them down.

"You would become so well-known to all of New York society," offered Blanche.

"I have been to New York and have seen your 'society'. I am already well-known where it is important to me. I can get into the papers without your help if I want to."

"Well, pardon me," said Blanche, offended. "It may not matter to you, sir, but did it ever occur to you that there may be some people who, for whatever reason, are unable to share in adventure except by reading about it? That is one of the many things the *New York World* promises its readers."

She was casting her journalistic bread upon a frozen lake. She could almost predict where his remarks were headed and she did not like it.

"Yes, I read about your Nellie Bly," he said, "a very resourceful woman."

She's not my *Nellie Bly,* thought Blanche. Blanche, however, had shown no scruple in using Nellie Bly's example to hammer home her argument with the *World*'s editor to give her a job. What could boost the *World*'s sales more effectively than to have another enterprising woman to ferret out stories in the wilds of the Canadian Rockies? Even as the words left her mouth she hadn't a clue what those stories might be, but she had confidence that inspiration would strike once she got there.

The editor, Julius Chambers, had been dubious. Other women had proposed a variety of stunts and expeditions—staged at the paper's expense, of course—and had been promptly dismissed. Blanche's notoriety had gotten his attention. The Ryder murder? Intimately acquainted with the killer himself? Already possessed entrée into society? Traveled widely? Lived in South America? Though her qualifications shot her to the top of the list of female candidates—and the paper was hardly squeamish about scandal— Chambers was not sure that even Blanche's publicity was of a type that would help the *World*. Why not let her write under her maiden name? she suggested. By the time a reader might equate Blanche Wilson with Blanche Alvarado, she would have brought home the goods and the additional publicity would do her no harm. The ability to persuade, seduce, bully, and brazen her way through the last ten years were qualifications she preferred not to catalogue in his presence, but she used them all, short of seduction. Blanche had herself a job on condition that she could produce a story that would make Nellie Bly but a distant memory.

"Are you not as resourceful as she?" asked Sándor.

Another challenge.

"Certainly I am," said Blanche. "I wouldn't be here if I weren't."

"Good, then perhaps you should come along."

"Come along? You mean with you? Up the mountain?"

"Yes," was his matter-of-fact reply. "What could be better than a first-hand account of a female reporter who has climbed the Canadian Rockies?"

For a moment, Blanche's resolve failed her as she gazed at the peaks that surrounded the Bow Valley. Very well. If he would push her, she would push back.

"Rockies—plural?" she asked.

Blanche took three steps to Király's two and faced him, halting him before her.

"Are you expecting to climb your way to Vancouver?"

"Perhaps," he said, standing at ease and casually holding his walking stick at both ends. "However, it is not my reputation that is in question here."

"I beg your par—"

"How can you claim to write about mountain climbing when all you've done is view them from a safe distance? Do you think I will sit on top of a peak and write down for you everything I see— every bird or wildflower or bit of lichen that sticks to a bit of rock, knowing you are sitting by a warm fire at the Springs while I do all the work?"

"When I came to Banff I expected to write about society," said Blanche, her indignation rising, "not the exploits of some arrogant Hungarian adventurer."

"Then perhaps you should stick to society. You will have no further need of me." He went around her and proceeded along the path.

"You have proved one thing already," he called over his shoulder.

"And what might that be?" Blanche called to his back.

"That you are afraid of a little discomfort, of being on horseback day after day—in any weather—and perhaps fishing for your dinner or shooting it and preparing it on the spot."

Afraid? What gall even to suggest it. Blanche silenced the retort on her lips. No, it wasn't fear, only a sickening distaste. The prospect of unending days on the trail conjured up ghosts she thought were long since laid to rest. The interminable weeks of struggle over the Argentine plateaus and into the mountains, through wilderness as beautiful and unforgiving as any on earth, and privations, cold, and hunger reared up before her like a ghastly specter. She had survived the humiliation of her husband's suicide and ruin and her flight from creditors in lawless country, entering remote village after remote village, bartering away her few possessions for bread, risking starvation on days when hunting for game failed, depending on her few friends to form the tenuous lifeline over South America. Even when she reached the relative safety of New Orleans, what she had to do to keep herself alive was sooner forgotten.

How could she tell Király all this—that in her own way she had probably covered more of the earth's map in her escape than he ever had in all his adventures? More than once she thought she might die of exposure and she had eaten things that Sándor Király probably couldn't look at. Was it any wonder that she should prefer the warmth and luxury of the Banff Springs Hotel, drinking champagne, and rubbing shoulders with all manner of society? How could she explain what it had cost her to transform herself from a fugitive into the refined, womanly image she thought would be the making of her? She thought of the toilette case in her room, full of the unguents of deception, and what she might revert to on the trail without them. In traveling through the mountains with Király she risked reliving the most painful episode of her life.

Blanche came to herself and was aware of Király's scrutiny. No doubt her silence had arrested his attention as much as her words. He had stopped and turned and was again at his ease, but he was watching her.

O'Casey had warned her often that she was not good at hiding her thoughts and feelings. She hoped that she had caught herself in time to erase whatever veil of pain her eyes might reveal. She looked at the mountains again and tried to assume an aspect of calm. When she looked back at Király, she felt as if the whole of her character and experience had been laid bare. His look startled her until she realized that in it was no judgment—no reprimand as O'Casey would have shown her—only knowing.

"If you are afraid of what you will look like in the morning," he said as if to divert her attention from her own true thoughts, "no doubt you will have heavier concerns than these. I don't look so good myself, if that gives you any comfort—and I am—how do you call it?—grouchy, and not fit to speak to until I've had my coffee. If you should forget this, I should certainly remind you with my grouchy-making."

He crossed the few feet of ground that separated them and smiled and considered her for a moment.

"You are not afraid of grouchy men, I think," he said more

softly, but still with the edge of challenge in his voice. "I can assure you that though I may be grouchy, I am conscious that others are not to blame for my grouchiness. I simply find the mornings to be a more contemplative time and am apt to resent any intrusion into the quiet inner sanctum. I realize other persons are not so and enjoy the vigor of the morning and can be quite loud about it. Even in the mountains, however, I try to observe the decorum of a gentleman, though you understand there will be times when our safety may depend on my judgment or that of my guides not being contradicted. No, in truth, I think there is not very much you would be afraid of.

"I will make the *New York World* a proposal that may perhaps help them to forget their Nellie Bly for a moment," he said, his tone changing to business.

Blanche threw another barricade of protest before him, however easily he might see that it was made of straw.

"Oh, yes? And will you be looking for backing from the *World?*"

"Not at all. I'm perfectly capable of backing my proposal, though you yourself will need clothing and equipment for which you may wish to acquire from your paper the necessary funds. No, I'm not here to make money off your newspaper."

"That will be a refreshing change for them," said Blanche, finding it an effort to restrain her sarcasm.

"I propose for you a big story," he continued, and with both hands sketched the gesture of a headline. "*Seven Peaks in Seven Weeks.* Of course, I would have to consult my guides to ensure that such a feat is possible and something you could accomplish with us."

The title's force lit a flame of excitement in Blanche that nearly made her gasp, the type of stunt that certainly might capture Chambers's attention. *That you could accomplish with us* was the part of which Blanche was less sure. Yet Király was right—it was the very part that gave the whole enterprise veracity. His own adventures might sell papers, but to have the *World*'s female reporter accomplishing these feats herself was as good as a guarantee. Her cheeks felt warm and her breathing stepped up a little faster.

"A large consideration is the travel time between our targets," he continued. "If we could begin locally here near the hotel, even beginning with this little Tunnel Mountain"—he pointed to what looked like a comparative bump on the landscape—"and perhaps Terrace Mountain here"—he gestured with his walking stick toward the much larger peak that faced the Springs—"they would help you get used to scrambling and to using equipment. It will take careful preparation. We shall have to consult Hector's and Palliser's writings and good local guides and maps. Whatever we do we must be able to accomplish it with good credibility for you and your paper—and of course for us. It will serve none of us if you don't succeed."

Blanche could hardly take it in—"succeed." *Success* was a word from an alien vocabulary whose meaning had been barred to her. Success belonged to a land where other people traveled, a destination for which she held no ticket. Until now the only significant variable in the equation of success was represented by the bank balance of the man to whom she was tied. Never had she thought of success in terms of liberty from such men, that success might be redefined on her own terms. Yet this man, this arrogant and irritating man for whom the word *success* was as commonplace as a table or a teacup had used the word and equated it with her. Moreover, he was willing to teach her the language and lead her into this strange new land himself. His confidence frightened her in a way that had nothing to do with mountains. The hope it awakened in her left her breathless.

"We should certainly consider many of the well-known peaks that the public may recognize—Cascade Mountain perhaps, if we save this for August and the clearer weather. Castle Mountain would be a challenge for you, but not out of the question if we ascended from the back side on the northeastern slopes. Of course there are still many unnamed mountains, but they don't have to have a name to include them on our itinerary."

"You're assuming I'll agree, then?" she said, playing for time to collect her thoughts.

"Indeed you must make up your mind soon or we lose any advantage of the summer months. Shall we say by dinnertime tomorrow night you will give me your answer?"

"My editor will have to agree."

"Of course, but your own agreement is of the first importance. Once you yourself are 'sold,' shall we say, upon the idea, it should be very easy to convince your editor. I'm sure you can be *very* persuasive when it suits you." The voice was serious but the eyes were almost playful.

"Tell me," Blanche said. She paused and put one hand on her hip, mimicking his easy posture. "You wouldn't be looking for an unnamed peak to christen as 'Mount Király,' would you? I suppose it is a possibility that would give the expedition even more cachet—scaling new mountains, fording new rivers, letting the public in on it, that sort of thing."

"You may be amazed to learn, Mrs. Wilson, that this object never occurred to me. I do not deny its appeal. However, there is another alternative that may be even more appealing to your readers than 'Mount Király.'"

"And what might that be? I'm prepared to have you amaze me."

"I was thinking perhaps of 'Mount Blanche.'"

July 2, 1891
New York, New York

My dear Francesca,

I hope this letter finds you well. I think about you often and hope that you are finding Banff to be the haven you had hoped it would be.

I wish I could have spared you the sad tidings of my telegram. I wanted to tell you myself at the earliest possible moment. I feared that committing this awful intelligence to a letter first, as would have been most proper, would allow time for you to find out by other means.

I cannot tell you how Edmund's last hours were spent, except that the authorities allowed his wife to visit him at the last, so he was not completely alone, as you may be wondering. Further than that, I cannot say. I have saved the newspaper accounts since your depar-

ture, but chose not to send them without consulting you. I would be obliged if you would tell me what you want me to do with them.

No doubt you will have noticed by the return address that I have removed myself from the 57th Street house and at present am residing at my club. Since the recent sad business, life at home has become very difficult. After a long and painful interval, my wife and I have come to acceptable terms but will take no legal action at present, and leave all avenues open. She remains at the house, should you wish to communicate with her.

I have decided to take advantage of Connor's proposed plan that the investors visit some of the newer resort hotels and will use this opportunity to put distance between New York and myself. I am sure you will at once be surprised and sympathetic. I will shortly be leaving for the Grand Hotel on Mackinac Island in Michigan. I have decided to go alone and will rely on the hotel's services for what I may need rather than encumber myself with servants. I shall leave in three days and do not plan to return until early autumn, which I understand is spectacular in that part of the country.

I have just reread the above. I am sorry not to have more cheerful news. I fear I do not have it in me to write very much at present. I will, however, send you a line from Mackinac after I am settled in.

Please take care of yourself.

Sincerely yours,
W. T. Jerry Jerome

Francesca read the letter aloud to Esther and Vinnie, who had joined her for a late breakfast in her suite. The day began cold and wet, postponing morning exercise in anticipation of the afternoon sunshine that usually followed. The small fireside table where the ladies sat perusing the early post had been laden with porridge, ham, eggs, and toast.

"I can't say I'm surprised," said Esther, looking up from her own letters, her pince-nez in one hand. "About Jerry, of course." She replaced the pince-nez and resumed reading.

The subject of Edmund Tracey that had played out in tears and condolence had settled into a dull silence in the days it took for Jerry's letter to arrive. Francesca thought he might have taken a little trouble to find out more, then she repented, turning the accusation upon herself for having left New York as much as she might accuse Jerry, who had stayed.

"I'm glad for Jerry," said Vinnie, looking sheepish as she spread marmalade on her toast and looked from Esther to Francesca. "For all her good points, Maggie must be a very difficult person to live with."

"I'm sure we're all difficult in our own ways, dear," said Esther.

"That's true enough," said Vinnie.

"Unfortunately," said Francesca, replacing Jerry's missive in its envelope, "it often happens that neither party knows the true nature of the difficulty until it is too late—or nearly so." The statement could be applied either to Jerry or to herself.

Esther continued to read her letter, though Francesca detected a slight movement that indicated Esther had heard and understood.

"I'm glad for Jerry, too, actually," she continued.

"Do you think they'll divorce?" asked Vinnie. "What a scandal that would be."

"I hardly think Jerry would put Maggie in such a position," said Esther. "For all his faults he's too much of a gentleman to allow Maggie to be branded a divorcée."

"A scandal generally involves a third party," said Francesca.

"You'll have to tell Connor about Jerry," Vinnie continued.

"He probably knows already," said Esther.

"Yes," said Francesca. "Jerry will have told Connor that he's going to Mackinac at the very least. If Jerry's mentioned that he's going alone I'm sure Connor can guess the rest. But yes, I'll have to tell him—officially—that they are"—she searched for a term—"giving things time to rest."

Francesca ate the rest of her porridge and poured herself a cup of coffee.

"It's hard to say what Jerry might do in the end," she said, sitting back in her chair and taking a sip.

"It's almost inconvenient that there's no third party," said Vinnie.

"Really, dear," said Esther.

"Well, it is, from a practical standpoint. There aren't many options left to him and I can't see Maggie letting him go quietly. As to a third party," said Vinnie, "I'm sure Jerry could remedy that if he has a mind to. I can't see Maggie perpetrating such a thing, though that's probably only wishful thinking on her part."

"Lavinia dear, how dreadful," retorted Esther.

"I can't blame Vinnie," said Francesca. "I've thought precisely the same thing. I sometimes wonder why Jerry hasn't if he's so miserable."

"Maybe you prevented him," said Vinnie matter-of-factly as she raised a forkful of egg to her lips.

"I?" asked Francesca, taken aback. "What on earth do you mean?"

"Just that you were in their house for two years," said Vinnie. Francesca's thoughts took a moment to adjust to this new way of approaching the Jeromes.

"You mean people think that Jerry and I—"

"Well," Vinnie replied, "not *exactly.*"

"What do you mean, 'not exactly'?"

"Well, for one thing, your being in their house may have delayed his leaving," said Vinnie. "He would hardly have left you alone with Maggie, would he?"

"No," said Francesca, continuing to take in the many facets of Vinnie's suggestion. "No, he wouldn't have done that."

"I know I'll regret asking, but what else are you implying, Lavinia?" asked Esther.

"Oh, Aunt Esther," said Vinnie a little disdainfully. She set her knife and eggy fork on her plate and looked at Esther as if she were addled. "Surely you can guess what half of New York was speculating about Francesca's relationship with the Jeromes."

"What half of New York?" demanded Francesca.

"The half of New York that minds other people's business, perhaps?" asked Esther, looking pointedly at Vinnie.

"I'm simply saying that having a handsome young woman in a house where the husband and wife are not on the best of terms was bound to make people speculate. How can you be so blind, Francesca? Weren't Maggie and Jerry constantly fighting about you?"

"Yes, but it was usually over my 'position' or finance or marriage or something. Jerry was simply doing what you yourself suggested—protecting me from Maggie."

"How do you suppose Maggie felt about that?" asked Vinnie. "Oh, Francesca, for heaven's sake. Jerry has been protecting you as long as I can remember. If enough of that happens—especially if it happens in public—it can certainly look as if he prefers you over his own wife. It doesn't take a great leap in the imagination to conclude—"

"Yes, thank you, Lavinia," said Esther with resignation in her voice. "Unfortunately, I'm afraid I have to agree on that point."

"Why do you think I worked so hard to get you out of their house?" asked Vinnie.

"Very commendable in the circumstances, Lavinia," said Esther.

"I can't think—"

"No," said Vinnie with emphasis, "that's just the point. You *couldn't* think. With Maggie calling the doctor every five minutes and doping you with laudanum till you could hardly stand up and Jerry in a state over you, I was afraid you'd either wind up in a scandal or an asylum—or maybe even dead." Vinnie breathed out a sharp sigh. "When the settlement opportunity came up, I thought it was heaven-sent—a sign that something could finally be done."

Francesca stared at Vinnie as the latter continued eating and regarded Francesca with a look of complete self-satisfaction. Vinnie took a bite of toast, chewed with deliberation, and sipped the coffee. Francesca and Esther could only wait.

"Father helped arrange it, you know."

"Your father?" asked Esther. "I thought it was pure rebellion on your part, dear. I had no idea."

"I was going to attempt it myself, but then one evening Father and Mother were saying how concerned they were for you, which gave me the chance to talk about the idea. Mother was dubious, but Father felt strongly that it was a solution, and one he could help arrange. I was more than happy to have everyone think as Aunt Esther has done—that it was my harebrained scheme—and no one need know Father and Mother were involved."

"Even Jerry didn't know?" asked Francesca.

"We couldn't risk it. If Jerry tried to protect you from Maggie, how much more do you think he would've tried to protect you from Forsyth Street and the settlement? The only thing to do was to get you out of their house altogether."

Francesca put her head in her hands, and rubbed her forehead and then her face until her hands met over her mouth. How could she have been so stupid?

"Was it you or your father who made the arrangements with May and the other servants at Sixty-third Street?" asked Esther.

"That was Mother. Father dealt with Forsyth Street while Mother dealt with May and Sixty-third Street. I think Mother was happy to be useful, especially when we realized how much effort it would take to orchestrate everything."

"And Anne and Michael?" asked Francesca.

"Oh yes, of course."

"I must say," said Esther, "this has given me a new appreciation for your fortitude"—she leaned over and touched Vinnie's arm— "and your friendship, dear. It's a great relief to my mind to know that your parents joined you in being Francesca's guardian angels. I admire you, Lavinia."

"Thank you, Aunt Esther."

"Do you mean to tell me that all this time you've let me think that you and Anne had gone out by yourselves and found a flat to let, and that you pulled up in a carriage one morning and whisked me away—all of your own accord? I can't even begin to fathom what I owe your family."

"Nonsense, Francesca, you know perfectly well you don't owe us a thing."

"That's not true," she said, despairing of her own failure. "You saw so many things I didn't have the power to see. Dear God," she said, "if nothing else I owe you my sanity. Quite probably I owe you my life."

"We were overjoyed that we could *do* something. We couldn't sit by and watch you suffer."

"I didn't realize how bad things had gotten," said Esther with regret.

"You couldn't possibly have known," said Vinnie. "What could you have done from Boston? You could hardly have come to New York to pick a fight with Maggie Jerome."

"Nevertheless, I do feel awful about it," said Esther. "It makes me even gladder that you were looking out for your friend—and continue to do so."

"Well," said Vinnie, looking at Francesca, "if you'll allow me to interfere—"

"After this, anything," said Francesca.

"Of this I'm certain—the sooner you marry Connor, the better off you'll be."

Esther sighed.

CHAPTER 48

A Common Ground

The utmost care should be taken that all the company will be congenial to one another, and with a similarity of tastes and acquirements, so that there shall be a common ground upon which they may meet.

—*Decorum*, page 93

"But my dear Blanche—I assume I may call you so, Mrs. Wilson? We agreed that by dinnertime you would give me your answer."

Sándor Király had met her at the entrance to the restaurant. The immaculate black tailcoat hugged his muscular frame. His handsome face glowed bronze above the white collar and tie, the coal-black eyes flickered with mischief, a shock of white hair crested into a wave like the snow on a majestic peak.

"Yes, Sandy," she said, matching him arrogance for arrogance and taking a liberty that had not been formally given to her. "I did agree to tell you by dinnertime *tomorrow*, not today. I have a previous engagement with friends this evening."

As she spoke she drew the folded fan of ecru feathers through her gloved hand and then swung it on its braided cord from her wrist. She played with her beaded bag as if making sure it contained the requisite lace handkerchief. Though the climate made a fan superfluous and the bag was nearly so, Blanche chose her accessories with care, finding them as handy for expressing emotion as an actor finds his properties.

"I'll meet you here at this time tomorrow," she continued. "If the answer is no, I'll be dining with other friends again. If the answer is yes, we'll dine together and you can order the champagne." She brushed the impeccable shirtfront lightly with the fan in a playful gesture of dismissal. Király bowed and called for the maître d'.

In spite of this bravado, Blanche had feared that dinner with Király would be a seven-course recital of his entreaties of the morning. Király had all but diverted their walk to include the Banff telegraph office to send Chambers a wire forthwith. With strenuous effort she held him to his promise of a day and a night to think and plan.

In fact, as soon as Sándor Király was safely in his room, she sent Chambers a telegram from the hotel. "Propose series. Seven peaks in seven weeks. Adventurer Sándor Király to guide self in small party. Please advise." Within hours the wire would reach the editor's desk in New York. She expected an enthusiastic reply, but needed to know before speaking to Király again whether she could leave the *World* on tenterhooks for seven weeks with little or no communication as each peak was conquered. Chambers would, no doubt, think of every problem, every angle—it was what she counted on. The *World* had endured periods of silence while Nellie Bly traveled from point to point for seventy-two days, but could Chambers wait for half so long before a word from Blanche Wilson? If she had misjudged the *World* and the answer were negative, she needed to know before tomorrow night. No, Király must wait.

The telegram dispatched, Blanche had felt at a loose end. To want to pour out her excitement and misgivings was only natural, but to whom? To seek out O'Casey was awkward and she had already strained any budding bonds of friendship with other guests by her incessant quest for stories. To her own amazement and annoyance, she found herself in need of something else, something she never had needed before—the counsel of other women. Not counsel perhaps—she knew what her answer to Király would be if Chambers agreed—but she needed something from them she could not quite put her finger on.

Blanche had always found friendship with her own sex difficult. From her point of view, women filled two functions: They either provided entrée or obstacle into society or competition for the attention of men. Being female, they understood Blanche and her motives too well to be either conspirators or confidantes. Now, however, with the prospect of weeks alone in the wilderness with a difficult man, cut off from the world, risking injury or worse, she needed someone more than Julius Chambers, or even Connor O'Casey, to worry about whether she returned. Whether anyone would bestow a blessing or a curse-and-good-riddance at her departure, Blanche felt she must leave with something. Moreover, a handful of ladies with the story from her own lips to keep her memory alive was more desirable than to become the minor subject of a few days' hotel gossip.

That afternoon she had sought the help of the one person on earth to whom she had never thought she would turn. Blanche left a note with May requesting the ladies' company that evening and hoped she did not sound as desperate as she felt. Francesca's short reply assured her that she, Esther, Vinnie, and Ida West would dine with Blanche.

Having dismissed Király, Blanche waited for them at the restaurant's entrance. A few moments later Francesca appeared, leading her small brigade. Francesca smiled and extended her hand, and with an amiable, "Good evening," shook Blanche's fingertips. She met Blanche's eye with a barely perceptible inquiring look, as if she were ready to take Blanche's cue whenever she chose to give it.

"Mrs. Wilson, I believe you have met Mrs. West," said Francesca. Ida and Blanche shook hands. "And you may know Mrs. Gray and Miss Lawrence, though I don't know if you've ever made their acquaintances formally." They, too, shook hands with Blanche.

"I'm very glad you could join me," said Blanche with mixed sincerity and trepidation. She felt some small talk was necessary, but feared her conversation might run dry before they were even seated.

"I understand you ladies went for a drive," she began.

"Yes," offered Vinnie. "We started before dawn, if you can believe it, but we had to. We had a long drive up the Bow Valley."

"The packers, poor dears, were up well before us," Esther chuckled, "but they had attended to all the provisions and the guides were waiting for us as we emerged from our *warm, comfortable* rooms," this with emphasis and a significant look at Francesca, "cheerful as anything, though I myself could hardly drag one eye open."

"A flask of hot coffee did the trick," said Ida, leaning forward on her walking stick and lowering her voice. "And a flask of something else to put in it later."

"Even I might have done with a hot toddy at that hour," said Vinnie.

"Bracing, I call it," said Francesca. "It was wonderful."

"In any case, they had us well wrapped up," said Esther, "and by midday the sun was very warm."

"What a lovely gown," said Vinnie, admiring Blanche's creamy velvet with its cascade of satin rosettes, seed pearls, and bugle beads across the bosom and falling to the hip. "Goodness, you two look like salt and pepper."

"Salt and pepper?" asked Blanche.

"Yes," Vinnie replied. "Your white gown and Francesca's black moiré. You complement each other beautifully." *Another first*, thought Blanche. The contrast was not lost on her—Francesca with her flaxen froth of hair, black silk gown, black beaded bag, and black gloves left Blanche feeling like the White Queen. The ladies laughed politely.

"Shall we go in?" Blanche said.

The elder ladies preceded her as she and Vinnie, and particularly Francesca, exchanged a few words as they made their way across the restaurant. With all eyes upon them, she was anxious to be seen as an intimate. As they passed, Király looked like a man whose bluff had been called, and Connor's astonished face softened into amusement.

Seating, presentation of menus, and the quick order of aperitifs left the ladies to themselves.

"I understand you've been kept quite busy with gathering stories for the *World*," Francesca began. "Successfully, I hope."

"Yes, thank you," said Blanche, drawing off her gloves and laying them across her lap. "Do you see that couple?" She indicated with a glance a handsome middle-aged man with gray at the temples in the company of a younger raven-haired beauty.

"Oh, yes," said Ida. "I've been wondering about them. Diplomat, isn't he?"

"I suppose King Leopold does need a good stock of diplomats," said Blanche. "Though I doubt that he's been employing them to good effect in the Congo. No, he runs some of the crown's business affairs there—the rubber plantations mainly."

"Pretty brutally, too, as I understand it," said Francesca.

"Yes, well, that's hardly a subject for the society columns," said Blanche. "They're here on holiday from the rigors of life in the Congo Free State."

"Not an easily negotiated topic," said Esther. "My hat goes off to you."

"What about those people?" asked Vinnie with a nod just past Blanche's shoulder. "They look as if they're trying to catch your eye."

As Blanche turned, the two people in question smiled broadly, the man nodding and the woman effecting a discreet wave of the hand.

"Don't mind them," said Ida, raising a hand as her glance met theirs. "They may not exactly be your idea of 'society' but they will be, if they have anything to say about it. It might be prudent if you got on their good side."

"Mining?" asked Vinnie.

"No, lumber—from the upper Middle West," answered Blanche, as if the American Midwest were purgatory.

"From what I hear they've added a couple of railroads into the bargain," added Ida. "I wouldn't underestimate the influence they may have if you're inclined to be charitable. Like most of us they're a little baffled as to how to go about it."

"Anyone exotic?" inquired Esther.

"As a matter of fact, yes, but I don't see him here. He tends to take his meals in his suite. An Egyptian gentleman, a cousin of Ismail Pasha a couple of times removed. Educated at Oxford, not Paris. A very polished and refined gentleman. He's here as part of his Grand Tour, having done Europe and North Africa already."

"How on earth did you get an interview with him?" asked Vinnie.

"I would like to think it was my magnetic personality, but I think it was the novelty of an interview by a woman that piqued his interest," admitted Blanche. "There's a gentleman dining alone on the far side of the room."

"Oh, yes," said Esther. "I see him nearly every night. He listens to the music after dinner and smokes a cigar. Occasionally I see him walk down to the town, but he's always alone and seems not to join in any activities. Has he no companions?"

"I happen to know he's a former intimate of Virginie Oldoini— the countess of Castiglione, you know. But that was a very long time ago. He haunts the Springs nearly as she haunts Paris at night. I doubt very much that he's here to make new friends."

"I noticed you in conversation with Sándor Király," said Vinnie. "What made him condescend to an interview? My impression was that he had no time for such antics." Blanche was grateful the subject had emerged so naturally.

"I imagine he hasn't been the easiest interview you've ever given," said Ida. "He's a cagy monkey and very hard to pin down."

"Yes," said Francesca. "You're lucky you were able to speak with him at all."

"I think he tests people to see if they can keep up with him," said Ida. "The only thing that saves me from that kind of test is my gamey lower extremity, if you'll excuse my mentioning it. Instead I put him through his paces in speaking English, but he seems good humored enough. Even so, he can't be an easy man to be around for long."

"As a matter of fact," said Blanche, with a portentous pause, "I am quite likely to be around him for a considerable time."

Clearly she had captured the ladies' attention, for they all stopped, exchanged looks, and then stared at her in silent chorus.

"Sounds intriguing," offered Francesca. "Are you at liberty to tell us?"

"I suppose not," Blanche said, "not really."

"Even more intriguing," said Vinnie.

"Oh come, Mrs. Wilson," Francesca said in a more relaxed tone. "You don't mean to invite us to dinner just to tease us, do you?"

"No, of course not," said Blanche. "Sandy Király has concocted a new expedition here in the Rockies and has invited me to cover it for the newspaper."

"Oh, Blanche—Mrs. Wilson—that's wonderful," cried Francesca.

"Now, please," said Blanche, holding up an arresting hand as similar exclamations of pleasure and excitement came forth. "I've wired my editor in New York and am waiting to receive confirmation from him." A sudden qualm overtook Blanche. What if Chambers did not confirm? "Of course, he may not like Sandy's project in the least," she added.

"Now you must tell us," said Esther. "How are we to judge his likely reaction? Do we not represent your readership? If we think it is a good idea, how can it fail with him?"

"If he balks, you can tell him we said so," said Ida. "Out with it. What has Sandy talked you into?"

A great weight lifted from Blanche's being. Unwittingly, the ladies had helped to frame the subject in such a way that for the present these events lay beyond her control. Moreover, if Chambers turned her down the responsibility lay with him.

"Sandy has proposed an adventure he is calling 'Seven Peaks in Seven Weeks.' He proposes to mount a small expedition to conquer seven peaks—and take me with him."

"Not climbing, too," said Francesca.

"Yes, climbing, too."

Again the ladies stopped and stared, this time with more caution.

"What is your own opinion of the scheme?" asked Esther, in a tone that hinted some misgiving.

"I must admit to a good deal of surprise when he suggested it. He said at once that many ladies of the best society in Europe have taken up mountaineering. He believes there are many peaks here suitable for a beginner—challenging certainly, but not impossible. He has also assured me that though he will certainly push me, he will not push me beyond my ability. I'm quite determined."

"Sandy may be keen on climbing," said Ida, "but he'll be equally keen on bringing you back in one piece."

"How many will you be?" asked Esther.

"Two guides, a packer who will also cook for us, Sandy's man

János, who has been his companion on many such expeditions, Sandy, and me," said Blanche.

"All men. Goodness," said Vinnie.

"No apprehensions?" asked Francesca.

"To be honest," Blanche replied, a little more subdued and trying not to betray the full extent of her misgiving, "I have many. Can a woman who is more fit for an opera box or a ballroom accomplish such a feat?"

"Have you promised Chambers that those seven peaks will be yours as well as Király's?" asked Francesca.

"Not as yet. One can only convey so much by telegram, which may be to my advantage."

"Seven weeks on an expedition in the Canadian Rockies may provide ample fodder for news, even if you only cover your companions' conquests," Esther offered.

"Thank you for that," said Blanche. "I do think my editor will hope for more—but yes, there will probably be many opportunities for stories besides teetering on the tops of mountains with a madman."

"What a wonderful opportunity," said Francesca. "This could be the making of you, you know. You'll never get this chance again. I'm confident that you will be able to make the best of whatever comes, and that you'll come back to us safely to tell us all about it."

Francesca's sincerity took Blanche aback. For a moment her eyes stung with the promise of tears, but Vinnie helped to check them.

"I think a lecture at the Springs would be in order, don't you?" Vinnie asked of the ladies. "Maybe even back in New York. Would the newspaper arrange such a lecture?"

"Perhaps a joint lecture with you and Király," said Esther.

"If he can sit still long enough," said Ida.

"You see," said Francesca. "We all know you can do it."

"You've packed me off for the hinterlands already," said Blanche. "I haven't even heard from my editor yet."

"That doesn't matter," said Ida. "Whichever way it goes, I think this calls for champagne." She raised her hand. "Oh, waiter."

CHAPTER 49

Leavetaking

❦

But when the time for departure has been finally fixed upon, no obstacles should be placed in the way of leave-taking. Help him in every possible way to depart, at the same time giving him a general invitation to renew the visit at some future period.

—*Decorum*, page 90

"Come in, my dear. I've ordered some tea."

Francesca had received the invitation from Ida West on a few minutes' notice—tea in Ida's suite at four o'clock. She had viewed the invitation with mild suspicion.

"Would you rather have something stronger?" asked Ida. She went to a small side table. "Scotch whisky or I have a little cognac?"

"Cognac, if you don't mind."

"That's the spirit."

Ida poured the cognac into the glass, handed it to Francesca, and then poured herself a whiskey. She handed Francesca a napkin before sitting on the settee in front of the tea tray on which was arranged plates of tea sandwiches and cakes. Francesca sat in the side chair opposite Ida.

"I had to cultivate a taste for tea, you know," said Ida, offering

Francesca a small plate with one hand and the plate of tea sandwiches with the other. "Of coffee or tea, I prefer good strong coffee. D'you know how we used to make it?"

Francesca shook her head.

"Sunday we ground the coffee and threw a handful into the coffeepot and boiled it on the stove. Monday, we threw another handful into the pot and boiled it. Tuesday, another handful—and Wednesday and Thursday and so on through the week. On Saturday, we cleaned the pot." Though boiled coffee was not unknown to Francesca, the thought made her wince. Ida chuckled to herself. "We made the best coffee you'll ever have in your life. Even Connor would say so."

The two ladies had little in common but their acquaintance with Connor, which made frequent references to him inevitable. Francesca suspected that in spite of the small talk, Ida West had a reason for speaking to her privately, and that reason might be her favorite subject. Francesca ate her sandwich in silence and was not displeased with the restlessness her reticence seemed to produce in Ida West.

"You're not a very curious woman, are you, dear?" asked Ida bluntly.

"On the contrary, my curiosity about some things can be insatiable," Francesca laughed. "I have found, however, that it's often more prudent to keep my curiosity to myself." She ate the last bite of sandwich and helped herself to another.

"Prudence and lack of curiosity can be very irritating virtues when a body has something to say," said Ida wryly.

"I suppose there's no chance that my devastating lack of curiosity will dissuade you."

"Hardly," said Ida, cutting a small piece of seed cake and offering it to Francesca on a fresh plate. "Do you want my advice? Never mind answering. You're getting it."

Francesca took the plate, but said nothing.

"Marry him," said Ida firmly.

"Did he send you as his emissary?" asked Francesca, trying to maintain her composure.

"We do talk a good deal. He doesn't confide in me, if that's what you're thinking. No, it's as much what he doesn't say about you as what he does say."

"Then why?" asked Francesca. She took the plate, broke off a piece of the cake, and ate with her fingers. "Why have you taken it upon yourself?"

"Because he's a good man."

Ida arranged a cushion, took the glass of whiskey from the table, and sat back.

"I didn't say he's a perfect man," she continued. "No man is— but he is a good man. What's more, he knows he's not perfect. Don't let him bluff you. He wants molding and shaping whether he admits it or not. You could be the making of him, and he knows it."

"Bluff" had struck Francesca as her first impression of Connor. She had even used it to his face and he himself had not contested it. Was this a signal that her first impressions were to be relied upon? For the present she was too annoyed to concede anything.

"I realize that I'm a comparative stranger to you," said Francesca, her equilibrium restored. "Your interests naturally lie on his side, but I have interests as well. What, in your opinion, will marrying Connor make me—a better woman?"

"Quite possibly," said Ida, taking a sip of whiskey. "You underestimate him so dreadfully. At the very least he can help you get what you want, and the whole business could probably mold and shape the both of you for the better. The fact that you don't need it is probably part of Connor's attraction to you. It won't be an obstacle to your life together."

Had Francesca not used a similar argument with Jerry when she told him about Connor and Banff? She stewed in silence and finished her cake.

"What's the matter?" asked Ida.

"Love is the matter," said Francesca, weary and angry at the same time. She took a large sip of cognac. "Or is love not in vogue this year? God knows I've seen enough loveless marriages. I had hoped I wouldn't have a loveless marriage myself."

"Then don't have one," said Ida. "It depends on you as much as on him. Now, if you want flowers and candy and somebody who'll salve your hurt feelings for you and protect you from the world, then indeed Connor O'Casey is not the man for you. If anything, he'll make you face life, not help you run from it."

"There's such a thing as being tired of life."

"You think he doesn't know that, too? You think he doesn't know the difference between running from life and needing rest from it? He doesn't want a mother, he wants a wife," Ida said with some impatience. "As for pampering, there's a time and place for that, and don't think there isn't." She stopped a moment and seemed to study Francesca.

"You can't make me believe that loveless marriages are the only marriages you've ever known," she said. "Are they?"

"Of course not," said Francesca.

How could they be, when the best marriage she had ever known was the marriage that brought forth her and her brother. Was she to be afraid of any marriage because of a few miserable examples? For nearly five years she had tried to reason herself either into or out of her fears until she no longer trusted herself to recognize what might truly make her happy.

"Did you love your husband?" asked Francesca.

"Walt?" Ida mused. "When I met Walter West neither one of us had a bean. He was a scrappy fella, though. I was scrappy, too, come to that."

Francesca recalled Connor's word for herself—*scrappy*—and understood now where he got it. Not argumentative necessarily, not difficult, or looking to pick a fight. Knowing Ida gave the word a different, perhaps truer meaning—toughness, stamina, an ability to stand on one's own two feet. In such a light the word was not as offensive as she had taken it when Connor first ascribed it to her. She almost liked it.

"We got on well because we understood each other," Ida continued. "We wanted the same things and weren't afraid of work. It was a good time in many ways. We were equals. We had to be or we'd've died, simple as that. Making money almost made things harder. Life changed. Our jobs became different—his in business, mine more and more in family and home, something I wasn't even sure I wanted. But we stuck with it. Turns out the children were the best part of us. No regrets there. Walter was good to me without assuming he knew how he should be good. I molded and shaped him, too, and it worked out fine for all of us."

"But did you love him?" asked Francesca, unwilling to give any ground.

"Yes," said Ida, "I grew to love Walter West very much."

A gray cloud passed across the sky as they sipped their drinks and curtained the room in shadow. A few drops of rain followed until a steady patter caused Ida to rise and close the window. She fetched her glass from the table and motioned to Francesca to hand hers to her to be refreshed. Instead Francesca rose, glass in hand, and followed her to the drinks stand and stood close by Ida as she poured more cognac and whiskey.

"I don't mean to pry or stir up bad memories," Francesca began more calmly, "but—"

"How did Walt die? And how was Connor involved?" asked Ida with her usual bluntness. "I expected you'd ask that sooner or later."

Francesca regained her seat across from the settee. Ida set her glass on the mantelshelf and stirred the fire to life. Francesca watched her as she put on another log—this solid, scrappy, self-reliant woman who, like herself, would not bother a servant to come and do a simple act she could just as easily perform, and do it without comment.

"Walt and Connor met working in the mines more than twenty years ago. They became fast friends. The boys scraped together enough to stake their first silver claim and hire miners of their own."

Francesca smiled at Ida's calling them "boys." This put Connor in a new light, and Walter, too, if Ida would use such an endearing term. Connor and endearing terms seemed out of place. No, that wasn't true, she thought. Had he not had the effrontery—no, perhaps effrontery was too strong a word—the audacity, that was it—to call her Frankie?

"They always had good relations with the men," Ida continued. "Having been miners themselves, they tried to do right by them. As they prospered, the boys took on investors—men who'd already made their money and hadn't set foot in a mine and weren't about to.

"Walt and Connor had a hell of a time with them—the investors, I mean. The boys knew how terrible and dangerous the conditions were. They spent a lot of time at the mine, keeping an eye on things, while the other investors built themselves fine homes in Leadville and Denver. The boys tried to keep up good relations and see that the miners were paid right—paid at all sometimes. When the investors came in the miners began to think that the boys had sold out. The miners had to blame somebody for their wretched conditions. Walt and Connor were the most visible because they were always there.

"It came to a head one day when Prescott, the chief of the investors, came out to the Five Star with a posse of bodyguards. The miners hadn't been paid in weeks, to the point where Walt and Connor were taking money out of their own cuts to keep them from getting too disgruntled—and discouraged. Those miners had families to support. Connor had seen Walt in the same fix, trying to support me when the mine owners wouldn't ante up. Sometimes Connor'd go with nothing for our sakes. When the boys bought into the Five Star they vowed it would be different, but they were bucked up against a majority who didn't want things to change, no matter how hard the boys tried to convince them. By the time Prescott arrived, everybody was too worked up to listen. The situation got out of hand and the miners rioted. Prescott's men killed at least half a dozen miners before the miners killed him and his men—all of 'em. Then they took all that pent-up fury out on the boys and beat poor Walt to death. They murdered him." Ida took a drink of whiskey. "They nearly murdered Connor, too. He was out cold, and broken in body, and had been left for dead."

Francesca was thunderstruck. For all her living in New York and her experience of desperate people in the tenements and the settlement house, she could hardly comprehend that kind of desperation. She felt terrified and desolate. Her imagination conjured up her life of the last nine months had Connor O'Casey not been there to challenge everything she hoped for and believed in. The expectations of the Jeromes and the Worths and all New York society became puny and insignificant and Edmund Tracey and Nell Ryder receded into a kind of moral oblivion. She felt herself breathing harder and a flush creeping over her cheeks. The last barrier was crumbling.

"Afterward, I brought Connor to Denver with me. It was a mercy for me to look after him and keep myself occupied. It took him six months to recover. I think the whole thing scared the liver out of him, if you'll excuse my mentioning it. Once he was on his feet, he came out fighting. You should have seen him. He didn't know how, but he was going to find a way to make something of himself. Not just money. That wasn't the same as making something of his life."

The patter against the window became more intermittent and clouds began to lift. A few tentative shafts of sunlight began to illuminate the room. Francesca turned and stood before the fire. Taking the poker from its stand, she jabbed it into the logs and released a new flame. When she again sat across from Ida, Francesca found her looking at her, dry-eyed and determined.

"Marry him, Francesca," said Ida with finality. "I've known Connor O'Casey for twenty years. You won't find a truer partner anywhere. He understands when the work has to be done to make something the way you want it to be. He'll work at his marriage with you. Oh, sure, there may be times when you and he don't like it very much—or each other very much, come to that. But he's never been a shirker and he knows when the work may be the only thing that gets you through. He knows a good thing and he sees that in you." Ida fixed a scolding eye on Francesca. "If you refuse him, I'll mark you down as the most foolish woman I've ever known." Ida left Francesca, still and silent, to stare at the tea service, the only movement the occasional sip of whiskey.

Francesca had not credited Connor with deep feelings, or with a deep sense of honor and fairness that she herself shared. When she sought him out to tell him about Tracey, it was to unburden herself to a human being who she thought could deflect a troublesome emotion and be done with it. Had she so misjudged him? Could anything allow even a particle of love to grow up between them?

What of the spark, that part of life she so wanted? What of romance? She had grown comfortable with her assessment of Connor. Now Ida West had fomented anarchy in Francesca's orderly emotions. She came to herself and realized she could not sit in Ida's room to work out what it meant.

"Thank you for the tea, Mrs. West," said Francesca, rising. "I must go. Thank you for the enlightening conversation." As she reached the door, she turned back, thinking to forestall future outbreaks, and added, "I trust we needn't repeat this topic in the future."

"Just remember," said Ida, calling after her. "He likes his coffee good and strong."

The glowing remnants of a northern summer dusk mingled with thin rays of golden dawn behind Terrace Mountain. Shadows moved in the great portico of the Banff Springs Hotel. Camping supplies, food stores, climbing equipment, and hunting weapons lay in ever-diminishing heaps on the pavement as the packers secured them to the horses. Király's man, János, went from horse to horse, taking final inventory, ensuring nothing was missed, checking straps and buckles, ropes and knots. Blanche and Sándor Király, heads bent over a map that shone in the lamplight, reviewed the first day's route with the two guides—a smooth-faced young man of the Stony nation and a middle-aged Swiss whose experience was carved deeply in a weathered face.

Blanche, unaccustomed to early nights and early mornings, had slept fitfully, caught in the anticipation of adventure and the fear that she had forgotten something. Between the ceaseless mental recitations of the contents of every saddlebag and haversack, she recalled with pleasure Chambers's enthusiastic telegram and the many well wishes she received at the expedition's champagne reception. How odd to return to her room to find it bare of all but her most essential possessions and to lay the electric-blue silk of evening next to the woolens ready for morning. The long hours of light and the short spate of semidarkness taunted her from behind drawn curtains. The knock at the door at four o'clock had startled her until she realized that her spirit had been ready long before.

Now, in the portico of the Springs, Blanche felt unusually alive to the voices of the men, to her breath in the cold air that mimicked the smoke from the men's pipes, to the warmth of her body cocooned in layers flannel and wool, to the prickle of her cold fingers around a hot mug of strong coffee.

The canvas-shrouded heap on the pavement was gone. Three hotel bellmen, well used to the predawn demands of life in Banff, emerged with flasks of fresh coffee, packs of the first day's meals, and full canteens of water.

Blanche broke away from the men and walked to a point where she could overlook the Bow Valley one last time from a safe vantage. She studied every river bend, every ridge, every curve of tree line like the scalloped edging on a dress that finally gave way to a gray-and-purple sheen like silk and finally to a mantle of snow. How different was this departure from the one that had catapulted her across the plateaus and mountains so many years ago, the one that faded from memory with each passing year. As she faced the Canadian Rockies and the adventure that lay ahead, none of it seemed real nor did the part she would soon play.

An old irony struck her—how many times had she encountered beauty in her life that had brought with it only hardship and danger? But what had been the greater danger, beauty or man? For a moment she thought of the human element with disdain and found relief in the notion that for seven weeks beauty, danger, and the peccadilloes of the human element might be more clear-cut. She thought of how far she'd come in spite of her own failings, or maybe because of them, and wondered what Blanche Wilson she might encounter in the mountains. The crunch of boots brought her back to herself. She turned.

"It's nearly time, Blanche," said Sándor. "Are you ready?"

She flung the last cold drops of coffee from her cup into the shrubbery and followed him back to the horses. As János and the guides began to mount, three figures walked toward them from the hotel—Francesca in a woolen skirt and cardigan, a shawl thrown over her shoulders, her nighttime braid pinned into a thick coil; Ida in her tweeds; Connor in woolens with a hastily tied muffler over his collarless shirt.

"I've been lying awake all night thinking about you," said Francesca. "We could hardly let you escape without seeing you off properly. I see we've caught you just in time."

Blanche was glad Francesca had not intimated the evening before that she would make this effort, lest she forget her promise, and was gratified by the unexpected kindness.

"Is one of those large leather bags full of paper and pencils?" Ida asked.

"Nearly so," said Blanche, laughing. "Though I was admonished to pack light."

"This may be a first, Király," said Connor. "If you can manage to get any lady to pack light, your expedition will have made a major contribution to mankind."

"Never!" jeered Blanche and Francesca together.

"Ladies always know how to pack for the occasion, do they not, Mrs. Wilson?" said Francesca.

"Indeed, always," answered Blanche. "Though I confess that packing for this occasion has been an education."

"That should be of great interest to your readers," said Ida. "It should give your ladies back East a whole new notion of what's essential to meet any occasion."

"He's allowed me a minimum of creature comforts," said Blanche. "I shall be quite the wild woman."

"Yes, but I've put the notebooks in oilskin," said Sándor with good humor. "The notebooks will be precious commodities, you know, and must be protected at all costs—not only now when they are empty, of course, but most assuredly when they are full."

"You've got quite an entourage, Király," said Connor, prompting Sándor to take him and Ida on a brief tour up and down the train, explaining the provisions as he went and leaving Blanche and Francesca to themselves.

"I hardly recognized you," said Francesca, pointing to the wide-brimmed hat that framed Blanche's face in a halo of drab wool felt. "It suits you."

"Does it?" said Blanche. "Sandy insisted on something serviceable—and it isn't the last thing he's insisted on. But there, I'm afraid I'll shock you."

"Shock me? Why?"

"He was appalled at my first attempt at mountaineering and blamed my 'impractical and unnecessary modesty,' as he calls it, in wearing a traveling suit. It was all I had for the purpose, much to his chagrin. On the second attempt he had the unspeakable gall to produce a pair of plus fours and puttees, which I patently refused, arguing that skirts and petticoats are much warmer. Unfortunately, I soon regretted it, to his immense satisfaction, and have now added a set of men's woolen all-in-ones."

Francesca laughed.

"So we have struck a bargain," Blanche continued. "I ride, camp, and hike properly and warmly attired in a skirt. On days we actually climb I subject myself to the humiliation of men's clothes."

"You poor thing. At least you won't be anywhere where women or other men will see you. I've often wondered what it would be like to try on men's clothes," Francesca mused, a confession that surprised Blanche. "They may not be ladylike, but they must be no end comfortable. I suspect men would be apoplectic with shock and indignation, but women—who knows? A good many of our sex might welcome it."

Blanche had not pegged Francesca for a rebel and thought with some amusement that Connor's hands might be fuller than he suspected.

"Nonetheless, the man's hat suits you," said Francesca. "You may start a new fashion—in more than one respect."

Then Francesca's light-hearted manner changed. Her eye met Blanche's with a look that gave her words significance.

"You will no doubt learn that a great many things suit you that you never would have realized without this opportunity."

"Yes, I am aware of that," said Blanche with some hesitation, "for better or worse."

"You think it won't be better?" asked Francesca. "To be given the chance to learn it is a great thing. I'm confident it can be nothing less."

"Meaning that anything is better than hopeless?" asked Blanche with an edge of sarcasm, then immediately regretted her tone.

"Don't be silly," said Francesca, calling her to account. "You're far from hopeless."

"So, you think I'm redeemable?" asked Blanche, trying to keep her tone light and looking away from Francesca's discerning eye. It was a serious question and one for which Blanche was surprised to discover she needed an answer, though she was loath to admit it, even to herself. Francesca seemed to sense what lay beneath.

"Redeemable? Of course, you are. You always have been. I think you know you are. I'll wager you'll be a different person when you return."

"Yes, I'm aware of that, too," said Blanche, somewhat discomfited. No one had ever cut so close to the bone.

"And is he redeemable?" she asked, looking at Connor as he and Ida and Sándor spoke with the guides.

"Connor?" Francesca asked, following Blanche's gaze. "You may be happy to know that according to the man himself, he's counting on it."

"Yes, he would be," said Blanche.

Francesca looked at Blanche with a start.

"You believe that?"

"That may be the truest thing about him," said Blanche. "It may be why he's right for you and not for me. I can see that now. I couldn't then—or I didn't want to."

They stood together awkwardly. Then Francesca reached up and unclasped a fine chain from the back of her neck.

"Take this with you," she said as she pulled the knotted scarf from Blanche's neck and secured the golden chain with the garnet pendant. "It belonged to my mother. I want you to have it—a talisman against injury, and to remind you of those who are thinking of you every day."

The gift startled Blanche. She looked at the garnet and was about to protest with words she was sure Francesca would instantly see through.

"Thank you," she said, taking refuge in formula. "That's very kind of you."

Before Francesca could reply, Sándor, Ida, and Connor came up to them.

"We must delay no longer, Blanche," Sándor said and turned to shake hands with Connor. "Good-bye, O'Casey, my dear fellow. Perhaps I shall book an extended stay at your new hotel when I return. Ida, my dear, *bonne chance.*" He turned and kissed her on both cheeks.

"Bless you, Sandy," she said. "Take good care of yourself—and this lady here."

"I will do my best," he replied. He took Francesca's hand and kissed it.

"Miss Lund, it has been a pleasure. I hope to see you again as well."

"I hope so, too—Sandy," said Francesca.

As Király and Blanche made for their horses, Connor laid his hand on Blanche's arm, arresting her step. This was one encounter she had hoped to avoid, but now that it had come, she found her courage rising.

"Blanche," he said, "I know the time for speeches is long past. I want you to know that I wish you the best of everything—truly. No one can be gladder than I to see you finding your way."

He seemed to hesitate for a moment, then extended his hand toward her. When she took it, he clasped his other hand over hers.

"Good luck, Blanche."

For a fraction of a moment, words caught in her throat, but she regained herself.

"Thank you, Connor," she said. "Take care of yourself, won't you?"

He merely smiled and stepped back. Francesca came forward and, with her hands on Blanche's shoulders, kissed her cheeks.

"God bless you, dear Blanche, and Godspeed."

"You think he'll find me, there in the mountains?"

"He never lost you." Francesca released her. "Good-bye, Blanche."

Like a bird whose cage had been unexpectedly left open, Blanche was released. With something like joy she mounted her horse and she and Király took their places at the front of the train with the Swiss guide with whom Sándor chatted away in German. The guide from the Stony nation and the packer urged on the pack horses as

János kept order bringing up the rear. With calls of farewell, they pulled out from the portico and made their way to the gravel path that led to Banff town.

As they made their descent, Blanche turned to look behind her and saw the three move down the path behind them, following the train to watch until the bend in the path cut them off from sight. She turned face forward and put her mind to her task as Király drew her into conversation with the guide or pointed out some detail or instruction. When she looked back again, they were gone. Of course they would be going in for breakfast, she thought, and she chided herself for the disappointment she felt. The sun was clearing the mountains when they came to the place where they would catch the last good view of the Banff Springs Hotel. Király raised his hand to draw them to a stop.

"One last look at this magnificent place for seven weeks, my dear Blanche," he said as he turned in his saddle and looked toward the Springs. "Who is that waving up there on the terrace?"

Sure enough, in the distance a fleck of white inscribed a wide arc over a tiny figure. Francesca, it seemed, had made her way to the terrace, the solitary sentinel on watch. Blanche took the long scarf from her neck and held the ends together in one hand and waved it over her head. The little figure stopped a moment, then waved the answering semaphore. Király raised his hat and waved it as the rest of the party followed suit.

"It must be your friend," Sándor said, as the party returned to the business at hand.

"Yes," said Blanche, tapping the horse's side with her heel. "It is my friend."

CHAPTER 50

Exceptions

The mode in which the avowal of love should be made, must of course, depend upon circumstances. It would be impossible to indicate the style in which the matter should be told. . . . Let it, however, be taken as a rule that an interview is best; but let it be remembered that all rules have exceptions.

—*Decorum*, page 185

The suite door opened and shut again.

"Jamie! It's about time you got back. Bring me my dressing gown, would you?"

Connor sat relaxing in the claw-footed tub, nearly shoulder high in steaming water, his arms resting on the tub's edges, a folded newspaper in one hand, a whiskey glass in the other with a cigar notched between two fingers. He was shielded behind the half-drawn curtain of the shower-bath. The door to the adjoining bedroom was closed. The marble washbasin and porcelain commode stood against the wall across from the bathtub. Freestanding near the foot of the tub was a cheval mirror and between it and the tub, a small stool, bearing the whiskey bottle, a cigar cutter, and a box of matches.

"Jamie!" Connor bellowed. "What about that dressing gown?"

Blast the man, he thought. Jamie was taking an unconscionable long time for the simple act of fetching a robe.

A hesitating step approached from the bedroom, unlike Jamie's quick, businesslike gait, accompanied by an unmistakable rustling of fine fabrics. A soft rap upon the bathroom door followed.

"Which one do you want—the dark blue silk or the jacquard flannel that looks like a blanket?" said a soft mezzo voice through the door.

For a moment, Connor was nonplussed—but only for a moment. The situation was not oft-repeated, for he considered himself a modest man, but that a woman should catch him at any point on the continuum of dress or undress did not faze him. That the woman should be Francesca—ah, that was a different thing. The possibilities presented themselves in wide array through his imagination. He smiled.

"In view of the company, I'll take the blue silk, thanks," he said, setting the glass precariously in the soap tray and taking a puff of the cigar.

Another moment passed. He heard her cross the room and pictured her calfskin-slippered feet upon the carpet as she retrieved the silk robe that lay across the bed. Through the cheval mirror he watched, amused. She pushed the door open and stood in the doorframe, peering in as if ready to avert her gaze. His movement as he took a sip of whiskey drew her eyes toward the curtained tub and her expression turned from caution to relief. Her hand was upon the doorknob and the blue robe over her arm, an ermine stole in her other hand. The evening frock of ice-blue-and-silver moiré hugged her figure, a watery-blue silk swag encircling her hips. The wide neckline left her shoulders bare, her long gloves nearly meeting the cap sleeves. Even in the mirror he could see the deep décolleté and the little well between her breasts—or did he conjure it, knowing it was there? He adjusted the glass in the soap tray and drew on the cigar.

"You'll excuse me if I don't stand."

At this she saw his movement in the mirror and an amused smile graced her lovely face.

"What a picture you are," she said, beginning to laugh. "I thought only ladies indulged in this kind of decadence. Reading, drink, cigars. My, my. Is this your usual state when bathing?"

She extended the arm that held the robe.

"I'll just toss it in your direction and leave you to it, shall I?"

"And have it end up in the bath? I'd rather not if you don't mind," he said. "You'll have to bring it in."

"You're enjoying this, aren't you?"

"I am rather," he said. "By the way, how do you come to be in this predicament?"

"I wanted to talk to you," said Francesca. "I thought I might catch you before we all met for dinner."

"I see. You have my full attention, I assure you."

"This is hardly the interview I expected."

"No doubt."

"It'll keep until later. I'll leave the robe on the rug just here."

"I'd rather that you didn't strew my belongings all over the floor. You can put it on the stool there," he said, indicating with the cigar. "Besides, I thought you were one of these modern, unflappable women."

His smile was returned with a challenging look in the mirror as she walked past the tub without looking at him and draped the robe across the stool. She turned and fastened him in a look of defiance.

Maintaining his air of nonchalance as best he could, he let the newspaper drop onto the floor, reached for a large sponge at the end of the tub, and floated it over his middle, at the same time drawing on the cigar in his other hand and blowing out the smoke toward her.

She burst forth in peals of laughter he never had thought possible in her. A gloved hand to her mouth, she threw back her head and rocked with pure mirth. Her eyes, at first wide in amazement, drank in the scene and closed tightly, as if all her attention were concentrated in merriment.

"I beg your pardon," he said. "Aren't you treatin' the gravity of this occasion a bit casual?"

In fact, the gravity was all on his side. Whether she laughed from embarrassment or his ridiculous posture, he was awestruck by her abandon. Not a feminine titter nor a childish giggle, but a ringing out from the center of her being, as if the form, cinched and restrained into womanly outlines, had finally taken leave to pop like champagne and froth over.

The day she told him about Tracey he thought the possibility of her ever laughing again had vanished—that some misplaced sense of decorum would prevent her from abandoning herself to joy. Moreover, he had feared that Tracey's handsome ghost would follow them through a lifetime of grief and self-reproach. At times he had wondered whether he could bear it, even for Francesca. To see her nearly helpless with mirth awakened the hope that he might someday make her happy. Whatever it might take to give her that laugh again and again over a lifetime, he vowed to himself, he would do it.

Her hair grew fuzzy in the steam and the flush in her cheeks made her face glow and her eyes dance. Connor thought he'd never seen her look so beautiful. He reached forward, grabbed her skirt, and drew her by silken handfuls closer and closer to him.

"Oh!" she cried. "Oh! Oh, no!" and tugged away from him— not very hard, he thought, or was it his imagination? With one last pull that nearly raised him to his feet he reached for the swag round her hips, threw her balance forward, and upended her feet. She landed across his body in a deluge of soapy water.

As the silk and linen layers submerged and covered him, she laughed like a drunken thing. He turned her and held her with one arm while he lifted her face to his and stopped her laughter with his mouth. Francesca's dripping skirts cascaded water over the side of the bathtub as she moved herself to cross him breast to breast. She propped herself against his chest and looked him in the face, then dropped her head as laughter overtook her again. He drank in the scent of her perfumed hair and reveled in the soggy, silken chrysalis that enfolded him. When she looked up he embraced her with his arms and with his lips.

The suite door again opened and shut. A knock came at the bathroom door.

"Mr. O'Casey, sir?" said Jamie's sheepish voice, as the man-servant stood frozen in the doorway, staring into the mirror.

"It's about time you got back here," said Connor over Francesca's head. "Would you please go to Miss Lund's maid and ask her, with my compliments, if she would please come and bring her mistress a new set of evening clothes?"

"Miss Martin," said Jamie to May, as the latter sat with Rosemary in their room, working at some mending. "If you please, there's been a slight mishap and Miss Lund requires a whole new set of evening dress."

"She hasn't called," said May, curiosity written on her face. "What have you to do with the matter, Mr. Lynch?"

"Well, you see," said Jamie, stepping inside and closing the door, "she's in Mr. O'Casey's suite."

Rosemary snorted a suppressed laugh and bent over her mending.

"I don't understand," said May, feigning ignorance and doing a poor job of it.

"If you please, May, there's no time to waste. Miss Lund requires a full set of evening dress—from the skin out, so to speak, and shoes and all. Perhaps it'd be best if you bring Miss Corcoran with you."

"I wouldn't miss it for the world," said Rosemary, wrapping her mending and laying it on the bedside table.

"The devil of it is, begging your pardon," said Jamie, "we've got to get it all up to Mr. O'Casey's room without drawin' any attention, if you take my meanin'."

Rosemary hooted and instantly composed herself.

"This is serious," pleaded Jamie. "We've got to go quickly. They'll be late enough for dinner as it is."

"We can wrap the dress in an overcoat and put the underlinen in a satchel," offered Rosemary.

"Best make it two satchels," said Jamie, "We'll need an extra allotment of towels."

The servants arrived to find Connor in the sitting room, nearly dressed, his tie hanging at loose ends and his cuffs without links, the mother-of-pearl cufflinks on a side table and his tailcoat lying across the back of the settee. He nodded to the maids as they bobbed slight curtseys, passed without looking at him, and followed Jamie through the bedchamber, where he motioned them toward the closed bathroom door. Permission granted to admit the maids, Jamie hastened back to Connor, closing the door that joined the sitting room to the bedchamber. Mixed expressions of horror and glee emanated from the bathroom.

"Oh, my God, miss," said May's voice to a fountain of giggles from Rosemary.

"Shhhh," Francesca admonished. "We've got quite enough to attend to."

The two men bent to the serious business of administering the cufflinks, not daring to look each other in the face, but each with an ear cocked toward the bathroom.

Rosemary appeared at the bedroom door.

"If you please, sir," she said, looking at Connor, then to Jamie, "Mr. Lynch, we'd be obliged if you could find us a bedsheet for wrapping the wet things. And if you'd be so kind as to deliver them, or see that they're delivered, discreetly, to our room while everyone's at dinner, we'd be most grateful."

"I'll see to it," said Jamie. As Rosemary returned to the matter at hand, May's voice again rang out from the bathroom.

"Oh, my God," exclaimed May again. "What are you going to do, miss? You'll have to marry him now."

"Shhh. That's enough."

At which, the two men looked at each other. Connor smiled and Jamie decorously dropped his eyes and helped Connor on with his tailcoat.

Connor tugged at his shirtsleeves, smoothed his lapels, gave himself one last look in the glass over the fireplace, and went to rap upon the bathroom door.

"Yes," said Francesca's voice in some surprise.

"I'm going out now. I'll meet you in the lobby. Jamie's leaving, too, so you ladies'll have the place to yourselves."

CHAPTER 51

The Universal Passion

❧✻❧

Love is the universal passion. We are all, at one time or another, conjugating the verb amo.

—*Decorum*, page 179

Francesca wrapped her stole around her shoulders and looked out over the landscape. The Bow Valley was filling with the last of the summer light like a great trough of gold that gilded tree and mountain as no Baroque artist could have bedecked a cathedral. In moments the gold would fade into twilight. A waning crescent moon had risen like a bowl filled with faint stars. An enormous calm settled upon her, a sense of well-being she could not remember feeling for many years. As she stood on the terrace, silent and still, watching the valley's colors change, birds headed homeward and insects tuned up for an evening rhapsody more tranquil than any music that echoed deep within the hotel.

Dinner was over. The large party of accumulated friends old and new had tested the hotel's culinary artistry. Francesca, transformed in a deep orchid silk gown of sweeping lines and void of ornament, floated above the conviviality with a light spirit. No matter where she went or with whom she might converse, she felt a pleasant connection to Connor, who always met her eye with a knowing smile that warmed her cheeks from an intimacy shared.

"What can this hotel be about?" complained Connor's elderly billiard partner to Francesca. "Here I am, dressing for dinner as per usual, when all of a sudden water starts leaking through the ceiling. Burst pipe or some damn thing."

"Problem, sir?" inquired Connor, who had caught the last few words.

"Just telling Miss Lund here that my man barely saved my wardrobe from ruin. Water all over. I can't think what the hotel can be doing. Had to move me to a different room till they could find the trouble." Connor was all sympathy and shot Francesca an amused look over the gentleman's head.

In the weeks since coming to Banff, New York had nipped at her heels like a mad dog. The telegram and Jerry's subsequent letter, even Vinnie's revelation about the Lawrences and her escape from the Jeromes, had upset the equilibrium she had hoped to regain in coming here. Then her interview with Ida brought her up short. She began to realize that although she might run away from a point on the map, she could not hide from herself. Ida and Vinnie and Blanche each had held up a mirror from which she could avert her gaze only at her peril. Each mirror showed her an ignorant, biased part of herself that mortified her. She wondered what possessed Connor to want someone as blind and willful as she and had stewed about it since Blanche's departure. A confession was nearly on her lips when she went to Connor's room, only to have her pious resolve evaporate into laughter. In spite of the restorative nature of confession, laughter had been the better tonic. She knew now what it felt like not to fret, that at least one person in the world existed to whom she had neither to explain nor prove. All that was left was to know whether he still wanted her.

A trickle of people began to populate the terrace. A familiar voice spoke in her ear.

"I came out to see if you might like a nightcap," said Connor, drawing up next to her and looking out over the Bow Valley.

"I don't believe so, thank you."

"You said you wanted to see me."

"Did I?"

"Don't tell me you've forgotten already," he said, clearing his throat. "I didn't startle you into forgetting, did I?"

"Oh, that," she said, smiling. "No, it was rather memorable." She reflected a moment and then added, "I suppose it doesn't really matter now."

"What doesn't matter?"

"I came to apologize for my appalling lack of tact in coming to see you when I got Jerry's telegram. No, that doesn't sound right. Not tact. I was so thoughtless. . . ."

"It's not like you to be thoughtless," he answered. His voice comforted her.

"I hope not," said Francesca. "I don't mean to be."

"I know that, Frankie."

"That's just it," she said in earnest. "You do know. I think I was counting on that from you."

"I did think it was a bit brazen of you to come to me and wondered what it meant—"

"But I *didn't mean* anything . . ." said Francesca, trying not to plead, for she knew she didn't need to.

"I know, I know. When you talked it out and I knew there wasn't anything behind it—anything—"

"To hurt you, you mean?"

"Yes," he said. "Well, then I was glad that you felt you could come to me—like a barrier between us might have come down somehow. Was I right to think that, Frankie?"

The name soothed her as it came off his lips, rolling over her in his mellow baritone.

"Yes," said Francesca. "I believe so."

They stood together in silence. Conversation now could hardly be private with so many there enjoying the evening, but Francesca knew not how to introduce the subject of more privacy. He seemed to read her thoughts.

"It's gettin' a bit crowded," Connor said. "Shall we take a little stroll?"

"You'll want a coat. It's getting chilly."

"Not for just a short turn round the hotel."

He offered her his arm. The living being who clasped her arm under his, the smell of pomatum and soap, the crunch of gravel under their earthbound feet comforted her.

"While we're apologizing," he said, "will you forgive me for anything hurtful or insulting I may have said to you? You're right that I bully people when it suits me, but I should know better than to bully someone I care for—" He stopped abruptly, as if catching himself before he made an exhibition of his feelings. "It's a stupid thing to do," he said in some confusion.

"To ask for forgiveness?"

"No, to treat people I care about as anything other than precious, that's all," he said. "I'm a fool that way. I am sorry, Frankie."

They had moved well away from other guests before he spoke again.

"Frankie, ought I to ask your forgiveness for Blanche?"

The question had never occurred to her before he uttered it. The fact of its total absence from her mental list of reservations about Connor O'Casey—the realization that she had never held anything against either of them—bestowed a sudden liberty upon Francesca that jolted her like a thunderclap.

"Heavens no," she said, dismissing the notion. "What right have I to forgive you for something begun before we ever knew each other? When I think of where we all were a year ago—even six months ago—how could any of us have foreseen anything that has happened? We'd have to be conjurors or prophets, and we're nothing like that, thank God. Being human is difficult enough without the burden of perfection that none of us can achieve anyway."

Ida West's words again rang in her ears. Francesca was not ready to grasp them then, but she believed them now.

"If you really feel that way, Frankie, that's more than I ever expec—"

"Of course, you realize I'll have to marry you now," Francesca broke in. It seemed the most natural thing in the world to say. She did not need to see his face to feel him register surprise. They were both quiet as she waited for his thoughts to catch up with hers.

"*You'll* have to marry *me?*"

She turned her head toward him and looked into his face.

"Yes. I've seen you in your bath," she declared. "How else am I to preserve your honor unless I make an honest man of you?"

In the waning light, she could sense the amused look on his face. He fastened his dark eyes on hers and held her there.

"I must admit, I hadn't quite thought of it in that way."

"Perhaps I shouldn't have jumped to conclusions," she said, a little embarrassed. "You do still want to marry me, don't you? Because if you don't I've just made a foolish—"

"Yes, Frankie, I do want to marry you—and strangely enough for the very reason you just said. I do want you to make me an honest man—at least a better man than I am."

"You know I can't do that for you. I can't be God for you."

What a thing for him to want of her. For a fragment of a second she thought of Edmund—a man who wanted everything around him to change for the better so that he could remain the same. Perhaps he had wanted to regain a man he had lost and mistook that journey for a treasure hunt. How different was he from Connor—a man who realized somewhere in his depths that if anything is to truly change for the better, it must first be he himself. Francesca hoped that this was so, that she was not deluding herself again. Yet was she not the one who asked him for honesty? If this request meant anything at all, was he not handing her his best intention as a basis for their life together?

"I'm not asking you to *be* God, Frankie," he chuckled. "Though I must say, your intimate acquaintance with the Almighty did give me pause. To be truthful, I'm not even sure that God is what I need. I am sure of one thing, though, and that is that in marrying you I'm sure to get closer to the both of you."

"The fact that you should even want to be a better man at all—"

"Now, let's not run away with the idea," he teased.

He turned her to face him and took her hand between both of his, as if sensing that a moment more of hesitation would undo her. Night was closing in—as much as night can ever do in Banff in late July.

"Francesca Lund—do you have a second name, by the way?"

"No, as a matter of fact."

"Truly?" said Connor in some surprise. "Not two or three? Right then." He drew her close so that her clasped hand rested on his chest and his face nearly touched hers. "Francesca Lund, will you do me the honor of becoming my wife? Can't we escape tomorrow morning down to Banff town and haul the minister out of bed if we have to and have him marry us in that little church? Can't we come back and demand that all your kit and caboodle be moved to my suite and spend the rest of our days here in honeymoon? Or would you rather that I take you off to another point on the edge of the earth where we can be together and say to hell with the rest of the world?"

"Are those your terms?" she asked, drawing her hands from his and walking from him a few steps. Her courage rose. "Because if they are your terms, I can't possibly accept."

"Not accept?" asked Connor, his voice full of bewilderment. "But you just said—"

"What a thing to ask of me," she said, the passion rising in her voice, and in her heart. "Do you think I want to slink away as if I'm ashamed of you and wed you in some hidey hole? To deny myself the pure joy of standing up before the multitude and showing off the man I'm going to marry? No, Connor. After all this time, after everything that's happened, after a lifetime of waiting for a man of whom I can be proud—and whom I hoped could be proud of me— elopement isn't good enough. When you first made your offer, you held out the challenge of my becoming the Notorious Mrs. O'Casey. Very well then. If I'm to accept that challenge, then you must accept the challenge of facing New York with me, in church, in front of all of society—in front of the world. Let them swoon, Connor, just as you said. We'll step over the bodies. Those are *my* terms."

His face bore none of the cockiness and self-assurance that she was used to seeing, nor entitlement nor dominance nor even fear. He stood in front of her again and took her hand.

"Could you really be that proud, Frankie, of you and me, together?" he asked.

"I am already," she said.

He closed his eyes and held her hand to his lips. Gratitude, respect, and regard seemed rolled into that one simple act. She felt he would take no further liberty until he had her answer.

"Then we'll do it your way, Frankie, any way you want, any way at all. Francesca Lund, will you be my wife?"

A plain man had delivered a plain question. All that was left was to give him a plain answer.

"Yes, Connor. I'll be Mrs. O'Casey—notorious or otherwise."

"Good gracious," exclaimed Esther in amazement. "How on earth did this happen?"

Francesca had joined Connor and gone off early with a walking party for morning exercise, leaving Vinnie and Ida West to join Esther for morning coffee. The latest cache of New York, Denver, Chicago, and San Francisco newspapers made their rounds through the ladies' hands as everything that was worth knowing was reviewed and discussed. Esther sat holding the latest edition of the *World* folded in quarters in her lap, her pince-nez in her other hand poised before her eyes.

"What have you got there?" asked Ida as she turned over a new page of the *Denver Post*. Vinnie merely smiled.

"'A union is planned between Miss Francesca Lund of New York, daughter of the late Mr. and Mrs. Jurgen Lund of New York, and Mr. Connor O'Casey, late of Denver, Colorado. The wedding is to be held in New York City in early 1892, followed by a European honeymoon.' Francesca never said she had told the papers already."

"Blanche sent in the story," said Vinnie, looking self-satisfied.

"And how, pray, did she manage it from the top of a mountain?"

"She wrote the story before she left with instructions to her maid to send it in the moment it was confirmed."

"Of all the cheek . . ."

"Nonsense," said Ida with a smile.

"It is true, you know," said Vinnie. "They are engaged."

"Well, I know, dear, but such a hasty announcement. It's not seemly."

"Nonsense," Ida repeated. She shot a look at Vinnie over the top of the newspaper.

"But who confirmed it to Blanche's maid?" continued Esther. "I can't imagine that Francesca would have done such a thing and with any luck Connor would have missed this small detail."

"I told her," said Vinnie.

"You didn't," said Esther.

"Certainly, I did," retorted Vinnie. "Blanche told me at the reception for the expedition that she had written several stories ahead to be posted back to New York at intervals. This was one of them—pending confirmation, of course. Funny that Blanche should have the last word about it."

"There's no sense in getting worked up," said Ida. "We all knew it would happen sooner or later. And I for one am glad that it happened sooner."

"What do you mean 'we all knew'?" said Esther. "I knew no such thing."

"Fiddlesticks," said Ida. "Of course you did."

"I knew," said Vinnie. "I knew the moment we made Connor's acquaintance that he was just what Francesca needed. I think it's splendid that they will be together."

"Oh, I don't know," Esther sighed. "I don't know what to think."

"What we think doesn't really matter. It's what they think that counts. Besides," said Ida, "there's no going back now. It's in print."

ACKNOWLEDGMENTS

In searching for a way to thank the people who have touched *Decorum*, I was tempted to save the best for last. Then I thought better of it. I have put the best first.

My deepest gratitude goes to my mother, Betty J. Christopherson, who one evening in 1999 said yes when I asked, "Would you let me tell you a story I'm thinking about writing?" I shared my sketchy notes about an Irish immigrant, an heiress, and a mistress that I hoped to turn into a novel, yet unnamed. The way she listened bespoke confidence that encouraged me to begin to write. Her enthusiasm grew with each scene she read for me. Her faith in my abilities spurred me on, especially through my periods of self-doubt. Thank you, Mom, for remaining my biggest fan.

Decorum has traversed a long road to submission of the final copyedited manuscript to Kensington Publishing in July 2014. In that time, versions of the manuscript in whole or in part have passed through many hands. My fear in naming people, of course, is that I may have missed someone. Nonetheless, I am grateful to all, including those named here: Sally Christopherson, Amy Christopherson Rempel, Pam Beard, Carole Aikman, Anne Alexander, Deborah Lloyd Allers, Susan Behnke, Judy Blair, Kathleen Dawn, Laura Kelly, Amy Martin, Vicki Moeser, Michael Mulcahy, Judy Parker, Byron Radcliffe, Terri Lynn Simpson, Chris and Catherine Schultz, and Martha Swearingen.

A critical turning point in *Decorum*'s journey occurred the year I joined a writing workshop led by the amazing Hildie Block. Few learning experiences have been as tough and affirming as that year of weekly discussion and critique. Special thanks to Hildie for her wisdom, encouragement, and good-natured badgering to find an agent, and to my fellow workshop students Jim Ball, Stephanie Brennickmeyer, Pat Everett, Christina Kovac Loebach, Judy Colp

Rubin, Joanne Schulte, Jane Tarrant, and Susan Woodward for their invaluable help.

Thank you to the many family members, friends, colleagues, and acquaintances who have kindly inquired, "How's the book?" through *Decorum*'s ups and downs. I am grateful to those who, in particular, have kept up the drumbeat of encouragement: Elayne Archer, Beth Bagnold, Linda Kay Benning, Melita DeBellis, Misha Galley, Kathy Gracenin, Kathy Green, Jacqueline Hess, Cindy Arciaga Hodor, Suzanne Kindervatter, Susan Lundquist, Art Sauer, Greg Saunders, Lonna Shafritz, Linda Sorkin, Pam Sutton, Jennifer Thorp, and Paula Tarnapol Whitacre.

To Victoria Skurnick, my agent at Levine Greenberg Literary Agency, many thanks for her enthusiasm, wise counsel, and common sense. To my wonderful editor at Kensington Publishing, John Scognamiglio, and to Vida Engstrand, Alexandra Nicolajsen, Michelle Forde, Jane Nutter, Paula Reedy, Peter Senftleben, and Gary Sunshine, thank you all for making the publishing experience for a Kensington debut author a good one.

Mollie Bryan, my great-grandmother, has been with me in spirit ever since I began using her etiquette book for reference, the 1881 edition of *Decorum: A Practical Treatise on the Etiquette and Dress of the Best American Society*, revised by S. L. Louis. What began as a simple search for facts soon gave the novel its organizing theme and its title. I am grateful that she acquired this book in 1882 and for its inspiration well over a century later.

Finally, to the Source, the Divine Spark at the center of all that is creative, my humble and heartfelt thanks.

DECORUM

Kaaren Christopherson

About This Guide

The suggested questions are included
to enhance your group's reading of
Kaaren Christopherson's *Decorum*.

DISCUSSION QUESTIONS

1. Every generation redefines what it means to "have it all." What do you think having it all meant to someone in the 1890s? What do you think it means to Francesca Lund? Connor O'Casey? Blanche Alvarado? Edmund Tracey? How do you think their servants would define it? How would any of these definitions be similar to or different from the way you would define it today?

2. Connor and Tracey each hope to make significant changes to his life as a result of marriage to Francesca. What does each man expect to gain if he marries her? What might he expect to lose? How does he feel about it?

3. During the conversation at Christmas dinner Blanche and Francesca discover that their respective situations with regard to men and marriage may not be as different as they may appear on the surface. How are their situations and choices similar? How are they different?

4. What attracts Connor to Francesca? Why does he not consider Blanche to be marriage material for him? What are Blanche's prospects if she doesn't marry Connor?

5. What barriers does Edmund Tracey face in attempting to improve his lot in life? Are their causes internal or external? Why does he make the choices he makes?

6. In an era when large families are the norm and many children a social value—and sometimes an economic necessity—how do you think Maggie Jerome feels when confronted with a large and congenial family like that of John Ashton and Isabel Worth? How has Maggie appeared to compensate throughout her life? How would childless women in general have coped in society in the 1890s?

7. As long as Francesca remains unmarried, Vinnie Lawrence is assured of companionship and equal status with another single woman. How do you think Vinnie feels once Francesca becomes engaged? What choices does a single, middle-class woman in her late twenties have in 1890?

8. Connor and Blanche both yearn for acceptance by New York society. Connor can move about in business while Blanche must wait for a visit from a society matron. What are their respective obstacles to being accepted? What are their respective advantages that might give him or her hope?

9. Marriage contracts were not that uncommon among the wealthy in the nineteenth century, yet Edmund Tracey is indignant over the marriage contract Francesca wants him to sign before they wed. Why?

10. In the nineteenth century, the "grand tour" became not only an imperative for wealthy young men, but a mania. Wealthy young women also traveled, but very often in more restricted circles and circumstances. How do you think Francesca is upholding or breaking tradition by proposing to go to Banff? How do you think Vinnie, who is not wealthy, feels about accompanying Francesca, as Francesca's guest?

11. Why do you think a woman of Francesca's social standing, personal values, and temperament would even contemplate Connor's unique proposition, which could lead to scandal?

12. Jerry confronts Connor over the latter's decision to follow Francesca to Banff and Francesca's consent to the plan. Why do you think Jerry does this, despite the fact that technically Francesca is of legal age and, being unmarried and orphaned, has no one else to whom she must answer?

13. What do you think will happen to Maggie and Jerry Jerome once Francesca, Vinnie, and Esther leave for Banff?

14. Blanche takes several extreme measures to turn her prospects around. What are they? Given her background, how might she feel that she's prepared to take risks? How might she be better equipped to meet these challenges than other women?

15. By the end of the story, Francesca, Blanche, and Connor have undergone a number of changes in situation, attitude, and outlook. How is each person different than he or she was at the beginning of the book? Did Tracey experience similar changes over his lifetime?